T0303816

New Yiddish Library

*The New Yiddish Library is a joint project of the
Fund for the Translation of Jewish Literature and
the National Yiddish Book Center.*

*Additional support comes from the Kaplen
Foundation, the Felix Posen Fund for the
Translation of Modern Yiddish Literature,
and Ben and Sarah Torchinsky.*

SERIES EDITOR: DAVID G. ROSKIES

The

Glatstein

Chronicles

JACOB GLATSTEIN

EDITED AND WITH AN

INTRODUCTION BY RUTH WISSE

TRANSLATED BY MAIER DESHELL

AND NORBERT GUTERMAN

Yale UNIVERSITY PRESS

NEW HAVEN AND LONDON

THE GLATSTEIN CHRONICLES

By Jacob Glatstein,
translated by Maier Deshell and Norbert Guterman
Edited by and with an Introduction by Ruth Wisse

Yiddish Book Center
Amherst, MA 01002

© 2023 by White Goat Press, the Yiddish Book Center's imprint
All rights reserved

Printed in the United States of America
10 9 8 7 6 5 4 3 2 1

Paperback ISBN 979-8-9852069-8-2
Hardcover ISBN 979-8-9852069-9-9

Library of Congress Control Number: 2022920123

Cover design by Michael Grinley

Cover photo from the Archives of the YIVO Institute for
Jewish Research, New York
Lublin, 1913. Jacob Glatstein (kneeling) with two of his friends:
Rottenberg (standing), a young poet later killed by the Nazis, and
Abraham Zimmerman (sitting), one of the early translators of
Western literature in Yiddish.

Previously published in 2010 by Yale University Press/New Yiddish
Library

Printed at The Studley Press, Dalton, Massachusetts

whitegoatpress.org

♦♦♦ *Contents*

♦♦♦ *Introduction*

RUTH R. WISSE

In June 1934, twenty years after he had arrived solo in New York City, Jacob Glatstein was summoned back by the family to the bedside of his dying mother in Lublin. Had he not been called for, it is unlikely that he would ever have returned to his birthplace. Glatstein at thirty-seven was then in the "middle of life's journey"—precisely in the middle as it later turned out—married and the father of three children, employed in the editorial and news departments of the Yiddish daily *Morgn Zhurnal,* and hotly involved in Yiddish literary initiatives. First and foremost a poet, a Yiddish modernist with a growing reputation, he was at work on his fourth book of verse. Even less conducive to a transatlantic crossing than his personal circumstances was the turbulent international climate. With Hitler newly installed as chancellor of Germany and anti-Semitism on the rise in Poland, Jews were frantically trying to get out of Europe rather than in.

The voyage turned Glatstein prophetic. Initially buoyed by his release from daily routine, he became increasingly aware at every stage of his trip of the political drift of Europe toward fascism, communism, and anti-Semitism. By the time he returned to the United States, he had assumed responsibility for the Jews trapped on the Continent. For the next four years he sounded the alarm in a weekly newspaper column that warned alike against Hitler and Stalin and against the political apathy of Western democracies that allowed murderous regimes to prevail. "Who is crazier," he asked in August 1935, "the maniac Hitler driving the 600,000 Jews of Germany to their death at 90 miles an hour or the impassive bystanders watching it happen?" Why were American Jews silent in the face of mounting anti-Jewish attacks in Poland? He hammered at Soviet Russia's repression of freedoms; the Arab pogroms against Jews in Palestine disturbed him all the more because Joseph Stalin hailed them as part of a Communist Revolution. With the nations engaged in constant swordplay over Jewish heads, he wrote, "the Yiddish writer feels like a strategist maneuvering invisible armies in legendary lands. No one has chosen him, yet he speaks into the wasteland where he hears only the echo of his own voice."[1]

Glatstein had always emphasized the subjectivity of poetry. No less subjectively, he now registered the growing threat. What became his most famous poem, "Good Night, World" (dated April 1938, in response to pogroms in Poland), slammed the door on the "big, stinking world" and made its way back to the twisted ghetto streets in an emotional-intellectual tangle of pride, sorrow, anger, regret, resolve, and dread. "Wagons," a much softer lyric of the same year, sounded "bells of silence" for a community of Jews approaching its final hour. More than death, each member fears to remain alone in a world without fellow Jews. Glatstein found multiple ways, through lyrical wit and transparent paradox, to express the ironies of a private sensibility that is nonetheless subject to the common Jewish fate.

The most obvious literary outcome of the journey home was the book before us—the fictionalized personal account of a Yiddish writer who returns to Poland in 1934. Apparently conceived as a trilogy, this project was begun shortly after Glatstein returned to New York. The first installment appeared in the little magazine *Inzikh* (In the self) in 1934, and the book *Ven yash iz geforn* (When Yash set out) was published three years later. The second volume, *Ven yash iz gekumen* (When Yash arrived), appeared in installments in the New York weekly *Yidisher Kemfer* and as a book in 1940. A 1943 collection of Glatstein's poems announced that the final volume of the trilogy was about to appear under the title *Ven Yash iz tsurikgekumen* (When Yash returned). But only a couple of fragments of that intended book ever surfaced, turning the missing third volume into the unresolved conclusion of the project. The "Yash" scheme was conceived as filial homage to Polish Jews and did not survive their destruction.

The narrator Yash, bearing the nickname of the author, is the central figure and consciousness of the two books. Though his name appeared only in the Yiddish titles, whatever we are told about him in the book corresponds to what we know about the life of Jacob Glatstein. In fact, we learn more about the author from these novels than from any other autobiographical source—about his childhood, family, voyage to America, early difficulties of adjustment to the new language and surroundings, and the various jobs that supported him as he wrote poetry. There are no apparent discrepancies between the author's biography and the parts of it he discloses here. Which is not to say that any great intimacies are revealed: as Glatstein told an interviewer in 1955, he did not feel comfortable with personal disclosures except through the veil of poetry, and could not write about himself, "or about my loves or about my non-loves—feelings about my wife or a beloved and things of that sort." Long after they had abandoned religious observance, the virtues of modesty inculcated by Judaism continued to influence most Yiddish writers, Glatstein emphatically among them. He supplies in these books only the kind of information about himself that conforms to the scheme of his literary voyage. Future biographers still have their work cut out for them.

The community register of Lublin, Poland, then under tsarist administration, records the birth of three Glatsztejns in 1896. The one who concerns us here was the son born to Icek (Isaac), aged thirty, and his wife, Ita Ruchla, born Jungman, aged thirty-two, on August 7 (or 19th, according to the Julian calendar still in use under the tsarist regime).[2] Yankev, Yankele, Yash, or, in English, Jacob, considered himself fortunate to have been born into a traditional family—his maternal ancestors were rabbis. He received a traditional religious education with incremental exposure to secular subjects as he matured. Raised in the shadow of the nearby Lublin fortress and prison, Jacob experienced the roiling political conflicts around him from inside a large, cohesive, and supportive clan. The paternal Glatsztejn (Glatshteyn) tribe of seven brothers accounted for a large part of the boy's education. One uncle ran the religious cheder the boy attended in the equivalent of third grade. A second uncle, a tailor, introduced him to secular literature, and a third was cantor of Lublin's largest synagogue. Following in their father's footsteps, his two male cousins became choral directors and composers, while he himself developed a vital attachment to music. His interest in literature he attributed to his father, who sold ready-to-wear clothing for a living but encouraged his son to read the latest Yiddish and Hebrew publications in the hope that the boy would become a writer.

Literature was a popular sport in the Russia and Poland of Glatstein's youth, and disproportionately so among Jewish youth, for whom many other competitive avenues were blocked. In describing his high school education at the Krinski Commercial School, the author underscores how futile it felt to prepare for professions from which Jews would be barred, and how much cheerier it was to spend the time in autonomous artistic and literary pursuits. Glatstein said he could not remember a time when he was not writing. His friends debated the merits of writers the way Americans did baseball greats. Relaxation of tsarist censorship after the abortive revolution of 1905, though only partial as compared with the liberties enjoyed in Vienna or New York, encouraged an explosion of talent in journalism, belles lettres, theater, music, painting and sculpture, secular scholarship, popular entertainment, and politics. From early boyhood, Jacob accompanied his grandfather on his visits to Warsaw, the cultural hub of Polish Jewry, and by his early teens, on his own, he made the obligatory pilgrimage of every aspiring writer to the Yiddish "master," Yitzhak Leybush Peretz. One of Glatstein's early stories was apparently accepted though never published by the mass-circulation Warsaw Yiddish daily *Fraynd* (Friend). Had he remained in Poland, he would probably have moved to Warsaw to join one of its burgeoning literary and intellectual circles.

As it happens, however, the family member who proved most decisive in Glatstein's life was the youngest uncle who had moved to New York. Polish nationalism, with its intolerant by-product anti-Semitism, persuaded Glatstein's parents to let him join that uncle very shortly before the outbreak of World War I. When he arrived at what was then the most crowded place on earth, his local relative could not leave his job in a cigarette factory to meet his ship. It took the eighteen-year-old some time to find his footing. While trading in one unsuitable day job for another, he attended night school, first to learn English and then to study law.

And yet New York was not altogether alien. With its critical mass of unsettled youth, the Lower East Side offered Glatstein the same kinds of literary opportunities he had found in Lublin and Warsaw. Yiddish, the common language of several million immigrants, generated newspapers, theater companies, publishing houses, humor magazines, a music industry, and an aspiring high literary culture. By the time he joined it, the local Yiddish literary community had already produced two literary "generations"—the so-called Sweatshop Poets of the turn of the century and the *Yunge,* the breakaway literary "youth," who emphasized their greater aestheticism, inwardness, and preference for quietude to socially relevant verse. World War I accelerated the independence of the immigrant community from its European origins, to the point that after the war cultural influences began flowing from the new world to the old.

Once Glatstein had started law school and saw that he *could* become an American lawyer, he realized that he did not want to, gave it up, and threw in his lot with Yiddish literature. Together with another law school dropout, Nahum Borukh Minkoff, and Aaron (Glants) Leyeles, he launched a new poetry "movement" called *Inzikh* through a manifesto and accompanying anthology of verse that demonstrated aspects of their theory in practice. As its name suggests, *Inzikhizm* or Introspectivism—the third indigenous Yiddish poetry "movement" in America—insisted that poetry filter everything through the prism of self, which, in turn, mandated the use of free verse so that every new poem could emerge in the rhythm appropriate to its subject and creator. "The world exists and we are part of it. But for us, the world exists only as it is mirrored in us, as it touches *us.* . . . It becomes an actuality only *in* us and *through* us."[3] The signatories declined to write on Jewish subjects or in a Jewish style simply because they composed in a Jewish language, or to use the accepted Hebraic spelling for words of Hebrew derivation.

Glatstein's first book, *Yankev Glatshteyn,* published almost simultaneously with the *Inzikh* manifesto of 1920, demonstrates some of the consequences of this insurgent spirit.

> Lately there is no trace left
> of Yankl son of Yitzhok [a traditional form of his name]
> but for a tiny round dot
> tumbling dazedly through the streets
> with limbs clumsily attached.

The violence of the age has done violence to the person he was. That tiny dot from the first letter of Glatstein's name alludes to "dos pintele yid," the distilled Jewish essence of the young man who felt himself exploded into fragments. The new poetry expressed the sensations of an immigrant whose language is all that remains of his formative world. But by reverse inference, fragments of Yiddish could also create a new cultural homestead. Disconnected letters, after all, do join together to form meaningful, complete poems. Glatstein was able in one of his poems to summon up a Jewish childhood through the mere syllables of Yiddish nursery speech, and in another to evoke the sweetness of Torah study through the remembered translation of a word from the Song of Songs.

The unsettling freedom of America comes across in the poetry, prose, and journalism that Glatstein wrote over the next fourteen years. Many a poem seems to be inspired less by a strong emotion, observation, or incident than by an exotic word, such as *Brahma, Sesame, Sheeny* (pejorative for Jew), or the random sounds of *Tsela-tseldi* that the poet is eager to try out in Yiddish. The term *experimentation* hardly suffices to describe the many subjects that Glatstein addresses, the poses he adopts, and the poetic variations he attempts. Unlike his Yiddish contemporaries and predecessors who were raised mostly on Russian, Polish, and German literatures, Glatstein also read Anglo-American literature, including T. S. Eliot, Ezra Pound, and James Joyce —expatriates like himself, who rendered the disintegration of their inherited traditions as masterworks of wasteland and exile. In a short essay, "If Joyce Wrote Yiddish," Glatstein demonstrates how playfully a Yiddish poet could write ultramodernist prose, by using the perceived breakup of his native language to reinvent it in new combinations.

Opportunities and liabilities of Yiddish writing in America were one and the same. Though only decades removed from what scholars marked as its "beginnings" in tsarist Russia in the 1860s, modern Yiddish literature was already dispersed with its speakers to Argentina and Australia, emerging under political conditions as diverse as Bolshevik Russia and British-ruled Palestine. Never before in history had more than ten million Jews communicated in the same language: to be part of Yiddish literature meant staying abreast of developments all over the world and reaching a potential readership from Berdichev to Buenos Aires. Migration and travel became prominent subjects. Yet the same freedoms that allowed Jews to write as they pleased in Yiddish encouraged most of their fellow Jews to start using the languages of their adopted lands, or at least to ensure that their children learned languages of opportunity and professional advancement. Had he been just a little younger when he arrived in New York, Glatstein himself might have written in English, joining a literary community with more American-centered concerns. For a writer, language is fate—his raw material at one end of the creative process and his marketplace on the other.[4] Glatstein came to understand that his fate as a Yiddish poet, in a Jewish language, was indivisible from that of its speakers.

The Glatstein chronicles stretch like a tightrope across a chasm. Book One, "Homeward Bound," opens as the poet sets out for his native city and ends with the train conductor's call for "Lublin!" Book Two, "Homecoming at Twilight," picks up the hero as he recuperates from his mother's funeral at a Polish Jewish hotel and ends with his impending return to America. Missing in between is the action that was the ostensible purpose of the trip. Where is the reunion with father and sister? Where is the pivotal deathbed scene? While we readers experience nothing like the narrator's bereavement, we lament the absence of the homecoming we anticipated but are destined never to know. The curtain remains drawn over the encounter between son and parents that was to have been the central "event." Instead, the *before* and *after* Yash chronicles frame the eclipse of his entire formative world. It is likely that Glatstein intended to feature the reunion with his dying mother as the centerpiece of the concluding volume, which would have dealt with his return to America. In lieu of Book Three he wrote a cascade of poems that wrestle with a catastrophe dwarfing the "natural" death of a parent. When Glatstein's father, brother, and family were murdered along with the rest of Polish Jewry, he evidently could not follow his intended literary scheme.

Yash begins his outbound journey in high spirits, delighted to be sprung from his daily routine. Pleasantly surprised by the fluency of his acquired English, he discovers that he is a consummate cosmopolitan, able to converse with passengers in Yiddish, Russian, German, and Polish, and, when necessary, to identify some sentences in Danish. As a professional newspaperman, he is curious about everything from the Sovietization of Russia to economic conditions in Chile, and as a student of the human heart, he is interested in the personal stories that flesh out the historical moment. Among the people he meets are a Schenectady socialist, a Jewish prizefighter, a socialite physician, a Wisconsin schoolteacher, members of a college student band, a pianist, and a painter. One of the passengers tells him, "You're such a great listener, you have golden ears. Your ears are worth a million dollars." This echoes what Glatstein wrote in one of his essays, "I have always liked human ears. I mean ears that can truly listen to someone else." Those golden ears are the reason Yash transcribes many more aural than visual impressions, many more conversations than painterly scenes. He reports on encounters during the stopover in Paris and the train ride across Hitler's Germany to Poland, encounters that convey the darkening mood of the continent.

But unlike the travelogue it otherwise resembles, this book moves simultaneously into the personal interior. On his first night at sea, rocking to sleep in his cabin, Yash is reminded of Fishl-Dovid, the overanxious hero in a story by Sholem Aleichem who is trying to make it home to his wife and children in time for the Passover holiday.[5] Fishl-Dovid has reason to worry, being rowed by a sadistic Gentile boatman across a thawing river. This momentary association discloses the world of Sholem Aleichem beneath the modernism of Jacob Glatstein, the nervous East European Jew who is embodied in the confident American, and the autobiographical impulse embedded in the reportage. The counterpoint between inner and outer voyages, past and present, literary inheritance and creative potential, continues from this point on. Memory interrupts and enhances the passenger's experience of the world; experiences trigger memory and self-understanding.

The book may be better described in musical terms than in categories of plot, characters, and dramatic action. No sooner does the ship leave the dock than the narrator feels himself subject to "marine law," whose function he had failed to appreciate when he was studying it in law school. The special qualities he attributes to life at sea are those of his prose: "Footsteps lighten, manners soften, voices lilt." People suspended at sea move gently, allowing for slower-paced narration. Whereas many a novelist uses a travel conveyance to heighten dramatic tension among strangers forcibly held together over a limited time, Glatstein relaxes the tempo and loosens the tension to allow for more genuine and prolonged encounter and reflection. The book's many allusions to music invite us to consider it in symphonic terms. Young and old, Jew and Gentile, European and American, male and female, coarse and genteel—the narrator arranges inharmonious voices so as to ensure that they do not drown one another out. The pulsating memories of the homebound Jew in troubled waters are like the solo instrument in this rich symphonic composition.

In boarding the ship, Yash has hoped to leave the newsroom and everyday life behind. "Maybe here I might succeed in ridding myself of the miasmas that had accrued to my being as a social animal, as a writer-for-hire, as Jew in a bloody world that—*pace* Shakespeare—demands only *my* pound of flesh." It is not to be. On the second day at sea, the ship's bulletin carries the news that Hitler has conducted a massive purge of the Nazi storm troopers (*Sturmabteilung*, or SA) and their leader Ernst Rohm. This would make it June 30, 1934. The news report suddenly sets Yash apart from the other Americans and Europeans he has been hobnobbing with and sends him in search of fellow Jews who will understand the menace to their tribe. Several days later, during his stopover in Paris, he learns of the death of the Hebrew poet Haim Nahman Bialik (July 4, 1934), who has provided the strongest spur and challenge to his career as a Yiddish poet. Thus, along with the travel encounters and the recovered memories, the third rail of the book is history-in-the-making—conveying the high voltage of the here and now.

Reviewing the first Yash volume shortly after its appearance, the not yet famous Isaac Bashevis Singer was dismayed by the absence of incident ("Jules Verne would not have wasted ten lines on a journey so bereft of adventure or romance") and by the book's apparently random organization ("At one point he lets his characters speak, and then, on a whim, he tells his own autobiography").[6] Adept at racy storytelling, Bashevis Singer failed to appreciate Glatstein's thematic approach to composition. The third chapter, for example, introduces a collection of Russians returning to the Soviet Union who try to impress Yash with the advanced state of their society. Expansive in the Slavic manner yet carefully toeing the Soviet line, they provide a truer composite picture of the USSR than the *New York Times* correspondent Walter Duranty was then offering the American public. These encounters in turn remind Yash of how the "revolution" first penetrated his consciousness when his father held him up to watch a workers' demonstration in 1905 and instructed him, "Yankele, never forget this." Juxtaposing the naïve beginnings of the Revolution as recalled by a Jewish child with the boasts of its newly minted Soviet citizens, including a Jew who veils his Jewishness, spares the author any need for disparaging commentary. The Communist boast crumbles under the forced optimism of its celebrants.

There is nothing random, either, in the contrast between the two parts of the Yash chronicles, the first moving out into the wide world, the second sealed almost hermetically inside Polish-Jewish society. Book Two is situated in a small Jewish sanatorium-hotel in a resort town between Lublin and Kazimierz Dolny recognizable as the real-life Naleczow, and as a literary knock-off of Thomas Mann's retreat in *The Magic Mountain.* Mann's imposing novel had not long before been published in Yiddish translation (by Isaac Bashevis Singer), and Glatstein must have derived bittersweet pleasure from transposing its Alpine loftiness into a miniaturized Jewish version. The sanatorium functions in both works as the symbolic setting for a civilization in crisis, and in each case the outsider falls under the spell of the hospice he has come to visit. But Thomas Mann shows the incurable infection lurking inside Europe's grandeur, while Glatstein uses a parallel scheme to disclose the irrepressible vitality of the condemned community of Europe's Jews. The opening sentence, pronounced before we know by whom, echoes the Bible's "De profundis": "Even from the muck will I sing praises unto Thee, my Lord." *Blote,* or muck, is the Yiddish self-deprecating substitute for the "depths" from which the psalmist reaches for redemption. The whole book negotiates between the heights to which Jewry aspires and the misery into which it has been forced.

The stationary setting of this second book allows for greater historical penetration than horizontal coverage. Already in the concluding chapter of Book One, Yash had met aunts and cousins who were trapped in a spiral of bigotry and poverty and unable to leave Poland as he had done two decades earlier. The gates to America were almost sealed by then, and though the "land of opportunity" was then also temporarily mired in the Great Depression, an American in Poland was like biblical Joseph from Egypt, minus the salvific granaries or political influence. The image of Yash as an impotent Joseph first appears when he is appealed to by a seductive, unhappily married female relative, and it is memorably reinforced when a dozen petitioners approach him to carry messages to their American relatives. As compared with Glatstein's actual voyage to Poland, which included arrangements for the publication of a volume of his poems, Yash meets with no fellow Yiddish writers but instead joins an assortment of Jews in a voluntary "ghetto" not strictly of their own making.[7] His sense of impotence grows with every demand on him that he cannot satisfy.

Framing Yash in the Polish chronicle are two powerful personalities, like older and younger prophets of modern Jewry. Steinman, whose "Even from the muck" sets the tone for the book, is a German-trained historian and custodian of Hasidic lore who serves the sanatorium guests as something of a modern Hasidic Master. He enthralls his listeners with stories of his life that are like a composite history of the East European Jewish intellectual, raised traditionally, exposed to the influence of the secular enlightenment, and drawn back to his endangered people. Steinman's magnetic personality and his ideas about the holistic Jewish people are reminiscent of the Yiddish luminary Y. L. Peretz, whom Glatstein had met as a boy, and traces of that encounter may be found in Steinman's paternal interest in this potential successor. Steinman excels at everything but succession: his devoted daughter is in no sense his spiritual heir, and there is no one remotely like him in the wings as he lies dying. Both the older man and the young writer realize that their personal affinity for each other cannot span the widening breach between the Jewish past in Poland and the Jewish future in America. The death of this public figure toward the end of the book signals the fading glory of Polish Jewry and allows Yash to experience the mourning for his mother that he had until then kept in check.

No less impressive than Steinman is a sixteen-year-old boy from one of the Hasidic dynasties that Steinman studies, a latter-day Nahman of Bratzlav (one of the early geniuses of the Hasidic movement), who wonders whether he might not be in the running for the assignment of Messiah. The boy invites the narrator home to visit his family—a rabbinic brother and rabbinic brother-in-law and their two wives—and to show off the literary fruits of his runaway imagination. The most dazzling of all the characters Yash encounters on this journey, the boy transcends the workaday world in his yearning to encompass all knowledge and to complete the work that God has left undone. "You're a stranger here, you'll go away soon, across the ocean," he tells the narrator. "You will think that a confused young boy has been talking to you. But don't be too sure." We readers can't be too sure either, for the boy's poems and ideas impress us with their precocity and verve. Yet his brilliance, like a firecracker's, threatens to explode in the process of shedding its light.

In the closing chapters, we meet a third representative of Polish Jewry, a well-to-do lawyer closer to Yash's age, who becomes his companion on an excursion to the nearby resort town of Kazimierz. A fully acculturated product of the big city, Neifeld becomes Yash's informant on Polish-Jewish relations just as Steinman was his guide to internal Jewish history and affairs. "Take deep breaths," Neifeld says, "Polish woods can cure the sickest heart." Both men would like to credit their native land with as much commendation as truth permits. But they cannot ignore the contrary evidence of Polish hostility, and the daylong excursion of Neifeld and Yash to Kazimierz, where King Casimir according to legend once cohabited with the lovely Jewess

Esther, becomes yet another of the several leave-takings from Poland that culminate in Yash's final farewell.

Among this book's several interwoven themes, let me highlight two. Neglect of the Jewish woman is implicit in Yash's inability to save his dying mother. At the hotel where he rests after the bereavement, a female relative comes seeking his help. He disappoints her, and then in a dreamlike dramatic sequence he feels helpless to rescue women from the predators who seek to harm them. One imagines that Glatstein visiting Poland must have experienced occasional pangs of guilt, yet they surface in the narrator only in relation to women who need his protection. At a later point in the book, Steinman and the narrator attend an evening dance that the hotel proprietor has organized for his guests. The sister-in-law of the young genius, one of the rabbis' wives, turns up, and explaining somewhat shyly that she loves to dance, invites one of them to take a turn with her around the dance floor. They decline and instead they allow her to be swept away by the most brain-damaged of the guests. When she leaves in dismay, they do not offer to accompany her home in the dark. "Neither of us was very gallant," Steinman comments, with good reason. Steinman also realizes that his spinster daughter has devoted her life to serving him. Finally, when Neifeld recounts how the Jews of Poland sacrificed Esther to King Casimir to achieve their ideal of Polish-Jewish symbiosis, he extends criticism of Jewish manhood to the national level. The narrator acknowledges his own and his society's failure to do right by their women, and rather than ascribe their failure of "manliness" to historical conditions, he takes the blame on himself.

In this connection, Yash is reminded of "a Spanish book I once read" —the allusion is to *Autumn and Winter Sonatas* by Ramon del Vale-Inclán. Like the momentary recollection of Sholem Aleichem's Fishl-Dovid at the outset of the journey, this evocation of the *Sonatas* at its conclusion adds a psychological and literary substratum to Glatstein's story. The Spanish work in question has been described as "decadent in every sense of the word": It depicts the last adventures of the Marquis of Bradomin, an aging Don Juan, who does not hesitate to seduce yet another young virgin despite the attendant anxieties of an arm lost in combat. As apparently alien to Glatstein's Yiddish culture as any work could be, this tale nonetheless reflects Yash's state of heart and mind on the eve of his departure from Poland. Though the narrator gives no hint that he (or his author) had indulged in sexual misadventures, he shares Bradomin's torment over his waning powers:

> It seemed to me now, in the twilight, that I had reached the autumn of my life. The whole day, the encounter with Neifeld, and even my mother's death seemed to coincide oddly with the downward movement of my own life, and all this was in step with Jewish life as a whole, maybe even with the twilight now settling over the whole world. . . .
>
> All of us—myself and everything I remembered, and everything I forgot—would very soon find ourselves in winter with a hand shot off. That would be the hand which, I had vowed, I would let wither if I forgot Thee, Thee and everything that had ever been reflected in my eyes and brain.

Yash substitutes the psalmist's "hand" for the fighting arm that Bradomin lost in combat. His vow evokes the Jews by the waters of Babylon, weeping as they remember Zion, unable to sing the Lord's song in a strange land. The psalmist says, "If I forget Thee, O Jerusalem, let my right hand wither . . . if I do not keep Jerusalem in memory even at my happiest hour." Yash had pledged his writing hand to an unnamed "Thee"—to the "Jerusalem" of Polish Jewry, since Jews were in the habit of re-creating their sacred space wherever they were permitted to sojourn. Familiar as he is with the works of decadence and modernism that insist on the untrammeled freedom of the self, Yash applies their libidinous passion to the Jewish predicament, which more than ever requires the allegiance of its cavalier. He fears that his writing hand will be blasted along with the object of his longing. Bradomin's need to prove his sexual prowess stirs Yash's fears of a shrinking talent just when he most needs his powers to do "Thee" justice.

Will the Yiddish writer fail his subject as the Jewish male fails his women? The book includes several auguries of such failure. On his deathbed, Steinman inspirits the Jews with a melody, but once their conductor ceases to animate them, they are like an abandoned choir that stops in mid phrase. The young Messianic genius writes eye-popping stuff, none of which has yet been published, and—we are made to realize—never will be. Neifeld seems to offer a promising artistic strategy when he draws the narrator's attention to the song of a nightingale they hear on the road. "There was no trace of degrading sweetness in the nightingale's song, no concession to debased popular taste." This tribute suggests an "utterly unsentimental" and "intellectual" aesthetic ideal for the book itself, yet shortly after he has described this ideal of song, Neifeld brings himself to tears singing a Rosh Hashanah melody of a cantor named Slowik (Polish for "nightingale") whom he remembers from childhood. What form of art, then, is adequate for the task that Yash knows he must assume?

As Yash contemplates his return to America, the packed suitcases beside his bed seem to him "the only real and solid objects in this world of shadowy forms." The voyager who had originally hoped to shake off the "miasmas" of responsibility now sees nothing so clearly as the baggage he carries back with him. The poet will have to do his best to deliver all the messages that were entrusted to him by desperate men and women. The hybrid form of autobiographical fiction allowed Glatstein to record the actuality of Polish Jewry through the conduit of his own experience, fusing memory and observation, the private and the communal, as intricately as Lublin and New York are fused in him. In place of the suitcases, Glatstein provided these books, "the only real and solid objects" he could retrieve from a world he was otherwise powerless to rescue.

Editor's Note: Although a bowdlerized English version of Book One, *Ven yash iz geforn,* was published in 1969 as *Homeward Bound,* I did not choose to adapt it for this edition but commissioned a new translation by Maier Deshell, retaining only the earlier title. By contrast, Book Two, *Ven yash iz gekumen,* had been finely translated by Norbert Guterman as *Homecoming at Twilight* (1962), requiring only slight emendations. Since Mr. Guterman died before I began this project, I took on the responsibility of editing his translation and of bringing both works together in a single volume.

These translations are as faithful as felicity will allow. One of the finest English translators from Yiddish, Maurice Samuel, believed that translations should never require glossary or footnote, even if this meant inserting explanations—lengthy explanations when necessary —within the text. The present work does not go quite that far. Given that history, geography, and cultural features may create difficulties for different sectors of our readership, we have preferred to provide explanations outside the text, without encroaching on the original. We had in mind the common reader, including students of literature, who want to discover a new American work as much as possible "as its author intended."

The title gave us the most trouble. When Glatstein called his books by the name of their otherwise unnamed narrator, he doubtless expected readers to make the association between *Yash*, the implied author, and himself. The English reader is, alas, scarcely any more familiar with the name of the author himself, so that calling the book *The Glatstein Chronicles* may produce an analogous effect. One of the passengers on his ship calls the narrator "Gladdy," but the nickname's Scandinavian provenance suits the speaker more than its subject. We use "Glatstein" in the title the way schoolboys might refer to one another, "Hey, Glatstein, how about that book you were writing?"

Translations from the poetry of Jacob Glatstein may be found in *Selected Poems of Yankev Glatshteyn*, trans., ed., and with an introduction by Richard J. Fein (Philadelphia, 1987); *The Selected Poems of Jacob Glatstein*, trans. with an introduction by Ruth Whitman (New York, 1972); *I Keep Recalling: The Holocaust Poems of Jacob Glatstein*, trans. Barnett Zumoff (New York, 1993); Jacob Glatstein, *Poems*, selected and trans. Etta Blum (Tel Aviv, 1970); *American Yiddish Poetry: A Bilingual Anthology*, ed. and trans. Benjamin and Barbara Harshav (Berkeley, 1986); and in other anthologies of modern Yiddish verse.

In the absence of a full-scale biography of Glatstein, readers may consult Janet Hadda, *Yankev Glatshteyn* (Boston, 1980); and Avrom Tabachnik, "A Conversation with Jacob Glatstein," trans. Joseph C. Landis, *Yiddish* 1 (Summer 1973): 40–53.

NOTES

1. Glatstein's column, under the pseudonym Itskus, ran in the *Morgn Zhurnal* between September 14, 1934, and April 29, 1938. This excerpt is from "A Writer's Day of Rest," November 27, 1936.

2. The date given in Jewish lexicons is August 20. I am grateful to Pawel Sygowski for his investigations on my behalf and to Monika Garbowska for her help throughout.

3. "Introspectivism," in *American Yiddish Poetry: A Bilingual Anthology*, ed. and trans. Benjamin Harshav and Barbara Harshav (Berkeley, 1986): 774.

4. I have treated this subject and these books by Glatstein in the following essays: "Language as Fate: Reflections on Jewish Literature in America," in *Studies in Contemporary Jewry*, vol. 12 (Oxford, 1996): 129–147; "The Yiddish and Hebrew Writers Head for Home," in *Ideology and Jewish Identity in Israeli and American Literature*, ed. Emily Miller Budick (Albany, 2001), chapter 8.

5. The Sholem Aleichem story is "Home for Passover" (Af peysakh aheym, 1903), trans. by Julius and Frances Butwin in *The Best of Sholem Aleichem* ed. Irving Howe and Ruth R. Wisse (1979): 89–102.

6. I. Bashevis, "Fun der bikher-velt: "Ven yash iz geforn," *Zukunft* 44, no. 3 (1939): 182, 183.

7. For a fuller description of Glatstein's actual trip to Poland and analysis of the *Chronicles*, see Avraham Novershtern, "The Open Suitcases: Yankev Glatstheyn's *Ven Yash Iz Gekumen*, in *Arguing the Modern Jewish Canon: Essays on Literature and Culture in Honor of Ruth R. Wisse*, ed. Justin Cammy et al. (Cambridge, MA, 2008): 255–298.

BOOK ONE
Homeward Bound

In Memory of
My Mother

A jak poszedł Stach na boje.
Zaszumiały jasne zdroje,
Zaszumiało kłosów pole,
Na tęsknotę, na niedolę . . .
· · · · · · · · · ·
· · · · · · · · · ·
Stach śmiertelną dostał ranę.
Król na zamek wracał zdrowy . . .

       And when Stach went out to battle
       The clear streams rippled
       The corn fields murmured
       Of longing, of misfortune . . .
       · · · · · · · · · ·
       · · · · · · · · · ·
       Stach received a mortal wound
       Home the king rides safe and well . . .
       —From "When the King Rode Forth
       to Battle," by Maria Konopnicka
       (1842–1910)

1

No sooner did the ship pull away from the dock than I instantly felt myself subject to maritime law. Only then did I begin to understand that which I couldn't quite grasp when I was a law student, the necessity for a separate body of jurisprudence pertaining to the sea. For just as the moon holds sway over the tides, or, as some would have it, over the whole human psyche, so does the ocean have an imperceptible effect upon those who would cross it. Footsteps lighten, manners soften, voices lilt. Aboard ship one suffers minor hurt rather than inflict hurt on fellow passengers. Gestures become more polished, behavior more formal. One lives under the mystical spell of the sea and behaves accordingly, altogether differently than on dry land. Parental admonitions that once went in one ear and out the other suddenly make sense. Everyone circles the deck, strolling like lords. A fine, silken cord connects one man to his fellow, even his fellow female. The merest exchange of greetings—"Good morning, good year"—spans the gap. I also began to appreciate the tenderness of the terms "shipboard brother" and "shipboard sister." Nor did this metamorphosis occasion anxiety, because it affected everyone to the same degree. Aboard ship, in contrast to their alter egos on land, strangers find themselves tossed together, and yet, wonder of wonders, God's world with its manifold souls stays in balance even here, where we tread softly and scarcely recognize the sounds of our own voices.

I looked for a secluded corner, away from the throng, where I could get a grip on my excitement. The red, yellow, and green flares of the launches that accompanied our ship like some exotic marine vegetation receded farther and farther away, extending our circle of solitude. We had escaped, leaving behind all sentimental reminders of relatives and attachments to terra firma. Now that the *Olympic* had pulled away from land, it formed its own little planet, with its own population, its own way of life, even its own invisible leader, the captain, whose existence you could deny without any damage to your peace of mind.

I stood leaning against the railing of the deck and had the audacity to cite myself. Somewhere I had written that the world is divided into two camps: those with the wherewithal to travel and those condemned to staying put. This notion pleased me now that I was putting it to the test.

Five young men were also leaning against the railing, looking back at the distant lights, the rank harbor smells still filling the air. They watched as the water thickened, turning blacker. The only sound was that of the wavelets, soft, playful plops against the ship like soap bubbles bursting. These stalwarts made up the orchestra, which had struck a minor key at our departure. "Why not a happy tune?" many of the passengers had demanded, as they waved a final exhausted farewell to relatives on shore. Parting was sorrow enough without this mournful accompaniment. Though each of the passengers had willingly embarked on this journey, the final wrench of the ship away from land seemed to rip them forcibly from their loved ones. There was no compensating pleasure as yet aboard ship, everything was still disorienting, undefined, and strange.

"Why don't they play a happy tune?"

The protest was taken up like a call to revolution. The members of the little band, mother's milk still on their lips, must have been intimidated by the passengers' displeasure and, in their confusion, blundered into yet another dirge, which tugged at the heartstrings. The passengers had no choice but to yield to the mournful melody. When

I told the musicians that I liked their little orchestra and that I particularly admired their courage in not playing something jazzy, they seemed to take heart. They had been somewhat depressed, thinking they were failures before the ship was barely out to sea.

These eighteen-, nineteen-year-olds hailed from West Virginia University, where they played in the student orchestra. By a stroke of good fortune, the dean had recommended them for a job as shipboard musicians, a two-week engagement crossing the ocean to Europe and back, with a free stopover in Paris. Four of the boys were tall, imposing, and handsome. The fifth, short and barrel-shaped, played the violin, not the drums as one might have expected. They all looked freshly hatched, in their brand-new suits and shoes, which seemed to show a mother's loving touch. If I am not mistaken, one face even bore the trace of a tear.

They spoke in a southern drawl that rolled right off their tongues, and they seemed to find the proper word for the proper expression. They reveled in my company as if I were some precious gem. After all, I was the first stranger to make their acquaintance, and I was gallantly passed from one to the other. They had no wish to sleep and were prepared to stay up all night until the last glimpse of land disappeared from view. They were full of excitement at the prospect of seeing Paris with their very own eyes, in the springtime of youth, their best years, when there was still pleasure to be had. I told them that I envied their good luck, and they laughed when they found out that I'd be in Paris too. Try as I might, I detected no trace in them of college-boy callowness. They fell into their new roles easily, with grace.

Suddenly I heard my own speech becoming more Yankeefied than it had been on land. My tongue was performing acrobatics. I sidestepped many of their questions and answered others not altogether truthfully. I was evolving into a different person, someone I hardly recognized. I sprouted wings and, like Alice in Wonderland, began to reel off adventures one after another, so that these five college students shouldn't mistake their first shipboard acquaintance as just anybody. I fell into my new role too, and played it as elegantly and as politely as I was able. The boys chattered on about college life, girlfriends, and parents, and about Paris, where one can lose oneself completely and still come up refreshed. They talked about their future professions and about their responsibilities to society. They asked me about New York and about Communism, and told me how much they admired President Roosevelt.

The next day I was distressed to find out that, while we slept, the iron hand of authority had divided all of us into separate classes. The holiday was over, and it was back to our destined stations. The way to the first-class deck was blocked, as was the way to second class, where I was booked, and likewise the way to third class, where the boys were quartered. When I later caught sight of the young musicians, all spiffed out in their finery, they were embarrassed by their lowly status, and I, in turn, was ashamed of my bourgeois privilege. It was only last night that we had parted with a casual "See you tomorrow."

2

Of all the passengers, the least interesting and most superfluous were those who came aboard as couples. It was as though, without missing a beat, they had simply exchanged their bedrooms at home for staterooms at sea. Strolling arm in arm, confident and proud, they already seemed to possess that which the others, eyes busily darting, were still hoping to find. Yet before long the couples began showing signs of unease. For everyone else, the ship was one big, happy hunting ground, whereas they, poor souls, were yoked together, performing their foreplay in full view of the other passengers. The female of the pair generally seemed grateful to her partner for this travel opportunity, and, no matter how tall she was, contrived to look up adoringly at her benefactor.

One by one, the couples drifted off quietly, leaving only the unattached to carry on. The males of the species engaged in brittle banter, their words dropping like dry bones. They inspected the females like bitches in a kennel, and a hushed, dreadful competition ensued until late into the night. I escaped to the bar, the male sanctuary, and fell into a padded chair. The swaying floor made me feel as if I were in a rocker.

Waiters stood at the ready. Subject to their gentle ministrations, I seemed to be dozing off in a barber chair, submitting to the soft hands of an expert masseur. I ordered a drink, and tossed a coin on the table with such a theatrical flourish that I was astonished by my own performance. The waiter bowed and walked off with mincing steps to tend to another patron. I was grateful that I had managed to cover up my inexperience and that my presence didn't publicly proclaim: "Listen, everyone. This is my first ocean crossing in twenty years—and how many such trips, I ask you, do you think a fellow like me takes in a lifetime?" Though my face didn't show it, I had the strange sensation that, for all the beneficences and transgressions of my adult years, only now had I become fully a grown-up. Indeed, it was just now, here at sea, with the floor shifting beneath me, that I finally felt myself to be my own man, secure in my own counsel.

Sitting at a side table against the wall were two pretty girls. The waiter had already come by five or six times to remove their empty glasses and bring them full ones. They were never without a cigarette and blew out the smoke in long streamers, like hardened veterans. Between puffs they sipped their drinks. They held hands and looked into each other's eyes like lovers, but their eyes were red and fear-ridden, as if they had already drunkenly squandered their virtue on the first night of the voyage. They moved closer to each other. Both were good-looking and fine-figured, though perhaps somewhat more buxom than the average American girl. For the most part they kept silent, and the occasional word they spoke was so hushed, hardly above a whisper, that it became somewhat dispiriting to look at them and their ample bodies, which now resembled a pair of passionate Siamese twins. The waiters looked away, as did the few other remaining drinkers in the bar. Only one roaring drunk—it was a mystery how he had managed to reach this state so early in the voyage—sat ogling the girls and laughing loudly. He kept this up until he drove them away. The two girls tottered out, arm in arm, and the drunk blew them a kiss.

Finally, he and I were alone in the bar. He called me over and insisted that I drink on his tab, all the while telling me to my face that he hated my guts. The devil only knows why he took it into his drunken head to think that I was German, and Scotsman that he was, he detested Germans. My protestations were useless. He wanted to know only one thing: Did I, or did I not, lose the Great War? Had I suffered total defeat, or was my nose still up in the air? Pulling a greasy British passport from his breast pocket, he slapped his chest and swore that if I didn't concede, I would pay for it dearly in the next great World War, when he would personally administer the coup de grâce. He told some witless jokes at my "German" expense, and whinnied like a horse. The man was large and sturdy, with a freckled face and powerful head and arms. His head kept drooping of its own accord with every drink, until his tongue could no longer form words. Nonetheless, he managed to order a fresh drink and promptly fell asleep over his British passport.

I lay on my cabin bunk, rocking back and forth. Sleepily, I thought of Sholem Aleichem's Fishl-Dovid the teacher, who was returning home for the Passover holiday in a little boat. I, too, was on my way home. Home . . . home . . . I said to myself, to the rhythm of the rocking, until I could no longer hold my eyes open.

3

The next morning on our second day out, that famous couple, water and sky, put in its appearance. By now a fixed routine had established itself, and everything was running with mechanical precision, as though we had been traveling for months.

I have never been any great shakes at orienting myself and now, aboard ship, for the life of me, I couldn't quite determine where I had walked or stood the night before. The sundeck at first seemed like the exercise path in a prison yard, though bit by bit one got used to the ritual of going round and around the deck after meals to take the air, until it began to feel like a real constitutional. But since the same smiling faces floated past on every lap, and the ship swayed lightly underfoot, the stroll around the deck with the sun stroking our faces seemed more like a turn around the dance floor. Even the passengers lolling in deck chairs, soaking up the sun, seemed part of the dance.

The ship with its barely perceptible movement began to feel like a giant yacht that had taken us all out to the middle of the ocean and then dropped anchor for a few days. It would have been hard to imagine a calmer sea, a bluer sky, or better company.

This was no mere voyage, but a dream. "One should travel to Europe only at the end of June, the beginning of July," remarked my neighbor on the warm bench we were sharing. His last crossing was in October, and aha . . . aha . . . did he have a tale to tell. He was as sick as a dog and vomited all the way, because the ship kept going like this —here he demonstrated with his hand how his ship had almost capsized. My neighbor spoke a meticulous English, but substituted an *s* for the *sh* sound, like one of those fully baked Lithuanian Jews whose speech was also marked by the same transposition. I was certain, however, that he was no *Litvak:* This specimen had rough hands, a broad back, a mighty head, propped on his neck like a cabbage, high cheekbones, watery-blue eyes, and thick, bushy eyebrows.

He looked like a laborer and talked like an intellectual, choosing his words as if he were sorting chickpeas and rejecting the inferior ones. He would settle on the precise noun and then deck it out with an exact adjective and an elegant verb. His raspy voice seemed to emerge not from his throat but from some region of the heart. He pointed to a wisp of cloud still in its swaddling clothes and said that he already knew to which category it belonged since, as he explained, he was a teacher.

"Of clouds?" I asked.

He burst into a hearty, peasant laugh. "No! Of geography, in a middle school in Schenectady."

I have always loved the ring of the word *Schenectady.* Schenectady! It sounded like the cracking of a hard Turkish nut. To show him that I had a head on my shoulders, I tossed in the name of Charles Steinmetz, that famous son of Schenectady.

What a question! Of course he knew of the electrical wizard. Now there was a man! And what a Socialist! What a noble spirit! So modest and unassuming, so friendly that he could chat up the meanest of men like a brother. My benchmate pronounced the word *Socialist* with a nostalgic gleam in his blue eyes. His hoarse voice spoke the word so tenderly that the dry term fairly quivered with emotion. He kept gesticulating with his rough carpenter's hands until he finally let one of them drop on my shoulder in a gesture of comradeship: "Yes sir, that was a Socialist!"

Suddenly, he pulled out his watch and, rising abruptly from the bench, said that, much as he enjoyed my company and would soon return to resume our conversation, he must now ask to be excused. It was time to go to the toilet. "Heh, heh! A person is only human." Chuckling, he gave me another friendly slap on the back. His bowel movements were at fixed times, calibrated to the minute. Should anything ever interrupt the routine, he would immediately take some measure to get himself back on track. This was very important, because a person was no more than a machine.

"Here, read something until I get back." He tossed me a pack of pamphlets and, already some distance away, doubled up in laughter when he saw how dumbfounded I was by the foreign language.

"Swedish?" I called out to him.

"No, Danish!"

I turned the pages. Complicated Scandinavian words, tough as nails, were underlined in pencil, with English comments in the margins. I kept turning the pages until the words assumed some familiarity and I was able to recognize familiar Teutonic roots under their Danish disguise.

On an adjacent lounge lay a young man, belly turned up to the sun, his face smeared with lotion to prevent burning. The melting grease glistened. A second young man lay on his side nearby, opening a nervous eye from time to time as if to check that his companion was still there. Over his bulging chest, the man taking the sun had on a tight sweater that seemed to be choking him around the neck. He chewed gum phlegmatically. He would doze off, snap awake, and then resume chewing. When I spoke to him, he didn't respond, and when he did deign to answer, his few words came out sleepily. Every time he spoke up to mutter three or four words, his sidekick would open a nervous eye as if to say, half entreatingly and half in anger, "Enough talking now." He would cut him off in the middle, ending the conversation.

The sunbather seemed somewhat put out with me. His broken nose, a collapsed, wooden ruin, snorted like a locomotive. It vexed him that I, alone of all the passengers, should not have known who he was. His companion, apparently some sort of manager, gave me a pleading look, miming me to stay away from his bread-and-butter. The sunbather fell silent, but then suddenly bestirred himself and, in open defiance of his Man Friday, laced into me, this time not sparing any words. Man Friday decided that he couldn't just lie there while his bread-and-butter was holding forth, so he sat up, the better to keep an eye on him.

"How come you don't know me?" said the sunbather. "Don't you go to the fights? You know who Barney Ross is? Well, I could have been a second Barney, if that black guy hadn't stopped me—*a finster yor af im.*" (The Yiddish curse was for my benefit). "A black year on his black head. I could take anyone down, but when it came to that guy, nothing worked. So I gave up boxing and opened a little store, but the store failed. Then my mother, may she rest in peace, died, so now I've decided to make a comeback. Yesiree, a comeback!"

Man Friday glared at his Hercules. He screwed up his face as if he had stomach cramps, but my interlocutor continued undaunted.

"The press mustn't find out about this. I'm going first to Paris, then to London, and after a few fights in Europe, I'm going back to get even. Damn him! Imagine, winning all those fights and then getting stopped by a black man. And you wanna know how come I know Yiddish? What am I, a Turk? I came over from Poland when I was twelve. My mother, may she rest in peace, was a pious woman. She couldn't make me *daven*—no way would I pray! But I did wear those fringes, the *tsitsis.*"

The greasy lotion dripped from his chin and from his collapsed nose. He fell back on his lounge, while the manager, who hadn't uttered a word, lay back on his side. But the fighter wasn't done yet. Again, he sat up abruptly, leaned head and shoulder toward me, and said, this time entirely in Yiddish: "Say, what kind of Jewish bastards are walking around on this ship anyway? They'd eat shit rather than admit that they're Jews. One Hitler isn't enough for them, the bastards."

Man Friday cocked an eye and the prizefighter lapsed into silence. He fell back on the lounge, and began, rapidly, to chew his gum.

4

Aboard ship it's easier to appreciate the individual's worth. Under the impact of the everyday, we tend to lose the sense of drama, tragic or comic, that is everyone's portion. The child's sense of wonderment dulls. You become the measure of all things, the star of the play, with everyone else reduced to bit players, mere extras in the great ego-drama which plays itself out in a million boring scenes that thrill no one else but you, the lead actor. Only when death cuts one of them down like a tree in a forest do you realize that your nearest and dearest have had dramas of their own. At that point you approach the empty space and try to reconstruct the missing life. You realize that it was full of incident. Trading anecdotes about the deceased, you see that he was the star in his own drama. But had this ever occurred to you when you caught sight of your wife sunk in a daydream, or your children lost in reverie by the window? You take them for granted as backup for your life, as satellites revolving around your planet.

Aboard ship it is different: there each person is a fresh discovery, every new face shines in the limelight. Though you may be as important as Moses, you get used to the idea that everyone else has a story to tell. During all those years when you had no idea of their existence, your fellow passengers were busy leading lives of their own, and naturally they are eager to share the details.

My Danish friend was orphaned at a young age and never knew either of his parents. He knocked around on his own and from early on put his little hands to work to earn his keep, since he couldn't depend on the kindness of relatives to whom a piece of bread was as precious as gold. He had much to tell and he wanted to tell it all at once, but he would rein himself in and begin with his first moment of self-awareness, which occurred when he lost his faith.

When he was a boy, faith burned in him like the flames of a hundred church candles. Every crucifix was a fiery thorn in his flesh. His heart yearned for the one who had died nailed to the cross and for the holy virgin who had given this martyr-god to the world. Then one day his fishing village was shaken by a horrible tragedy. A fishing boat capsized, drowning all eighteen aboard. The wailing of the mothers, fathers, brides, children, wives, and the peals of the church bell in the center of town ringing out the misfortune—this was familiar from all the ballads about the hazards of life on the sea. One need only recall Charles Kingsley's "Three Fishers":

Three fishers went sailing away to the west,
Away to the west as the sun went down;

Each thought on the woman who loved him the best,
And the children stood watching them out of the town.

Drownings are not uncommon in fishing villages, but when they occur
they send a shudder down your spine and children stare terrified at the
waters lapping the shore as they would at a cold-blooded murderer.
Eighteen drowned was a considerable haul, even for the piratical
North Sea, and all of Denmark was in a frenzy. A prominent clergyman
was sent down from Copenhagen to eulogize the unfortunate fisher-
men. When he learned that the drowned men had belonged to another
Christian denomination, he condemned them to eternal damnation
because they had impudently strayed from the true path. The priest's
eulogy caused a scandal and all the newspapers seethed. The priest's
sermon was salt on the widows' wounds. They wailed like cats at the
thought of their husbands, fathers, and brothers roasting in eternal
fires of hell. It was then that our young Scandinavian spat on belief
and set out for America.

My new Danish friend spoke with great passion. He was one of those
introspective types, with a dash of Dostoyevsky, though he was no
epileptic but rather, physically vigorous. Religion, God, Woman, Purpose, Afterlife—he was burdened by a mass of confused ideas, and
spoke of his loss of faith with heavy heart. Although he pretended to
have closed a chapter in his life, faith was as necessary for him as
breathing, eating, or sleeping. It was such people whom Mary Baker
Eddy must have had in mind when she founded her theological labo-
ratory of Christian Science.

He became a Socialist, transferring his passion from God to a faith
in human brotherhood, especially the brotherhood of the proletariat.
The austere, overintellectualized Karl Marx, with his precise, almost
mathematical social axioms, became the young Dane's fount of inspiration. He yearned for the utopian Red heaven, but his hopes were
dashed when first the British Socialists and then the Germans began
—here he apologized—"to shit all over themselves," and all that remained of his one-time political faith was an interest in the cooperative
movement and a hope in Roosevelt.

But he was getting ahead of himself. When he first came to America he worked like a mule in small factories. Then came the awful war, and he saw action as a seaman. After the war he was finally able to escape from a life in the miserable shops and became something of an intellectual, with a refined profession, though his bones still ached from all the days and nights of hard physical labor so that he almost lacked the strength to enjoy his new status. Still, going from sweatshop to teaching was like entering the millennium, like paradise on earth. "When you're a teacher in a middle school instead of a workhorse in a factory, you come home and—the devil take it—there's time to look into a book and to think about the mysteries of the world. As the poet Dehmel said, 'Nur zeit, zeit, zeit'—let there only be time, time, time." He confided that with a refined profession also came "a better class of friends."

He would never forget his dear friend, now deceased, a priest and "jewel of a man." He may not have been a Marxist, but he had an ingrained sense of justice. A true American, he interpreted strictly the declaration that all men are created equal. This priest had an odd weakness for globes. He was a geographer and had amassed a wonderful collection, the most beautiful globes of their kind, which he loved to spin while contemplating the variety of lands and peoples and God's blessing on all.

One day, our Dane noticed a new acquisition that was exceptionally beautiful, an artistic triumph. "This must be the globe you have been looking for all your life," he exclaimed. "Why, it's exquisite! Who made it for you?"

"Nobody," the priest said simply. "It created itself."

The Dane thought the priest had lost his mind, but the latter stuck to his guns, insisting that the globe was indeed self-created, until, taking pity at last on his atheist friend, he said: "When it comes to this wooden globe, which is merely a mechanical representation of the earth, you cannot believe that it created itself. Yet when it comes to the great, big, beautiful, wonderful universe, with its millions of stars and planets, you are willing to swear by Darwin and Marx that this miraculous world created itself, out of thin air."

"Now wasn't that a superb lesson in religion?" the Dane said with a smile, "Slightly primitive perhaps, but moving in its child's logic.

That's how he was—a man of faith to the end, until he departed this life."

My talkative friend went on with his story, telling me that he was past forty when he married. His wife, a quiet woman almost his age, was content to be a housewife. She cheered his evenings at home, and in due course, twins arrived, a beautiful, blue-eyed boy and girl. Needless to say, he was wild with joy. He had found purpose in life. Life was crazy. You ran around like a hen, pecking for food, peck-peck, knowing that sooner or later someone was going to come along and wring your neck. Still, you kept going, and crazy as life was, you wanted to be a father, a husband, a grandfather, as well as a citizen in good standing, so peck-peck, you kept pecking away like a hen.

"Tell me, Gladdy, my friend," he said with sudden intimacy, devising a diminutive of my surname, "is there an afterlife? Or is it all just an empty dream, and the foolish hen lays down to die and sleeps forever? Well," he sighed, "the twins didn't live long, only three days, and both died almost at the very same instant. You know the reason— mother and father over forty. But biological facts don't heal the wound.

"I stood there looking at the lifeless little faces," he continued, "grieving over my loss, until the last rays of the setting sun fell on their waxen figures and, all at once, I saw a great light. These infants—this little boy and this little girl—were miniature man and wife, my own father and mother who had abandoned me so early in life. Now they had made themselves visible to me in order to restore my lost faith. The dolls' faces smiled serenely and I bowed my head at the revelation. When I told this to my wife, she made no response. She was in a state of shock, and her melancholy silence lasted several months. But my suffering was peaceful because I had my faith back with renewed clarity.

"Well, to make a long story short, we had another child that, mercifully, lived, but my wife became seriously ill. Doctors advised her to return to her native town in Denmark, and she's been there with the child ever since. Every summer now, for the past six years, I've been going over there to be with them."

His was no easy life, to be sure. His wife was an invalid, albeit gentle and devoted. In the course of his summer visits, they slept together only five or six times, and that was it for the year. He was no longer a young man and couldn't change his ways, even in the face of the temptation that came his way in the shape of the fluttery middle-school girls, who thrust their young breasts right up to his nose, making his head spin. He was aware of what went on in schools between male teachers and female students, all those stories about orgies. But he was self-disciplined, not for nothing was he Scandinavian. One had to be very careful not to slip. So each day he went home to his room, to his old maidservant, who cooked him his meals, to his dog, his radio, and his books on cooperatives.

I asked him to join me for a drink. "No, thank you," he said. "I don't drink, just the occasional beer, and I only smoke four or five cigarettes a day." And, he added, whenever sinful thoughts invaded his mind, teasing him and disturbing his equanimity, he thought, who knows, perhaps if he were younger he might act on the impulse and write to his wife, explaining everything clearly and explicitly. She would understand and forgive him.

"But, Gladdy my friend," he said, winding up his tale, "I'm losing my hair and teeth, and something else doesn't work as well as it did in my younger days. I'll just have to get used to it. The only question is: Are we making fools of ourselves? Is there an afterlife, or is the joke on us?"

All that night I thought about the twins and the reborn father and mother who had sentenced themselves to nine months of anxious gestation and to a second death so that they might bring a measure of hope and encouragement to their orphaned son. It was like some Hasidic tale, but with a Scandinavian twist and a whiff of salt air, joined to a death-fugue, rising and falling with the waves of the sea. I even attempted to write a poem about this, but it came out sounding more like John Masefield than a proper Yiddish poem.

Chapter 2

1

Only one and a half days out to sea, and already I feel released from obligations to family, society, even from the gamut of political credos with which, for professional reasons, I had found it necessary to stock my brain, merely to sustain myself, earning me my livelihood—a modest share of oxygen to fill my lungs and drink sufficient to water my gut. It was for just such "luxuries" (though perhaps also for the roof over my head, a garment to cover myself, a bit of warmth, and a wife) that I immersed myself in all those poisonous ideologies.

There was a time, years back, when for me introspection meant philosophizing about the meaning of existence, a private pleasure, like the cud chewing of a self-absorbed and sated cow in a sunny meadow. But these past few years my mind is mired in the bloodstained world of politics. "I think, therefore I am" is no longer enough. Am what? One must legitimate oneself by announcing a political creed: I am a liberal, a Fascist, a Social-Fascist, or a Communist, a Trotskyite, a Lovestonite, a Zionist. Hecklers shout down from the gallery, demanding to know, "Are you with us, or with our enemies?" Events move so quickly that *we* and *the enemy* shift kaleidoscopically, and yesterday's friends change into today's foes too swiftly to let you catch your breath.

Worse yet is when hecklers turn into the voice of your conscience. You pretend it isn't happening, until one day you are afraid to reach for a glass of orange juice without reckoning all the political implications. And how dumb this politicking is! You no sooner locate your political absolute than along come the world leaders to season your ideals with executions, slaughters, and betrayals. We are baffled. Should we shout hurrah! and join the happy ranks of loyal recruits, or find ourselves a new political creed?

I feel aboard this ship as Jonah must have felt in that first moment when he thought he had escaped God's wrath. I breathe easier, having at last broken free from the whole abracadabra of my existence. Maybe here I will be able to scrape off the scabby crust that had accrued to me as a social animal, a writer-for-hire, a Jew in a bloody world that—*pace* Shakespeare—only demands *my* pound of flesh. Now all is well, and the sun beating down on the deck feels so beneficent that I don't want to admit any thought that might claim me. For what is thought but clarification, and I want no clarification—only to see and hear for myself, without comparisons or conclusions.

By now my fellow passengers, in contrast to our first day aboard, treat me with the same nonchalance that I accord them. I feel no need to speak to them. I look at them with half-closed eyes and attend to them with half-closed ears, and if it pleases me, I devote more attention to a speck of dust than to the group gathered beside me. All's well and good, I've divested myself of the little I possess. I am a poor man who has accumulated such a store of poverty that I can afford to jettison the bits of knowledge I've acquired, the meager passions, the entire claptrap of my little world. And should faces from my past swim into view, they break apart like reflections on the water's surface as I toss in pebbles to make them disappear.

The sea, until now a frozen, immobile surface—"a painted ship on a painted sea"—suddenly came alive with porpoises, leaping and cavorting alongside our vessel. Anyone privileged to have once seen these creatures in motion will never forget the sight. They rise from the water by the tens or even hundreds in graceful arcs, heads plunging into the waves, but always in pairs, like two elegant hands. Arched in the air, they mirror themselves in the sun so that their every leap is a cascade of color. It is a marvelous sight, as if the sea had opened a porthole into its secrets to reveal the wonders just below its surface.

The thought that had been teasing me all this while finally let me in on the secret that I was lucky to be away at this peak time of Jewish organizational politicking. For the height of summer was when the leaders of the community swung into action, furiously jockeying for place. And here was I, well out of it, on the high seas with not even so much as a newspaper assignment demanding my attention.

This trip had occasioned my first face-to-face encounter with a boss. Until this last job, I had worked for the kind of organizations or companies that did not require dealing with the man on top. Since the bread I earned, with or without the butter, fell like manna from heaven, I had never seen my exalted provider and thus never felt any great divide between me, the "means of production," and the boss, the absolute controller of my modest income. When I worked for the American Surety Company, a huge corporation that employed hundreds of people, I could observe the vast hierarchy of subordinates and superiors, the assorted ranks of lower-level toilers overseen by inspectors and superintendents, but I never got to see the shining face of our almighty ruler. Once, an arrogant type with just the right configuration of bald pate and gray fringe came by and looked us over, smacking his lips, as if he were counting his sheep. He seemed so unaccountably important that I was disappointed to learn he was a mere vice president, one of a score.

My fellow toilers were white-collar workers, a collection of meek men and dolled up young women, the latter mostly from poor towns in New Jersey, where bathtubs, it would seem, were in short supply. They took the ferry every morning to metropolitan New York, to the city of golden opportunity, not so much to get to work on time as in the hope of fitting into Cinderella's glass slipper, or at least winning a fur coat from the boss for favors granted. On hot summer days, for all their good looks, they reeked of sweat. It broke my heart that women with such pretty faces and such tiny, dancing feet should emit these pungent smells, as if nature had bestowed rank odors on beautiful little female animals in order to repel predatory males.

One seductively sunny day, I looked for an excuse to say goodbye forever to the dusty documents accumulating on my desk. The opportunity came with a "fatherly" note from a supervisor, reminding me of all the duties I had neglected. He warned that unless I completed these duties I would be ineligible for promotion to higher positions in the company. I replied with a rude note in kind—for that's how business was conducted at American Surety, in the grand manner, with an exchange of memoranda between subordinates and supervisors and vice versa. The superintendent lost no time in sending for me and demanding my resignation, in just those words. Given the munificent sum of seventy-five dollars a month that I was pulling down (to say nothing of the vague opportunity to "work my way up," in the good, old-fashioned American way), the demand that I resign had such an official ring to it that I complied and strode right out of the superintendent's office with head held high.

My white-collar comrades with their finely tuned antennas promptly got wind of my revolt. These colleagues, purportedly buddies, buried their heads deeper in their documents lest, God forbid, their bidding me farewell be taken as a sign that they identified themselves with my insurgency. The only one with the courage to say goodbye was a Scotsman, whose vocabulary featured an all-purpose word, "horseshit!"— an exclamation he employed, with varying intonations adapted to the occasion, to signify both approval and displeasure, equal verdict on the rotten eggs that were served up at Child's restaurant and on the pretty, friendly waitress who had brought them. He ran after me, pressed my hand warmly, and uttered his trademark expression, a "horseshit!" so deep-felt, filled with such sorrow and regret, that—loosely translated— it seemed to say: "Don't take it to heart, my friend, because it's all vanity of vanities, *vanitas vanitatis*. You'll certainly find another job." The one magic word conveyed all that, and more.

It was midsummer. To reach the exit, I had to walk past the desks of a whole row of female workers. The scent of their makeup, simmering in perspiration, followed me out the door.

When I was a university student, I worked for a union local. At that job I never saw the "big boss" either. To be sure, I had a supervisor, but I felt that my true employer was the working class, even though it didn't exactly keep me in clover. For ten dollars a week, my job was to stand behind a grille, facing a clutch of resentful workers who had just put in a week of hard labor and now had to suffer the further indignity of lining up to pay their union dues. The dues payers would often let their anger out at me and scream across the grille that I was draining their blood, gorging on the fruit of their toil, and sucking the marrow from their bones. The job ended when my supervisor sent me to buy a few bottles of whiskey for a little banquet the labor leaders were throwing in their own honor. Inasmuch I was given no money, only instructions to go to a nearby saloon and charge the purchase to the union's credit, I persuaded myself en route that, as a university student–turned–whiskey–errand boy, my dignity was being trampled on. It was a good excuse not to return, and so ended my union job, without my ever having laid eyes on the top man.

As teacher in a Jewish school in a remote town in the Catskills, I was apparently working for a commune. I had been hired to provide spiritual nourishment not only for the children, but as well for the mostly tubercular adults, who endured winter days in their little business establishments, with not a cent of revenue coming in, waiting for summer's redemptive bounty. During the long winter nights, after a day spent instructing their children, the teacher was milked for whatever he could provide in the way of literature, history, Jewish lore, culture, and other edifying fare. Sunday evening was the highlight of their week, the time of the weekly meeting, when they assembled to transact community business, all dressed to the nines, the men freshly shaved, their wives grotesquely fat or grotesquely thin. They made long-winded speeches and proposed various resolutions, quarreling among themselves, insulting one another, and spreading slander. The women took a lively part in the proceedings, violating all parliamentary procedure and forcing me, as if at gunpoint, to declare whose side I was on. They weighed my every smile, trying to guess at whom it was directed, and why. Only a Disraeli could squirm his way diplomatically out of this embarrassing situation.

After I had successfully negotiated the slippery terrain, treading neutrally among the competing factions, I was given my reward. In my presence, the parents of the children would solicit contributions for my weekly salary. They were usually two or three dollars short, and this would lead to a long, oppressive pause. The women would throw me a look of pity and sigh over my plight. But invariably, always in the same heroic fashion, a savior would step forward, a veritable Lohengrin, and, every inch the proud philanthropist, toss down the missing few dollars. The expression on his face, however, warned that such largess would not be repeated and was not to be expected the following week. His generosity would be greeted by thunderous applause. At last the greasy bills—from the butcher, the shoemaker, the plumber, the blacksmith, the gas-station owner, the shopkeeper, the tailor, the grocer, the flour merchant, the hotel owner, the furniture dealer, the bootlegger, as well as a childless widow married to a Gentile, who donated her dollar to the cause of radical Jewish education in the mistaken belief that this would secure her a place in Paradise—would be thrust with a triumphant flourish into the teacher's hands.

I had many "bosses" in the Catskills, but the chief boss, the one who wielded the whip and threw me crumbs, spent his winters in warmer climes, and him I never had the good fortune to see.

My latest employment was—and remains—that of writer for a Yiddish daily. I had worked there for eight long years without ever seeing my boss, the paper's owner, who remained a phantom presence until it came time to negotiate a leave for the present trip. He was a shrewd businessman who knew that I hadn't asked to see him to foment revolution, so he dispensed with me quickly. I sat scrunched down in the chair opposite him and he was obviously as eager to get rid of me as I was to have done with the whole uncomfortable business. I felt awkward and insignificant in the presence of the mighty one, who held my livelihood in his palms and brandished it over my head, as God did the Torah over the Children of Israel at Sinai—accept My Law and live, otherwise perish! I probably looked to him like some miserable child. My rectitude, my talent, my three slim volumes of poetry, my convictions—were all as naught when I imagined I heard outside the office door, clear as a bell, the pleas of my wife and three children not to make a false move or utter a wrong word, God forbid. The sun might be shining as brightly as it did that day when I walked out on my job at American Surety, but there must be no more talk of resignation. I was now a paterfamilias and must bow to the special demands of the role.

"I'll think it over," said the supreme authority.

"Thank you. Good day," I replied.

There was no rejoinder, but I had finally seen the provider of my sustenance, seen, too, that he considered me only a debit in his account book, a mere inkblot in his business ledger. Coming out of his office, my left ear burning and cheeks aflame, I ran smack into my supervisor. He threw me a sympathetic look, well aware of the agony I had just undergone, but he quickly drew himself up so that I, in my helplessness, shouldn't think him a friend and cry on his shoulder.

So the small joy that I felt at the prospect of my first trip abroad in twenty years was reversed, and I was seized by a strange foreboding. The fear persisted as I prepared to board the ship.

2

In the morning, informed by the ship's newspaper that Hitler had done away with his closest associates in the so-called Night of Long Knives —apparently taking to heart Mussolini's advice never to share your rule with the fellow revolutionaries who aided your rise to power (by the same token, rather than pay back a debt owed to good friends, it might be easier to slaughter them)—I went looking for Jewish faces among the passengers.

The paper, an attractive miniature version of its counterparts on land, conveyed the news simply, without commentary, as if this were no more than a sensational tidbit, the severed heads of a dozen or so Nazi pederasts served up on a silver platter for the delectation of the passengers after their rich breakfast—yet another item on the ship's program to stave off boredom. The effort was wasted on the Gentile passengers, who got no thrill from the news. They thumbed the scant pages, reading the jokes, the sports items, the announcements of afternoon activities, barely pausing over Hitler's bloody purge. When I tried to elicit some reaction from them about this report that had traveled from land to us at sea, many admitted that they hadn't seen the news at all, and those who had said things like "Hitler's a damn fool!" "Let them knock each other's brains out!" "Hmm . . . this is just the beginning!" My Scandinavian friend gave me a sharp lecture on Marxism, exclaiming, "By God, the Danes hate the Germans! It's high time Roosevelt said something about this."

None of these responses cheered me, lacking as they were in Jewish understanding and feeling. I realized that to the Gentiles, Hitler meant something altogether different than he did to me. My non-Jewish fellow passengers, whether provoked to anger or not, regarded Hitler as merely Germany's dictator. To me, to 600,000 German Jews, and indeed to all the 17 million Jews worldwide, Hitler was the embodiment of the dreaded historical hatemonger, latest in a long line of persecutors that stretched from Haman, Torquemada, and Chmielnicki to Krushevan and Jozef Haller, a beast with a murderous paw, wielding a bloody pen that was writing a dreadful new chapter of Jewish history.

The casual reaction of my Gentile fellow passengers to the Hitler-news was the first slap in the face I had received as a Jew on this floating international paradise. I felt isolated, even offended that news of such importance to me should fall on such indifferent ears. I longed for a "warm Jewish heart" to share my emotion. The boxer had complained about the "bastards" trying to pass for *goyim*, but I began to discern a few Jewish faces. Perhaps under the impact of the Hitler-news, they were coming out of hiding and also looking for company.

My first such discovery was a dignified gentleman in house slippers, a prosperous-looking man with a trimmed beard, sitting on a bench, poring over a sacred text, soundlessly mouthing the words. He was altogether an exemplar of Jewish aristocratic bearing. His beautiful, delicate hands hesitated before turning the page he had just studied, as though he were sorry to leave a passage still so full of immeasurable wisdom. He had sought out the quietest corner of the deck, apparently unwilling to let even his whispers reach the ears of an alien, hostile world, not, God forbid, because he feared that world but because of its undying hatred of Jews. "The whole world is our enemy," he declared, when I buttonholed him for his reaction to the Hitler-news. The Nazi bloodbath was no special concern of his. With fine Jewish humor he explained that such events were family squabbles, as at a wedding to which we Jews were not invited either by the groom's side or the bride's. The moral of the Hitler purge was that they all hated us. How this followed from the massacre of Nazis slaying one another he didn't say, but he assured me that all the enemies of Israel could be made to disappear by studying a sacred Jewish text.

The man looked to be about seventy, on the cusp of the Bible's allotted span of years. He radiated a serenity that could not be bought for a king's treasure. The rabbinic dictum "The day is short and the task great" didn't seem to concern him. In leisurely fashion he studied the sacred texts for the sheer intellectual pleasure this gave him, engaging in the holy activity for its own sake. He considered the reward of the world to come beside the point, and besides, the world to come was still far off. It was refreshing to find an American Jew who fit Lao Tse's aphoristic descriptions of wisdom, in sharp contrast to the more general type of American Jew, who didn't question the average life span cited in actuarial tables positing that one would drop dead like an exhausted horse in one's fifties, and who consequently thought it necessary to speed things up, discharge one's responsibilities with dispatch, and gulp down the bit of pleasure that life affords. This type did not believe in getting too wrapped up in children, either: What was the point of forming close relationships with them, if you would be a father for only—twenty years?

This slipper-clad Jew emitted the same aura of Sabbath calm that descended over our house like a secret when Mother and Father would shut their bedroom door for a nap following the Sabbath-afternoon meal, a stillness that would prevail until darkness fell and the time came for Father to take down the iron bolts and bars from his shop. The smell of the rusted metal, the clanking of the frozen keys, and the appearance of the first customer of the new week—these were the signals that the God of Abraham had rekindled all the lamps, marking the end of the holy Sabbath and the start of another care-filled week. Suddenly, this gentle Jew studying his holy texts on the ship's deck seemed a bridge linking my first seventeen, eighteen years at home with the present journey back to it—a return voyage to see my dying mother. "Her ears are as yellow as wax," my aunt had written. "Pack your things and come immediately, and may God help us all and bring you here in time to find her still alive."

The ship seemed to be carrying me back to childhood, as though it were sailing backward in time. The two decades I had passed in America crumbled to dust between my fingers. Suddenly, all that mattered were the first years of my life, now straining to link up with the home that was awaiting me, like the two parts of a toy that need to be joined. I was awash in memories. Hitherto I had strongly resisted the temptation to submit my early years to the scalpel. I thought I should wait another twenty years and postpone any autobiographical exercise until I was sixty, by which time the fortunes of Yiddish letters would probably have sunk so low as to preclude any interest in serious literature and left nothing for a writer but to become a purveyor of old gossip, satisfying people's curiosity about other people's lives. Now here I was, making some concession to the evil impulse and beginning to root around in my memories in a way that I hadn't done since I had left home.

Imagine a place with no dragons, no scorpions, no buffalo or bison, no lions or leopards, not even a ram or deer. Who can fathom the misery of a child in a town devoid of such fauna? Elsewhere the wide world holds many such blessings, but not Lublin, which contains nothing but a town clock and a fire warden who, every quarter-hour, sounds the hours until midnight, when everything slumbers but the flitting shadows around the synagogue. My Lublin didn't appear on small maps, and on the larger ones was only a faint, barely legible marking. Really big maps, however, showed not only Lublin but also a tiny squiggle indicating the Bystrzyc rivulet (known to us by its Yiddish equivalent, the Bistshitse), a minor tributary of the Vistula River that flowed through Warsaw, home of the big-city branch of our family.

Long before I was conceived, there was a paternal great-grandfather with the German-sounding name of Enzl, and a grandfather called Yosl Enzls, neither of whom I knew. Enzl was just a name to me, and it sounded more like a nickname. The family archivists—that is to say, my older uncles and aunts—described him as a soft-spoken, sweet-tempered man, who earned his meager living as a sexton and who was reputed to be one of the thirty-six secret saints by whose grace the world is sustained. Grandfather Yosl Enzls was a more fleshed-out figure in my consciousness. He ran a workshop that sewed ladies' garments for well-to-do customers—the high-born daughters of the gentry and of the governor, as well as wealthy women in general. A softhearted exploiter of the working class, he employed thirty or so girls, who ate and slept on tables in the shop, where they also warbled their love songs and collected their dowries, courtesy of the employer, when they left to get married.

This grandfather was no great scholar, but he scrupulously observed all the Jewish laws and attended daily prayer services. He prayed with even greater fervor when he knew that there were carriages pulled up outside the shop with customers waiting for him to return and personally fit them for wedding dresses—and wait they would, he was sure. Those who knew about such matters claimed that he wasn't much of a craftsman, just an ordinary tailor, who got by on personal charm and his winning ways with people. He left behind seven sons, sturdy as oaks, and no inheritance, unless you count poverty a bequest. When he died of a stroke—brought on by the grief of seeing my father, his sixth son, go off to serve in the tsar's army—all that remained was an empty, decrepit workshop.

My mother's side boasted a line of small-town Polish rabbis, and a great-grandmother Drezl, also the wife of a rabbi, who was widowed young. Drezl was six weeks pregnant when her husband died. Since this might have led to ugly gossip, she announced her condition before the open grave, to forestall any dirty rumors that might be spread about her—God forbid! For added insurance, she named the daughter born to her, Bine, after her late husband, Binyomin.

As a respected rabbi's widow, my great-grandmother was given an important community appointment, attendant at the *mikve*, the women's ritual bath. I have clear memories of the meticulous way she would go about fulfilling her duties. My mother must have regarded my prepubescent masculinity as of no moment when she took me along to the mikve and sat me down on a wet bench while the women, young and old, splashed in the water, performing their ritual ablutions under my great-grandmother's stern and competent supervision. During a break from her duties, she would press a coin into my hand, with the wish that my little heart be as open to Torah as was God's Holy Temple.

When she died at the age of one hundred, her son, my grandfather, poor soul, was left an orphan at seventy. Grandfather Avrom was a widower, who lived with us for as long as I can remember, as much a fixture of the household as my father, mother, and brothers. He had a beautiful white beard that had become slightly stained from all the snuff he had pushed up his nose, and he owned a number of snuff boxes, all of them plain, proletarian ones, made of wood or bone, not silver, let alone gold. It took Grandfather longer than a prima donna to perform his toilette. Before going out, he would polish his boots, comb out his beard, and look himself over in the mirror. When he was already standing in the doorway, he would call me over for a final inspection, to make sure that no bit of feather still clung to him. Every Friday afternoon he went to the bathhouse, returning home with time to spare for a nap, before going to usher in the Sabbath at his Hasidic rebbe's synagogue. It was our custom never to touch the braided Sabbath loaf, the *hallah*, until Grandfather had come home to recite the *kiddush* blessing over the wine.

Grandfather was a goldsmith. He had all sorts of strange tools, the strangest being a bellows used in the melting of gold that left a coating of soot over the whole house. He made his services available, gratis, to all in the family, repairing and cleaning their rings, earrings, and brooches—the only exception being Mother, who had to hound him for weeks before he would attend to her jewelry. Sometimes, he would set out with his tools to nearby villages, returning with a deficit that took several glasses of brandy and a hearty meal to overcome. After such indulgence, his cheeks turned red as beets, his blue, carefree eyes started to blink, and soon he would be stretched out on his bed, snoring rhythmically into his lower lip, his beard rising and falling on his chest. The children of the house were ordered to walk on tiptoe, because, as Mother loudly declared, as much to provoke him as to command our attention, "Grandfather, the great breadwinner, has returned from afar and is taking a nap."

The ship was barely rocking. The slipper-clad Jew had dozed off. The air grew sharper and a wondrously cool fragrance rose from the sea, of saltwater long warmed by the sun.

3

The second Jew caught in my net proved less complaisant. I found him strolling arm in arm with a Haitian diplomat who spoke a heartrendingly beautiful French. In his polite yet proud demeanor, the diplomat, a light-skinned mulatto, might have been the great-grandson of Toussaint-Louverture, the black slave who, in 1801, rebelled against Haiti's white masters and gained independence for his country, so electrifying the world with his military genius that in Europe he was dubbed the Black Napoleon. The diplomat spoke in a loud, flirtatious voice so that all could hear how beautiful the pearly vowels of French could sound. He drew on all his powers to convey the subtleties of the language. Absorbing every word, his companion was in seventh heaven when he was able to interject a French sentence of his own, which in turn elicited from the Haitian a fresh torrent of elegant phrases. He pursed his lips like a fish, and every word he uttered was a kiss, sent into the air like a bird freed from confinement.

The diplomat was slender, with polished features and a long, bumpy, almost Jewish-looking nose. He had shrewd eyes and theatrical gestures. If he had to beg someone's pardon for the slightest inadvertent contact that might be mistaken for a shove, he would gallantly bow his head in apology. In sum, though he represented a small, poor land, he was the very model of a diplomat, with all the requisite savoir faire.

Since his companion was much shorter than he (and nondescript looking, to boot), the tall diplomat was constantly bending down to reduce the distance between them, in yet another gesture of tact and courtesy. When, in my quest, I interrupted the pair to solicit the shorter one's reaction to the news about Hitler, he stopped in his tracks like a stunned rooster. For a moment he froze, then suddenly let go of the diplomat's arm. Whereupon the latter, without missing a beat, caught the arm of a passing woman in a motion better suited to the dance floor, and, graciously, with his new companion in tow, continued his stroll around the sundeck, while his erstwhile companion gazed after his departing hero like an orphaned child.

"How did you know I was Jewish?" he asked, as if some misfortune had befallen him. "Well I am, but not one of those common Polish Jews. I'm Dutch."

One of his eyes had a tendency to wander, and kept going into and out of hiding. He was a phlegmatic sort, who spoke English well enough, choosing his words with a slow, deliberate care that complemented his stiffness. His hands hung lifelessly by his side. His step was heavy, and his thoughts, translated from Dutch into his distinctive English, heavier still. He treated our conversation as a fencing match, expecting me to take the offensive.

"As it happens, I'm a Polish Jew," I said, rising to the challenge.

He responded with that great Gentile compliment, "You don't look it." When I asked him to tell me something about his ancestry, he was unwilling to discuss even so recent a forebear as his great-grandfather. Not for him, it would seem, the grand heritage of Dutch Jewry—no Spanish Jews finding refuge in Holland after the Expulsion of 1492, no Polish Jews with their own illustrious history, who, in more recent days, had immigrated to Holland, and certainly no Baruch Spinoza. He was a Dutch Jew, pure and simple, a descendant of generations of Dutch Jews—end of story.

I then tried to steer him to another subject, and asked whether he had ever heard anyone in his own family, or possibly in the Amsterdam Jewish ghetto, speaking the old Judeo-Spanish dialect, Ladino. But he shook off this question too, as if afraid I might suspect him of association with matters that weren't properly Dutch. He merely allowed that he came from a family of rich merchants and that he was returning home from a three-week visit to the United States, to rejoin his father in the family business. As for the Jews of Holland, he would preface any remarks with the standard lecture that they were Dutch citizens first and foremost, Jews only secondarily. They took a deep interest in politics and were fervent patriots, and only after they had carried out their civic duty to the full, so that no one could accuse them of disloyalty, were they also Jews. But their Jewishness was only a minor part of their identity, the merest tip of the iceberg.

"What keeps them connected to the Jewish people?" I asked.

"Nothing!" he exclaimed, delighted by this opportunity to expound on the special nature of the Dutch Jews. "They are an entity unto themselves, a sort of thirteenth tribe of Israel, without a history or traditions. Maybe somewhere there's buried archeological evidence of their origins."

He was an intelligent man, who obviously preferred innocent banter to confronting unpleasant truths. Ultimately, however, it all came out.

No less than their Christian neighbors, Dutch Jews detested the Polish Jews in their midst. With their long, scraggly beards, the Polish Jews who shuffled about the streets of Amsterdam in their ridiculous garb were an embarrassment to the Dutch Jews, to say nothing of the Christians, generally patient and tolerant souls. The Polish Jews were doing great harm to their Dutch coreligionists, and their presence was a slap in the face, because no matter how hard the Dutch Jews tried to keep their distance from the Poles, the Christians felt that the Dutch Jews bore some responsibility for the behavior of their eastern brethren.

"Why have they come to disturb our longtime peace and order?" he said. "I swear, I turn red in the face whenever I see a Polish Jew. Why must they always attract attention to themselves, with their stubborn insistence on being different?"

"But why should this disturb you?" I asked with feigned innocence. "Are you bothered by a Chinaman? A Hindu? A black man? You can't be the free and tolerant Dutchman you think you are if you're ashamed of a Polish Jew on the street with whom you don't even claim kinship, who's neither your uncle nor your nephew."

He ignored my barb and began to describe how safe and secure the Jews of Holland had always felt, how deeply rooted, until "this Hitler" began to act up. "So far, there hasn't been any anti-Semitism in Holland," he said. "Everyone is equal. There are Jewish cabinet ministers, judges, and prominent businessmen. Everything would be fine, but with Hitler so close by . . . The Dutch don't even like the Germans, but who knows what will happen? Until Hitler came along, everything was fine."

"So you're afraid of Hitler?"

He admitted that Hitler gave him pause.

"Then doesn't that make you want to rejoin the Jewish people, to become a brother to the other twelve tribes of Israel?" I said, with a thrust of my imaginary foil.

"No! Not at all! As I've already told you, above all, we're good Dutchmen."

I was growing weary of this parrying. No doubt my young, two hundred percent Dutchman was sure that his were original thoughts, but to me his words gave off the same rusty, familiar clang sounded so often by other deluded Jews in other lands, with the same misplaced faith. I couldn't resist a sarcastic retort.

"But no matter how Dutch you think you are, my good friend," I said, throwing him a big smile, "according to the latest research on race being conducted by German scientists, you aren't an Aryan. The Nazi racial doctrine, a 'proven scientific' fact, will reach out to get you no matter how Dutch you may imagine yourself to be. It has condemned not just the 600,000 Jews of Germany but all 17 million of the Jews in the world. When we look at ourselves in the new Teutonic mirror, you, the Dutch Jew, and I, the Polish-American Jew, are equally non-Aryan."

I made a move to leave but he wouldn't let me go. He wanted to talk some more about Jews and Jewishness, like someone picking at a scab. Again, I restricted myself to questions and posed the following puzzler: "When you hear about Chinese being persecuted in China, or Jews in Germany—which concerns you more?"

"I struggle with myself," he replied. "As a civilized person I want to care, or not care, about them equally, but I must confess that the news about the Jews hits closer to home."

"Why?"

"Why?"

We had spoken simultaneously.

"Well," he said, "this may be a personal fear, but I worry that Jewish calamities elsewhere might find their way to us in Holland, and that wouldn't be fair, because we Dutch Jews are different, as I've already explained. We're Dutchmen first, Jews second."

As he pounded away on his single theme, he grew more talkative, but his voice remained a steady drone. On and on he went, marshaling his meager learning, bandying about the names of philosophers, writers, musicians. I became deaf to his monotone and all I could think of were the hackneyed reproductions that hang in kitchens—a Dutch windmill, heavy wooden clogs with upturned toes, impossible flaxen hair, and clenched fingers busily milking a cow. Needless to say, this was not the sum of Dutch culture, which has a long and rich tradition. That culture also has Jewish resonances—Rembrandt's substantial Jewish patriarchs, for instance, and even the sour Judeo-Christian taste of Spinoza's *Tractatus Theologico-Politicum*—but if my Dutch friend was in any way representative, these seemed to be lost on the "thirteenth tribe" that he imagined Dutch Jewry to be.

Lately, he droned on, Dutch Jews had begun to suffer from the affliction of Zionism, which was spreading among the youth like an epidemic. "Imagine," he said, "sitting in Holland and dreaming of Palestine!" A cousin of his, a well-educated young man from a wealthy family, had thrown everything away to become an ordinary worker in the Land of Israel. "His parents want nothing more to do with him," my Dutchman continued, "but he sends them letter after letter, telling them how happy he is to have found solid ground under his feet. Now why would someone like that, who was on the point of converting to Christianity, suddenly become a Zionist? The devil only knows!" Actually, he noted, a number of Jews, who were more Gentile than Jew, had begun to identify actively with Zionism, which seemed to attract the most assimilated elements of the community. "It's probably the panic about Hitler," he said, more to soothe his disquiet than in agreement with me. "The good Dutch Jews look askance at this Zionist flirtation. It's hurting us. It can undo the respect of our Christian neighbors, which we've worked so long and hard to cultivate. If the Dutch were to find out that our hearts lie elsewhere, beyond the borders of Holland . . . "

"Why then don't you convert?" I interrupted.

He wasn't in the least insulted. For the first time his mismatched eyes showed a glimmer of longing. He confessed that he was strongly attracted by the romanticism of the Catholic Church. A number of times he had consulted his father on the matter, who had advised him against conversion, though he couldn't give any good reason. "One of these days I'll take it up with him again," he said. "I just love the incense and the theatricality of Catholicism. Then again, maybe I'll go check out the Land of Israel, to see what all the excitement is about. Maybe," he laughed cheerlessly, "my heart will begin to throb with a biblical beat if I get to crush rocks on native soil. Ha, ha, I might just become the Columbus of the Jewish homeland. Yes, I might just hear a diapason in a Jewish mode, summoning Jews home from the far-flung Diaspora."

Diaspora! Diapason! Lovely musical words. But wouldn't the words of Jeremiah, if only he had known them, better have expressed his sentiment? "A voice is heard in Ramah, lamentation and bitter weeping; Rachel is weeping for her children."

Finally, as our conversation wound down, he cautioned me against visiting Holland, should the notion ever occur to me. "There's nothing to see," he said, swiveling his afflicted eye as if to emphasize the point. I suspect he didn't want yet another Polish Jew setting foot in Holland, lest he tip the balance and ruin everything for the Dutch Jews.

4

"To tell you the truth, I envy the way you can sit there so calmly, talking to such a jerk. If I ever caught a Jew like that in my city, I'd give him the thrashing of his life, and I'd add two slaps in the face for good measure."

The speaker was a tall, broad-shouldered man, with a powerful set of teeth that could easily grind a whole loaf of bread to bits, long, sturdy arms, and mocking cat's eyes, whom I had nonetheless failed to notice all the time I was talking to the Dutchman. "I know some English," he said, "enough to make out what that weasel was talking about. What can I tell you? He's just the sort of Jew who needs our boys to teach him a lesson. They'd knock some sense into his head, either that or finish him off altogether."

What was he talking about? What city? What boys?

He apologized for beginning in the middle, without first taking the time to inform me that he was from Colombia, from its capital city, Bogotá, with the accent on the *a*.

"You see," he said, launching into his tale, "I'm from across the River Sambatyon, where the Ten Lost Tribes of Israel ended up, and my blood boils whenever I hear the name Hitler. Along comes this nincompoop who has no use for Judaism. Yet this Dutch noodlehead is no less a Jew than the Gaon of Vilna. Go figure it out!

"Have you any idea where I hail from? When you hear the words *Colombia* and *Bogotá*—accent on the *a*—even if you were a mapmaker you wouldn't know what these places are like. Only *Sambatyon* can begin to give you some inkling. Do you think you'd understand it better if I said 'South America'? One man's South America is not another's. You're from New York—isn't that right?—so I'll try to explain where I live in relation to where you live. Let's say you suddenly go mad, poor man, and decide that you want to go to Bogotá. You'd board a ship in New York and sail seven days till you reach the small port of Cartagena. That would put you in Colombia, but don't lick your chops just yet, your troubles would just be beginning. Next, you'd take the train to the Magdalena River—your true Sambatyon—and those nasty, little Red Jews on the far bank, those are us, the chimps, or what you in the States call peddlers, the guys who have to wheel and deal to earn a meal.

"So, here we are at the Magdalena. You navigate it by boat, or what passes for a boat but is actually a wreck, a piece of floating lumber that idles down the river for a day, two days, three, four, five—and suddenly you're on another train. How come? Because the Magdalena has a slight obstruction, it runs smack into a waterfall, and waterfalls, as you realize, don't welcome either boats or passengers. Only a train can get you past this obstacle. Then it's back to the Magdalena till you reach a small village where—can you believe this?—you get on another train, but finally one that takes you all the way to Bogotá (accent on the *a*).

"The train crawls uphill, until you're four thousand feet above sea level. You pass coffee plantations, some barely cultivated, others lush, with heaps of coffee beans drying in the sun. The coffee bush likes the cold mountain air. No taller than a man, it loves to enslave the human species. The energy it takes to put even a spoonful of coffee on your table is like what it took the Hebrew slaves to build the cities of Pithom and Ramses in Egypt. The coffee bush needs pampering, nursing, and feeding before it makes the grade. Its berries look like red cherries. You have to pick them by hand and throw away the soft, fleshy part, leaving the hard kernel—the bean. Well, what do you know? You're off to Bogotá so you've gotten a free lecture—bully for you! The train keeps going for hours and hours, passing one pretty little village after another, until, finally, you arrive at your destination.

"Now, try telling me that I don't live across the River Sambatyon! Better yet, here's my check, go ahead and smack it. Don't be afraid, smack it real hard. I can take it, and I bloody well deserve it, because across the Sambatyon is where I buried the best years of my life. Don't go thinking that I went bust there. I've actually managed to put away a tidy little sum, but that's worth no more to me than a pinch of snuff. What matters to me more than the $80,000—maybe $100,000—that I've scraped together is my mother's longing for me, back in Bessarabia, and my longing for her and for my old home. What is a man, anyway? Just a money-grubbing pig—or shouldn't he be doing something worthwhile with his life besides making money?"

Having opened the spigot, the burly Bessarabian went on to recount how he had come to Ecuador in 1922 as a bachelor of twenty, and gone on from there to Peru, where straight off, in his very first year, he made $10,000 as a peddler. Why Ecuador and Peru? Better not ask questions of life. A friend had dragged him out there, and thanks to that same friend he had made his fortune, but right now the fortune sticks like a bone in his throat.

In Peru he found a thousand others like him, young Jewish men working as peddlers, and since he had always been something of an entrepreneur, a real hustler, he became their manager, selling them supplies, lending them money, and making his thirty percent profit. It all went belly up in 1925, when the climate in Peru toward Jews suddenly changed, and the peddlers scattered, naturally forgetting to pay their debts. He was ruined. But Chile was another prospect, so he went there next and ended up in the fur business, netting a $25,000 profit. "As you can see," he said, "God is a Father and He takes care of a tough guy like me." In 1929 he picked up again, took his money to Bogotá, and opened a new chapter in his life called "Colombia"—damn it to hell!

There he found some Russian Jews who had worked their way up to becoming coffee magnates, as well as several hundred young Jewish men, or "boys," as they were called. Why "boys"? Because they were all unmarried, which was the root of the problem.

"Imagine," he said, "some four hundred young male peddlers on the prowl, all making a decent living, but should they wish to set up a 'house in Israel,' as it says in the Bible, and start leading a proper family life, there's no one to do it with. Put yourself in our shoes—a whole country without Jewish brides—no *shadkhen*, no *badkhen*, neither matchmaker nor wedding entertainer. The four poles of the wedding canopy stand orphaned. For these miserable young men, it's all pain and sorrow, because there's no Jewish wife with gentle Jewish hands to grab them by the forelock and say to them: 'Time to start living like grown-ups.' Without a wife, life is humdrum, rootless. Jewish homes stand forlorn, and so do the trees around them. With no Sarah, no Rivke, Rokhl, or Leah, no Dvoyre, no Braindl or Zlote, you just rattle around like an empty shell. There are only half-men wandering about in Bogotá, with their missing half nowhere to be found.

"Oh sure, there are about thirty established Jewish families in Bogotá, but they haven't been in the country long enough to produce grown daughters. The few girls that were old enough for marriage were snapped up, and now we're waiting for the young ones to grow up, the way you wait for the Messiah. What else can we do? There aren't any other Jewish girls in the whole country. Some of the boys who ventured into mixed marriages with Spanish or Indian or Negro girls found no great blessings there, and hardly set an example for the others.

"Why don't we import Jewish girls? Well, if they were willing to come, even if they were as dark as night and ugly as sin, cross-eyed and pockmarked, they'd all be beauties in our eyes. We'd fight over them, serenade them, and give them the moon. But what Jewish girl would be crazy enough to let herself be lured to Bogotá? (As you now know—all the way to the Magdalena and across the Sambatyon.) It's a real pity about those boys, pining away their lives. One could write a whole book about their loneliness."

But apart from that, I asked him, how was Jewish life in general in Bogotá, accent on the *a*? The Bessarabian took his time answering. Then, slowly and deliberately, but with an onrush of words that seemed to have been stored up deep inside him and were just now being released, he tried to stir my sympathies for this far-flung Jewish tribe of his and to lay on my shoulders the heavy burden of responsibility for these newfound relatives, whose obscure habitation could be located on the map of Jewish sorrows somewhere between Warsaw, Jassy, Berlin, Vienna, Istanbul, and Salonika. I could feel my shoulders sagging under the weight of Jewish brotherhood, kinship, solidarity, as if I were carrying the entire Jewish world on my back. Saying "Jews" now meant not just my coreligionists in Romania and Poland, America and Russia, Holland and France, but also Indian Jews in Calcutta, yellow-skinned, almond-eyed Jews of China, Yemenites, Falashas in Ethiopia, Arabian Jews in Algiers, Sephardic Jews in Greece, and, as if this wasn't burden enough, the Bessarabian was adding to my load the exotic touch of Jewish travails in Colombia.

"Jews," he continued, "aren't much liked in Colombia. We're considered Russians, and Colombians hate the Russians. They like the Germans. Those backward Colombians go wild over German technology and German machinery. When this Hitler business started and the local Germans began spreading Nazi propaganda, they found a ready audience. We're afraid to do anything about it. If you even think of suing a German in court, forget it. You know in advance what the verdict will be.

"Even the climate is against us. It may suit the natives, but not us— cold, rainy, dreary weather that gets under your skin and drives you nuts. In Peru it doesn't rain very much, but in Colombia it pours, and when it does, life and limb get swallowed up in the deluge.

"What keeps the Jewish young men together? Loneliness, mainly, and maybe the fact that the Colombians consider us Russians. Let's see, what else? We've founded a mutual-aid society called Ezra, to set a man back on his feet in case of need. Also, Yom Kippur warms us a little—though we gather mostly out of the fear of *not* getting together on that day. The occasion lacks any real Jewish flavor, but since we still remember how to recite the Kol Nidre and some other Yom Kippur prayers, we rent a room and mumble a bit of the liturgy. The rest of the year we're far removed from religion. We observe no Sabbaths, no festivals, we just work like mules.

"You think we have a *shokhet* to slaughter our meat in the proper, kosher way? There's no ritual slaughterer for the thirty or so families and for us boys, so gradually we got used to eating nonkosher meat, hoping that it wouldn't go any further and bring our Jewishness to an end. As a matter of fact, we've just taken steps to provide for our eternal Jewish souls and bought some land for a Jewish cemetery. This we learned the hard way. When some of our boys bit the dust, young as they were, and we had to bury them in the Christian cemetery, we decided to do whatever it takes to get our own little plot for when we hit our own hundred and twenty.

"So we're squared away with death, but life is still bitter. Which doesn't mean that I'm pining away for a shokhet or a synagogue. I just wish we had other 'ideals,' to use a highfalutin word. If not prayer books, let there at least be other Jewish books, or a Jewish newspaper. But without anything Jewish to latch onto, we're becoming boorish. If not observant, let's at least be educated Jews, but we're neither one nor the other.

"Now we're back to where we started—healthy young bachelors, who can't set up households, but don't want to go hungry either. So dangling from the arm of each boy is a Colombian mistress. These dusky women are lovely as sin—tall, willowy, and so graceful that you think you're going to be the luckiest man in the world if you get to the bottom line, but the truth is that these gorgeous women are useless in bed, cold as icebergs. They just lie there, like royalty, turning those glorious moist eyes on you, and not moving a muscle. Still, as they say, you take what you can get, and since these are the only available women, you make do. Everyone knows that Yankl is living with his mistress, and Shmuel too, and Haim likewise. They furnish a house for these women and live as man and wife, but there's no public acknowledgment of the fact.

"Are the women faithful to these boys? The devil only knows. It seems so on the surface, but it's unreasonable to think they don't have other men on the side. The minute there's a grievance with the Jewish lover, up pops a Colombian guy. So where did he come from? Did he drop from heaven? The boys live with their women for a few years till they get bored with them and then go on to others. But the Colombian women are expensive treats and don't allow themselves to be toyed with.

"I lived with a dark-skinned woman for a couple of years and it ended up costing me five, six thousand American dollars. All of a sudden, things cooled between us. Actually, what happened was that I'd hooked up with somebody else and thought I could play a double game. But when the first woman realized that I was fooling around, she chewed me out like a regular wife. So I let her go. Right away I realized that I was deeply in love with her—I'm ashamed to admit it, not only in love, but I had gotten so used to her I couldn't live without her. That temptress even warned me that this would happen, she knew her own worth. To be honest, I went crawling back to her on my hands and knees, begging for forgiveness, but she burst into tears, sobbing that I had stabbed her in the heart. When she cried herself out, she showed me the door."

He took from his breast pocket the snapshot of a mulatto beauty, tall and full-bosomed, with a regal bearing. "This piece of tail ripped me apart," he said. "I handed my business over to strangers and traveled around the world to get her out of my system. That's how a Colombian whore can ruin your life. When I try to figure out why I felt the way I did, I think it's because all the other women I knew were such cold fish, and she was such a perfect fit. All I know is, I'll never find anyone like her again—it's over and done with."

He sighed heavily and hitched up his pants, looking less the burly Bessarabian than a picture of defeat. He took out his handkerchief and blew into it noisily, as if trying to hold back the tears. For a moment he had forgotten the Jewish woes of his wretched Bogotá, and he spoke with such feeling about his loss that I began casting about for some words of comfort, man to man. Since he himself had called his Colombian lover a whore, I tried casting a shadow on her character, but apparently only he was allowed that privilege. A beaten and helpless steed, he leaned on the ship's railing and looked mournfully out at the sea. He kept fingering the Colombian's photo until he finally returned it to its place near his heart. Reliving the tragedy of this romance had almost brought him to the point of breaking down completely. Suddenly, though, he caught hold of himself and realized that his personal story had undermined his responsibility as chronicler of the small Jewish settlement of Bogotá, with its four hundred lonesome boys.

"So that's how the boys live, with lovers instead of real wives," he resumed his tale. "You don't bring these women into society, but though you try to hide your secret behind seven locks, their existence is an open secret. The non-Jewish residents of Bogotá know all about it too, who belongs to whom, and when you break up with your woman, you have to be—what do you Americans call it?—a 'gentleman,' and do it nice and quietly, leaving her a tidy sum; otherwise she might hire someone to bump you off, or if she's not too lazy, do the job herself, because these Colombian women are very handy with a knife.

"As you can see, this whole sex business is a mess, but what can you do? A healthy young guy can't be expected to sleep in an empty bed night after night. You can't thumb your nose at your baser instincts because they don't let themselves be fooled. Some boys are so desperate to find a wife they will keep an eye out for a little Colombian schoolgirl, declare their intentions, and raise her to womanhood. For the child's poverty-stricken parents, this is a stroke of luck. The Jewish guy pays all her expenses and gains himself a wife. We have several such couples. In some cases, the girls even converted to Judaism, and so far, so good. One of these girls, a delicate child, fainted twice last year, fasting on Yom Kippur, but she held out to the end. The girls get used to their Jewish husbands from childhood on. Disregarding the fact that they're much younger, they become attached to these men who, literally, raised them, like nursemaids. But these are the lucky exceptions. How many people have the patience to take in a little girl and wait for her to grow up?

"So you see, it's anything but a good life. And you Americans talk about settling Jews in our part of the world—in Ecuador, of all places. Forget it. Ecuador's a poor country and there's no future there for Jews. As for Colombia, now you know the score. A curse on any Jew who goes there, even if he does make a pile of money. To sum it all up, a young Jew in Bogotá can't expect a decent family life. Come holy Sunday, he makes his rounds all morning long to collect the week's payments due him. The afternoon is devoted to cards, and he's not just playing for amusement. It costs him dearly, sometimes to the tune of two, three hundred dollars. He takes a break to wash off the week's accumulated dirt, then sits down again at the card table. At night he hangs out in the dance hall, where you can rent a girl for six cents a dance. If you don't have a woman of your own, you take home some poor Colombian girl, who comes around the next morning to collect her payment in goods. That's Monday morning, when you wake up with a bitter taste in your mouth and start working again like a mule.

"Passover, we get a bit of a break. Forty or so of the boys gather in someone's house and we stuff ourselves and get drunk. Eating and drinking is our holiday, without resorting to the Haggadah. There you have it—our entire spiritual life. It's lucky that our Jewish cemetery is blooming, waiting to gather us in.

"Nevertheless, we're still a cut above that Dutch jerk you were talking to. Our Jews may be crude, but at least we've got a spark of Jewish spirit. But that guy is some kind of Jewish freak. Oh, would I love to see him fall into our hands!

"Lest you think all these matches with the Colombian lovers have come to nothing, let me inform you that in Bogotá alone there are about two thousand young boys running around—our little bastards. We can't take credit for all of them, but we can claim a hefty share. These kids run wild in the city, with nothing to do, nowhere to sleep, nothing to eat. Naturally, they end up doing the only thing they can— shining shoes. You never know, that snotty-nosed kid you just tossed a coin to for shining your shoes might very well be your own son. The female bastards are luckier, the Red Cross finds homes for them. But the boys are left to God's mercy, maybe because they're too rebellious to be taken in hand by the pious wardens of the Red Cross.

"Many years ago, there were still a few Jewish brothel keepers around, plying their sleazy trade, but we shut them down. We thought then that we could make something decent of ourselves, but nothing doing. Nowadays, we even have among us a few preachers of Communism, who somehow drifted to our remote corner of the world. Believe me, their propaganda doesn't bring us much good. That's all we needed! It was bad enough to be blamed as Russians without being charged for ruining the country with Bolshevism! I'm sure that Stalin doesn't give a damn about us and Karl Marx would have turned up his nose at Bogotá, but our handful of Reds think they can turn Colombians into Stalinists—a job that would take several army regiments.

"I may be a citizen of Colombia, but I'm still drawn to Bessarabia, where my mother writes tearful letters to her dear Yosele. Look at me now, some Yosele, huh? But to my mother I'm still a little boy, scrawny and frail, who used to get fearful lickings from his father. My father, may he rest in peace, had a hand broad as a board, and whenever he laid that paw on me, Mother would cry out that he was killing her Yosele."

A gong summoned us to supper. It had grown cooler on deck, but the Bessarabian wasn't yet done with his tale about life across the River Sambatyon. "I must get away from there," he cried. "Tell me, what can a Jew like me, with my capital, do in New York? Let's say I came for six months, met a nice girl, married her, and, thanks to her, settled down. What would I do in New York? I'm not going to become a scribe who sits there writing out mezuzahs. What could I do with my money?"

"You could publish a Yiddish newspaper, maybe a quality weekly," I blurted out. This crazy notion popped into my head at the embarrassed thought that I was being entrusted with someone else's $100,000 fortune.

"Me? A Jewish newspaper? You must be joking. With all due respect, I'm just a simple boor."

I tried to reassure him that in the newspaper business education didn't matter. You could get along just fine without it, without any formal schooling at all. Indeed, the newspaper business, as I explained, was a business like any other—and the word *business* he certainly understood.

♦ ♦ ♦ *Chapter 3*

1

Except for a sallow-faced spinster who puffed nervously on a cigarette and raced round and round the deck alone, as if afraid that someone might catch and rape her, and several other chronic recluses whose curt, pinched "Good mornings" and "Good evenings" indicated the limits of their social wants, the rest of the passengers were getting acquainted, forming friendships, even cliques. With raised antennas, they searched for counterparts and found more or less what they were seeking. Cardplayers formed sets. Talkers met up with patient listeners. Debaters sniffed out other debaters to argue points of mutual interest. Aggressive women unearthed bashful men, and suave men with romantic inclinations and courtly manners attracted the attention of delicate women, who spoke mostly with their eyes, caught, as they were, in a rapturous trance of their own inducing, that the ship was going nowhere and would never anchor. What remained after this instinctual pairing were the dregs of both sexes, who had no alternative but to settle for one another's company for the duration of the voyage.

A wealthy dress manufacturer was a recluse of a different order. He kept his distance from everyone, even from his daughter, who was accompanying him on the trip but didn't join him on his promenades.

His doctor had informed him that he was dying, telling him point blank how much time he had left, whereupon he decided that he would take one last ocean trip. But he felt about the sea the way a Jew does about the mud stream into which he empties out his sins, symbolically, at the New Year. He hated the ocean, and every time he looked down at the water, he heaved a mighty gob of spittle overboard, with the same pleasure one might take in spitting an enemy in the face.

He was much aggrieved by the prospect of imminent death. He was not afraid, his face betrayed no sign of stock-taking, no hint of sorrow, no grimace of regret, no benevolent smile, no shadow of resignation— the usual marks of a person who knows for certain that his days are numbered. Some people in these dire straights become mild-mannered and gentle and quickly jettison the ballast of meanness that has weighed them down. Not so our dress manufacturer. His flushed face registered only anger at having to die before his time.

According to his daughter, he had been a regular bon vivant, not letting any morsel of pleasure get away, from the spicy meat rolls and brandy of the Romanian restaurants he frequented to the high-heeled beauties strutting in his factory's showroom, modeling clothes, whom he snatched away from his workers. Now he must leave all this to others who would go on laughing, singing, dancing, and making love, while he lay rotting in the ground. He looked at death as a personal insult, a lousy, unfair deal. He had always vented his anger on hired underlings, but now he felt like a chained dog. The other passengers tried not to look at him, because if they caught his eye he would stick out his tongue at them. Furious at the sight of happy laughing couples, he called after them, "Sons of bitches, you can kiss my ass." Luckily for everyone, this condemned madman spent most of his time lying in his cabin and seldom ventured out, for many a young Galahad had wanted to toss him overboard for insulting his frightened damsel.

Just as some passengers hung back and withdrew into themselves, others were naturally outgoing and gregarious, what Americans call "good mixers." Such a one was my Danish friend. By the end of the first day, he knew everyone on board, and had learned everyone's life story, eliciting their comedies and tragedies. He was even something of a matchmaker, bringing together heavy-hearted members of both sexes. He liked to keep things at a merry boil. So successful was his matchmaking that some of his pairings endured for the entire length of the trip.

One day he proposed to set me up with a real Russian, one of his tablemates. He felt that Jews and Russians were somehow related and that the two of us would get on like a house afire. The Russian, named Khazhev, was actually delighted to meet me since the meddlesome Dane, despite his enthusiasm for Socialism and the great Soviet experiment, was becoming too much of a burden. For his part, the Dane was relieved to divest himself of the Russian, busy as he was with many other social duties that precluded paying too much attention to any one person. Besides, he was already light years removed from his youthful radicalism, and uttered the words "Soviet experiment" mechanically, "to make conversation," as the Americans put it.

Khazhev took an immediate shine to me, as if we were indeed related. His tiny, almost Mongolian eyes looked at me warmly, trustingly. As for me, I had never been in either the old Russia or in its newer incarnation, and knew Russians only from the Polish city of my youth, then under Russian rule—a Russified town with onion-domed churches, long-bearded Russian Orthodox priests, Russian high-school teachers, and Russian government functionaries. But one look at Khazhev and I knew that standing before me was a different Russian sort, the new Soviet man. The three years he had just spent studying electrical engineering at Cornell University had done nothing to "Americanize" or refine him. Indeed, very little of America had stuck to him, and he spoke English as if he were rolling pebbles around in his mouth. He often had to rescue himself from his sputtering by falling back on a good, old Russian word.

He was happy to be going home and especially pleased that he had completed his four-year plan in three, saving the Soviet government a full year's expenditure on his behalf. He wished that poor students of all other nationalities should have it so good. In addition to his tuition, the Soviet Union had provided him with a monthly stipend of $150, for students a princely sum. On top of that, during his overseas studies, the Soviet government supported his wife and two children. Now the Soviet motherland was expecting him back, and he was proud to be returning, with not just a diploma but a body of knowledge that could be put to immediate use in regular development projects. He looked forward to showing that the money spent on him had not been wasted. He had seen a great deal of America—the Ford motor plant, the General Electric Company, and other models of industry and capitalism. He had many good things to say about America, but he wouldn't settle there for all the money in the world because . . . Here he chose his words as tactfully as a diplomat. He was grateful for the education he had received in America, but since he was now leaving the country, why badmouth it? He thought of himself as an ambassador whom the Soviet government had sent to a friendly country, and he didn't want to embarrass his country with an unnecessary remark. Decked out like a tycoon, Khazhev was bringing home cameras, suits, several pairs of shoes, a typewriter, a phonograph . . . But he wished he were already home.

"You see," he explained, "my older son was born mute. He was five when I left, and had never spoken a word. He just sat there, looking up at everyone with his warm eyes, but his silence was heartbreaking. He took after a mute uncle, a sensitive man with an inborn appreciation of beauty. This uncle never made those shrieking sounds you sometimes hear from mutes. He spoke sign language with his fingers, laconic in his way. Our little boy never made such sounds either, he just sat there, silent as a giraffe. But during the time I've been away, some important Soviet professors have been working with him, and so far they've taught him to say a single word—'Papa'! Now, when I get home, I'll be able to hear it with my own ears. I can hardly wait. You can't imagine what a joy that will be. Up to now, my mute little Misha has been struggling to say 'Papa' with his eyes, lips, hands—you should have seen the agonies he went through—but now he will say it out loud, with his mouth."

Tears ran down Khazhev's cheeks as he spoke, in true sentimental Russian fashion. He spoke not only as a loving father but also as a proud son of his motherland, blessed with professors who were making great strides in medicine, performing real miracles.

Khazhev's father was a peasant who had always been a revolutionary. Though he scarcely knew how to read or write, he knew full well the meaning of *laborer* and *peasant,* and of the tsar's whip. Thanks to several prison terms, he was now, at age sixty, half paralyzed and a broken shell of a man. The government had granted him a pension, and he sat around all day, crying tears of joy at having lived to witness such a miraculous time. "You should have seen how happy the old man was when I went off to university, studying the whole day," said the Russian. "After taking a drink, he would often grab a heavy physics or chemistry textbook and order: 'Read, Vasya! Let's see how a peasant's son reads and gets smart.' I'd have to read whole sections to please him. And, peasant that he is, with a bit of religion still in him, he'd listen to the strange words and sob: '*Slava tye gospodi!* Praised be the Lord!'" As for his mother, she was illiterate and had labored all her life. Her hands were always red and swollen, her heavy legs bloated, and her eyes puffed up from grieving while the father sat in jail and the children were sick, and there was scarcely a piece of stale bread in the house.

This was his background, and now his country had done him a great favor, opening all doors for him—Khazhev, a peasant's son. Under the tsar, what could he have been but the filthiest piece of dirt? The Soviet Union had transformed him into a choice student, had sent him abroad, with the confidence that he would learn enough to be able to assist in developing the motherland, so that it could set an example for the world and become a model of a new way of life for future generations. Of course he was grateful. How could he not be? And not for selfish reasons alone. Across the length and breadth of his land, a new life was beginning. To be sure, it was still a hard life for many millions of people, but there were already signs of a better future. As he set about listing all the Soviet benefactions, he made sure—and was very clever about doing so—that the virtues he cited would underscore American shortcomings, which he wouldn't criticize directly.

"And not only the sons of peasants should be grateful," he said. "Jews, too, should be dancing in the streets, yes, dancing in the streets! What were they before the Revolution? Nothing! And now they are everything! The same goes for every citizen of the land." He said this not like a Gentile proving his love of Jews but simply, without apologetics, proud of the fact that his Soviet Union had corrected a grave injustice. He was well informed on details of Soviet-Jewish life. He knew about the Jewish schools, Jewish collective farms, Jewish writers, and he spoke glowingly of the Yiddish theater. These developments were offered not as curiosities, as a Gentile might visit a synagogue to hear Jewish melodies, but as great national achievements.

He was thirty-four years old, of medium height, with genuine Slavic cheekbones. He looked the typical peasant, peasant face, peasant hands, gray peasant eyes, but every peasant feature had undergone refinement, just as Maxim Gorky's peasant face had softened over the years. His shrewd, warm eyes were shrouded in a mist of true Russian sorrow. Warmth! That was the word to describe him, he simply exuded warmth. Khazhev spoke to me with the affection of someone who is wholesome and secure. He talked on and on, describing his country, which he had crisscrossed from one end to the other. And if he threw in the occasional, regretful remark about as yet unremedied Soviet shortcomings, he did it so artlessly, and with such brotherly goodwill that I didn't want to offend him by seeming to notice.

Only once, in passing, did he mention the "Supreme Leader," but the reference came unadorned, unaccompanied by the obligatory praise. He sincerely believed in the great Soviet experiment and, in his peasant naïveté, regretted that other countries were not following the Soviet path.

After treating me to this elegant propaganda, he let me know that, in addition to himself, there was also a sizable Soviet colony aboard ship, all returning home. He pointed to a corner of the deck where a woman lay on a deck chair with legs outstretched, not the delicate, shapely legs of a femme fatale, but legs unquestionably feminine all the same and not badly turned out either, a tribute to their Creator, whose infinite ingenuity could lend a touch of allure to a thickened ankle. The portrait was completed by a group of young men at her feet, looking up at her adoringly, like medieval troubadours.

She was the only one on board to be stricken by seasickness. The days and nights were so glorious that the rest of us were growing healthier by the minute, but she alone had fallen victim to the malady. Her pitch-black hair, parted in the middle, her dark, Jewish eyes, and her full, almost swollen, lips—all attested to her suffering, or rather, seeing that she was surrounded by a crew of melodramatic Russians, her "agony," which she gave herself leave to express. The young men looked up at her, vying with one another to ease her discomfort, tossing off flowery phrases and chivalrous compliments. They called in reinforcements, quoting from Lermontov, Pushkin, Nekrasov, Mayakovsky, and Yesenin. The Russian-Jewish woman was in seventh heaven. She wasn't a beauty, nor was she that young, yet she was the object of all this royal attention, her seasickness gaining her the favors of all these cavaliers. There were prettier women on board ship, but the Russian young men ignored them, preferring instead the enchantments of Russian cadences as they emerged from a Russian woman's soft lips, on an English boat, amid alien surroundings.

"Children, take your dream-stricken eyes off the elegant Sonya Yakovlyevna and spare a word for this worthy gentleman," said Khazhev good-humoredly and with exaggerated formality. "Let me introduce you."

Four young men leaped up, as if by military command—a fine young specimen with a straw-blond head of hair and a wide Russian mouth, whose Chaliapin bass voice seemed to be issuing from a cello; another with the face of a dullard, but with remarkably friendly, merry eyes; a third, with a beret atop his head and a pair of fidgety, restless hands; and a fourth, with slightly stooped back and the mien of a serious student. Sonya Yakovlyevna extended a hand that made the quick metamorphosis from housewife to coquette. In less than a minute I was welcomed into the ship's Soviet colony.

"*Pozhalusta*, welcome," boomed the towhead, the most Russian of the group, in the rich baritone that only a Russian youth can allow himself. His unhurried gestures, his open manner and thundering resonance brought to mind Turgenev's Bazarov, Artzybashev's Sanin, and a score of similar literary heroes who reflected not so much the Russian reality as the creativity of their authors in supplying models for a whole generation of the Russian intelligentsia. And yet, this blond young man with the voice of a Russian cathedral bell was a new species of Russian intellectual, the product, nay, the exemplar, of a new way of life. He had a keen grasp of political-economic issues. His comrades clearly respected his mastery of dialectics and his ability to apply Soviet dogma to various contemporary situations. Whenever his colleagues made a doctrinal misstep, stumbling over the Party line, he would correct them good-naturedly—"That's not exactly how we would handle it, comrades"—and lead them step by step through the ideological maze to the necessary outcome.

He and two others of the group had spent only six weeks in the United States, where, as electrical technicians, they had been sent to inspect plants and factories. They had seen and learned much in the course of their whirlwind tour. The fourth member of the group, the one who seemed a dullard, had won a factory lottery for a trip around the world and a year's vacation. He had been everywhere and was now going back to his job. Oddly enough, even this laborer, who worked in a steel mill, with the callused hands to prove it, took a personal interest in economic questions and was knowledgeable about the driest, most complex issues of world economic affairs. Apparently this had become some sort of sport, a version of crossword puzzles for Soviet youth, which afforded them deep satisfaction. They seemed to know their way around, understanding where to be gentle and where to get tough. Each saw himself as a representative of his country, ready to take up the cudgels for the motherland and do battle with any unbeliever.

The four young Soviet stalwarts, who had spent only a short time in the United States, were far less reticent than Khazhev to openly criticize America, always prefacing their remarks with, "We don't want to give you"—that is me, the American—"any advice on how to run your country." There followed a litany of complaints about dirty streets, filthy theaters, and public places littered with cigar and cigarette butts. By contrast, Soviet theaters were spotlessly clean and the workers approached them as reverently as worshipers once did a temple.

"When you were in the States, did you come across activists, or attend any Communist meetings?" I asked.

They recoiled at the very idea. Taking their cue from the blond pacesetter, they replied, almost in unison, "No! What does that have to do with us? We are Soviet citizens and we were guests of America. We know nothing about the American Communist movement except what we hear." Their relief was palpable: they had acquitted themselves well as Soviet emissaries in a foreign, but diplomatically friendly land. Then, relaxing a bit, they suggested that perhaps Sonya Yakovlyevna might be the better person to tell about the American Communist movement. She had spent twelve years in America. Her husband had returned to the Soviet Union two years ago, to take up an important post. Now she, too, was returning and was delighted by the prospect, because all the time she was in America, she had clung to her Russianness—her name, her patronymic, and her rough but succulent Odessan Russian, with its rolling Yiddish r's.

I invited them all into my cabin for a drink, explaining that I had more bottles of liquor on hand than I could possibly finish off by myself. They fell silent and looked to their blond leader for instruction, unsure as to whether Soviet citizens should let themselves be talked into drinking by a stranger. He laughed uncomfortably and blinked several times, narrowing his eyes at the thought of the drink. After wrestling with the dilemma, he arrived at a compromise between the urgings of the evil impulse and Soviet dialectic, and handed down his ruling: "*Nyemnozhetchko!*"—indicating just how tiny a drop by the minuscule shape between thumb and forefinger. We all trooped into my cabin, even the ailing Sonya. After the blond young man had downed several hefty nyemnozhetchkos, the cabin began to ring out with the exuberance of Soviet song.

2

The singing grew louder. The blond young Russian danced around my narrow cabin with the stout Sonya Yakovlyevna. Someone brought in a portable gramophone and a pile of records of Russian popular songs, each ending on a high shriek, like the bark of a sergeant-major shouting out orders, indicating that the song was over, that life itself had come to a halt, and one might as well stretch out, close one's eyes, and go to one's eternal rest. Staid, curious American passengers poked in their heads to stare at our merrymaking, as if at an orgy of friendly cannibals. The drunken whoops, the gramophone's shrieks, Sonya Yakovlyevna's tipsy laughter amid all these men, the raucous shouts of masculine camaraderie that had an almost homoerotic charge—all this cacophony spilled out into the corridor, seeking more room for itself. I, meanwhile, none too sober myself, was saying in my mind, not questioningly, not assertively, but with a drunken insouciance: "This is it" —this is the new, happy breed of romantic materialists, the products of victory, of waving flags, captured barricades, endless struggle, of revolutions and communes. This is the glorious song of fulfillment. That I happened to find myself here among the victors was no mere happenstance. I had arrived at this revolutionary point, having experienced all the revolutions on the books, with the names of the revolutionary martyrs, the working-class slogans, all engraved on my child's brain, as my native city, suffering under the harsh rule of Tsar Nicholas, had contributed to the overthrow of the tyrant.

Brothers and sisters, let us march together.
A plague on Tsar Nicholas and his mother.
Hey, hey, down with the police.
Down with the Russian oppressor.

I used to taunt my grandfather with this revolutionary Russian jingle which class-conscious dressmakers, seamstresses, embroiderers, carpenters, lathe turners, tanners, and apprentice butchers would sing under their breath. This was my childish rebellion against his fear of incurring the wrath of the authorities. "Go rub your nose in a fart!" Grandfather would exclaim, breaking out the obscenity he reserved for times when he was truly angry. "We'll all be sent to Siberia because of this rascal!" I paid him no heed and recruited my little brother, who was two years younger and barely able to pronounce the words "Russian oppressor," to the class struggle.

I was five or six at the time. My friends were snot-nosed kids with hanging shirttails and narrow-brimmed Jewish caps. The ground, as I recall, shook underfoot, as we tottered about, playing "Knock down the King." We must have looked like a yardful of penguins.

I don't mean to brag about my revolutionary credentials, but even then I knew that the huge fortress-prison that loomed over the city was not reserved for thieves alone. The ferocious-looking soldiers, rifles at the ready, patrolled it day and night. It was visible from all points below, from every Jewish street, stretching as far as the main synagogue. Jews going to pray had to make their way under fearful government scrutiny, in full sight of the weapons flashing on the hill above.

At the foot of the prison stood the Krasutski factory, where coughing cigarette and cigar makers, stooped and exhausted, toiled. Between factory and prison, particularly the section that housed the political prisoners, there was a living bridge—the Krasutskis' gentle daughter, who was lame. She wore glasses, and her earnest face could have been taken for either Jewish or Gentile. At dawn she would step out on her balcony and fearlessly chat with the prisoners who appeared, from the neck up, at the little barred windows of the prison.

My concept of revolution was garnered from the heroic tales Grandfather would tell me about a certain Berek Joselewicz, who defied the Russians, about the Jewish tavernkeepers who hid Polish aristocrats from the Russian authorities, and even the joke about those same aristocrats, who would crawl out from behind the oven after the Russians had departed, twirl their mustaches, and shout at their protectors, "Jews, off with your hats!" Grandfather, who was nothing but a realist, would also tell me that when the Cossacks would catch a revolutionary, they would cut off his most important member and hand it to him with a bow: "*Kuritye pozhalusta*—here, have a smoke." He also had a pack of tales about stubborn guerrilla battles in thick Polish woods, about gallows, lances, daggers, and Cossack whips.

Then came the first steps of actual revolution. Late at night, long after midnight, not in the well-to-do suburb outside the city but right on the crooked, timorous Jewish streets, there was a sudden eruption of singing. The flimsy houses, held together by spit, trembled awake but stayed silent, not taking sides. We understood what was going on, but were afraid even to look out the windows and kept our heads buried under our featherbeds. The revolutionaries were trying to gain control of the city by force, one street at a time, hoping to get the job done before the arrival of the troops. Meanwhile, members of the Polish Socialist Party were pouring into the streets, from the Hess foundry which manufactured heavy scales, from the brickyards and the sugar refineries, carrying torches, waving flags, and singing:

Workers to the barricades.
Raise aloft the red flag.

At first they marched slowly, then the pace quickened. The torches flashed by the windows, followed by an ominous silence that seemed like a cry for help. Suddenly, there was the sound of angry hoofbeats, as the fiery Cossack horses came galloping in. Enraged at having missed their chance, the Cossacks relieved their fury by firing into the air a shot that pierced the Jewish night like a red-hot nail.

Another time, on the fast day of Tisha B'Av, when everyone was at the synagogue mourning the destruction of the Holy Temples in ancient Jerusalem, the comrades decided to show off their revolutionary fervor by marching upon the synagogue courtyard, waving their flags. Soon the Cossacks rode up, lashing away with their whips. The synagogue doors were hastily locked. For several hours thereafter, we could hear the Cossacks sniffing around like angry dogs. They didn't dare enter the synagogue, while we were afraid to leave. Long after we had finished reciting the various laments, we remained huddled in the synagogue through the night.

What a Tisha B'Av that was! We actually relived the ancient destruction. The lights in the synagogue flickered. The cantor remained sitting on the steps leading up to the ark. I half-dozed on a hard, overturned lectern, rummaging in the straw on the floor with my stocking feet, delighting in the fleas that tickled the soles of my feet in their frenzied attempts to reach a child's warm flesh.

In the center of the synagogue, the fearful shadow of a hanging lamp swayed back and forth, like a body dangling from a rope. In my mind I kept hearing stray echoes of the plaintive lament for Zion and her devastated cities that the cantor had just led the congregation in chanting. I was desperately hungry, and thought about the starvation we had heard described in the Book of Lamentations, that drove the parents of besieged Jerusalem to eat their own children. Like our ancient forebears, we too were under siege. Titus and his legions were on the prowl, about to pounce and devour me. I looked in terror at my father, who was nodding off, stroking me with a sleepy hand.

I can't remember exactly which pogrom it was—Kishinev, Bialystok, or some other bloodbath. Father had come home with a newspaper and was weeping so uncontrollably that everyone in the house joined in, my mother, my brother, and even the maid, who was mute—everyone, that is, except me, whose heart gets hard as flint when it comes to shedding a tear. I looked at the black-bordered photos with their caption, "Martyrs," and thought of the Ten Martyred Sages, the rabbis of old who were tortured to death by the Romans and whose sorrowful fate we recall on Yom Kippur, recounting how the Romans tore the flesh from their bodies with iron combs. The newspaper pictures showed a dead synagogue sexton holding a Torah scroll, dead, glassy-eyed children, and shredded sacred books. My swirling thoughts had already formed an idea of what a Jewish revolution should be—on the one side, Tsar Nicholas and his pogroms, and on the other, the young people in their blue, black, or red peasant shirts, with their sashes and tassels. These Shirts would some day topple the Tsar from his throne.

I conjured up an image of Tsar Nicholas sitting atop a high throne, like Pharaoh in Egypt, every word out of his mouth a decree against the Jews. Like Ahasuerus in the Book of Esther, he holds a gold scepter in one hand and a wand in the other, and instead of going to wash in the baths, bathes in Jewish blood. As he is about to issue his next evil decree, in rush the two whirlwinds, Yankl, the redheaded carpenter, and Yosl, the pockmarked locksmith. First, they pay their respects to the monarch and rattle off all his imperial titles, then, without cere-mony, they say: "Get the hell out of here, my lord king, you've ruled long enough." They toss him off the throne, fire a few bullets into him, spit three times, and shout: "Take that, for the Jewish blood you've spilled!" They grab a pole, press a spring, and out pops the red flag. At once, they're off to Russia, where they march up and down, singing:

Hey, hey, down with the police,
Down with the Russian oppressor.

And yet, when the Shirts once took over the synagogue and stood there "slandering God," as my Hebrew-school teacher later explained, my heart was heavy. To oppose Tsar Nicholas was one thing, but to op-pose the Jewish God? What sins had He committed? Those were His scrolls of the Torah being stomped on and ripped to shreds, His Jews being massacred. What claim could you have against the God who went into exile with His people and never enjoyed a worry-free mo-ment, except, perhaps, on the festival of Simhat Torah that celebrated His Law?

This Jewish God of mine looked exactly like Rabbi Avremele Eiger, the Hasidic master of Lublin, a gaunt, soft-spoken man with a long, white beard, dressed in white stockings and slippers, who didn't know what money looked like, who accepted no fees, who fasted every Monday and Thursday, and got by on next to nothing all year long, whose cracked voice was always lamenting Jewish disasters. This was the Jewish God of my tormented, childish imagination. What could one have against such a God, who was ready at any moment to hasten the Redemption, but whose hands were too short and weak to bring on the Messiah?

It was on a Purim night, when Jews were in the synagogue observing their ancestors' deliverance from the evil Haman, that the Shirts invaded the premises, seized control, and bolted the door. Their leader, a youth with long black hair, mounted the rostrum and launched into his harangue: "Comrades and citizens, today is Purim. They want you to believe that on this day a miracle occurred, that God—in a pig's eye! —saved the Jews from a pogrom . . . "

"Get down from the pulpit, you infidel, you sinner, the devil take you. Get down!" The voice resounding throughout the synagogue was that of Moyshele Glisker, a *Kohen*, scion of the priestly line of Jews, a man with a hot temper and a forehead that turned red as a rooster's comb when he was angered. "Get down from there," he shouted, ignoring the threats of the Shirts, that they would knock him dead, that they would put a bullet in him—and to prove their point, they even aimed a gun at him. But he kept on shouting, as if in a burning blaze, "Down from there."

I plead guilty that in this particular struggle, between the blasphemer against God and Moyshele Glisker, the unalterable opponent of revolution—and by "revolution" I meant against Tsar Nicholas for shedding Jewish blood—I sided with Moyshele. To me he was a hero, like Mattathias, father of the Maccabees, wielding a sword and shouting, "Who is for God, unto me!" I myself became a little Maccabee, and together we fought the Lord's battle on His behalf, since He Himself had grown weak and tearful, too compassionate, a shadow wrapped in a prayer shawl, spending His days weeping.

To this day I cannot abide defiance against God. No matter how often I repeat the Marxist gospel, that religion is the opiate of the masses, it doesn't help in the least. Whenever I see someone insulting the sheer, innate goodness that lies behind that mysterious misery we call life, I feel deeply offended by their confusion of the kernel with the husk. I know that my children will never be bothered by such concerns, having encountered neither Avremele Eiger nor his noble, gentle colleague, Rabbi Hillel Lifschitz, and thus denied the privilege of hearing the good Rabbi Lifschitz's sigh-laden discourses on Rosh Hashanah prior to the blowing of the shofar, or his cracking voice calling out the sequence of staccato blasts to the shofar blower, my uncle Khiel-Osher, who executed the broken *Shvorim* sounds with a poignancy beyond compare.

Nonetheless, following the Purim incident, I began to sense the presence of a new force in town. Until now Jewish power had resided in the underworld, the toughs who were handy with a knife—Avreml the Torpedo, Mordkhele the Bastard, with his patent-leather boots, and other such gruff specimens. What they said they meant, what they threatened they carried out. When they beat a whore almost to death and she pleaded with passersby, "Jews, children of mercy, save me!" the merciful children hurried past, pretending it was not they who were being entreated, afraid they might be beaten up, too—you didn't want to mess with those guys. But with the advent of the Shirts, the underworld lay low. I once saw some members of the Jewish Socialist Bund beating up a thief who had stolen a couple of rubles from a servant girl. "Give back the money!" They pummeled the miscreant until his blood streamed like red soup and he returned every last groschen, as the poor girl, her hands like frozen apples, cried, "Enough!"

This was a new form of power, exercised in the service of an ideal, though I became confused again when this new power pumped a few bullets into Elye Taub because he refused to give his employees a raise. Young and old wept at his funeral. Elye Taub had been a tailor and himself not a rich man. When I saw his black casket being carried through the streets of the Jewish quarter, it occurred to me that his transgression against his workers paled in comparison to his punishment. His wife tore her hair, his children wept, and the schoolboys following the coffin chanted the traditional verse from Psalms, "May righteousness go before him." I weighed his sin and his punishment on my child's scale of justice, and somehow the two didn't balance.

Elye Taub's death sent a shock throughout the community. For the first time, it began to feel as if the vaunted Jewish unity, as expressed in the precept "All Israel are brethren" and voiced so keenly in the New Year prayers for the collective well-being, no longer extended through the rest of the year. There were now two camps, workers and bosses. The first salvo had been fired in our town's class warfare.

The workers sang their songs with growing pride and joy, and whenever eight or nine gathered, a tenth would invariably spring up from somewhere to preach to them, always beginning with, "Comrades and citizens." Elderly Jews, passing such gatherings, would mutter disapprovingly under their breath, "If things don't get better, they'll surely get worse."

Thus it was no great surprise to me when one day the new powers brought Shimen Berger over to our house. Reb Shimen, my father's employer, was the owner of a large clothing store. He sported a broad, flaxen beard and lived in a beautiful home in the best part of town. Father would call on him on holidays to pay his respects, but it took the new powers to bring him down from his lofty perch to our lowly dwelling in the shadow of the jail, on an ordinary weekday.

Several young men whom I didn't know were seated around our big table under the lamp. Their stern faces showed that they meant business. At the head of the table sat not Shimen Berger, as might be expected, mopping his brow, but my father, who had been assigned the heavy task of arbitrator. The new powers respected his decency and fairness, even if his class-consciousness was not yet fully developed.

Reb Shimen, it turned out, had slapped a clerk in the face, and the powers were demanding justice. The aggrieved party, who was among those present at the table, a youth with the piping voice of a choirboy, kept jumping up from his seat to shout into his boss's face. Reb Shimen wiped the sweat from his forehead and tried to answer, but my father cut him short, saying, "Keep still, Reb Shimen. Have you forgotten Elye Taub?" That was enough to quiet him down for a while, until the young clerk again began leaping up like a bantam rooster and Father once more had to invoke the ghost of Elye Taub. As a sign of how peaceful class warfare could be, a revolver lay on the table, the weapon's blue steel reflecting the flickers of the overhead lamp.

My father handed down his ruling: Shimen Berger must pay such and such a sum to the workers' party, in compensation for damages. The young clerk was to be given a pay raise of half a ruble a week, plus cloth for a new suit of clothes. Furthermore, Reb Shimen was to promise henceforth to keep his hands to himself, because, as the young clerk had observed, "These days, you don't go around smacking people!"

Reb Shimen accepted the judgment. The workers were satisfied and left. Reb Shimen remained sitting across from my father, a murderous look in his eye. After a moment, he rose and began pounding his head with his fists. "Itskhok," he shouted at Father, "I'll kill myself, I'll hang myself. If you can no longer beat your own worker, then the world's come to an end. If I can't have the pleasure of slapping such a little snot-nose on both cheeks to show him who's boss, then who needs this lousy life?"

Yes, long before Tsar Nicholas, Shimen Berger felt the heavy hand of revolution coming down on him, and submitted, never raising his head again. He went about stooped, gloomy as doom, giving the revolution its first sweet victory.

Days of unrest followed. The comrades, flush with success, next began a campaign against an offending janitor, no ordinary caretaker but a Cerberus of his courtyard, zealous in his eagerness to serve the tsar. He looked down on his broom and pail as merely incidental to his higher calling of informer, keeping a sharp eye out on the comings and goings in his building, constantly on the lookout for suspicious, illegal behavior. His own children went about in rags, begging for crusts from the Jewish children. In reverse of the usual pattern, in his case it was the wife who was a drunk, often to be found sprawled next to the garbage bin, cursing out her husband and children. The janitor himself was always sober. He suspected that schemers were plotting revolution right under his nose and he took his spying duties with the utmost seriousness. But early one morning, the career of this most loyal of the tsar's local servitors was brought to an end.

After this promising beginning, more janitors, an occasional policeman, and even an assistant to the mayor met their fates. I remember once hearing on our street several dull claps, like the hasty raps of a stick against a shutter. A policeman, who had just bought a bag of flour, fell several feet from where I stood. The contents spilled across his face and soon dried clots of blood began to appear in the white, chalky mass, looking like chunks of raw liver and lung. The policeman lay there for a long time in his lifeless, polished boots, and Jews felt as if he had been thrown there as faked evidence in a blood libel, until the law arrived from its station on the other side of the clock tower, wrote up an official report, and took him away.

Then there was the affair of Abele Tsimring. No Jew in town sported a longer beard—it was a triumph of facial adornment. He always walked slowly, as if out for a stroll, his hands folded behind him, resting on his posterior, his large, black eyes peering out from under bushy, black eyebrows. He was already as gray as a dove, but his eyebrows refused to follow suit. As he looked around, from time to time he would remove his right hand from its resting place to give his gray beard a good stroking. His gaze was a form of inspection. As he continued on his way, he would call over to the first youngster whose eye caught his, saying: "Sonny, no one ever got anywhere by staring. Have you prayed today? Here's a groschen, go buy yourself some candy." No boy ever took up his offer. Abele's benevolence sent a chill down the spine.

Abele was a Jew who had entrée to all the official sources of civic power—the courts, the town hall, the provincial government. He was in cahoots with the authorities, and it was no secret that he was an informer, whose unholy labors had already netted him several valuable properties. In his earlier days he had made a living from hunting down young men eligible for forced conscription, but later he moved on to informing on political offenders. People cursed his very being but shuddered before him, afraid that his ominous look might land on them, as he strolled about the Jewish streets in his long, satin caftan, spying.

But no bullet, it seemed, could fell him that easily. The first time he was shot he was only slightly wounded. Within a few days he was back on the job. A second time, he was wounded more seriously, but the Jewish hospital, where he was taken, soon issued the glad tidings that he was improving and would fully recover. For purposes of security, the authorities had him transferred to the Russian military hospital, which was surrounded by high, thick walls, and heavily guarded. Nevertheless, a few of the young comrades managed to sneak in and pay him a bedside visit, making sure that he would never rise from his sickbed.

Abele's funeral was an occasion for cheer. All the Jewish schools closed in his honor. Although in his lifetime he was something of a government personage and a figure of fear, as a Jewish corpse Abele belonged entirely to us. His remains got a good shaking up on their way to the cemetery, as young and old threw stones at the passing casket. Abele, along with his formidable beard, was buried among the outcasts by the fence of the cemetery. For weeks thereafter, Jews took satisfaction in how things had worked out, quoting the biblical verse, "You shall extirpate the evil from your midst."

It was then that the Russian authorities decided the time had come to show their full might, and scare us into thinking twice before embarking on any further antigovernment ventures. It wasn't just a matter of who had one revolver more or one revolver less, because they were the real force, and to prove it, they pulled out all the stops, sending out an awesome parade. Leading the march were the drummers —boom, taraboom, boom, taraboom—calling the townspeople to witness what was obviously intended as a display of military might—artillery, infantry, grenadiers, and Cossack cavalry. The Cossack horses were so wild that they wouldn't stay in step and broke ranks constantly, spinning round in circles. It was a wonder that the Cossacks, armed to the teeth with rifles, lances, swords, and whips, didn't fall off and break their necks. Other riders on tamer mounts, fitted out with machine-guns, were followed by open-jawed cannons bumping along the unpaved streets, swaying every which way. The soldiers' stern, cruel faces were directed at the darkened houses that lay swaddled in fear. Row after row of soldiers marched past in formation, interspersed with the drummers—boom, taraboom, boom, taraboom.

The townspeople, however, for whom this display had been intended, not only failed to line the streets but disappeared behind bolted doors. As the ominous drumming resounded, they knew instinctively that this was no ordinary exhibition. Already the nights were long and terrifying because of a military curfew and now, as people exclaimed, they were coming to poison the days as well! The Jewish shops immediately closed their doors—there was no business to be had anyway. The men scattered, the women collected their children, like mother hens rounding up their chicks. One gate after another slammed shut. The Jewish streets looked like an abandoned town.

I was the only one not quick enough to make it through the gate into the courtyard of my Hebrew school. The gate was quite high, and I must have looked like a small, frightened kitten, pressed against its length, shivering through the whole long while that it took for the parade to pass. I may have been the only living soul around from the entire Jewish neighborhood. Officers winked at me. Cossacks, the better to scare me, stuck out their tongues. Wise-guy soldiers pointed their rifles in my direction. As the drummers marched by, they beat out their boom, taraboom even louder, as if in my special honor, as the blood drained from my body.

When the last soldier was gone from view, all the gates began to open, slowly, stealthily, as if testing the safety of the streets. My teacher, Yankl Peiletz, ran over to me and hugged me as if I had been lost and was now found, tickling my face with his generous beard. My classmates surrounded me and begged me to tell them everything that had happened. Even the teacher's assistant, who ordinarily ignored me, paid attention as I spun my—fantastic—account, not forgetting to mention how the soldiers had tried to take me captive, to turn me into a Cossack, and how I drove them off by reciting the *shma yisroel,* the declaration of faith—"Hear, O Israel, the Lord our God, the Lord is One."

How I envied the cobblers' and tailors' apprentices, guys of fourteen and fifteen, who by day lugged heavy tubs of water for their employers, but after work dressed up in brightly colored shirts, cracked pumpkin seeds, and romanced girls. They belonged to the youth wing of the Bund. When someone needed slapping around, they were the ones to do it. When a shop owner was in violation of the regulated business hours, they were the ones to break his windows. More than once I told Father that I envied them, but he snapped back that the revolution would get along just fine without me. Mother, for her part, agreed, and Grandfather sought to buy me off with a three-kopek coin if I would recite for him a chapter from the Five Books of Moses. He was no great scholar, so it gave him much pleasure to hear me rattle off a scriptural passage, even throwing in a bit of commentary. Grandfather believed that there was no better talisman against revolution than a biblical text. "Let the revolutionaries tend to themselves."

By that time I had discovered the treasure trove in my Uncle Velvl's house. He owned hundreds of books, from popular novels to the latest proletarian literature, but would sooner lend you money than let you borrow one of his books. He claimed that whenever he loaned out a book, he felt that something was missing from the house, as if a chair or a table had been removed. You were welcome to sit in his house and read—that with greatest of pleasure!—so long as you didn't carry off one of his precious books.

Velvl was my proletarian uncle, as opposed to Uncle Khiel-Osher, who, by that time, had become my teacher. Uncle Khiel-Osher, eldest of the seven brothers, was a tall, handsome man, indeed, the handsomest man to be seen in the bathhouse. The black hair of his beard still vied for supremacy with the gray, and his eyes were youthful looking. His only blemish was a bulging bit of intestine on the right side of his body that he kept in place with a truss.

Khiel-Osher's school was considered third-grade level. Its studies included a smattering of Talmud, as well as some biblical Hebrew. On Christmas Day, when Jews customarily refrained from the study of sacred texts, he would take out a grease-stained volume of the Talmud, as if it were some kind of contraband, and read to us the account of how that person—referred to as Yosl Panderik—the man who would be God, was toppled from his glory. He read on and on, until the ultimate punishment was pronounced, eternal immersion, said Uncle Khiel-Osher, "in boiling let's-not-mention-it-by-name."

Uncle Khiel-Osher was a good-natured soul, with little jokes for every calamity. He allowed his pupils, literally, to crawl all over him. This didn't bother him, nor was he irked that his second wife didn't do right as a stepmother by the daughter of his first marriage, devoting herself entirely to the twins they had together—and that she henpecked him to boot. The twins would have crawled all over him, too, but the two baby girls were still creeping on their stomachs. They slithered about like snakes, always moving in tandem, turning at the same time, with never a hair's breadth between them, and ate off the floor. Because of their disdain for the stepmother, the schoolboys had no warm feelings either for the two little worms crawling about, and would surreptitiously step on a little hand or foot, taking delight in the stepmother's shrieks: "Damn that Khiel-Osher. They're killing my twins!"

Uncle Velvl, my working-class uncle, stitched gaiters for a living. His fingernails were discolored, his hands corroded by acid. He pounded away on strange, tall, wide-bellied Singer sewing machines, singing as he worked, popular theater tunes by Abraham Goldfaden. He was very poor and had a reputation in town as an enlightened person, almost a heretic, although his entire heresy consisted solely of the fact that he sometimes talked during services in the synagogue. His place stank of leather. Unfinished pieces of work lay scattered everywhere and gave off a smell that almost tasted of salt. He had no apprentices and did everything himself, standing humped over the sewing machine, like a camel, singing out loud. He was the first among the brothers who unapologetically raised his children to be workers. One daughter became a seamstress, his son a housepainter, and another daughter he even saw fit to marry off to a shoemaker.

The seamstress, Beyle Perl, was a Socialist Zionist, who actually tried to recruit me to the cause. I must have been about seven or eight and she was probably seventeen, a strapping girl, with long, thick braids. She talked to me about Dr. Theodore Herzl, about the workers' struggle for a better life, and arranged for us to meet one Sabbath afternoon to visit the organizational headquarters, just off the new road. However, my younger brother betrayed me, and my pants and boots were confiscated to prevent me from going out. Father commented that the Zionist revolution would also carry on without me. As for me, I could swear that those impounded boots forever destroyed my chances for a political career.

Be all that as it may, Uncle Velvl's free library was still at my disposal. I threw myself on the Socialist pamphlets, but they turned out to be somewhat dry and hard, like brittle cookies. I looked into "heretical" books, but they didn't give me as much pleasure as did the storybooks and the writings of Sholem Aleichem.

The books drew me to Uncle Velvl's on Sabbath afternoons. Aunt

Bine, who was related to us in several ways—she was Uncle Velvl's wife, Father's sister-in-law, and also my maternal grandfather's sister —was a short, pious woman, a kindhearted soul, who asked no more from God than her share of poverty. By the time I would show up, she had already set out a plate of gooseberries, currants, pea pods, and beans. Uncle Velvl lay napping, nose up, snoring rhythmically, a sleep-inducing sound that spread through the house, like a cricket's chirping. Aunt Bine, who always had a pious word on her lips, sat by the window, reading her Yiddish Bible aloud, in a drowsy, singsong voice. She knew that the books in the room were somewhat improper and would try to persuade me that, for a clever little head like mine, the study of Talmud was a far healthier pursuit. However, after this bit of edification, she returned to her Bible, spelling out each word meticulously and leaving me to share the perils of *The Family Tsvi*. I relived the horrors of the pogrom they had experienced, as I chewed the mealy beans, the sour currants, the reddish gooseberries with their tiny filaments, and the fleshy sour cherries that filled my mouth with the winy taste of a bounteous summer. I read the poems of Dovid Edelstadt, the Yiddish-American "proletarian" poet, returning to the front of the book, after each reading of a poem, to look at his picture, admiring his refined face and handsome beard. His "working class" seemed to me a tribe of princes who suffer like water carriers under their heavy burden. I had trouble making the connection between Edelstadt's "working class" and the begrimed laborers of our own city.

One Sabbath afternoon, while I was caught up in Edelstadt's verse, I heard several shots, followed by sounds of running in the streets, shouts, and wails. I rushed down the dark stairs of my uncle's house. On the ground floor lay the bloodied figure of a man, half-seated, half-reclining. His head was hidden by a cap. There was blood on the stairs. Within a minute, the whole town became aware that young Atlasovitch had been shot. The next day, hectographed fliers, plastered throughout the city, proclaimed that he had been executed for betraying his party's secrets.

Young Atlasovitch was the son every Jewish mother in town dreamed of having. A pious youth, with curly, blue-black hair, fair skin, and deep-set, almost girlish, eyes, he was a good student, and from a fine family. His stern father was a man of few words, but secretly proud that the young boy he was raising, his only son, was somebody special. He kept quiet about it, for fear of the evil eye, but he was certain in his heart that one day his son would brighten the dark Exile.

Suddenly, young Atlasovitch had strayed from the path. His father turned gray overnight, but otherwise gave no sign of his anguish. He remained stolidly silent and withdrew into himself. The old man could scarcely be persuaded to attend the funeral. He walked proudly, head high, not at all like a mourner, while his wife, the unfortunate mother, beat her head with her fists. Strangers wept over the young tree cut down before its time, a sacrifice to the unruly times, but the father still walked on proudly, looking straight ahead. After all the respects to the dead had been paid and the time came for reciting the mourners' kaddish, as all were waiting with lowered heads, old Atlasovitch drew himself up, spat several times into the grave, and, instead of proceeding with the prayer, cried out, "May his name and memory be erased." Then he turned his back on the mourners and returned home, his stride quick and unwavering.

After all the many rehearsals, after all the woes, the revolution, when it finally arrived, burst upon us like some grand festivity. Waking up that morning, one knew that the day was going to be exceptional, a blessed day—knew it as the child does who opens his eyes and, in a haze of sleep, before his first conscious thought, feels a sweetness coursing through its limbs at the realization that today was a holiday and there would be no school. On that festive day, the sun struck the windows with so much light that it almost shattered the glass. There was sunshine and joy in every street and on every face. Officers kissed Jewish girls, aristocrats fell on Jews' necks. People walked about freely, carrying the red flag. Everybody was singing, music played. Father raised me high on his shoulders, over everyone's head, and, pushing through the crowd, said to me, "Don't ever forget, Yankele, that you were lucky enough to see all this with your very own eyes."

A slight, skinny kid, riding aloft on my father's shoulders, I felt light as air, like a flag fluttering in the wind. The tsar had granted a constitution! Soldiers fraternized with the crowds, Cossacks laughed, Kalmuks with leathery faces flashed their white teeth, the sidewalks sang.

All day long there was marching. Girls' braids flaunted red ribbons, red banners waved, people cried for joy, knelt in the street and made the sign of the cross. Young Hasidim with goatees and billowing coats hopped and sang as on the festival of Simhat Torah. Many shops and stores hung out red flags, commerce was at a standstill. My little heart was bursting with joy. Perfumed hands tickled me with flowers and showered me with confetti. Father lifted me so high that I felt unsteady in his grip. Any moment he would put me down and I would be crushed by all this happiness, by the high heels of the women's shoes, and the Cossack horses that, for the moment, were standing quietly on the sidewalks among the crowd, amiably neighing. I devoured it all, excited by all the activity that swirled around me.

Hundreds of comrades had gathered at the jail to talk to the political prisoners through the barred windows. The knitted, creased faces of the prisoners were visible, crying and laughing. Any moment now, the gates would be flung open! People were singing and shouting, embracing, laughing aloud at our boundless good fortune. Women, who otherwise would never be seen in the vicinity of the jail, were now singing beside the soot-covered workers of the iron foundry:

Workers, to the barricades,
Raise aloft the red flag.

And all the while, my father was saying, "Yankele, never forget this."

But moving through the crowd like shadows were several pious, gray-bearded Jews, separated from the tumult and exhorting us to leave. These killjoys had darkened faces and bent backs, as if crushed under the sorrowful weight of the massacres of 1648 and all the many other Jewish catastrophes. Jeremiahs, prophets of doom, they wandered through the crowds, warning, "Jews, go home! This is not your celebration."

The next morning, awash in shame, heartache, and fear, people spoke about the long night of terror, of the bullets that rained down on the workers gathered at the jail, of the raging Cossacks, the flowing blood, the packs of roaming officers and soldiers, of spies and hundreds of arrests, of how Tsar Nicholas had signed the constitution with his right hand and abrogated it with the left. Last night's joy had turned into panic, its tattered remnants still strewn on the streets. Janitors swept up the dirty confetti.

The revolution was suppressed and almost driven from my childish consciousness. As we grew older, all that remained were stray reminiscences. The revolutionary resistance, which had started out with such hope and joy, was dead, its spirit gone. The workers had lost all courage. They had had their golden opportunity, and lost it. When would there be another? Spinsters, aging by the moment, instead of songs of revolution, sang of bridegrooms who could never be. Garment workers, backs bent over their sewing machines, heads bowed, sang snatches from Yiddish operettas, finding consolation in such devil-may-care sentiments as: "Oh, money's nothing but sorrow, / Here today, gone tomorrow." There were poverty-stricken engagement parties and even shabbier weddings. Young women covered their hair and donned wedding veils for any man whosoever. Poverty became widespread. Scrofulous children with bulging eyes, massive heads, and wide little bottoms splashed about in the mud. From time to time, typhoid fever came calling. Several of our sensitive young men, who had read too much Schopenhauer, took that pessimistic hypocrite literally and committed suicide. Funerals increased and the revolution was yesterday's dust.

We, the city's golden youth, refined young men with too much time on our hands, consoled ourselves along the dark paths of the Saxony Gardens by reading Maxim Gorky's *Mother*. We saw the shadows of the blackened workers, the gloomy factory walls. We heard the call to strike. We admired the posters of a working-class mother, a towering figure with upraised fists, a proletarian Joan of Arc. But now "revolution" took on an aesthetic tinge. We subjected its protagonists to our critical eye, analyzing their actions to determine whether they were "psychologically consistent." Our literary gauge was Ibsen's Nora, slamming the door on her unhappy marriage—should she have left her husband or not? We debated Knut Hamsun's *Hunger* and Gerhart Hauptmann's *The Weavers*. While the other side of the park was swarming with aristocrats, brokers, and Jews pecking like hens at crumbs of a livelihood, we went about like Hamlets, twirling our walking sticks—a twirl this way, "to be," a twirl that way, "not to be."

This is how we turned out: One became a bookkeeper in a sugar factory, another, a process writer's assistant (the first later went off to the Academy of Art in Kraków, the second, to the Warsaw Conservatory). A third became a Hebrew teacher, a fourth worried about what he would do with his diploma in the absence of a gold medal and about how his father would receive the news were he to convert to Lutheranism. A fifth sent off his poems to the journal *Niva* and passed around the encouraging letters from its editor, the kindly Vladimir Galaktyonowicz.

As for me, I threatened to commit suicide if my father wouldn't underwrite a steamship ticket to America.

3

Sonia Yakovlyevna lay stretched out on the small sofa in my cabin, her weary, danced-out feet propped up on a chair. The blond young Russian stood over her, smoothing her disheveled hair and stroking her cheek. Her eyes were closed, but it was evident that she was enjoying the touch of his gentle hands. He moved on to massage her feet with expert strokes, as if trying to erase their fatigue. He began to croon, like some sleepy-voiced singer on a phonograph record, one of Lermontov's lullabies, "Bayu, bayushki, bayu," adding after each verse, in recitative, the refrain from a once-popular song, "Cover your pale feet." The steward, who had been invited to the party to add some proletarian flavoring, sat off in a corner, clutching a bottle, drinking by himself. He had a professional reputation to uphold and couldn't afford to get too friendly with drunken passengers who might make trouble once they sobered up.

For my part, I kept repeating the words, "This is it," which, if they had any meaning to begin with, were now lost in a drunken haze. Like a drunk who latches onto a thought that he won't let go, I kept repeating, over and over, "This is it." As my head cleared, the myriad thoughts swirling about in my brain began to dissipate, but one took hold and stayed firm—that those remembered sufferings from my childhood, of Lublin in 1905, had nurtured my fine young Russian shipmates and eased their way. All those tailors of my youth, the shoemakers and seamstresses, long since in their graves, had seen their bellies swell with hunger for the sake of this liberated generation. Once I sobered up, I remembered that I had asked the October Revolution to toast the Lublin of my youth. I had cursed and blasphemed, mustering all the Russian I still retained. Moscow should not be so high and mighty: It was about time that everybody knew there was a Lublin in the world and that Moscow owed it a debt. My native city deserved the Order of Lenin.

Hey, hey, down with the police.
Down with the tsarist oppressor.

That night, half-sober, we sat fraternizing in the bar. We played chess and I kept losing, but far from taking a sadistic pleasure in their victory, the young Russians turned out to be pacifist players and pacifist victors, who, after each of my defeats, sought to assure me that I was doing just fine, out of fear that I was perhaps one of those competitive players of the old school, who played the game to the death and might do himself harm if he lost. We drank Scotch and soda at a large, round table and felt the floor barely moving and the chairs slightly swaying. In fact, we forgot all about the sea. Everything seemed saturated in whiskey, which lent a lilting tone to our conversation, as though we were not talking, but slowly waltzing. The strains of an operatic medley drifted in from the ballroom—some Wagner, bits of Puccini, snatches of Verdi, reaching a crescendo with Pagliacci's sobbing lament.

Sitting at our table, besides the Russian colony that of course included Sonya Yakovlyevna, were several other women who were attracted to our company by the lure of the exotic. One of these could claim a connection to the group—a Latvian-Jewish woman of about thirty, who, though her face was not completely rid of girlish traces, wanted very much to play the lady. She spoke six or seven languages, including a decent Russian, which she pronounced with a German accent. She had lived in America only three years and was returning for a visit to her family in Riga. Her husband was a wealthy importer, with a house in the prosperous Flatbush section of Brooklyn, and she could well afford the luxury of indulging her homesickness.

The lady from Riga had the manners of a grande dame and, accordingly, passed her time aboard ship in the company of the Haitian diplomat. They promenaded the deck arm in arm, carrying on a polite flirtation in French. Her good breeding was everywhere evident, in her dress, her demeanor, her olive complexion, her delicate hands and smartly shod feet. However, she had one annoying habit. Whenever she loosened up a bit, she would invoke her absent husband, working the phrase "as my husband says" into every conversation, as if to emphasize that she was a devoted wife, above suspicion, or perhaps as a necessary safeguard against indiscretion. Her delicate fingers toyed with her Scotch, and her dark eyes glistened as she looked from one person to another around the table: "*Nu, shtosz, tovarishch, nye plokho zhit na svyetye*—well comrade, it isn't that bad, it's great to be alive!" Sonya, on the other hand, was growing increasingly melancholy. She was the sort of woman who brightens when she is the only female among male company. Women like Sonya, when there are other women present, turn off their lamps and withdraw into the darkness.

An Englishwoman, well past forty, whom I had met through my Danish friend, was also at our table, and exclaimed in amazement: "Aren't these Russians perfectly exquisite!" She understood nothing of the conversation, but she had one great virtue, she could drink up a storm. The blond young Russian, who in his aspect of cavalier was not only a gracious Slav but also a humanitarian, anxious over the fact that the Englishwoman was being neglected by his indifferent comrades, singled her out for his attentions. He paid her lavish Russian compliments, and though he was old enough to be her grown son, bombarded her with expressions of his love. Flushed from the Scotch and aglow from the compliments, she kept assuring me that "these Russians" were "perfectly exquisite."

Another female guest at our table was a Finnish-American woman, whom I impressed by inquiring about the *Kalevala,* the Finnish epic, rattling off the names of its main characters, the heroes Väinäimöinen and Ilmarinen, and the arrogant Lemminkäinen. She was especially taken with me when, straining all my musical talents, I sang her excerpts from Sibelius's *Swan of Tuonela.* Far from young and farther still from beautiful, she also boasted a long, pointed nose that seemed to have a life of its own, like a bird or some other small creature. She told me she was a nurse, and thanked me profusely for recognizing her national origins. To most Americans, she observed, the word *Finland* was a meaningless sound with no associations. To show her appreciation, she invited me to visit her in Hoboken. True, she had only a small room with a narrow bed, but even the doctors at her hospital had told her that she wasn't ready yet to be tossed aside. It's worth taking a chance, she urged, squeezing my hand, what did I have to lose? She, too, bubbled over the Soviet youths.

Also gracing our table was an American woman from Wisconsin, thirty-three years old and a head taller than tall. She was a French instructor at a women's college, with the spinsterish air that seems to mark the females of the profession. To appear even more serious, every so often she would put on the pince-nez that dangled on a silver chain from her long neck. To break the monotony and restriction of the school year, and perhaps to take a vacation from her earnestness, she spent each summer in Paris, where for ten weeks, as she put it, she played the bohemian (though what that implied for an American schoolteacher, God only knows). In Paris, she said, she became a different person, a new soul in a new body. In place of the Wisconsin teacher was a woman who burned up ten weeks like a single day. The hardest part was avoiding her older students, who also "hopped over" to Paris in the summer for a taste of freedom, which is why she found it necessary to stay on side streets in second-class hotels.

Here, aboard ship, the schoolteacher felt that her Paris blossoming had already begun. When she removed the pince-nez, you saw her clever face, and her smart self-control on the point of yielding. Her old-maidish demeanor was encased in an athletic body. She radiated physical vigor, as witness her strong and alluring arms and legs. She confided that in Paris she had many close Russian friends, but they were of the "other," White Russian kind. She was therefore pleased with this opportunity to meet the "other side of the Russian coin."

"The Russians you know in Paris are the worn-out side of the coin," I ventured.

Khazhev, overhearing our exchange, chimed in more ardently, blurting out in English, "They ought to be shot!"

"Why?" she said angrily. "They're fine, upstanding, warmhearted people," and to snuff out the light that suddenly flared up in her eyes, she slipped on the schoolmarmish pince-nez, so it would look as if her outburst were more on the order of a dry disquisition on the characteristics of White Russians. "You are all dear people. All Russians are wonderful," she continued, taking on the mission to reconcile the old Russia with the new.

Khazhev would have none of it. With his limited English vocabulary, he stood his ground and insisted, "Your friends should be shot!"

She gave an embarrassed laugh, as if seized by the fear that the death sentence was real and about to be implemented. There stood all her Franco-Russian friends, lined up against the wall and bang!—they were gone! All those marvelous summers in Paris—1930, 1931, 1932, 1933—that gave her the strength to endure the harsh winters somewhere in Wisconsin, all blasted in an instant! "Why should they be shot?" she asked in a maternal voice, as if pleading for her own flesh and blood. "*Podzhalusta*, please," she said coquettishly, in her stilted Russian, "*Ya vas lyublu, spasibo*. I love you, thank you!" Having exhausted her entire Russian lexicon, she sat back, pleased with herself, but with only one regret, that she hadn't been able to make peace between her White Russians and the Bolsheviks at our table.

I was pressed into the role of interpreter between the young Bolsheviks and the American teacher. The blond Russian gave Khazhev a friendly chiding for his talk about shooting. "Shooting," he said, "is not a fit subject for conversation. One should never talk like that. Shooting is often necessary, but so long as one is still talking, one doesn't resort to shooting, and even then, not without good reason. Give the good lady to understand that we are not murderers. Shooting comes later, much later. First we talk, in a humane way, and only if we can't find common ground, and someone poses a danger, only then, little brother, when there's no further recourse, do we perform our revolutionary duty and apply the maximum sentence." Thus the blond young Russian discharged his Bolshevik obligations.

As I was translating this little speech, the middle-aged Englishwoman, who by this time had lost track of the number of Scotches she had tossed off, was so moved that she leaned over to kiss her blond cavalier-cum-dialectician and exclaimed, for the umpteenth time, "You have to admit it, the Russians are cute! Perfectly exquisite!"

Couples were conversing quietly on couches along the walls and in all corners of the room. It was past midnight, the hour of laconic wisdom and meaningful silences, when eyes, hands, and nudging shoes do the talking. But in the bar of this English ship, even these muted activities were being conducted with Anglo-Saxon reserve. The hushed sounds drifted toward us from the distance, like fragments of some sentimental song, several times removed. Our table, which stood in the center of the room and which, until now, had been going full blast, also couldn't help but yield to the spell of the murmurings. Someone at the table observed that all these disparate couples seemed to constitute one collective romance. The worker who had won the trip around the world began to whistle a Schubert song.

"Comrades," shouted the blond young Russian, "you can stand me against the wall and shoot me like a dog for being sentimental, but what he's whistling, that's exactly how I feel. He hit it on the nose. Any other time, that song about nightingales would have the flavor of marinated herring, but tonight I'm ready to get on my knees and sing Schubert songs to one of these lovely ladies. Long live Soviet power, and long live love." He snuggled closer to the Englishwoman and joined in the whistling.

It was during this lyrical outburst that I was approached by one of the Russians—as was Joseph by his brothers—who told me what was anyway obvious, that he was a Jew. He tried to be as casual as possible about the revelation, but once the secret was out, decided to go for broke and tell me everything. May the gods of internationalism forgive me, but, amid this colorful, multinational assemblage, his words sounded especially homey, redolent with the Jewish aromas of freshly baked hallah, hot, peppery fish cooling on a platter by the window, mouthwatering chicken soup with floating globules of fat, and homemade horseradish that hits you smack in the nostrils—all this, from the moment he began to unroll his genealogical chart, starting with the fact that his father was a melamed, a Hebrew teacher, in a small town somewhere in Poland.

He spoke softly and quickly. He was certainly an integral part of the

Soviet group, but it seemed as if he wanted to take me aside and tell me that, although he was just like the other comrades at the table, give or take a hair, there was something he had to get off his chest. It was about his father, who was living in poverty, on the verge of starvation. He— the son from the Soviet Union, where thousands were dying of hunger in the streets (he threw this in without a trace of irony)—sent money to his father every month to help him keep body and soul together. He was lucky that he himself had been able to get out of Poland in time, had studied engineering, and was now holding down a responsible position in a factory. The factory had sent him abroad for six weeks—a shame it was only six weeks—whereas he would have liked to spend at least a few months in America. He would have learned English, well enough to speak it properly, not like Khazhev and his stammerings— this last said in a loud voice, so that Khazhev and the others could hear the good-natured jibe.

"*Yevreyskaya golova*, a Jewish head!" I blurted out, paying him an innocent compliment. This is what Russians themselves used to say when marveling at Jewish accomplishment, but the words now fell with a thud. He paled and tried to extract me from the gaffe I had perpetrated, but I sank in deeper and deeper. As the others smiled in discomfort, he apologized for my use of an expression that was a relic from tsarist days. It seemed to me that, in one stroke, I had lost both worlds of my newly formed friendship with the Russian colony—the Russian and the Jewish—but worst of all, I had embarrassed the single Jew among them, as if I had slapped him in the face with my unhappy compliment. It was the faux pas of the evening, and it took some time for the embarrassment to lift.

Only slowly, very slowly, did he pick up the thread and resume his account, telling me how he, a Polish Hebrew-school boy, had managed to escape from that dung heap into the wider world. Had he waited just one more year, he would surely have become his father's assistant, dragging unwilling, wailing children to the classroom. Instead, look at him, he'd been to America as the representative of a great land, the workers' motherland, and was returning home to enjoy its blessings. In passing, he let slip that he had traveled to America on a German ship.

"A German ship?" I asked in astonishment.

"Yes," he replied with perfect equanimity, as if my question was merely routine. It tore my heart to hear about his German passage, but he spoke about it so casually that I almost envied him. Here was a truly emancipated Jew! His father is a melamed in a small Polish town, and the son, in the era of Hitler, travels without qualm on a German ship!

"The food was delicious," he said, smacking his lips, "and we never talked politics. They were very careful about this, and we, even more so."

"But how does it feel nowadays to be a Jew on a German ship?" I asked, unable again to restrain myself.

He gave me a pitying smile and said, "That's a sentimental question and we don't have time for sentimentality."

Once more I had occasion to envy my liberated coreligionist and proposed that we drink to the new Jew in Moscow, who doesn't fall ill when he hears that Jews are being beaten in Algeria.

"A toast to the new Jew!" I cried out in a burst of masochism, as if sticking needles into my flesh.

"More sentimentality," he rebuked me. "Let's drink instead to the new man!" He went on to describe life in the Soviet Union, a veritable idyll as he saw it.

"You work hard," he said, "but for whom? For yourself, of course. If you work real hard and show ability, you are rewarded with vacations, trips, special theater performances, the ballet, reserved seats at the movies, stays in sanitariums, and free medical treatment. And if you want to work extra, you get paid for every bit. Take me, for example. After I put in a day at the factory, I'm a lecturer at the university, for which I get paid again, and on those evenings when I'm not at the university, I often go back to the factory to work on a project. The Soviet Union is built on work—sweet work, because you work for yourself. Some people earn so much that they can't spend it all and are able to save a good many thousands of rubles. But don't worry, we're not breeding millionaires. What do we do with the extra money? We help a friend, we give it away, we give it back to the government by buying government bonds."

The picture he painted of the good life in the workers' paradise was like watching a Soviet film—fields heavy with grain, plump cattle with udders bursting to the full, laughing faces, everybody happily at work, singing all the while. Behold the millennium!

Dance music was now drifting in from the ballroom, along with clip-clops from the swaying dance floor, rocking gently on an unseen sea, to which no one was giving a second thought. It seemed as if the music and the dancing were accompaniments to the Soviet idyll as described by my Jewish engineer friend.

"You understand?" I said to him. "I honestly don't know if I can untangle all the strands of my life story in a way that will make sense to you. I come from Lublin, a small city in Poland, and I remember the revolutionary songs which the workers in my town used to sing, what their hopes were, and the look in their eyes when they spoke of the social revolution. In fact, the revolution was watered with their tears. They, the downtrodden, wanted to stand tall, alongside a Rothschild, a Shereshevsky, a Brodsky, a Wissotsky, and our own local millionaire, Sheinbrun. But life is a lousy midwife and child delivery a hazardous business. In the course of being born, someone's skull can get crushed, someone else's hands and feet can get mangled, and the devil knows what else can go wrong. In a happier instance, the midwife delivers a perfect infant, patting it on the head and tying a red ribbon around its wrist. One such healthy baby grows up smooth-tongued, another can't put words together properly and from birth on is destined to become the slave of those who tell him what he can and cannot do, what he wants and doesn't want. One grows up with clever hands, another bumbles through, a third grows up dull-headed, while a fourth proves a mathematical genius. Such is the despotism of tens of thousands of blackened years, the genetic heritage of great-great-great-grandmothers and -grandfathers, aunts, uncles, and the devil knows who else, going back all the way to our Cro-Magnon or Neanderthal ancestors."

I was now wound up. "You Bolsheviks," I continued, "play right into the hands of that miserable midwife. You accept her decrees. You reward talent, while the helpless among you, the damned, the incompetent, are left to fend for themselves. Those with ability get to drink wine from the Caucasus, those without are lucky if they see a piece of bread. All those begrimed tailors and shoemakers, with their tear-stained cheeks, have achieved nothing. Where are the luxury liners for them? When do they get to celebrate? And yet, they are in the tens of millions, and you, the talented ones, members of the Party, are in the minority. Where is their recompense? Their downtrodden lives, their tearful stammer won the revolution for you clever, intelligent types. Believe me when I say, in all sincerity, that you are terrific engineers. Yet here you sit, enjoying the best, while all those unfortunate millions remain sunk in their misery. Their revolution, my friend, has yet to come.

"Take your comrade here. He had to get lucky and win a lottery in order to be equal to you and earn himself a break. He had no other alternative. Neither capitalism nor Communism wants to pay for his lack of ability; he must always be dreaming of winning the sweepstakes. Yet that unfortunate creature is your true millionaire, the salt of the earth. He isn't cunning, he doesn't know how to play politics, he can't make speeches, he's no brilliant mathematician, but the truth is that he helped build the new society, which isn't merely for the blessed, talented, lucky few who've jumped onto the bandwagon and now hold the reins."

We all went up and walked round and round on deck. The night was so bright you could make out every feature on every face. An invigorating breeze rose up from the sea to lift our spirits and gladden our hearts.

"You are a sentimental bourgeois and an enemy of the Soviet Union," said the Jewish engineer, placing a friendly hand on my shoulder, "and I have no idea what you've been babbling about."

A ship outlined in lights came out of nowhere and began to accompany us, like an orbiting moon. For the first time, we had the feeling that we were not alone on the vast sea but one part of a greater whole, of a grand, oceanic scheme. Sonya Yakovlyevna was so moved by the ship's appearance that she danced for joy, like Robinson Crusoe at the sight of his rescuers. Khazhev and the tall Wisconsin teacher stood leaning against the railing and stared at the lights of the vessel, now moving alongside ours. The Finnish-American nurse sang a Finnish folk song. The lady from Riga kept reciting verses of sea ballads in five or six languages. The middle-aged Englishwoman, walking arm in arm with the blond young Russian, disappeared with him every so often into a dark corner. Each time that she emerged from hiding, she would say to me, in a breathy whisper, "Aren't these Russians perfectly exquisite!"

Chapter 4

1

Should you want to conjure up the aroma of our British ship, you must begin with the salty breakfasts that permeated the large dining room with disagreeable smells of frying bacon, kippers—grilled, baked, or fried—and herring.

At my table, inhaling the pungent odors, sat a deaf professor, munching on a piece of dry toast. Next to him was a student, of middling height, with broad, athletic shoulders, big hands, and full cheeks. The professor held up an ear trumpet pointed toward the student, listened to what he was asking as if he were on the phone with him, and answered with a mouthful of food and in a high, squeaky voice that was in sharp discord with his commanding head and steel-gray hair. The student was also something of a surprise. His appearance suggested some sort of athlete, but he turned out to be an economics student, indeed, a whiz on the subject, and he bombarded the professor with questions about supply and demand, tariffs, international agreements, farm production, all bolstered by tens of citations that were as dry as the toast the professor was attacking with his false teeth.

The professor, who was on his way to do research at the British Museum, was visibly impatient with the student's importuning. He would have preferred to engage in lighter conversation with others at the table, but the student was intent on monopolizing his attention and moved on from economics to pestering him with details about student life at American universities as compared with the European, all of this replete with statistics. The student ate quickly, never looking around him or down at his plate. He kept his gaze fixed on the professor, giving the poor man no chance to turn elsewhere. Like some giant, omnivorous whale, looking to scoop up its fill of knowledge, the student must have belonged to the school that holds one mustn't forgo any opportunity for instruction. Even later on deck, when the professor had finally managed to get out from under his clutches, the young man sat off in a corner, head buried in a book, taking notes. Here, too, he didn't glance up or return the smiles directed his way. He seemed to have decided exactly how he wanted to live and how to make every moment count, for a career doesn't just stand there waiting, it must be cultivated, otherwise somebody else will snatch it.

At table, whenever the professor, wanting to be polite, threw some good-natured remarks my way, the student made a face, showing signs of impatience, only waiting for the strategic moment when he might reclaim the professor for himself, reattach himself like a leech, and resume spouting. Only after the two had left did things lighten up. The thirteen-year-old girl at our table didn't lose a moment and immediately started imitating the professor's high, squeaky voice and the student's bass drone. She strung together meaningless sentences with ten-dollar words, mocking the elevated discourse of the learned duo. Her father, a hardworking American, with a red neck and an even redder face marked by an outbreak of eczema that divided his countenance into peaks and valleys, ordered her to stop, but couldn't help himself and laughed so hard that he spit his tea back into his saucer. He coughed and choked, but his daughter persisted in her comic performance and answered him in the professor's falsetto voice.

This American workingman, with his calloused hands and scarred face, who seemed lost among all the big-city sophisticates in the dining room, also began to loosen up and became rather animated, as if he had just bidden farewell to two gravediggers. Between sips of tea, he told me that he was a widower, raising on his own the little girl his late wife had left on his hands. He explained that his daughter, now thirteen, had emerged from childhood with a rare combination of boyish and girlish traits—mischievous as a boy and flirtatious as a girl. Since she was the only female in the household, she felt she could act the coquette with her own father. Her split nature was reflected in the contrast between her sturdy body and her plump, round girlish face, with its laughing, mischievous blue eyes. The girl was dark-complexioned and healthy looking; she looked as if she had been cast out of tasty rye bread. She behaved toward her father like one pal to another, speaking to him as an equal, and also chewed him out like a little wife, as well as watching over him to make sure that he wasn't eating too fast or too much.

For his part, the father kept his strong sentiments for his daughter under layer upon layer of protective armor, afraid that he might cry at the mere sight of his playful kitten, babbling away at the table, and self-assured enough to interrupt the deaf professor when she felt like it. So to mask his feelings he acted toward her as buddy-buddy as she did toward him. He was on his way to England, he told me, for a yearlong stay with his parents. He wanted to give his child a holiday that would also get her acquainted with her grandparents. He, too, needed a good, long rest. Other than the joy his daughter brought him, he confided that he hadn't had a single carefree moment in his entire life. He worked like a horse and worried about raising his little girl, which was the toughest job of all, since he was father, mother, and cook, as well as breadwinner.

He was employed in a gold mine. "You don't get much sympathy from ordinary blokes when you tell them that you work in a gold mine," he said, in his broad British accent. "They hear 'gold' and right away think that you must be rich, because how can it be that some of that stuff doesn't stick to you, and besides, gold is such a nice, refined metal, mining for it can't be all that hard. None of that, of course, is true. Gold is as hard to mine as coal. The gold goes to the mine owners, and we get the copper, that is, the few lousy coppers they pay us, for which we work like slaves."

He had certainly earned his rest, he said, and all he wanted to do on this Atlantic crossing was to lie in the sun, warming himself, like a hound. He complained bitterly about the aloofness of the passengers, so different from those on the ship that had brought him from California to New York. Now there was a lively voyage, because everyone aboard was an American—friendly people, not like the teachers, doctors, and professors of the present company, who began to stink of Europe the moment they came aboard, second-class people the lot of them, trying to pass for first-class. "I'm not an educated man," he said, "but I know all about people like that, and I don't like them."

He was one of the loneliest persons on deck. Even his daughter had made some friends, girls her own age, but he connected with no one. When he was sure that his daughter wasn't looking, he sneaked into the bar and quickly downed one whiskey after another. And when his daughter next saw him, she smelled right away that her father had let himself go too far and gave him a few good smacks in his red face, as he swore on his life to this plump little girl with the sharp tongue that this was positively his last drink: If she ever saw him take another, she would throw him to the sharks.

On deck there was so much sun that everyone seemed to be encased in a thin layer of sunlight, like cellophane wrapping. There was sun between every exchange of smiles, between exchanged Good Mornings. Sun everywhere, on hands and necks, bare backs, and faces. Everything looked brighter and more transparent—suits, dresses, stockings. The slight hairs on women's bare legs, stretched out on deck chairs as if on display, quivered in the sunlight like tiny blades of grass. Downy motes flew by, like precious diamonds of sun-dust that sometimes streak on the tail of a comet of sunlight into a sun-drenched room.

The prizefighter who had spent his first days slathered in oil, sunning himself, was now up and about, beaming at everyone. He had become more acclimated to shipboard life and had abandoned his former habits. With a woman on his arm, he now promenaded the deck, just like everybody else, neglecting to swagger or thrust out his chest. He still wore the same sweater knotted around his neck, and a cap at a jaunty angle, but his muscle was no longer intimidating. On the contrary, the companion he had picked up looked more the prizefighter. She stepped down heavily on her sandals, weighed down by her considerable bulk. Her red-painted toenails, rouged cheeks, painted lips, several gold teeth, and her ample bosom sagging under clanking chains were all so well suited to the fighter's bashed-in nose that no one could have found him a better match. Trailing him, like Sherlock Holmes, was his manager and Man Friday, looking as if his head were in the clouds, but all the while, not once taking his eye off his bread-and-butter. He walked alone, too much the concerned businessman to bother with the ladies—his head filled with plans, calculations, and strategies.

The doctor who had been stalking me for days finally caught up with me. Unceremoniously, he motioned to his wife to go off and leave us alone, and immediately launched into an account, sparing no detail, of how he had discovered a cure for that incurable affliction, Addison's disease. With his fat little hands and round face, he had the look of a clever pug. His cheeks here and there sported bluish-red blotches. He was a short man, and when he spoke, he bounced up and down, thrusting himself into the listener's face. His medical practice was divided between America and Europe, half a year on each continent. "Europe used to mean Germany," he sighed, "but that's now off limits." He was therefore on his way to Austria, where he would be attending a medical conference, at which he would disclose his cure for Addison's disease.

He explained to me, in his grotesque Yiddish-German English, interspersed with some well-worn Hebrew phrases, that, in general, doctors were actually—he finished the sentence with a vulgar word, spoken with the utmost relish. He then struck a questioning pose, to ascertain what impression his shocking word had made on me and whether I had caught his opinion of his colleagues, who, to his mind, were no great exemplars of wisdom. He repeated the offensive word several more times, smacking his lips and shouting it aloud so that all might hear.

"Dat's vot doctors are. You tink," he said in his Germanized English, lapsing into a Yiddish intonation, "that a doctor is a clever man, but the truth is"—this he confided to the non-Jewish woman who was walking beside me—"a physician is a —." Again he concluded with the same Yiddish vulgarity and the same display of Hasidic rapture. It was a word which for him was the ne plus ultra for conveying the unmitigated stupidity of doctors. The woman looked to me for protection from the incomprehensible remark, which the doctor urged me to translate for her. "Tell her what it means. It's no shame! It's human."

Sensing that some indelicacy was being bruited, the woman took fright lest I actually translate, as requested, and very elegantly slipped away from us and disappeared.

"You see," he said, rubbing his fat, little hands with satisfaction, "I chased her away. I hate it when women mix in when men are talking about serious things." He then digressed and proceeded to lecture me, now speaking entirely in Yiddish, on how one should behave toward women. One must practice thrift.

"Sure, flirt with them," he expounded, "make them happy, don't make a fool of yourself, but above all—preserve your manly energy, your vital fluids. Never dissipate your powers. Learn how to get pleasure out of life, but always practice thrift. Life isn't that proverbial 'inexhaustible fountain.' A great doctor is telling you this, not some little pipsqueak who thinks he's a doctor, but who's really . . . well, you already know what."

But he couldn't take the risk that I might have forgotten and told me again. Just then his wife happened by and he decided that she should also have the pleasure of knowing. She smiled tightly and continued on her way.

The Latvian lady passed by and greeted me. I introduced her to the doctor and he immediately took advantage of the opportunity. Asserting medical privilege, his hands made a quick tour of her figure, as he noted her lovely throat, healthy skin, well-developed bust, and truly proportioned back. His fat, little hands moved up and down, until she realized that this was more than a medical occasion and she excused herself. "Well," said the doctor, "I've just given you an illustrated lecture. I can't say that I don't enjoy a pat here and a pat there, but the main thing is to conduct yourself like a man and preserve your source of energy." He then explained to me that the most fatal mistake doctors make is to speak of specific diseases.

"The truth," he declared, "is that there are no separate diseases. People are divided into two categories—healthy and sick. This is elementary, but doctors have messed it all up with their complicated theories. A healthy person contains within him all diseases, but he is master over them, he keeps all his body parts in harmony, he sets a rhythm to his life. In a sick person, all the so-called diseases erupt simultaneously and they become the masters. There's no such thing as cancer alone. When a person falls ill, he becomes susceptible to cancer, to tuberculosis, he can die from pneumonia—in short, he can get any and all the diseases in the book. A doctor—and you know what kind I mean—pokes around, looking for a specific ailment, and lucky him! A diagnosis! Right away he begins to bombard the ailment with all manner of junk medication, overlooking the larger picture, the entire human body. This is how an amateur operates, not how life operates, and it is, in fact, downright inhumane. He pokes around in the dark to cure the 'illness' while everything in the patient is going wrong. He doesn't understand that it's all a matter of harmony and disharmony. He puts a stethoscope on the chest and listens to the heart—do you know what a heart is? Neither does that doctor. You might as well be whistling into his ear. When you listen carefully to a heart, you hear—what can I tell you?—you hear a Wagnerian opera. Now it's pumping away as triumphantly as the ride of the Valkyries across the heavens. Then comes the *kol demama daka*, the 'still, small voice' of the High Holiday prayer —Liebestod. Blessed be the true judge!"

He dragged me over to a corner and took out a brochure from his breast pocket. "Let me read you a lecture I delivered in 1900," he said. "It was later published, and created a furor in the whole medical world. It immediately put me in the front ranks of the great doctors of our generation. Why am I suddenly reading you a medical lecture? Because I want to show you that medicine is the highest form of poetry. First, listen to the beat and cadence of words that are recognized as classics of poetry, that no one doubts are rhythmic song:

She walks in beauty like the night
Of cloudless climes and starry skies;
And all that's best of dark and bright
Meet in her aspect and her eyes.

Every schoolboy knows that this is poetry—'She walks in beauty like the night.'"

He almost chanted the lines, tapping out the rhythm with his feet, stressing the accented syllables and muting the unaccented. In his recitation he strove to demonstrate how beautifully chiseled each line was. "Keep in mind that same rhythm, that same music, and you'll see that it's exactly the foundation for my paper," he said. "Remember, 'And all that's best of dark and bright.' Now concentrate, it's not that easy to understand. Free your soul, take your paws off your soul and let it sing to you andante cantabile."

He was transformed. His eyes turned moist, like rain-streaked windowpanes. His coarse features lightened, his foot beat time to the verse. His face flushed in a mix of shyness and pride. He looked like some provincial author, reading from a work into which he had poured his heart and soul—which was reason enough to set him ahead the table of the immortals, where they are served slabs of praise and leviathan-sized hunks of recognition and, as Hasidic Jews do from their rebbe, grab leftovers from the fingers of Shakespeare and Homer.

Long after the Byronic enchantment of his lyrical model had faded from my mind, he continued to intone his medical masterpiece. He sang out the multisyllabic medical terms denoting all sorts of ugly, loathsome diseases of the blood, skin, digestive tract, and liver, to the tapping of his little, Terpsichorean feet, as though they were words in a dream, music for a dance.

He read on and on, growing more and more flushed. After an hourlong performance, he returned the brochure to his breast pocket, remarking that he only wanted to show me what medicine is, its mystique, its music, its poetry, its intimation, provided that it's being practiced by "a real doctor not a —." He opened his fleshy lips wide and cackled as he once again pronounced his beloved word. His face regained its bluish-red blotches, everything returned to type. He shouted out the word again and again to make sure no one failed to hear it, and with the same exuberance that he had just spoken of Byron's poetry— adding a dollop of national pride—he exclaimed, "A plague on the goyim, they should only have such a fabulous word!"

2

Sitting on a nearby bench, with two girls in tow, was a man with a square, gray beard, wearing a French yarmulke, a beret, that is. He had just finished a phlegmatic set of exercises and was now relaxing, flirting with the young women, who flirted right back. They looked the old man straight in the mouth, which issued a stream of youthful, seductive sounds, as if he were playing the flute. His voice was morning fresh and clear and held us all in thrall, particularly when he remarked that he had made sixty-seven Atlantic crossings but couldn't remember a more delightful one than the present. "The air is like champagne," he said, breathing in and out several times, with studied regularity.

The doctor wasted no time in practicing his wiles on the young women, but they both fled, like frightened hens. After their hasty retreat, the graybeard, finding himself in exclusively male company, let pass a gross word at the expense of the girls, still in the same flutelike tones. He talked on and on about himself, but the more he talked, the less one knew him. His name was Lawson, and at one time, he said, "I came this close to being a millionaire. Today I'm a—who knows what I am?"

But if he didn't know what he was, he certainly knew everything else, and made no bones about it. "I know everything," he declared, in his self-assured way and in the same flute-tone. He spoke four or five languages fluently. He was Gentile but was well informed on Jewish affairs. He knew everything there was to know about Zionism, he even knew the names of Yiddish newspapers . . .

"I like Jews," he said, "but they have to be real Jews. I don't like bluffers. I can bluff with the best of them. I once told Otto—we were on a first-name basis—that he was a louse, neither Jew nor Turk." I presumed he meant Otto Kahn, the famous investment banker. "'Otto,' I said, 'you're a louse.' And he answered me, 'Vincent, you're right, but we live in this world and have to make a few dollars.' That's why that rabbi of yours is such a prince. 'Stephen,' I said to him"—surely this was Rabbi Stephen Wise—"'it must be very hard on you to be the leader of such a stubborn people,' and he laughed in his deep, bass voice. Now, Felix"—this I took to be Supreme Court Justice Felix

Frankfurter—"was an altogether different sort of Jew than Otto. And ah, yes! I knew old man Jacob, that little Jew with the German accent, who raked in all that gold in America, the philanthropist who left a pittance to Jewish charities." Was he talking about the revered Jacob Schiff? "But one shouldn't speak ill of the dead, *de mortuis nil nisi bonum,* and all that. Of course, Otto's dead too, and I'd like to know what saints he sat himself down with in heaven. I bet he snubbed your holy men and went right for the Christian martyrs. I love Jews. I must have a Jewish soul. Ninety percent of my lovers were Jewish, as were my first two wives, neither of whom asked for a cent in alimony. I once said to Roosevelt, 'Who are you kidding? You talk Socialism to the capitalists and capitalism to Socialists!' The president doesn't mind being teased. He's a politician through and through, also a great statesman, a real American. What's a real American? First and foremost, a family man. Had I been a good family man, I'd be on top of the world now. Unfortunately, I've got wild blood in me."

The doctor, who was forced into silence by this verbal deluge, at last saw his chance in the notion of "wild blood." He began to lecture on how one must learn to curb impetuous behavior. Mr. Lawson interrupted with an authoritative medical lecture of his own. This was too much for the good doctor, and when I saw that he was ready to explode, I took pains to inform Lawson that we were in the presence of one of New York's most eminent surgeons. But Lawson wasn't impressed and was ready with a tale about his own close friendship with Doctor Alexis — Before he even had a chance to say the surname, the doctor jumped up, his bluish-red blotches filling with blood, turning his face as purple as eggplant. "Tell your Alexis that he's a —," he sputtered, pronouncing his beloved word with such force that even a non-Jew might grasp its meaning. "Do you know what that is?"

"Does Lawson know?" the graybeard chuckled. Indeed, he knew full well, and the mere fact that a non-Jew understood the meaning of his precious word calmed the doctor somewhat. "Don't work yourself up," Lawson continued. "Your pulse must be beating like a jackhammer."

"Don't you worry about my pulse," said the doctor, calmer now. "Leave that to me. And what, may I ask, is your profession?"

Mr. Lawson replied with as many as twenty answers, but both the doctor and I were left none the wiser as to what it was that he actually did. There was a hint of involvement with high finance, Wall Street, money—money that grows and money that sinks into the ground. One day a yacht, and the next, a gas pipe or a rope around the neck. "It's a jungle out there," he said, "full of wild beasts that go for your throat, thieves who steal millions from you with a smile. But I know how to play their game. Take copper, for instance."

"Let's not," the doctor retorted, again jumping up from his seat, as if he were about to have a heart attack. "Don't tell me about copper! You're a fake, a scoundrel, a liar! I lost $250,000 on copper. All my hard work and toil, gone up in smoke, because of copper! And Mr. Marcus and his bank took the rest, emptying me out. That will teach you about copper. Liar! Wall Street thief!"

Just then, the doctor's wife happened by and tried to quiet him as best she could. The doctor was shaking. He was especially upset by the fact that Mr. Lawson was sitting there calmly, a smirk on his face. Grasping at a straw, he called out, "So, he thinks he knows about copper, too, that —," giving his beloved word a final spin, as he let himself be led away, like a child, by his wife.

Mr. Lawson was unruffled. In his finest voice, now pitched to a key of compassion, he was ready with another roulade. "There they are," he trilled, "the sacrificial victims, in their tens of thousands, all across America, the trusting souls who spat back the whole Coolidge prosperity and the Hoover two-chickens-in-every-pot, right back into the pockets of Wall Street. I feel pity for the doctor. Had I known, I wouldn't have mentioned copper, not for a million dollars. Poor man! Such people are bound to get hurt." He spoke with counterfeit zeal, and it was obvious that he didn't give a hoot, not even about the humiliation he had inflicted.

The doctor was now circling the deck, and as he passed by, he threw angry stares at Lawson, who looked back, still in his phony pitying mode, with the same poisonous smirk on his face that said he wouldn't give the doctor a nickel even if he were about to go under. On his third circuit, the doctor stopped and, as if nothing had happened, addressed Mr. Lawson. "Do you play chess?" he asked. "Ah good, you do. If you're such a smart man, let's see if my knight can take your rook." Turning to me, he said, "Come join us, you can kibitz." I declined the pleasure and remained on deck, joining the promenaders instead.

The Bessarabian Jew from Bogotá caught up with me.

"Hey," he said, "I've been looking for you for days, but couldn't find you. Where have you been hiding? With whom have you been keeping company? *Goyim*, I bet, especially Gentile women, shikses. You see that shikse over there, the one with the bare legs? She sits there knitting, damn her, and won't give you the time of day. I've been circling around her since the first day aboard. You think I'm the only one? There's a whole pack of hungry wolves after her, but she won't look at anyone. You think that that little minx doesn't know she's being looked at? Oh, she knows! She lives for this, she loves it! If you think she's a beauty, forget it. She's no way what people consider a beauty. In fact, she's as far from being beautiful as I am from Bogotá. She's all skin and bones, with legs like snakes. Look how she twists and untwists those legs, how she twines one around the other. She knows all the tricks. She even has hooded eyes, from all those sinful thoughts of hers. What's the matter? You don't believe me? I know what I'm talking about. I'm an expert on these matters. I'm ready to bet that all those great beauties you read about in history books weren't really beauties at all. Your Helens, your Cleopatras, they were all emaciated wretches, like that one over there. They're wicked, they are! They've swallowed hellfire and don't deign to smile at any man, lest it give him pleasure or, God forbid, give them some pleasure, too. They keep on swallowing fire, until they catch the right fish, the one they've been on the lookout for, and, poor sucker, he has to pay for the sins of his gender. They drive him crazy and burn him to death. You think I don't know that I should run as far as I can from those witches? Yet I've been circling this shikse like an idiot for days, with no more notice from her than she'd pay to a radish or an onion. Anyway, you be well. I'm going back to my circling. I know it's hopeless, but maybe something will come of it."

Nearby, a heated discussion about books was in progress, and my Danish friend, who was among the participants, used every trick to draw me into the conversation. He asked my opinion on this and that, casting a variety of nets in the attempt to land me. I resisted with all my powers.

A rail-thin young man, with a small, narrow head, was giving his expert opinion of the American publishing business, of Greenwich Village and a brother who'd fallen into its clutches—a professional free spirit who had already been an anarchist, a Wobbly, Socialist, Communist, and was now a homosexual. The Dane had earlier given me the lowdown about this skeletal young man—first, that he wasn't as young as he appeared, that he was stuffed with money, and that he was head of a long-established American publishing house, inherited from his father and grandfather, that specialized in textbooks for colleges and high schools. He was also twice divorced and had had two children with each of the wives. This was his first vacation in twelve years. He was on his way to Germany to acquaint himself with German publishing and make business contacts. He was constantly sending radiograms to his firm, uneasy about having left it in strange hands. As someone who worked hard himself, he wanted to make certain that his employees were doing the same.

I also happened to know that this publisher was something of a Jekyll and Hyde. His days aboard ship were spent exclusively in the company of men, not even looking at a woman, but at night he would dress up and proceed to the ballroom to pick up female companions whom he would then drag to the bar and from the bar to the deck, and there into the darkest corners. At night he suddenly turned nearsighted and recognized not a single one of the men with whom he had spent pleasant afternoons. Similarly, in the daytime he never acknowledged any of the nighttime women. He practiced double-entry bookkeeping. The days were for serious thinking and sharpening his wits, the nights for lovemaking.

The group that had gathered around the publisher kept growing, but the Dane was still bothered by the fact that I was keeping my distance and kept trying to bring me into the discussion. He therefore directed everyone's attention to me by announcing: "Be careful what you say, there's a writer over there who's eavesdropping on every word you say. He may want to write about you." The tactic worked and the Dane got what he wanted. Now it would have been impolite of me not to join the circle, so I did, but not as a participant, only as a reluctant listener. The publisher took it upon himself to reassure everybody.

"Here on the water, we have no fear of writers," he said. "The sea has immunized us against all authorial onslaughts. A writer needs real people to base his characters on, and we are mere passengers. That's a wholly different category. Passengers at sea are rootless, whereas fictional characters must have solid ground under their feet. The sea is solid ground only for sailors, so to speak, whereas for us the sea is happenstance. Perhaps the sea represents all our unconscious fears, but what's a writer to do with that? How can he capture us? How can he create conflict, when we're all so careful not to step on one another's toes? What problems can he attach to us, when we are all without problems? And if we do have a real moral and ethical past rather than just a virtual existence, we have left it behind on shore. What is most important, though, is that our meeting at sea was not planned but a random accident. We're joined on the *Olympic* by chance, which is not enough to bind us together. If we like, we could talk ourselves into believing that we are the last morality-free generation on earth, without roots, but with an unspoken fear that the ship might sink and we would then meet our common fate. In other words, that fear might be our bond. But this theme is so trite that no writer, I'm sure, would want to touch it."

A discussion ensued about the respective attributes of sea literature and its dry-land equivalent, and everybody wanted to hear my opinion on the subject. I was rescued by a sudden, unexpected turn in the discussion, initiated by one of the participants, a high-school principal from somewhere out west, with large, tobacco-stained teeth, a prominent jaw, and big fists, which he pounded each time he wanted to make a point.

"Writers are poisonous snakes," he pronounced. "As members of society, they're the lowest of the low. They should be confined to iron cages, and whenever they let out a cackle that they are about to deliver themselves of a manuscript, their composition should be taken from them between the iron bars with the same obstetrical care that a venomous tongue is removed from a snake. Their works belong to the people, but the psychopaths themselves should be isolated from society, and not just from society, but from one another, because they devour each other, like cannibals. Being a writer is the most egocentric thing you can imagine. Writers are all sick people, a bunch of degenerates."

The Dane looked worried for my sake, fearing a scandal. He was sure that I'd feel mortally insulted and sought to ease what he thought was my discomfort by softly letting me know that a writer had stolen the principal's wife and that the two had run off together. However, the principal had decisive views not on writers alone. He also railed against New York and New Yorkers. If it were up to him, he probably would have consigned New Yorkers to cages as well. "New Yorkers are a poisonous race," he said. "I was once in New York for a few days and it was a nightmare, a city of pirates. New Yorkers even begrudge one another their wives. You're never safe walking down Broadway with your own wife. At every corner, there were men leering at her, even men who had women of their own. It's just pitiful to see those creatures fighting their animal natures to preserve a semblance of civilization. You're in constant fear that someone will knock you over the head with a hammer and make off with your wife. Disgusting! New York's one big pornographic city, fit for just dime-store romances."

Among the group that had formed around the combustible principal, who had now seized the reins of the discussion, were a dentist and his seventeen-year-old son headed for the Soviet Union, who spent their days aboard ship reading from the same book. The dentist was going to study the problem of hygiene in the Soviet Union and, so as not to arrive there totally ignorant, was reading the currently popular *Red Medicine*, and also urging it on his son. The son read faster than the father and was constantly waiting for him to catch up. The boy kept looking up at the sky and down at the sea, and daydreaming. The father was in no hurry. He read the same page twice, even three times and covered it with notes. The boy stuck out his tongue and left it there. He warmed himself in the sun and made darting, boxing movements at his father, who never noticed the flying fists, impervious to the danger. When the father finally turned the page, the son gave it a quick glance, sucked up the contents like an electric vacuum cleaner, and was again free as a bird.

The dentist spoke rough English sprinkled with Russian words, as a kind of dress rehearsal for the Soviet visit. He had a Park Avenue practice, one of the fanciest, and had chosen not to sail first class only because he was a democrat. He had once hung out on the Lower East Side, he had known everyone, but that was long ago and it all now seemed like a dream. He inquired fondly after the famous Yiddish playwright Jacob Gordin.

"He must be an old man by now," said the dentist. "What? Dead, you say? I pull teeth on Park Avenue and assume that the world is standing still. I began pulling away from the Lower East Side some forty years ago. Gordin, I remember, had a fine beard and went about with a thick walking stick. He had a temper. He expected an actor to obey him strictly, and if he didn't, knew how to give him one or two whacks with that stick. He spoke a beautiful Russian, but could swear like a sailor. I remember he wrote problem plays, but I've long forgotten both the plays and the problems. I myself speak a good Odessa Russian, but my Yiddish leaves something to be desired—I've just about forgotten most of it. So, how's the poet Morris Rosenfeld? And the operetta writer Abraham Goldfaden? And that other old rhymester —the one who wrote verses about the blessing in the plow— *In der sokhe ligt di mazl brokhe?* And let's not forget that old drunk, the one who wrote 'Hatikvah.' What was his name—Imber? And little Louis Miller, the labor leader who rode around in a carriage pulled by a team of horses that tore up the East Side? *Tchto vy govoritye,* you don't say! All dead? The whole East Side is dead. My entire youth is dead. And here I am, pulling teeth on Park Avenue, and thinking that the world is standing still, waiting for me! Say, but what about the editor of the Socialist paper, that Yiddish daily, Abe Cahan of the *Forward?* He's alive? Thank God. He used to hurl insults at Miller and Gordin, at everybody —a real *molodyets* he was, some brave man! And how are the anarchists doing? I remember how they used to stir things up with their Yom Kippur balls, their free love, and their birth control. Ah, I've just remembered old Doctor Solotaroff from my youth. He must also be dead—*yey bogu,* this is no joke—everyone from my younger days has up and died and here I am, sitting on Park Avenue. Do you take me for a spring chicken? I'm also getting ready to pack it in. Still, I want to take another look at Odessa, Mother Odessa, *yazhnaya krasavitsa,* Odessa the beautiful. I want my son to see it too, to see where his father's crib once stood. He thinks that everything will be as it was, but in the meantime, we've had the Bolsheviks—a big problem. But I have to see how things are being done now. At home I belong to a club of dentists and doctors, where we discuss social problems. We've already examined Bolshevism from every angle. Maybe you can come and give us a lecture sometime, let's call it 'A Greeting from the East Side,' or maybe 'from the Hereafter.'"

The dentist edged over to the discussion circle and began defending New York against the attacks of the principal, who declared that, this time, he had stopped in the city, before boarding the ship, only long enough to spit on it. "You're all jealous of New York," said the dentist, and to the principal in particular, "That's why you're so angry. New York is a city of culture. In fact, New York is the only real metropolis in the whole country. It's a city of freedom and openness."

"That's precisely it," the principal screamed. "That's what appeals to you, freedom and openness! The freedom of the Constitution isn't enough for you. You feel you're being choked by all the repressions of American society. Congress, the Senate, the Supreme Court—aren't these freedom enough for you? You want still more freedom? Why don't you come right out and say the word *Bolshevism*. Go ahead. Why don't you mention Lenin, Marx, Stalin, and all the other saints of materialism?"

The dentist was taken aback. Moreover, his Russian accent wasn't helping any either. The principal spoke with a western twang, filtered through his crooked, yellowed teeth. Yet when he pronounced the word *Bolshevism*, it was with a mock-Yiddish inflection. Lenin, Marx, and Stalin came out sounding like a band of what he would probably have called "kikes."

"Roosevelt saved the country from Bolshevism," the Dane interrupted. "When he was elected, America was on the verge of revolution."

"Ridiculous," the principal spat back. "That's what all you immigrants say. If you knew the real America, you would know that we don't give a damn about your revolutions. Our revolution is the ballot box. If you don't like an administration, just take a broom and sweep it out, but make sure that the broom is constitutional. When you New Yorkers export your products to us—Socialism and Communism—we say, 'To hell with them.'"

From there the discussion led directly to the subject of Hitlerism. Doctor Schwartz, an American-born Christian of German descent from Milwaukee, with whom I had already spoken several times about Fascism and who kept apologizing to me for Hitler, called out suddenly, "To hell with Hitlerism."

"Young man," said the principal paternally, "we don't want and don't need a Hitler here, but you have to understand Germany. Hitler is a great leader; he united the German people and saved them from Bolshevism."

A woman with a pious face, who spoke in a nasal voice and who had pushed her way unnoticed into the group, began to berate the principal with all the evils that the Nazis had committed against the Jews, the people who had given the world Jesus and both Testaments, the Old and the New. "It's simply dreadful," she said, "how those unfortunate people are being treated. How un-Christian! My God! They're the people of the Bible!"

"Hold it!" the principal thundered. "There's no way to compensate the Jews for the Testaments. In any event, my testament is the American Constitution, and there's nothing in the Constitution that says I can't hate Jews. But as an American, I draw a line between what I would call passive hating and active hating. I'm against pogroms, but I have the right to hate. Hitler is a fool to be making all that fuss, but Jews, as it so happens, love a fuss and know how to make an even bigger one."

"No! You have no right to hate, even passively," Doctor Schwartz exclaimed. "You poison the world with your hate. You already smell of it and it stinks up the world. Hate the Negroes, hate the yellow races, hate the Catholics, the Protestants, the Jews—it's all right for you, a school principal, to hate passively, but a truck driver may not be so fastidious and his hate can turn active. You speak in high-flown phrases, you use the Constitution as a shield. Okay! But should a Hitler show up in America, you'll find support for him in the Constitution. He'll eat your Constitution and shit it out on your head, and all of you will shout, 'Heil!' Your hate is worse than syphilis. You're disgusting."

All respect for the principal suddenly came crashing and everyone applauded the young doctor, whose cheeks had turned red with excitement. It was obvious that he wasn't well. His hands shook and his thin, well-formed nostrils quivered. His lips were still twitching from the burning words they had spoken. Indeed, he still seemed to be speaking, but there was no sound. The applause did not let up, and the pious woman wept aloud. The dentist found the courage to speak up. "That is America," he said. "That's the real voice of America!"

"Young man," the principal, now somewhat chastened, spoke to the doctor, "you're entitled to your opinion, but —"

Doctor Schwartz couldn't calm down. He walked off quickly, stopped at the railing, and bending over it, nervously tossed into the water scraps of paper he had torn from a letter. One by one, the group began to wander off. The principal, realizing that he was beaten, took a softer tone with the last remaining member of the group—the Dane—whom he tried to prevent from defecting with the rest. But the Dane also laced into the principal with a stream of accusations. "The trouble with you," he shouted, "is that you never received a radical education."

The principal undertook to restate his views. "It all has to do with a war of ideas," he said, "America versus New York. New York, at the threshold of Ellis Island, smacks of foreignness. It's alien to the rest of the country, which lives by good American values."

"But you're disregarding economics," the Dane shot back. "Since you didn't have the benefit of a radical education, you should read Bebel."

"To hell with Bebel. Jefferson is good enough for me," the principal retorted, and was the first to bolt when the gong sounded for lunch.

3

Lunch was greasy, spicy, salty, and sweet. The various fish and meat dishes, even after cooking, tasted of the ice in which they had lain in their raw state to keep them fresh. When the serving platters were brought into the dining room and the metal covers removed, all those fried and roasted concoctions made heads spin with seasickness. The English pudding swam in a red, blue, or green puddle of sweetness. It required a postprandial walk on deck to relieve some of the heaviness, and after several turns we had burped away all that greasiness, spiciness, and saltiness. The warm breeze gently slapped our faces, ruffled our hair, tickled the forehead, and slowly brought us back to life, as if from a near-faint.

"The best complement to a meal is a brandy," said the tall piano player when he saw me standing at the rail, catching the breeze that blew in from the heaving waves, rejoicing in each splash of spray that hit my face. From the look of him, it appeared that he had already taken his own advice more than once. We hadn't spoken before. Indeed, throughout the entire trip he had been avoiding me, and not me alone, but everyone.

By day he walked the deck holding a book, always with a finger inserted to keep his place, but no one had ever caught him reading. He strolled incessantly. At night, in the salon, while others socialized, wrote letters, read, played bridge or chess, he sat at the piano and played Chopin, only Chopin. When he first sat down, people assumed that he must be some kind of prankster—but only for that moment. It soon became evident that we were in the presence of a virtuoso. Some women even recalled his name and that he had performed in New York. He was tall, with a proud bearing, but at the piano he sat hunched low, his head almost touching the keys, as though searching for something. It seemed as if he wanted to curl himself into a corner and play for himself alone. A group of women always gathered around him at these nightly concerts, staring rapturously at his hands. At the conclusion of the performance, he stood up to his full height, made his way silently to the bar, where he sat by himself, again hunched low, this time, with his head in a glass.

Ordinarily, he would have been pacing the deck restlessly, but now he seemed more relaxed, as if he had just gotten up from a nap. He even smiled at me. "Journey's end!" he said, repeating the phrase several times more, to make sure that I didn't miss the reference to the famous play of the same name, the play about the Great War. But no sooner had he raised the specter of the war than his smile vanished.

"You Americans," he said, "saw the war only on stage or at the movies. By the time you joined in, the war was practically over. The Hun was already done for, and you were just being toyed with when you were told to fire the last bullets to finish him off. You convinced yourselves that you were the ones who brought down the kaiser. But we're the ones who lived through the whole bloody war. It'll take us years to get rid of the blood-soaked stench in our skins."

He gesticulated with his big, well-formed hands, which were somewhat too hairy for his almost girlish face. Even his fingers were covered with tufts of golden-blond hair. His face was flushed from all the liquor he had poured into it, but for all that, he remained in control of his feet, walking steadily beside me. I learned that he was an Englishman who had immigrated to America only five or six years before, and in several New York concerts had made quite a stir with his Chopin interpretations, becoming a welcome guest in the best houses.

In New York he led a restricted life and saw nobody, except for music-loving women, crazy, hysterical creatures. "Heavens," he said, "how did New York come to be filled with so many middle-aged women!" They clamored for his attention day and night, and he did nothing to protect himself from their advances. "Well, maybe a little," he conceded, "but it was passive resistance, sort of like Gandhi." The houses of the rich in New York were always stuffy, the windows shut, the heavy curtains drawn, the rooms filled with the smoke of the women's cigarettes, mixed with the sweetish aroma of cosmetics and sweat, a swirl of bellies and backs confined by straps, laces, and corsets about to burst their bounds. He was fondled by so many motherly women, that he began to feel like Oedipus, playing the hapless role every day.

"Do you know what poverty really is?" he asked. "English poverty? If you've ever read Arthur Morrison's *Tales of Mean Streets,* you'd have some idea. English poverty means wallowing in garbage, in hopelessness, human beings reduced to their basest condition—bellies swollen from hunger, filth, and squalor. I had to trick my father and mother into giving me a piece of bread. I learned to get up early, before my father did, so I could gobble the soured, leftover pigs' feet. Of course, I knew that my father would later beat me up for this.

"I was too young to go to war, but nevertheless, I carried the war on my back. I even wore a torn, lice-ridden greatcoat—a shirt was out of the question. I slept in barracks, I heard the frenzied rejoicing on the evening before the soldiers left for the front, I saw the half-crazed Tommies returning home on leave, the truckloads of the wounded, the crippled, and the glass-eyed blind, I heard the macabre music that sounded the prelude to slaughter, I crouched in cellars to be safe from enemy planes.

"I got drunk and, a mere squirt, began to consort with low women in return for a hot meal. I stole, yes, stole. I went barefoot on sharp stones. I became like a dog, always on the lookout to snatch a bite. This is how I lived, until one day a major's widow took pity on me. We came across each other in a pub. She was more than twenty years older than I. Her husband and only son had both been killed in the slaughter, and I was to replace them. By this time my own parents and brothers and sisters had become like something in a bad dream. She was a good woman, though a bit on the hysterical side. When she got drunk, she would drive me from the house, calling me a liar, screaming at me that I wasn't her husband, that I wasn't her son, and that she would shoot me like a dog. But when she was sober, she was a tender, loving soul, and believe me, that was a time when I needed a bit of tender loving. She hired tutors for me. In her house, my limbs began to thaw, like after a frost, and my mind grew clearer. She nursed me until she had weaned a milord. To see me now, you'd find no trace of my louse-ridden origins. She even changed my name.

"What's the use of pretending? I'll tell you plain and simple, I've been a whore all my life, and it was only after I came to New York and fell in among the music-loving women that the whole business began to disgust me. My God! They pampered me and praised me to the skies, but I knew I was a burned-out case, and not just I, but my whole postwar generation. We'll never amount to anything. How can we offer the world beauty, even artistic ugliness, when we ourselves are so thoroughly worm-eaten? Our greatest artist is possibly James Joyce. He grabbed hold of Ireland, dressed it in top hat and tails, and then dropped its trousers. But Joyce is older than us. At the time of the war he was already old enough to be an observer, but we were smack in the center of that damned maelstrom, and saw nothing and heard nothing. The war cast up the dead and the not-quite-dead. Those New York women, as well as the critics, tried to convince me that I was a genius, but I know what it really means to play the piano. Did you ever hear Józef Hofmann?

"I escaped to Delaware. I now teach music at a rich all-girls' college. Only females! That seems to be my fate. But these females are different. They're young girls who usually get a crush on a teacher and send him anonymous mash notes, with quotations from Keats and Shelley. It's a small town and the loveliest thing about it are the woodland paths, where I enjoy going horseback riding. Even when there's a girl riding beside me, prattling about Dreiser, Shaw, or Mencken—they still swear by Mencken in Delaware—it doesn't disturb me and doesn't keep me from gazing up at the brilliant sky."

The Wisconsin teacher came by, but even before she had time to greet us, the pianist excused himself and walked away abruptly. She stopped short and let out a high burst of laughter. "Why is he always running away?" she asked. "I've been chasing him for days. I'd really like to get together with him for a talk, but he won't allow it. You're a connoisseur, you see how handsome he is, but he's a hollow man, without heart or lungs—a marvelous robot, a zombie."

"So, why do you chase him?"

"He's intriguing, and it would be wonderful to draw him out, like warming your ears after coming in from the cold."

"Or maybe like rubbing the cold feet of someone you love."

"Exactly! But he is a bit cheerless."

"He hates women, truly detests them."

She sighed. "Who knows how many he's hated!"

A couple walked by. She was young and pretty, but only in left profile. She was quite otherwise seen from the front. Her right eye was blind, covered by a patch that was heartbreaking to see, making a shambles of her pretty mouth, magnificent head, and the other bright, blue, frightened-looking eye. Her husband was older and altogether decrepit. He waddled on flat feet as if on crutches. She held on to him tightly, as to a sole support, and he clung to her adoringly, like the answer to his prayers. Their love was touching to behold.

"Maybe it's because the trip is almost over," said the teacher, "but I feel sad. I'm going to have myself a good cry tonight. Be warned, it may be on your shoulder. Everything makes me cry. You saw that couple? When I think of how that half-blind girl must have grown up carefree and mischievous, until the mirror told her clearly that she'd have to make compromises, and of how she's accepted her situation, old husband and all—well, it makes me want to cry. I tell you, I only feel this way because the trip's almost over and my mind is jumping ahead, and it depresses me. I see the whole summer slipping away all too quickly and coming to an end. I see myself standing at the train, bidding farewell to my new friends and to my little bit of Paris freedom. Another wonderful summer gone, and it's time to return home! Each time I take a trip, it seems to me, I'm already returning. Who knows how many good summers I have left? Who knows when I'll have no other alternative but to latch on to some old man for security? Do you want to know how old I am?"

The pianist hurried by again, book in hand. She looked at him longingly. "Do you know what?" she said. "Let's kill some time and go down to third class."

"A great idea!" I concurred. "I even have some young acquaintances there, the ship's musicians. They were the first people I met, but we became separated by class."

We stood at the companionway leading to third class. It was only a half-flight down, but during the whole time at sea, its passengers and ours only gazed at each other as though through a telescope. They looked up at us, just as we did at first class—a whole other world. Down below, on the narrow stretch of sundeck allotted to third class, the days passed quietly and indolently. Their activities seemed the same as ours—shuffleboard and sunbathing—but a cloud also seemed to hang over everything, or so it appeared to us. There was little joy below. For us the journey was a pleasant interlude, a time for relaxation. Not so for the third-class passengers, if one was to judge from their worried expressions, which said that the voyage itself was an ordeal, because awaiting them were destinations that anxiously preoccupied all their thoughts.

But even from above we could see that the sunniest ones below were the students of the ship's band. In their white summer jackets and dark trousers, they looked out of place among their doleful fellows. When we descended, the young men gathered around me, instantly recognizing the passenger with whom they had spent the first hours at sea. Since we had come just at the moment when afternoon tea was being served, they invited us to join them as honored guests. My companion took to them right away. For her, the young students represented a greeting from her everyday life. True, that was the life she was happily running away from, but it was also nice to be reminded that somewhere there was a place where she mattered. She talked with the students about college life and they exchanged campus stories, which were like inside jokes, boring to outsiders but hilarious to those in the know. The students were overjoyed; this was the first time they had ever had such intimate contact with a teacher. The anecdotes began to take on risqué overtones, but the professor withstood them handily, which delighted the youths, barely pushing twenty. They laughed loudly, an unrestrained, earsplitting, boyish laughter. All the barriers between teacher and student fell, and it wasn't long before she was sitting on someone's lap and being called by her first name.

The musicians slurped their tea and, like true cavaliers, fussed over the teacher, who was pleased with all the attention. I noticed, however, that one of the students wasn't joining in the laughter. It was like the scene you sometimes see in a burlesque house, when the line of naked chorus girls prances out and they begin to sing in their nasal voices, shimmying like mad. They kick their legs, shake their hips, their bodies quivering like fish jelly. They lob allurements at the loge, the orchestra, not ignoring the balcony—just put out your hands, boys, and catch. The beat of the drums and the clash of the cymbals are like hot coals under their feet, like whips lashing their bodies, inciting them to turn up the heat. Suddenly, amid all this tumult, you notice one dancer who is separate from the rest, going through all the motions, but mechanically, like a calisthenics routine. She moves a bit faster than the others, kicks higher, upsetting the group's harmony, and the more you look at her, the more you become aware that she's mocking the simulated gaiety of the performance.

The mirthless student caught my eye and drew closer. Out of thin air, he asked if I was Jewish. "I beg your pardon," he said, "for sticking my nose into your business, but I simply have to know, because I'm Jewish and it seems to me that you're also a member of the tribe."

"Is that really so important to you?" I asked.

He didn't answer directly, but instead told me that his father was a doctor in a small town in West Virginia. He'd once made a fine living but that was no longer the case. Behind the doctor's back, a quiet boycott was organized, and most of the Christians were now going to the other doctor in town, also a Christian.

"It was a good thing," he said, "that my father put away some money for a rainy day and we're able to manage. As for the university, being Jewish isn't really a problem, because there are so few of us. Still, as few as we are, there's no great love for Jews. Maybe you can explain to me why. My father didn't teach me any Hebrew or any prayers or any Jewish history. He never even instilled any desire in me to learn about Jewish history. I actually know very few Jews—my parents and a few aunts and uncles, all very fine people. You're from New York, there are lots of Jews there. Maybe you've got the key to explain why Jews are so hated. I don't understand it."

I attempted to accommodate his puzzlement as best I could. "There are many keys," I said. "Take your pick, whatever suits your temperament best. There's a nationalist key, a Marxist key, even a masochist key. Many Jews exaggerate their own faults in order to rationalize away the hatred toward them. And then there's the genetic key. After so many generations of hating Jews, it's simply transmitted in the blood. A child suckles hatred from its mother's breast, from the breast of the priest. Say, are things bad for you here?"

"God forbid!" he hastened to assure me. "Everybody here treats me wonderfully, like royalty. We play only one hour in the afternoon and a few hours at night. The food is good and the other band members have to be especially nice to me since I'm the pianist, the leader of our little band."

"There," I said, "there you have another key, if you will. You are the leader and they must behave themselves, that's like a taut string that has to snap. They need your leadership. But maybe it's time we let them lead themselves. Let them be the leaders for a few hundred years and we'll see what they achieve. And what should one do with one's natural talent? What if you really are a good doctor, a good pianist, a good economist? Should you suppress your talent, because that's what the goyim want? What should you do when you're propelled to the front because of your innate abilities? That particular key is not to your liking? Well, pick another. But the problem, I see, has grabbed you by the throat and won't let go that easily."

Two middle-aged women came over to our long table and sat down to drink their tea. One wore a large, black crucifix. Both had sallow faces, work-worn hands that looked like dead branches, and feet so crooked and twisted that not even shoes could conceal the disfigurement. The leather was stretched out of shape by swollen toes, corns, bunions, and all the other woeful adornments that ornament bad feet. Their hands were clean, as were their necks and faces, but the cleanliness was streaked with grime so embedded in the skin as to give it a special pigmentation—a grime that bespoke years of scrubbing laundry and floors, cooking and cleaning, and that had burrowed itself deeply into their thick flesh.

Both women were speaking Polish. I turned away from my Jewish pianist-friend and his problems and threw some friendly remarks their way. The woman with the cross didn't answer at all. Her companion did, albeit with an air of suspicion, even though I spoke their language. I finally managed to win a measure of the latter's trust once she discovered that we were both on our way to see mothers and fathers in Poland. She was headed for somewhere in Galicia, now part of independent Poland and no longer under Austro-Hungarian control as formerly. Her parents were very old and very poor. The hovel they lived in was on the verge of collapse, and the rain poured into it. She was bringing them money for repairs, or even for building a new dwelling, if possible.

"Do you miss Poland?" I asked.

"No, I don't. I have grown children in America," she replied without hesitation. Nor did she miss the little town in Pennsylvania where her husband and two sons worked in the coal mines. "I'm too worn out from work for all that," she sighed. She examined my face for a few minutes, then suddenly burst out, "What I do have a longing for is Russia, the worker's motherland."

"You're a Communist?"

"What if I am?" she said, looking away. "My husband's a blockhead, always drunk. He has no idea how we're going to take over the coal mines and leave the bosses to rot there and blacken, may they suffocate to death, may the walls fall in on them. But my sons are different, they've read the Communist literature and had no trouble convincing me. A mother's heart understands. They're wonderful children, serious young men. They don't drink, they bring home the little they earn, when there's work. My daughter's a different story. All she knows is painting her face, lazing around, and thinking about boys. Phooey— American girls! My sons are perhaps a bit too serious. 'Why do you always look so worried?' I ask them. 'What's not to worry about?' they tell me. 'We're waiting for the day when you, Mama, will live to see a Soviet America. It's about time. They've stepped on us long enough. Now it's time for us to step on them.'"

The woman with the big crucifix around her throat, who had been silent until now, burst into tears and sobbed in agreement, "It's time for us to step on them." The Communist mother told me that the sobbing woman's husband had died in a mine accident a few years earlier. She had one son, who supported her, a strong, handsome young man, who had no interest in marriage, not wanting to leave his mother alone. That woman was also on her way to somewhere in Galicia, where her uncle had left her an inheritance worth a few hundred dollars in American money.

It was almost time for supper, but the university instructor could barely tear herself away from the students. They promised that they would sneak over to our deck later that night, after they'd finished playing, so that we could all spend our last night at sea together.

4

I couldn't get the third-class tables, chairs, and floors out of my mind. Everything there was neat and tidy but smacked of institutional cleanliness. True, there was no trace of the poverty, the sheer hell, of what used to be called steerage, which I myself had never experienced but had heard about from older immigrants. However, the whole time that I sat there in third class, I couldn't rid myself of the notion that somewhere a door would open and somebody would poke his head in and shake it from side to side, to signify bad news, which would leave everyone stunned. We would all rise from the benches, feeling ourselves to be most unfortunate. Indeed, in its very neatness third class smacked of a waiting room—in a hospital, say, or an unemployment center, or the office of a society offering free loans, as necessary to the petitioners' well-being as air for breathing. Soon the door would again open and someone would again shake his head in refusal: "No."

In my continued imaginings, the two Polish women get up. Their twisted, misshapen feet are barely able to support the weight of their ample buttocks and pendulous breasts. Their heavy feet are worn out, the first of all the overworked body parts to capitulate. The toes are entangled one with another; the little toe, minus a toenail, is curled over a second toe, the second having buried itself in a third, which, over time, has made a place for it to lie comfortably, as in a sheath. One big toe, unusually large, with a distressed black nail, protrudes from the side of a shoe, looking to burst out. The shoe itself is crinkled and worn. Both work-weary women are about to get down on their knees to scrub the floors with huge brushes, which they dip into pails brimming with soapsuds.

On deck it was already dark. You could scarcely see the water. You had to lean far over the railing to make out the white spume glinting on the black sea, like a mouthful of white teeth in a dark face. The air was damp, and with every shudder that passed through me I heard the words of Aunt Gnendl's letter about my mother. "Her ears are as yellow as wax," she had written. "Pack your things and come immediately, and may God help us all and bring you here in time to find her still alive."

My mother's ears . . . I remembered them as of twenty years ago—small, with tiny holes for large earrings, narrow slits. As a child, whenever I thought of how they had pierced her ears with a red-hot pin when she was a little girl, I would have to shut my eyes and I'd begin to tremble. Her face—serious, tearful—was sallow-complexioned but beautiful. She seldom laughed, preferring a smile. Her forehead was bright, becoming even brighter when she took off her wig. Now her ears were yellow as wax. I was seized by a profound feeling of hopelessness. It was now twenty years since that night when she stood in the dark at the railroad station, wringing her hands, awaiting the train that she believed would take me straight to America, without stopping. Twenty years . . . and now I was coming home to look at her yellowed ears.

No matter how strongly my mother had campaigned against my leaving, she nevertheless had to give in. My father's clothing business —by this time he had left Shimen Berger's employ—was going down the drain day by day, and soon he would be forced to close up shop. Even his partner Ezra was beginning to show signs of surrender. Ezra had a proud, Gentile face, but his aging hands trembled, as did his round gray head and trimmed gray beard. He could neither read nor write but still considered himself an aristocrat, because his second wife was of vaunted Lithuanian origin and didn't cover her hair, and because his son attended a Russian high school and spoke an ungrammatical Russian and Polish, but with the proper pronunciation. Common Gentiles and Jewish customers he would leave for my father to wait on. However, very often Father would also have to attend to Ezra's refined customers, because if any of the latter began to haggle, Ezra would become touchy and let loose with a jab, "What do you think this is, the targ?" Targ was the Gentile market where secondhand clothes were sold almost for nothing.

Now, even proud Ezra bowed his head whenever odd customers showed up, peasants in coarsely woven coats, whom, in the better days, he had chased out, scattering them like frightened hens: "Go on, beat it! This store's not for you. There's nothing here for you." Ezra himself did not as yet deign to wait on such customers, closing his eyes as Father pulled overcoats on and off, sighing like the Hasidic master Levi Yitzhak of Berdichev remonstrating with God: "A fine old age You've given me. What's there to say, oy, Master of the Universe!"

This was the time when Poles had begun to settle a score with the Jews for having helped elect the labor deputy Jagiello to the Russian parliament, and not the out-and-out anti-Semite they had favored. The ensuing anti-Jewish boycott, begun as a jest, soon took a more serious turn, biting into Jewish businesses, which ground to a standstill. Even the prosperous Khazanov store passed many a day without a single ruble in sales. The money exchangers fled. Father sought to save himself by advertising in the Polish newspaper *Zhemya Lubelska*. Its rival, the *Polyak-Katolik*, reprinted the ad with an editorial raking *Zhemya* over the coals for carrying a Jewish notice.

My steamship ticket already lay in a tin box in the bureau. I counted the months, the weeks. By this time, even Mother would have liked to speed my departure, afraid that the business might eat up the several hundred rubles that had been set aside for my travel expenses. "Itskhok," she kept reminding my father, "this money is sacred. It can't be touched."

"Ite Rokhshe, who's touching it?" Father would reply.

In the evenings I was a regular at the café run by the Turks, whom we called Greeks. I drank lukewarm milk and broke off pieces of the thin, saffron-infused pastry, studded with raisins. I even confided to one of the proprietors that I was going to America. He asked me, when? I was always eager to show off my small stock of Turkish and answered, "In hon weeks"—"weeks," of course, spoken in Russian. Then, for his benefit, I rattled off all the numbers in Turkish, from one to ten—bir, iki, üçi, dört, besh, alti, yedi, sekiz, dokuz, hon. The Turk beamed at my numerical proficiency in his language, which I had acquired from an appendix to a teach-yourself-Esperanto textbook. I even tossed in yirmi—twenty—and elli—fifty—so that he would know how far my Turkish extended.

The last few weeks prior to departure, I passed my days in the Saxony Gardens, where spring was in full bloom. My friends and I went about Lublin with our heads held high, like the heroes of Hamsun's *Growth of the Soil*. Our group included: the painter, one of his eyes milky as herring milt, who had just returned from the Kraków Academy; the poet, recently back from Warsaw, bearing a stack of testimonials; the bushy-haired violinist, who had just completed his studies at the Warsaw Conservatory and had already appeared with the Hazamir orchestra; our "pessimist," a professional cynic and misogynist, with moist palms and long, dirty fingernails, the eldest among us, who dabbled in the Upanishads, cited Schopenhauer and Weininger, and boasted that he preferred onanism to making love to women; the friend who'd spent a year and a half with a sister in Siberia, in far off Ufa, and therefore affected a Siberian accent when speaking Russian; and several well-read youths who were preparing themselves to becoming critics and who went around with volumes by Taine, Saint-Beuve, Belinsky, and, especially, our Brandes.

We strutted about like peacocks, as unreal as characters in literature. These were my Bazarovs, Nekhlyudovs, Karamazovs, Oblomovs,
Sanins, Hamlets, and Don Quixotes. We were surrounded by spirited
Gentile life, rather, by several such, Russian and Polish, each at dag-
ger's point with the other. There were also the many strata of Jewish
society divided like Hindu castes, from the Untouchable paupers to the
Jewish rajas, who rode around in carriages drawn by fiery horses. The
surrounding streets churned with tailors, shoemakers, tinsmiths, cigarette makers, laborers in brickyards and sugar factories, tanners, iron-
mongers, teachers, water carriers, maidservants, stocking makers, glove
makers, seamstresses, musicians, hairdressers, tycoons, religious-court
adjudicators, rabbis. Oblivious to all of it, we sparred with ready-made
phrases and went home to mama for supper and some pocket money.

The poet recited a poem about spring. His sad, lilting voice caressed
and smoothed out the inharmonious lines. Strongly influenced by
poets of the sort that asked "the little birch trees to pray for me," he appealed to the flowers and spring breezes to bestow I no longer remember which of their favors on him. We all thought highly of him
and placed great hopes on his becoming our local star. Even I, who had
already written whole packs of poems and stories, considered myself
his inferior. I envied his melancholy lines that quivered like a stammer and proclaimed themselves poetry before one grasped the sense of
the words.

The poet's father was a wealthy man. The family lived in a non-Jewish neighborhood in one of the new apartment houses with mirrored
hallways and couches on the landings, one of those buildings that
everyone had run to gawk at while it was under construction. Their
apartment was something to see—large, mirrored drawing rooms,
heavy furniture, blue and red plush chairs, tall vases, cages with
singing canaries, and a young, good-natured stepmother who looked as
if she might be the poet's older sister and who perfectly suited the modern decor. She went out of her way to be nice to her "child" and his
friends. The poet had an ornately carved writing desk, where he kept
his cache of poems, all copied in his meticulous handwriting. His very
first poem, which he declaimed to me tearfully in his beautifully furnished study, was called "The Young Mother Is Dead," and as its title

suggested, it was a free adaptation of the Yiddish poem, "The Old Cantor Is Dead." The poet made no secret of his debt, indeed, he boasted about how well he had mastered its melodious tone, and I commended him on his fidelity to the original. I simply found it hard to reconcile his tearful melancholy with the rich household, and felt that even if he was truly mourning his mother, it was ungracious of him to write an elegy when there was such a kind, agreeable, and understanding stepmother on the premises. At the time, I was writing nationalistic poetry and erotic fiction, but I regarded myself as a lower-ranking member in our little group of literary talents, and all because I envied the poet his divine gift for sorrow when, it seemed to me, he had everything in the world anyone could want.

We all enjoyed the poem about spring, even more than the actual season itself. The only dissent came from our professional cynic, who dismissed it with a coarse jibe, citing whole passages from Homer in Russian and Heine in German to bolster his case. However much we took pleasure in his epigrammatic proficiency, the poem in no way suffered in our esteem.

We also talked about my forthcoming journey, and my friends admitted to envy, though they also pitied me for falling into the "land of yellow journalism." At night, we continued our walks to the Saxony Gardens along class-divided routes, one street serving the proletariat, working men and women, the other, the route of high-school students of both sexes, externs, and assorted functionaries. Once inside the Gardens, we took to the dark paths, chasing every silhouette of a brown-skirted schoolgirl uniform.

On some mornings I took walks across the fields, going as far as the sandy stretch where my rich Aunt Khome lived in her own cottage, with her own chickens, a few ducks, even an occasional turkey, and two fair-sized maidservants, with calloused bare feet and hands that smelled of parsley, onions, and parsnips. The older one would often drag me to a secluded spot far from the house, across the tracks by the train station. There she would look into my eyes, her breath hot as fire, and sing me peasant love songs. Should I try to snuggle up against her, her voice took on a cold, husky tone, as she admonished me, "No, Yankele, no."

Two weeks before my departure, I received a piece of bad news that dashed all the anticipated pleasure of the trip. All along I had been expecting that I wouldn't be traveling alone but with a ship's companion, a female one at that. She was a year and a half younger than I, tall, slender, and fair, with a turned-up Gentile nose and such deep brown eyes that whenever I saw her I couldn't get over the contrast between her warm eyes and her icy blond hair. She already swayed like a woman, her haunches moving rhythmically, like millstones. She had unusually lively, chiseled legs, a rather wide mouth with thin lips that compensated for their thinness with a smile as bold as a wink. Her people were common stock, a family of butchers. Her mother and father, uncles and aunts, all had red hands with big, blood-stained nails, red faces, heavy feet, and coarse voices. She alone was delicate and refined. Her smile bore the traces of generations of forebears who knew what they wanted and knew how to get it, but on her lips the coarser desire emerged as gentler insinuation, with an added "I beg your pardon."

They were our neighbors on the new street where we had moved, across from the butcher shops, both Jewish and Gentile, that displayed hanging calf and ox heads, with their pitiful, open, dead, velvety eyes. Even their family name—or, as we called it, "the German name"—was butcherlike.

In those days, many Jewish high-school girls were under the influence of Tolstoyan morality, and before it even came to a kiss, one had to wade through long passages from the New Testament: "Whosoever looketh at a woman to lust after her hath committed adultery with her already in his heart." One had to negotiate a complicated process of moral deliberation before one could even think of committing a sin—and sinning in this instance meant no more than holding hands, looking into the beloved's eyes and declaiming poetry in the dark. I no longer remember which came to us first, the chicken or the egg, meaning Saninism or Tolstoyism, but both codes swirled around us, like the fiery swords protecting the Garden of Eden. At times one inclined to the hedonistic Sanin, with his urgings to seize the moment; at other times, to Tolstoy, with his belief that every action in this life must be a preparation for the Kingdom of Heaven to come. When all this morality-playing became tiresome, one let go a bit of one's dignity and made the acquaintance of a seamstress or a stocking maker. Of course, their fingers were notched with needle stabs, but they more than made up for it with their heartrending Jewish folk songs, arms ready for a warm embrace, and the modest request that you "Fear God and the tongues of the righteous." Everything else in the joyful union of two young people came to pass with no need for prefatory babblings from the New Testament.

My mother was aware—but derived no pleasure from the knowledge—that I had my eye on the butcher's young daughter. She worried that the infatuation might lead to a match, and this didn't sit well with her because, in addition to everything else, there was a blot on the butcher's family escutcheon—a cousin of the girl's had converted to Christianity and married a Gentile boy, a young butcher, and to spite her parents and drain even more of their blood had opened a Gentile butcher shop with her new husband, right next to their own. The unfortunate parents went about red-faced and ashamed to lift their heads in public. As for the bride, her belly kept swelling as she busied herself selling pork, with rare adroitness. My mother was afraid that I might fall in among such a family. Up to then I had exchanged perhaps a dozen words with the girl, but I grew excited when I learned that she would be traveling on the same boat with me to America, to join an uncle. (Her mother knew that in Lublin the family stain would haunt her forever.) We would be traveling together on the same trains and on the same ship, disembarking together at New York's Castle Garden, the immigrant's gateway to a new life. The girl's mother was delighted that her child would be in the company of someone familiar, a respectable boy, who would keep an eye on her (and on her smile? I couldn't help adding).

But for some reason—and to my utter misfortune—her plans changed and her departure had to be moved up by two weeks. The blow was totally unexpected. We ran into each other in town and she said with a smile, "You know, I'm leaving tomorrow." There was nothing in her tone or expression to suggest that she was feeling the blow she had delivered. I was devastated. I felt abandoned and began to dread the long journey that lay ahead of me and that I would now be making alone. She gave me her hand, with its long, slender fingers, and said, "I'll see you in New York." That night I felt that I had just lost my first love.

Up to that time, the longest trips I had ever taken alone were from Lublin to Warsaw, to visit my Aunt Gnendl. My grandfather had showed me the way and we made the trip several times together. Only after he died did I begin to travel to Warsaw and back by myself. Naturally, with Grandfather we traveled fourth class. The train crawled along and managed to stretch a four-to-five-hour trip into twelve. We'd start out in broad daylight and arrive long after midnight. We'd ride and ride, past fields and villages, and all day long there was an unending parade of travelers. Fourth class cost almost nothing. Even so, there was frequent haggling with the conductor. It broke my heart to see grown-up, full-bearded, dignified Jews, who could ordinarily deliver a slap that would send you reeling, scurrying to hide under benches, their backsides in the air, like supplicants in the synagogue on Yom Kippur eve, awaiting the penitential flogging. Should an inspector board the train and catch sight of one of these stowaways, the unfortunate soul would be dragged to his feet and thrown off at the next station. I couldn't stop worrying about this poor Jew, imagining him all alone in some peasant village, wandering about the tiny railroad station, chewing on his black beard, mulling over the commerce he was hoping to transact and how hard it was to make a living, as difficult as splitting the Red Sea. Circulating among the down-and-out riders of fourth class were also the gamblers and cardsharps, looking for dupes.

My grandfather had a fine travel routine. En route, he would untie his kerchief and take his refreshment—a hard-boiled egg, a hunk of bread, a purple plum, and a golden pear that dripped juice down his beard, all the while conducting a conversation with me: Why in the world was he dragging along a rascal like me to meet the Chofetz Chaim, the great rabbi he was planning to see, and why had he wasted a half-ruble to buy me a sacred book, when I never looked into it? But Grandfather was by no means angry. This was merely pleasant chit-chat, because "a person has to let off a little steam" before dropping off to sleep. The train wobbled and Grandfather likewise, until he began to snore into his beard. As the train chugged along, I would drink in the passing fields, the forests, and rivers. When night fell, the passengers stretched out on all the benches, even under them. The silence was broken only by the conductor, with his smoking lantern, calling out, "Have your tickets ready."

Sprawled on one of the benches lay an impressive-looking young man with black whiskers, patent-leather boots, and a cap with a shiny visor, his nose pressed against the dark window, humming a sad, heartrending tune. Heads rose from all sides, feet wrapped in rags stirred, and people shouted, "Quiet!" But when they saw the sort of person they were dealing with, the passengers turned over, sighing and groaning, as if to say: "Oy, dear Father in Heaven! Some fine specimens You've filled Your earth with! But we had better keep our thoughts to ourselves."

The young man, who looked like a pimp, sang with his nose pressed against the window:

O Feyge my dear, Feyge my love,
Enjoy all the good things that come from above.
And when I ask that you turn down your bed,
This shouldn't trouble your sweet little head,
Shouldn't trouble your sweet little head.

A few taps on the train window were followed by Feygele's reply, in a high, thin, plaintive voice:

There, I've turned down my bed,
But with whom shall I now lay my head?
With a low, mean, dirty dastard, that's plain,
And a whore I shall always remain,
A whore I shall always remain.

Clickety-clack, clickety-clack . . . The wheels of the train vibrated on the rails in the rhythm of the refrain, "A whore I shall always remain." The young man continued with his song, tapping his fingers against the window each time he paused between the man's importuning and the woman's replies. He sang his ditty all through its many verses, to the very end, to Feygele's final plaint: "A whore I shall always remain." (A Feygele of this description was soon to appear among us in Lublin, circling the town clock, with her shawl drawn over her head, jingling her keys.)

As the train approached the city, the lights on the bridge over the Vistula River seemed not to be moored on metal supports, but rippling in the water. More green and red lights . . . and then we were in the Warsaw station. Now Grandfather and I began to drag ourselves through the dark streets until we came to a gate, where we rang a rusty bell and waited to hear the clatter of the porter's wooden shoes over the cobblestones, and his cursing that continued until Grandfather proffered a coin. Grandfather then led me by the hand across a long courtyard and up a set of stairs, and knocked on a door. My aunt appeared, kissed me with a sour-smelling mouth, as if she had just risen from sleep, and rolled me into bed, covering me with a heavy quilt. I could scarcely fall asleep, filled as I was with the excitement of the train ride and of finding myself in a strange city, far from home.

In the morning, I began to orient myself to the wonders of the big city. The first marvel was the water closet in the hallway, a space with peeling walls and a drain that gurgled but did little else. Then there was the large courtyard, with its four or five separate entrances. It reeked of tar, lime, urine, a malodorous white disinfectant, and sewage. My aunt's kitchen boasted a gas stove that emitted a smell so nauseating that it felt as if one were being choked by poisonous green fumes, or vapors from the kerosene rubbed into braids as a remedy for nits. There must have been a leak in the gas pipe, but no one thought to fix it.

My uncle, a dealer in oxen, knew that he had to bring home some tripe from the slaughterhouse because about fifty years ago in a local dispute a rabbi had declared tripe not to be kosher—a prohibition that remained in effect in Lublin while elsewhere it was permissible to eat tripe to one's heart's content. And even though I had no taste for those tough chunks of meat that were as hard to chew as fried goose skin and that curled up like pages in an old prayer book, nevertheless I devoured them with relish, intrigued by the notion that simply by getting on a train and traveling a few miles, I was able to indulge in a food that was taboo in one place and permissible in another. In my honor as guest, my uncle also brought home pieces of udder, a delicacy calling for special preparation in an earthen pot that was destroyed immediately after the cooking, because udder is a sort of mixture of both milk and meat, rendering the utensil unfit for further use. My mother under no circumstance would let herself be lured into the adventure of cooking udder, but my uncle wanted to show me Warsaw and all its wonders. I ate the udder, too, with particular interest, because I wanted to experience a forbidden drop of milk in meat.

My aunt actually lived not in Warsaw but in the suburb of Praga. The lantern outside bore the house number 12, stenciled in tin. The huge building, containing perhaps a hundred families, was managed by a Jewish lawyer who lived in the building, a man with waxed, pointed mustaches in the Polish style, who also had a side business writing petitions. He wore a greenish-black frock coat, was tall and thin, and sought to give the impression of being an aristocrat who had fallen on hard times. In the manager's house everybody spoke Russian and Polish. The eldest son gave English lessons. He had spent several years in America and returned home threatening either to commit suicide or to convert. The second son, because of restrictions on the number of Jewish students allowed to attend Polish schools, to his misfortune ended up in the Krinski Business School. He roamed about in his school uniform, complaining that he had to attend a Jewish-run school, where, in addition to everything else, he was made to study Bible and Hebrew. The mother of the family waddled around like an infirm member of the nobility. The manager liked his drop of whiskey and when he was drunk, took to taunting his wife with the information that while she, the old battle-ax, darkened his days at home, the famous cabaret singer Kevetska was helping him pull on his socks in her dressing room. This frequently led to pitched battles, the sons siding with their mother and physically attacking their father, who was agile and could give as good as he got.

Outside the house, the young commercial student was the very picture of refinement, walking with measured steps, doffing his hat and bowing, as if he were descended from generations of Polish nobility. The hands that had just pummeled the father now made graceful, studied gestures. Their owner lectured me on manners, warning me never to speak with my hands. The primary function of manners was to mesmerize one's public, because the born aristocrat aims to be a leader, and a person without manners cannot aspire to authority. He confided that it had taken him a full year of practicing before a mirror to perfect the smile he offered in greeting, which must never be too intimate or effusive, not even when encountering one's closest friends. To show that one was well disposed, a smile should reveal only a glimpse of the teeth—of which this young man had a fine set, with tiny gold fillings, the ultimate in dental artistry of the day. He taught me the tricks of hat-doffing for all occasions: greeting an acquaintance (hat turned toward or away from oneself, depending on whether one wanted to stop and chat or effect a quick dismissal), greeting a girl, an old woman, a friend, an elderly gentleman, a person of indeterminate station, as well as how to avoid a greeting, because deliberate disregard was also part of good manners.

When I told him that I had taken a correspondence course in hypnotism, that I owned a crystal for use in hypnosis, that I had put my brother into a trance in which he could barely pull apart his hands, the student became my devoted friend. We took long walks down St. Petersburg Boulevard, across Walenska Road, and in the small park by the bridge, not far from the tracks, where a toylike little trolley chugged along, taking on real passengers. As we walked, we talked about hypnotism, mesmerism, and the occult. We crossed the bridge from Praga into Warsaw proper, into the packed Jewish neighborhoods filled with pickpockets, secondhand stores, old-clothes sellers, food vendors, and peddlers, where the streets stank of dry leather from all the tanneries. We continued all the way to Nalewki Street and Simon's Arcade, location of my friend's place of learning, the Krinski school. We stopped in at Friedman's for their special mustard-covered sausages—hot, fatty, salty, juicy—that popped in your mouth.

In addition to these walks, I also had social obligations imposed on me by my grandfather, who, wanting to show me off, dragged me to visit his rich Warsaw relatives, leather merchants, men with huge haunches and long beards, married to wives with goiters, pudgy hands and feet, wide hips, thickly rouged cheeks, many chins, and heavy earrings that pulled at their ears—a distant branch of the family, belonging to that special class of Jews, wealthy-Hasidic, with polished boots.

The men of this class would engage in important commerce, while the women developed rich-lady ailments and went off to spas, seeking cures. My grandfather even arranged a visit to a relative who was a traveling salesman, a tall, clean-shaven, well-turned-out man, who wore a derby and was the repository of so many vulgar traveling-salesman jokes that he had to share some of the latest, hot off the griddle, with me. His house sparkled, his clothes were in the latest style, his children sweet smelling, his wife tidy. Yet, the family name was Schmutz —in Yiddish, "filth." A brass plate proclaiming "I. Schmutz" was attached to the door, unmindful of its irony.

My grandfather and I scoured the stalls in the market until we found Shloymele the Busybody, who sat there conducting his trade. Shloymele knew about all the doings of our family in Lublin. In his squeaky voice he had a ready disparagement for everyone after whom he inquired: "How's that prick of a teacher? How's the thief? He's not in jail yet? How's that intellectual?"—all said with a pious look and a saccharine tone.

Warsaw nights . . . the distinctive nocturne of the clang of the trolleys, with their cheap wooden benches and their worn plush seats, separate sections to accommodate the segregation of the populace, five kopeks for the plebeians, seven for the aristocrats . . . the wooden omnibuses rattling over the cobblestones, that seemed about to break apart, like barrels . . . tall, lit street lamps, like slender trees heavily laden with fruit . . . the walk there and back on Walenska Road . . . flirting in the courtyard with the high-school daughter of the neighboring Tyomkin family, slim and freckled, with spindly legs and thin, strong hands, a not too pretty face but with a dear mouth that offered delightful kisses in the dark, who squirmed out of my embrace and still had the audacity to wish me, in Polish, "A peaceful night."

The train ride back to Lublin . . . street lamps floating in the distance . . . long dark stretches of night, a far-off whistle . . . the rising sun tinting the windows rosy-red . . . the sun high above a meager field, a village sun that called to mind dairy foods, sour milk, noodles with cottage cheese and cinnamon . . . a cow lazily raising its head toward the rushing train, contemplating a moo and then thinking better of it . . . shuddering rails under wheels that clacked out the rhythm, "I've turned down my bed . . . a whore I shall always remain" . . . the Tyomkin daughter's warm hands . . . a peaceful night . . . I sat up with a start. It seemed that the train had passed over a ditch, lurched momentarily, and then quickly righted itself. Apparently, I had dozed off and was just beginning a dream whose full action had not yet begun to unfold, and all I had managed to dream were the unraveled possibilities.

Then, that other train journey, the first leg of my emigration to America . . . I kissed my little sister goodbye, and took off for the station. It was just before midnight. Everything looked like a soot-blackened lamp. Everyone seemed to be nodding off, on the verge of falling asleep. The station was filled with my friends, family, young men and women. I was waiting for a certain someone. It was already a year since we had spoken, and though I couldn't break through my stubbornness to bid her farewell, I nonetheless had hoped she might come to see me off. Her appearance would have meant something, exactly what, I wasn't sure. I kept searching for her in the dark, but it was getting late, and becoming very clear that she wouldn't be showing up.

My father pretended indifference and cracked a joke. His lip trembled, to the point of twisting his mouth. My mother wrung her hands. The stationmaster, in a red cap, came out to meet the approaching train. I was soon aboard, my bags smelling of my mother's pastries— rugelach, egg cookies, and strudel. "Goodbye, goodbye!" sleepy voices called in the dark. "Goodbye . . . goodbye . . . " The calls grew fainter, like fading farewells to departing troops, until they could be heard no longer, as the train, gathering speed, began to huff and puff, like bellows blowing on a flame.

At Sosnowicz I got off and took a public carriage to the house of the smuggler who would be arranging the next stage of my journey. "Hello, young man!" he greeted me. "What's your name?" He took out a letter and compared its contents with what I told him. Everything was in order. I lay down to sleep on a hard bench, and only after daylight broke could I make out my surroundings, a large room set up with old wooden benches and plank tables. A young girl of about fifteen or sixteen entered, her bare feet in loose slippers that kept flapping against the floor. As she walked, she plaited a braid and, when done, threw it back over her shoulder. She was pale, with large black eyes, and her

half-uncovered arms, bare feet, and bit of revealed neck were enough
to arouse my desire. "You're the American?" she said. "My father's dav-
ening and will be in right away." She handed me a battered copper dipper and pointed to the water barrel, indicating where I could perform
the ritual washing of hands. She brought me hot water and milk and
several buttered rolls. Each time she drew near, I sensed the aroma of
a warm bed, or kneaded dough redolent of sweet-sour yeast. "You're really to be envied," she sighed, tears forming in her eyes. "You'll do well
in America."

"What are you, a fortuneteller?" I asked. But she didn't hear me and
repeated her remarks in a forlorn and faraway voice, looking off into
the distance, almost to my America. I stood over the rotting barrel, my
reflection floating on the black water. I filled the dipper and poured
water over my fingernails, once, twice, and as I performed the ritual I
recalled the story of the Jew who goes to Egypt to study magic. On the
way, he stops at an inn, and when the innkeeper learns the purpose of
his guest's journey, bids him first to wash his hands before eating. As
the traveler is standing over the barrel, dipper in hand, the innkeeper
casts a spell on him, conjuring up the Jew's whole future—marriage,
great wealth, capture by pirates, deliverance, descent into poverty. The
innkeeper, in stunning detail, leads the traveler through scores of years,
into misfortune, old age, and decrepitude, until, as he is approaching
his death, the innkeeper breaks the spell, and the Jew realizes that he
has been standing over the barrel for only a few moments, during
which he experienced his entire, frightening life to come.

I imagined that this girl, too, would cast a spell on me that would
keep me here forever. Who needs America? Why go off on so long a
journey? Stay here, I fantasized, marry the smuggler's daughter, wear
a satin dressing gown, sit at the Sabbath table with its savory braided
loaf, sweet fish, beans mixed with farfel, a fat portion of meat with
horseradish, carrot compote, stewed prunes, and a golden glass of Wis-
sotzky tea. And as the fantasy candles flicker in their tall, silver cande-
labrum, I, half-asleep in the semidark stillness, kiss my young, bashful,
pregnant wife . . . Drip, drip . . . I saw my face floating in the black
water of the barrel.

I sat sipping my hot drink, as the girl stood over me, looking as lonely as only a Jewish daughter can who has suddenly grown to maturity and whose mother and father have yet to take this new fact into account.

"You're really to be envied," she said again.

The smuggler entered, still in his prayer shawl and *tefillin*. He touched the arm phylactery, the head phylactery, kissed his fingers, then silently pointed to his mouth, as if to say, "Have you eaten?" I indicated, also in pantomime, the glass of hot water and milk. He pursed his lips in a grimace. "Rokhl!" he barked at his daughter. "Nyah, bring some sour cream, a green onion. Oh, that girl"—he pointed to his head—"no sense at all." Young Rokhl, slippers flapping, fetched the sour cream. The father then touched his phylacteries, by way of asking if I had prayed yet. When I hesitated to answer, he gave another quick snort—"Nyah"—pointed at his behind, then at the ceiling, and shook his head, meaning "No." The message was clear: he wouldn't be whipped in heaven for my transgression. He stationed himself for the silent recital of the Eighteen Benedictions, and after rushing through the prayer, took the customary steps backward, treading heavily, as if he were being released from a yoke.

Later that day, after it turned dark, a young man arrived who was to be my guide, dressed in hip boots with tops that reached over his knees. Then another young man showed up, a deserter from the Russian army. He quickly threw off his uniform and changed into civilian clothes, including a pair of glasses. The soldier sat there impatiently, like on hot coals. "When will we finally get moving?" he cried out. "You want to kill me here? Do you have any idea what can happen?"

The young man with the boots was in no hurry. He first asked for some herring and some whiskey. He kept stuffing his mouth with rye bread and pouring one drink after another down his gullet. After each glassful, he tried putting the soldier at ease. "Don't worry," he said, "you're in good hands."

At last, the smuggler reminded him of his duty, saying, "Rakhmiel! Let go of the bottle. You'll need all your wits about you." Only when it grew very dark did the smuggler settle his accounts with us. He wished us a pleasant journey and reminded our guide to keep his head on his shoulders. "Go in peace," he bade us farewell, putting on a devout, priestly face, as if he were about to make the sign of the cross over us. The girl suddenly appeared at my side, extending a cold hand. I groped for a warm reply, but my tongue was tied.

"Are we ever going to get out of here?" the soldier began to complain like a woman. "You're killing me. I may as well hang myself."

"Go in peace, in peace," the smuggler repeated.

The girl scurried off to a corner like a cat. The guide threw open the door and we stepped into the darkness.

"Rakhmiel, you devil," the smuggler called after us, "remember, a head isn't the same as a behind."

We passed through backstreets. A dog barked in the distance. The night was very dark. We trod with soft steps on soft ground. The young man with the boots walked ahead of us, somewhat unsteadily, muttering to himself, "He gives me a herring head, a lick of whiskey, and half a ruble and thinks he's making me rich. That cheapskate! He should burn in hell!"

The soldier kept blabbering that if the operation, God forbid, didn't go off smoothly, he'd kill himself. We walked and walked, not looking at one another, until things began happening as in a fairy tale. First, the guide disappeared, then the soldier. I began to walk faster. I seemed to be the victim of a ruse, tricked out of my money and left stranded between a black sky and the desolate earth. I walked faster and faster, holding my head rigid, like someone on the verge of a breakdown.

The muddy ground soon gave way to tidy, narrow sidewalks. I kept plunging forward, never veering from the main road, until I came to a cluster of neat little houses with occasional lighted windows. Before long, I found myself in the center of town, with wagons and trolleys rushing by. Everywhere I looked I saw the same Gentile faces, Gentile mustaches, and Gentile mouths as in any Polish city, but the surprise came when those mouths opened to speak. I looked at the coarse faces and couldn't stop marveling when I heard the sounds *ja, ja* coming from their lips. I approached a policeman, who looked like one of our own policemen, but even before I came near, he greeted me, "At your service." I mingled with the crowd in the street and it began to dawn on me, that, yes, I had made it safely across the border. *Ja, ja,* the geography had changed. No bells had rung, no cannons had fired, nevertheless, I had crossed over from Poland, where every second word was *pshakrev,* "son of a bitch," into Germany, the land of *ja, ja.*

Most of the people were tipsy. A peasant, not much older than I, pulled me into a smoke-filled bar. I drank thick, foamy, dark beer from a tall, slender glass. There was much singing and spitting. I was afraid to ask point-blank where I was, but through some sly maneuvering, I finally discovered that I was in Mislowitz and that there was a streetcar that ran directly to Katowitz. I managed, though not without difficulty, to tear myself away from the friendly drunks, dashed from the tavern, and reached Katowitz that same night.

Trains . . . trains . . . and more trains. Hanover . . . Frankfurt . . . a few hours in Berlin . . . another train, filled with happy, singing students in green Tyrolean hats. I was exhausted, my head dizzy from lack of sleep. At last I got to Bremen, where my vagabond appearance identified me as an immigrant, and things were taken out of my hands. I came under official scrutiny, but this didn't bother me much because, in my sleepy state, I saw everybody through the wrong end of a telescope. I could hear what people were saying, but their words oozed by like soft tar, devoid of meaning.

That night I slept on a stone ledge that called to mind a stair in a cold bathhouse. Each time my face or my hand touched the chilled stone, I awoke with a start. It was pitch black. Men and women were speaking some kind of incomprehensible Yiddish, of which I couldn't make out a word. There was a woman sleeping next to me, breathing into my face. One of her heavy, bare legs lay sprawled across me all night long. I was afraid to move. Only in the morning did I discover that all those men and women with whom I had bedded down, and whom I assumed to be Jewish, were actually speaking Flemish.

I was made to undergo an official interrogation and given a shower, and before I knew it, I found myself on a salt-encrusted boat, reeking of pitch, old rope, rusted iron, and disinfectant. The deck was strewn with sacks and barrels. The food was unspeakable, and following the meals, everyone retreated into his own, private hell. After a day and a half of this agony, your bowels feel about to come spilling out of your nose and mouth. I looked around for a sympathetic face but saw myself surrounded by what appeared to be only enemies. It ceased to matter whether it was day or night.

At last we landed safely in Hull, on the east coast of England, and all the Jews, men and women, were immediately rounded up for a blessing by a Reform rabbi, who held forth about the wandering people of Israel and Jacob's feet grown weary from his travels. We were then taken to a damp hall and fed at long, dark tables. My stomach was still churning from the short sea-crossing. I chewed with trepidation on a hard crust of bread, taking care lest each bite bring on a catastrophe, and sipped cold, weak tea.

Again a train . . . Liverpool . . . a hostel with several rooms that were really one, the spaces divided from each other by steps—a few steps down and to the right, a dormitory set up with beds; a few steps to the left, a dining room. I met a young man there, who introduced me to his sister Liza, a redheaded girl with freckles, and to her friend Sonya, who was toying with two long, black braids, braids so black that they practically glistened. The young man struck me as peculiar, since he was headed not for New York but for Connecticut. He and his sister sang heart-melting Russian love songs. The four of us chattered away in Russian and spent our three days in Liverpool together, prowling the streets.

We boarded the *Aquitania* and stood on the deck, watching the baggage being hoisted aboard by big-muscled stevedores who joked as they worked. Next to me stood a tall man of about sixty, with a sizable shaved head and a clean-shaven, somewhat hermaphroditic face, without a trace of hair, only a maplike network of reddish veins. He was trading quips with the stevedores, calling down to them and sending them into peals of laughter. They called back to him and he let out a boom, like thunder. I didn't understand a word of their exchange but took in the tonalities of the new language. The tall, big-headed man was a German-American farmer, returning to the United States after a trip to visit his birthplace.

Later, he and I chatted and he made good-natured fun of me and of Jews in general. Every Jew in the world, he said, seemed to be headed for New York, where each had an uncle who worked in a factory that manufactured either cigars, shirts, or pants. He advised me to forget about my uncle and go with him to the open land, where he raised horses, cows, pigs, and chickens. He was prepared to take me with him and would even pay my fare from New York. I was still a young man, he said, and there was no need for me to end up in a miserable sweat-shop when I could lead a wholesome life, doing healthy work. He talked to me of the American prairie, of clean air for shriveled Jewish lungs, of restful nights, of strange birds that call out "whippoorwill" all night, and—this with a knowing wink in acknowledgment of my youth—young girls not averse to a romp in the hay.

A Jewish cook in a white chef's hat didn't let the Jewish passengers forget that it was Shavuoth, the Festival of Weeks, and favored us with excellent dairy dishes, the foods customary to the holiday. My young friend and I, along with the two girls, strolled on deck until late in the night, singing Russian songs. Liza, who was slightly anemic, turned in before us, but the black-haired Sonya was made of sterner stuff. She kissed both me and my friend, who paid her the compliment of calling her a Nietzschean superwoman. Sonya swore eternal love for me and I for her, my friend bearing solemn witness. She then swore sacred and devoted love for my friend, with me as witness. We could barely tear ourselves away from her to go our separate ways to our cabins. Upon debarking, Sonya, my shipboard soulmate, fell right into the arms of a butcher, an American cousin, who had brought her over to be his bride. Later, I would often see her peering out of a butcher shop in Harlem, standing at the window among the sides of beef, looking like a tearful calf, with large, foolish, yearning eyes. As for me, I didn't go off to the prairie with its whippoorwills but settled in New York with my uncle the cigar maker, who never even came to the boat to claim me, afraid of losing a day's wages.

I felt sick at heart, my entire pose of worldliness suddenly crumbling in the face of the warm commotion around me, the kissing and em-bracing, the joyful welcomings. My entry into America was hardly tri-umphant. A man wearing a badge from a Jewish immigrant-aid society shepherded me around all day in search of my uncle, who had moved several times since sending me the steamship ticket. Fortunately, the official was a patient man, but nevertheless I watched him like a dia-mond, afraid that at any moment his patience would give out and he would abandon me. The German farmer's mockery, as it had issued from his gold-filled mouth, followed me all that day: "Every Jew is looking for an uncle."

Overhead, gloomy elevated trains clattered. Heavy wagons rumbled by. A gramophone in a store sent a Yiddish song wheezing into the street: "The prayer shawl is my only consolation." A sob froze in my throat. That cruel welcome to America hibernated within me for many a year thereafter, leaving its ice-cold imprint.

5

The Bessarabian Jew from Bogotá spotted me on the deck and practically kissed me. "You have no idea how I've been looking for you," he said, "like hunting for a treasure. Since this is the last night of our trip, I can allow myself to confess that I love you like a brother. Why do you think I love you so much? Because you're such a great listener, you have golden ears. Your ears are worth a million dollars. You sit there and listen and listen and listen. You could bury me six feet under, my words could be going in one ear and out the other, and still you'd be sitting there, listening with your pair of golden ears. I'm a broken man and when my heart grows too heavy, I have to talk it out, but go talk when nobody is listening. I open my mouth to speak and see that there's another mouth about to open and speak too. This talking at one another is a disaster. Do you think I'm any better? I've no patience either when somebody's yakking away at me. But when I talk to you, I know that I'm talking to a real pair of ears. You hear that? You're not the best judge of your own worth. If I had your ears, I'd have them insured."

From off in a corner came the lilt of a Hebrew song, starting with a young female voice, soon flanked by two tenors.

"Do you know who they are?" the Bessarabian asked. "They're fine Jewish children, Hebrew teachers, a young couple and a friend. They had good jobs, but they gave everything up and now they're on their way to the Land of Israel. You can't imagine how jealous I am. Ah, the Land of Israel! The Machpelah cave, where the Patriarchs and the Matriarchs lie buried . . . Rachel's Tomb . . . the Western Wall. Ah, when

I think about the Land of Israel, my mind begins to spin. I remember my first Hebrew teacher, a pious Jew with a long, gray beard, who himself looked like one of the Patriarchs. Do you remember the scene of the aged Jacob lying in bed, surrounded by his twelve sturdy sons, each capable of striking a blow if necessary? They're all standing there, and Jacob addresses Joseph in his weak voice, 'Bury me with my fathers and their wives in the land of Canaan, in the Machpelah cave, something I was unable to do for your mother, Rachel, whom I had to bury by the wayside.' It's a beautiful story, as you may recall. For me, though, it's as if everything was poured into a sieve and the Yiddish words sifted right through. But those young people over there, they're speaking Hebrew as if they'd just stepped out of the Bible. Well, excuse me, I have to go change. Tonight's the last night and everybody's going to be on late watch. I want to catch a dance. You hear? I believe in grabbing what you can, since you only live once before they push you under. But, for God's sake, let's make sure we see each other in the morning before we leave the ship. I must shake your hand and thank you for those golden ears of yours."

The ballroom was jammed, the dancers were one on top of the other. The reek of perspiration assaulted anyone who stepped into the room, but nonetheless the dancers glided elegantly across the packed floor. The tall pianist wandered about, looking bewildered, trying to reach the door leading to the bar. "*Et tu?*" he exclaimed when he saw me. "You're also here in this Turkish bath, with all these women?" He grabbed my hand and deftly maneuvered us out of the ballroom.

The bar, too, was crowded. The pianist found us an empty corner somewhere and we sat ourselves down. This well-bred Englishman had already had one glass too many and his laughter rang out louder and looser than usual. Yet piercing through his noisy cackles, I could hear the crooning baritone of the blond, young Russian: "*Sonyetchka, ti otsharovatelna,* you are absolutely bewitching." The large center table was occupied by the Russian colony, with the queen bee, Sonya Yakov-lyevna, presiding. For the occasion, she was decked out in a Turkish shawl, wrapped around a colorfully embroidered dress. She wore heavy, black drop earrings that made her large head look even larger. "*Sonyetchka, ti otsharovatelna,*" the blond Russian kept purring.

At a second large table, youth was having its fling. Three unusually beautiful girls, aged fifteen or sixteen, with rouged cheeks and mascara-touched lashes, sat drinking with several young men. The girls wore absurdly long dresses, cut low front and back. They flirted with their companions, making good use of their bared shoulders and the quicksilver path that trembled between their three-quarters-uncovered breasts. They played with the high-heeled shoes they wore on bare feet, revealing long, slender, almost boyish-looking legs. Their chaperone was sitting nearby, a woman with a hard, shrewd face and wiry silver hair. Her watchdog duties notwithstanding, on the very first night out, she had found herself a tall, elderly man and became so taken up with her conquest that her three charges were left free to dance, get drunk, and disappear into strange cabins. Now the girls were sitting with five or six young men in tuxedos. The whole group looked as if they were very capably imitating their elders, dressed in Father's trousers and Mother's gowns. The chaperone was already quite tipsy. Every so often one of the girls would get up and go over to her, give her a peck on the forehead, exclaim, "Darling!" and return to the group. The chaperone, drunk as she was, was still in sufficient command of her senses to comment to her elderly swain, after another swig of her glass: "I have to watch over those young bitches, but who knows if there's anything left that's worth guarding. Take a look at those tall, magnificent whores. Well, you should see the three of them in the shower. I simply cry just looking at those taut, glistening bodies and those delicate feet. I say to myself, 'Goodnight, Mary, it's time to go to sleep.'"

"I could live, but they won't let me"—suddenly I heard Yiddish sounds, the lyric of a popular song, no less. It was the prizefighter, whispering into my ear and pointing at the three girls. "For a threesome like that I would consider converting, as sure as I'm a Jew," he said with a conspiratorial wink, as he was led away by his Man Friday, still dogging his every step.

The bar was growing more stifling and crowded. Overheated couples spilled in from the ballroom. My pianist friend, who had already downed more than a few glassfuls, began to stare at me with glazed eyes. "You hate me!" he shouted. "You, too!" He stood up on his shaky legs and stumbled out of the bar. Only now, left alone, did I feel the slight movement of the floor underfoot, and it struck me full force that this was the last night we would be spending on the water.

"No sleeping tonight. Tonight we'll guide the boat to shore with wide-open eyes." It was the Wisconsin teacher, who had tracked me down. "Am I disturbing your solitude?" she asked. "You know? The young musicians have shown up, they're waiting on deck. It's such a beautiful night. Let's get out of here, it's suffocating." She took me by the hand and led me away, without waiting for an answer. As we passed the Russian table, the young, blond Soviet jumped from his seat and called out, "No, no, this won't do. This is no time for individualism. Tonight we are a collective. No private love! No private passion! Tonight we all love one another." To illustrate his point, he started a song in his booming voice, the entire Soviet colony joining in, including the earnest Khazhev. "*Vsamom dyelye*," said Sonya, "stay with us." We made our excuses and barely managed to escape their friendly clutches, telling them that we'd meet later on deck.

On one of the steps leading to the upper deck, the Wisconsin teacher came to a stop. After a moment, she buried her head in her hands and began to sob. It all happened so quickly that my throat choked up and my hands began to tremble helplessly. I tried to calm her, in a quivering voice close to tears that betrayed my own distress. She stopped her crying as suddenly as she'd begun. "Pardon me," she said, wiping her eyes like a little girl. "I'm just an overgrown fool. But, I warned you, didn't I, that I was going to cry." We continued in silence. She clung to me and I had the feeling that something significant had just taken place between us, that she had confided something of importance, though what exactly I wasn't sure.

It was cool and spacious on deck, but my heart jumped at my first glimpse of the water. The sea's vastness, its terrifying expanse, had shrunk into something much narrower. Small islands, some round, some square, and some shapeless, appeared on the water as if great chunks of sea had been bitten off and transformed into land. Also gone was the sea's bottomless depth, the turbulent abyss. The water was now calm and smooth. Our ship moved like a rowboat, its engine no louder than the slap of oars. Red and green lights blinked from afar. Not only did everything look as it did when our journey began, it even smelled the same, the shoreline aromas of pitch filling the air. Our ship moved slowly, with the leisurely strokes of a confident swimmer.

Everyone spoke in hushed tones. The tall Haitian diplomat promenaded with his Latvian lady, bending down every now and then to whisper something into her ear and plant a kiss. The young book publisher walked arm in arm with a heavyset woman whose large, cheerless cat's eyes shone in the dark, almost as though illuminating her companion's impatient expression. The young musicians stood at the railing, staring into the water. A narrow band of light appeared in the distance, warming a stretch of the sea and indicating where the sun would rise. I felt a sudden weariness in every fiber of my being. Our ship's whistle sounded, and its echoing call was answered by several nearby ships. I brought the Wisconsin teacher over to the musicians and excused myself.

Sleepy deckhands were washing down sections of the deck, barely moving and not exchanging a single word. The soapy water brought out the musty smell of the wooden planks. The deckhands swayed back and forth as if in their sleep. I asked one of them how much time we still had before docking. Several replied in unison, like automatons, "A good six hours."

I felt that I had to stretch out on my bunk and close my eyes for a few hours. The passageways, already barricaded with piled-up suitcases and heavy trunks, looked darker than usual. Couples were slinking along the walls, crawling over the mounds of luggage. Three tall youths were leading, practically carrying the three tall girls through the obstacle course. The girls' heads were thrown back, resting on the boys' shoulders. A cabin door opened and they all disappeared inside. The blond Russian escorted the middle-aged Englishwoman, pulling her faster, as if afraid that the ship would be docking any moment. She trailed him like a calf, with bold, little steps. She was drunk and murmured between belches, "Darling, no one has ever treated me like this before. I have sons almost your age. Where are you taking me?" To which the Russian kept replying, "Yes, yes," as he continued to drag her to his door. Stewards sat atop the heavy trunks like Buddhas, puffing on their pipes and impassively observing the scene.

My neighbor, an elderly schoolteacher of about sixty, was standing at the door of her cabin, fiddling with the lock. When she saw me, she began to speak, as if to herself: "This year I'll be in Spain. I was in Spain last year, too. For the past thirty years I've been going only to Spain. We are all creatures of habit, and Spain is Spain. Anyway, what's the difference? Is Italy any more interesting? I'm a Spanish teacher, so I go to Spain. If I were a German teacher, I would probably have gone to Germany. Going to Spain in that case would have been remarkable. My fate is bound up with Spain. But what kind of fate is that, when even after thirty years, I still don't have hold of it? Are you married?" She yawned and fiddled some more with the lock. "*Buenos noches*, as they say in Spain."

I lay on my bunk, rocking, trying with all my might to keep my eyes open, as if I were afraid of missing something . . . When I awoke, I felt strange. My entire body had suddenly become heavier and had lost the sea rhythm to which it had grown accustomed. I sensed a physical change in all my parts and realized, instinctively, that the ship had docked.

♦♦♦ *Chapter 5*

1

As the passengers debarked, their separation from each other took effect almost immediately, far faster than the bonding that followed embarkation. We all stood before our open suitcases in the huge customs shed and avoided looking at one another. If by chance any eyes made contact, we smiled guiltily, as if ashamed of the bacchanalia of friendship and intimacy that had raged among us for five whole days. Each one of us now stood alone, reverting to a previous order of things, to the social standings that prevailed on the other side of the Atlantic, with their attendant privileges, responsibilities, and prejudices—all of which had been suspended for the short duration of the voyage. People were embarrassed at having indiscriminately entered into friendships that must now be severed. The more tenderhearted exchanged what-is-there-to-say smiles, implying: "Don't hold this against me. The ocean's the ocean, and land is land. Now we are no longer thrown upon each other's friendship and must behave accordingly, politely and properly." The hard-hearted types broke off the shipboard relationships with an arrogant abruptness, casting icy looks, as if at a stranger. Their expressions bore something of the air of Cain after he had done away with his bothersome brother. The very sensitive types (male and fe-

135

male) felt themselves used and discarded. They experienced an after-taste as of some bitter cigar. For them the cold cessation of friendship was a painful bit of surgery.

The faces of the passengers were now as cold and drawn as those of the customs officials rummaging through the suitcases. Everyone had changed into different clothing and looked oddly overdressed. A strange hat had sprouted on a head you'd previously known only as a mass of red hair blowing in the sea breeze. You never expected that a new hat, or overcoat, or other article of clothing could so change the countenance and spirit of someone you had seen daily in more casual, intimate attire. The easygoing shipboard interlude, which the majority of the passengers now wished to forget, lay packed away in suitcases, along with snapshots and other mementos. The customs officials me-chanically inspected every item twenty-five times over, and each time the small reminders of the voyage were fingered, the more detached from them you became.

Yet despite our splintering into discrete individuals, we still retained something in common, a feeling of helplessness, of immigrant anxiety. The strange uniforms of the customs officials and the porters, the rapid patter of a different tongue, gave everyone the feeling of knocking in vain at the gate of a foreign land. We proud Americans felt ourselves dazed, even somewhat criminal, under the suspicious glare of the French officials. As certain as we were that we were not bringing in contraband cigarettes, we still answered their question with a shaky "No." I was reminded of the stringent border search of Father Jacob's sons and of the silver goblet that had been surreptitiously slipped into Benjamin's sack. Who knew what lay in our own suitcases!

Not until we were on the train, racing to Paris past ugly, sooty vil-lages and scraggly fields, did a slight bit of bonding recur. The porter had tossed all the baggage into the first carriage he saw, and in the scramble to reclaim our bags, a selection began to take place. It opened with a question: "Where is a Jew headed?" The answers came fast and furious. "Poland." "Romania." "The Soviet Union." "Lithuania." What had happened to all the passengers who were on their happy way to Paris, Italy, England, Switzerland, and Spain? "Where is a Jew headed?" Where did all these Jews suddenly come from? One had never seen them aboard ship. Now here we all were sitting together, as if herded into the Pale of Settlement. The Jewish faces were troubled. The rich, smug uncle on his way to visit an impoverished relative had already begun to resemble the unfortunate kinsman he would soon be meeting. He was remembering how it was. Twenty, thirty, forty years of Americanization were dropping away. Once again the returning Romanian Jew, Polish Jew, Russian Jew, Lithuanian Jew reverted back to who they had been when they left home. Other carriages carried pleasure seekers; the passengers in ours were burdened by what awaited them at their destination.

I studied the glum faces and it occurred to me that in twenty-five years such travelers returning to pay respects to the graves of forefathers will have disappeared. These were the last of a generation. Fathers and grandfathers were nearly gone, and one by one, the sons were also beginning to die off. Should *their* children ever think of visiting Soviet Russia, Poland, Lithuania, Romania, they would go as one might visit Paris, Switzerland, or Italy. They would not be returning home but traveling to see the sights so that they might slap yet another sticker on their suitcases. The familiar Poland will have died, and with it the longing or the hatred for that Poland. There will be tourists, but no one going home to see a dying mother or father, or to mourn dead parents.

A case in point among my traveling companions were a father and son, the father on his way to visit brothers and sisters in Minsk, but the son headed for the brave new world of the USSR. There was a chasm between their expectations. The son had delicate features. A native of Boston, he had earned an engineering degree at the Massachusetts Institute of Technology but ended up working in his father's garment factory. "A Jewish engineer has a Chinaman's chance of finding a job," he said to me sadly. To get beyond such Jewish hopelessness and uncertainty, he looked to the great opportunities for educated young people that existed in the Soviet Union.

"That's America for you! Go ahead, don't become a radical, spend your best years studying, become an engineer, and see how those Boston snobs and anti-Semites react if your name happens to be Goldstein, Cohen, or Greenspan." This was the father talking, a former labor supporter who had become something of a boss in America. "They write a lot about the critical situation of Jewish youth in Poland, Romania, and Germany, but they're silent about what's happening to Jewish young people in America. There's a new Inquisition at work there—fathers who make their sons doctors, lawyers, and engineers are leading them to the slaughter. Forget it! There are simply no opportunities for Jews. My son graduated with honors. He's a mathematical genius, just what he needs to work in his father's tailor shop! That's why you've got to hand it to the Soviet Union, though I disagree with many of the things they're doing over there. They've done away with that whole dirty Jew-Gentile business. But I'll tell you the truth, it could be much worse. When I remember my son's friend, Faber, I hold my tongue. That man was absolutely brilliant. I tell you honestly that my son, who's no slouch himself, was only fit to shine Faber's shoes. If he hadn't been born a Jew, by now Faber would have been the most famous engineer in America. So, where is he now? Sitting on death row. It just tears my heart, when I think about that young man. I'm sure he acted out of sheer bitterness. Here was a Jewish engineer, utterly hopeless—something must have snapped in his head out of desperation. On top of that, he fell in with a bad crowd that also ensnared his younger brother, and instead of becoming a famous engineer, he became a famous thief and murderer. Now for sure he'll get the electric chair and nothing, no doctor, can help him. There's no cure for him anywhere."

"You shouldn't exaggerate American anti-Semitism," interjected a Jew with a pointed beard, speaking in a Galician accent. "All the professions are overcrowded. It's an economic problem facing the whole country, nothing to do with anti-Semitism, God forbid. Anti-Semitism is when there's a direct assault on Jews from the government, when it's a matter of legislation, when there's an organized attack against Jews, when Jewish blood flows, may Heaven protect us. Let us not be sinful or ungrateful. American Jews have much to be thankful for."

The fields rushing by were dusty and poor, the grass yellowed and dry. Laughter rang out from the other coaches, but our little ghetto resounded with Jewish sorrows. As crowded as our car was, one Jew after another kept stumbling in. "Where is a Jew headed?" we asked one another. "Poland? Romania? Czechoslovakia, you say? Really! Where . . . where . . . where?"

As the train pulled into the Gare Saint-Lazare in midafternoon, a heavy rain was falling, and even though it was the beginning of July, every drop imparted a cold bite.

2

The porter carried my bags on his back from the station to the hotel, a distance of a few streets. He turned into a packhorse under the heavy load, his figure bent, his bandy legs moving one step at a time, like an elephant's. From the hotel window, everything looked uncommonly common. The rain had something to do with this, there being nothing like a downpour to wash away the distinctive features of houses, roofs, and passersby. A side window looked out on a little crooked street, twisting between brownish houses with peeling walls. A man in a beret, hands thrust into his pockets, scampered like a cat between the narrow walls, turned around, and ran back. Everything began to take on the aspect of a scene from a novel by Eugène Sue. A woman walked along the narrow sidewalk on high, crooked heels, tottering back and forth, as if she were clambering up a wall. She moved so unsteadily that it seemed as if the dirty little street was going to spew her out, like slops from a pail, against the opposite wall, and send her little straw hat, perched on her head like a beret, tumbling to the ground. I felt uneasy. The woman looked up at the window and yawned. Her face was impassive and sad.

The rain never stopped. I lay on the bed, wondering what key might unlock this new city for me, but the rain washed away all thought. A maid, a woman of about thirty, entered the room, handed me soap and towels, and ran me a bath. She came in and left, scarcely looking at me. I felt uneasy again. I heard her rustling in the hallway, and all I could think of was her indifference. Something was bothering me. I was becoming more anxious by the minute, and it took me a while to admit that I should take hold of myself and maybe probe the reasons for my anxiety, even though it was easier to just lie back and give in to my mood of rain-soaked weltschmerz. But once I opened the door to self-questioning, there was no going back, and I had myself a heart-to-heart talk. I asked my idiot self whether I didn't resent the fact that

Paris, from the first moment of our encounter, had not shown me its full Maupassantian and Balzacian face.

The maid returned, turned off the faucets, and shut the door behind her. I splashed in the tub and gave in to my feelings of disappointment. There was a large clock across from my hotel window that marked the steady passage of the minutes. I was scheduled to leave Paris that night and time was running out. How best, in a brief span, to experience this foreign city? I took a taxi to hunt down my addresses, one address, a second, a third—everyone was away on vacation. I was alone in a rainy city, among rain-drenched monuments. (It occurred to me how much the foreignness of a city is marked by its monuments and police uniforms.) The taxi rattled over a bridge and the driver half-turned to me, gesticulating with short movements of his hand. When he spoke, his facial muscles tightened, as if he were in pain, though his speech was soft and musical.

The Café Dome was quiet; only a few banquettes were occupied. People were sipping coffee and reading German, Russian, French, and English newspapers. A painter, who had been to America several times and whom I recognized, was sitting by himself. He was short and stout, with tiny legs, like a dachshund's, and a dour, Oriental face with slanty eyes. I went over to him and told him that I had just arrived from America. This made no impression and he gave me a cold look. But once I'd begun the conversation, I felt I had to plow on. My being a writer did not impress him either. Under no circumstances would he allow his place in the artistic firmament to be diminished by association with an artist of possibly lesser standing and, to establish my credentials, he asked what kind of writer I was and did I know so-and-so. When I told him that I knew this one and that one, he still wasn't sure of me, but he must have decided that his reputation would suffer no risk from a civil chat. Accordingly, he said, in an almost friendly tone: "I have some terrible news for you. Bialik is dead."

I was stunned. He pulled out a telegram signed by Meir Dizengoff, a founder and longtime mayor of Tel Aviv. "Old Dizengoff won't survive this," said the painter. "He's a sick man himself, with maybe one foot already in the grave." The news hit me like a bolt of lightning, the shock one always feels whenever one hears of the death of a fellow writer—a blow to the stomach, dread, and finally relief that you're still alive. "A great Jew!" the painter continued. "What am I saying? The greatest Jew, a truly great man." I was afraid to say anything lest I break the mood of his lamentation. "Haim Nahman Bialik was the greatest Jewish poet since Yehuda Halevi," he shouted. "He was certain to receive the Nobel Prize." I screwed up my courage and ventured to join in the threnody: "He had such youthful eyes, an imposing head, a thick neck, like a laborer's, and slightly stooped shoulders that bore a good part of the Jewish national burden."

"You knew him?" the painter asked, narrowing his slanty eyes.

"I didn't know him, I only saw him. Three times," I replied, and waited for the painter to ask for the details.

The painter, however, was awash in his own sorrowful memories, swimming in his tears, like a fat duck on a pond. He labored to inform me that there was a vast difference between his dead Bialik and mine. For me it was the national Hebrew poet who had died, of whom every Jew in the street could claim a part. But for the painter, whose life was closely bound up with the Land of Israel, who was himself a national artist, a poet of the palette one might say, who was an intimate of the deceased and a frequent visitor in his house, a regular at the poet's famous Saturday-afternoon gatherings—for him Bialik's death was a deep, personal loss. To what could he compare it? It was as if he had lost an uncle who was also a great scholar. The whole city might be mourning a stately Jew, a great personage, and a noble being, but this was, after all, his own beloved uncle. Did I understand?

I was vanquished and capitulated completely, especially when the painter informed me that he owned considerable property in the Land of Israel—"real estate, as you Americans call it"—all of it bought from the sale of his paintings. "Real art sells," he said, "despite what those foolish fellows here in Paris want you to believe."

I had no choice but to offer up my own meager scraps of Bialikiana. I recalled the first time I saw him in the midst of a noisy gathering, a banquet tendered him by Yiddish writers to honor the great Hebrew poet. Bialik addressed us—no, spoke rather, in an intimate, conversational voice, like a spider spinning a web, sending out strands in all directions, fine, delicate strands, well-chosen biblical verses, talmudic phrases, as well as worldly observations, without overstepping the bounds into alien territory, only enough to indicate how much world culture a contemporary Jew should help himself to in order to stock his own reservoir of particular Jewish wisdom. The important thing, he said, was to cultivate your own vineyard, because it contains all and all can be found in it. Everything he said seemed spontaneous, but there was a plan to this apparent spontaneity, he was weaving the fine strands into a deliberate design. This we realized only after he had sat down. While he was speaking, it all seemed pleasant enough, like words heard in a daze. Only after he had concluded his talk were we aware that all those innocent strands he'd been spinning were, in effect, a spider's web and that the fly he had trapped in it was—the Yiddish language. It lay in the web the poet had spun, almost suffocated to death, and stirred memories of all the tens of Jewish languages mentioned by Bialik, which Jews had created in their millennial wanderings and which had all disappeared. One Jew in the Land of Israel, he averred, was worth ten in the Diaspora.

After Bialik took his seat and we Yiddish writers realized that he had read us out of existence, the room erupted in Jewish warfare. God! What a sorrowful war! Barbs flying in all directions. Bialik sat serenely through the tumult, more secure in his convictions than we in ours, but less appealing in his self-satisfaction. Unable to pierce Bialik's calm, we grew angrier and more belligerent—more tragic and, therefore, perhaps more in the right. Among us there were also idealists, the descendants of Jewish martyrs who were prepared to go along with Bialik. Eyes zealously ablaze, noses atwitch at the smell of their sacrificial offering, they were ready to bring to the altar their hybrid-tongue, the last Diaspora jargon, as a sacrifice to Hebrew, the one, eternal language of the Jewish people. Others agreed with Bialik for reasons of their own and took sadistic pleasure in his remarks. They sensed a golden opportunity to dump their colleagues' assets. They themselves had invested very little in Yiddish. Why, then, should it bother them if Yiddish were to be destroyed? Let it burn on the altar! Let the smoke rise to the heavens! Yet another group sought to match the attacker's eloquence and proclaimed themselves exemplars of "the republic of Yiddish": let the "enemy" see just what greatness Yiddish has produced. Much of their talk fell with a thud, like counterfeit coin. The most tragic were those struck dead by shame, as if their tongues had been cut out. They stood facing Bialik, in mute protest, pounding tables and, if I remember correctly, raising their fists. I was among the shamed and humiliated. I grieved for my own handful of poems, which stood to be destroyed in the war of the languages, and I pounded the table along with the rest.

Bialik's cheeks reddened, his forehead glistened. He did not look us in the eye. When he finally spoke again, it was with something of the air of the Grand Inquisitor. If he had felt wounded by our demands that he give us back our mother tongue, he merely hunched his shoulders lower, under the weight of our complaints. Yet he had no words of comfort to offer. He threatened us with the cruel inevitability of history on the march, as if to say: "Poor, little calves, you tremble. Alas, you don't want to be led to slaughter. Nevertheless, slaughtered you will be."

A few days later, I found myself sitting with a colleague in a corner of a quiet hotel. Bialik sat between us. The colleague had been assigned by his newspaper to interview the great Hebrew poet. It turned out that Bialik clearly remembered my standing across from him in protest. He averted his eyes from me, as if he felt guilty over taking something from me that he couldn't return. However, whenever I turned away, I noticed him stealing a glance at me. This was followed by a heartfelt Jewish sigh.

The third and last time that I saw Bialik, he was sitting on a platform among Hebraists. When he opened his mouth to speak, another war erupted, this one a civil war, you might say. Voices screamed out: "Speak Hebrew with the Ashkenazic accent!" Others: "No, the Sephardic accent!" Bialik defused the hostilities by shifting from one accent to the other. Present at this Hebrew event were young men and women, Hebrew teachers, and a few elderly gentlemen wearing yarmulkes, who sat there beaming, eyes shut, savoring every word that Bialik uttered. For them the content was irrelevant. It was *loshn koydesh* that mattered to them—Hebrew, the Holy Tongue. The younger members of the audience sat openmouthed, scarcely believing they were in the actual presence of Bialik himself.

When I finished relating my few, fragmentary recollections, I noticed that the painter was no longer at my side. He had slid down the banquette to join a plump woman. I could see only his profile and I searched there for a trace of his former grief. But his wrinkled profile, which looked to be kneaded from black pepper, revealed only a broad smile. The plump woman was unattractive, but I had to conclude, according to an old novelistic recipe, that for the painter she represented the symbol of life, erasing the death of the national figure who had been to him like an uncle.

I suddenly felt someone's eyes on me. To my utter surprise, sitting two tables to my left was the French teacher from Wisconsin, nursing a half-empty glass of beer. We stared at each other for a few moments, as if trying to determine the extent of our mutual detachment since leaving the ship and to what extent we should remain distant. In my surprise, I failed to greet her. She picked up her glass and sat down beside me. "You know," she said flirtatiously, "it's not nice of you not to have left yet on your trip. What are you? A spy? Had I known that you were one of those types who come to Paris and head straight for the Dome, I wouldn't have spoken a word to you on the ship. As for me, the minute I unpacked, I rushed right over here. Disgusting, isn't it! I can't bear to look at myself."

I explained to her that I was a member of that miserable guild—journalists—who have a string of Domes in our collection. Whenever one of us takes to the road, the first thing we seek out, in whatever big city, is a Dome. How we ever expect to meet a real person under such circumstances is a mystery. Nevertheless, we file dispatches and write books, and people think they're getting real slices of life, but all they're getting are pieces of a Dome.

"If that's the case," she said, "let's get out of here," and led me off to a nearby restaurant. We took a table outside and sat looking silently at each other. "There's something about the Dome that's missing here," she said at last. "Courage, for example. At the Dome I had more courage. There's something about its atmosphere that would have let me say, oh, just about anything. Here I feel all proper again, shorn of my wings."

"Should we go back?"

"No! I've missed my chance. Let's eat. I'm starved." She ordered an apéritif. As she moistened her heavy lips with the viscous drink, I caught a good look at her close up—a tall, oversized woman, with long arms and feet, with wide-open eyes and trembling lips.

"Are you a Jew?" she asked. "I know nothing about Jews."

"What makes you think that there's anything special to know about Jews?"

"I'm sorry, you're right."

"No, I'm wrong," I teased.

By now she had drunk several glasses of wine and talked very little, but suddenly she lit a cigarette and resumed the conversation, speaking in a lazy voice. "How long will you be staying in Paris?" she began. "Let's say five, six days. The first day, you'll let me get to know you. We'll walk through the streets and talk and talk and talk. The second day I'll fall in love with you. The third day, I'll think that I'm happy, excuse the foolish word. No, we'll think that we're happy. The fourth day, you'll fall in love—no, not yet. The fourth day, we'll still be in our happy place. By the fifth day, however, you'll fall in love with somebody else and I'll be as jealous as a shrew. On the sixth day, you'll toss me aside."

"A fine script, except that I'm leaving at midnight for Poland," I replied. "My mother is sick, very sick. It's been twenty years since I've seen her. I owe her every minute I can spare. I'm only waiting for the train. I even thought of taking a plane."

"Take me with you," she said. "No, don't, you'd have a big parasite on your hands. The playing out of our script will have to wait until your return trip, if I won't be too busy, that is. Give me your Polish address and I'll write to you. It'll be greetings from the Dome, maybe also a greeting from the English language, since you'll be speaking Polish over there with your family."

"No, Yiddish," I set the facts straight.

"Yiddish! Yiddish!" she exclaimed. "I've always been intrigued by languages. The French speak French, the Turks Turkish, the Jews Yiddish, and Americans will soon be speaking American. It's a curious thing, but quite natural. Each of us speaks in our own tongue, in the language in which we were nurtured. It's as personal as breathing, no translation required, you just open your mouth and out come the words of your native folk songs and lullabies. I like these old, plain words, like bread, water, butter, milk, cows, grass, heaven, heart, sun, stars, and love. I hate fancy, pretentious words. Each language should stay simple and pure, sealed from others, and resist all those foreign, illegitimate imports—those careerists that invade and poach on other languages. A grandchild should be able to speak exactly with the same words as its grandfather."

She took a few quick drags on her cigarette, tossed it away, and resumed: "I once went back to a little village in Sweden, to seek out my origins. My parents were born in Wisconsin, but my grandfather, my father's father, returned to his birthplace as soon as my father and the other children were able to stand on their own two feet. He could never get used to the new land. In that little Swedish village, you didn't even need an address to find my grandfather. He kept pinching my cheeks, but his second wife, my step-grandmother, shot me angry looks. She may have been afraid that I'd come for my inheritance and was concerned about providing for her own children whom she'd had with my grandfather. Several of these children—I didn't count them—were even younger than I. Other branches of the family came to see me, six-foot-tall uncles with thick mutton chops that looked like they'd been pasted on. They drank to my health, laughed very loud, and talked a great deal, even though I couldn't understand a word. At night a strapping, idiotic boy, a relative, stole into my bed. I don't even remember how we were related. He stank of sweat and leather, and I quickly decided that with such an idiot, it was the better part of wisdom not to put up a fight. Why scream theatrically and create a scandal in a small village? Better to submit for a few minutes and be rid of him. But it seemed that young man was so smitten that the next day he wanted nothing else but to marry me. He even sent my grandfather over as matchmaker. My grandfather pinched my cheeks and kept talking up the match in the broken English he still retained. I fled from there without even saying goodbye."

My thoughts ran along parallel lines, and I said: "I, too, came close to fleeing from the city of my youth, but there was no escape. I wanted to become a new man in a new land. Instead I was a hybrid. I couldn't forget that I had left behind a mother and a father on the other side of the ocean. For a long time, I wandered around in an unfinished state, trying to toughen myself up. I had fled as you would from a place of horror, because that's what it was. A Jewish child in Lublin was raised on terror. The Gentiles of our town filled us with terror with their frightening images of the crucifixion. Many of our own festivals did the same, the candles representing flickering souls. Our funerals were scary affairs, with the corpses returning as the living dead to frighten the children. Even in dreams you had to keep your wits about you and remember how to respond when a corpse grabbed you by the hand, saying, 'Come with me!' In our building, in the basement, there lived a Jewish baker, who also attended to the dead. He washed corpses for burial, preparing them for the hereafter, where all of us must stand in Final Judgment. With the same hands that washed corpses, he kneaded dough for the rolls that my mother bought each morning. For me these were rolls of death and they often stuck in my throat. But worst of all were our dark, black, tearful funerals. If you've never as a child seen a small-town Jewish funeral, then you don't know the meaning of terror. Even the dogs howl in fear, because the Angel of Death is abroad, and the Angel of Death, as every Jewish child knows, has a thousand eyes, and pulling the heavy quilt over your head is of no use at all. I remember that once my mother fell sick—she was never very strong—and I prayed to God—I don't know if half-asleep or dreaming—that if she could not be spared, let her be granted a few more years, at least until the time when I would leave for America. (Even as a child I dreamed of going to America.) I thought I would never live through a funeral in my own house, my mother's funeral. Now my mother is very sick. She summons me home, who knows for what reason, probably for the funeral that awaits my arrival. I've already covered two-thirds of the journey. I wanted to escape my mother's funeral. But how could I? This is my fate, I have no choice but to go. Look, it's getting late. Come see me to a taxi. I mustn't miss the train."

On the way to look for a taxi, as we again passed by the Dome, I ran into a young painter, a New Yorker, who had been living in Paris for the last few years and would come occasionally back to New York to visit family. "You're here in Paris?" he said. "Finally! When did you get here?"

"Just now," I answered, "and I'm also just about to leave."

"You should be ashamed of yourself. Paris and I will never forgive you."

"I'll be back."

"In that case . . . "

The Wisconsin teacher looked at both of us, glad for the opportunity to extract herself from the too hasty intimacy that had sprung up between us. She stood there, staring coldly at me and the painter. My friend stared back at her with the open-faced audacity that only a painter can pull off and said to me in Yiddish, "Who is that . . . that . . . shikse?"

"From the ship."

In New York, I had probably exchanged no more than ten words with this painter, but now, standing outside the Dome, he suddenly seemed so dear to me, as if a good deal of the reason for my coming to Paris was to see him. This had nothing to do with any feelings of loneliness on my part, but was owing rather to the warmth he exuded. In New York we considered him somewhat affected, with his long hair, his mincing steps and overly polite way of talking. Here, in the vicinity of the Dome, he seemed remarkably natural. Even his little steps didn't suggest weakness but their opposite, as if he was eager to conserve his strength. "A shikse from the boat, and straightaway to the Dome? There's something improper going on here," he said in a talmudic chant. He then spoke to me in English, overwhelming the Wisconsin teacher with the sudden switch from the stream of Yiddish to perfect English sentences. "So what's happening in New York?" he asked. "How are all the good and decent people faring?"

"I'll tell you everything on the way back," I said. "It's almost eleven and I don't want to be late for my train."

His face took on an earnest, worried look, as if he'd suddenly assumed all my cares. He summoned a taxi and told the driver to take me to my hotel, not far from the Gare St.-Lazare. The Wisconsin teacher stood a few steps away, looking uneasy and forlorn, having been shut out by the unexpected encounter with the painter. I recognized her bewilderment and called out to the pair, one foot already in the taxi, "Introduce yourselves, a painter from New York, a French teacher from

Wisconsin." The painter was hurrying me along, "You'll be late for your train. We'll introduce ourselves."

Before the taxi door closed, I saw the two of them standing together, without me, and noted the strong contrast between the two strangers I was leaving behind, whom I had thrust upon each other—she, tall, blonde, vigorous, the essence of Gentileness; he, short, dark, and unmistakably Jewish. She suddenly broke away and sprung over to the taxi, again looking bewildered. "I hope," she stammered, "that all goes well with your mother." She spoke with tenderness and sincerity, sending warm greetings from a woman from Wisconsin to a town in Poland. It wasn't what she said that touched my heart so much as her spontaneous, deeply felt gesture of concern, setting aside her self-absorption. She had spoken as warmly as it was possible for her to do. She remained standing as the taxi started to pull away, her eyes downcast, looking as if she wanted to add something that she couldn't quite express. And as the taxi swerved to the left and the right, almost knocking down tens of pedestrians, a thought crept into my mind, that maybe the right thing to do would be to turn around and spend another day or two in Paris. Even when I was already in the waiting room at the station, I still couldn't rid myself of the feeling of an opportunity missed.

3

Aboard ship, thoughts of my old home had stayed pretty much in the background. They came to the fore only at those moments when I felt troubled and confused and began to conjure up scenes from my past, to reassure myself that I wasn't rootless. Mother, father, brothers and sister—all belonged to the past. To be sure, my mother's illness bobbed up constantly, like the refrain of a sad song, but she herself was no longer quite real to me. Each time I called her to mind I had to uncoil a great ball of memory, rolling it out to considerable length to reach back to my beginnings. I had sent a cable to Poland from the ship, but that was prompted in large part by the wish to play with the magic of technology. Nevertheless, the wireless dispatch created a thin bridge between me aboard ship and the family back home. The bridge held fast for a while and then disappeared like a mirage.

However, once I debarked from the ship, my old home became my destination. What had once been the past now lay ahead, with all the tantalizing mysteries of the future, a future I was impatient to confront. I was even prepared to forgo weeks and months of my life in order to bring that future closer. This is how an invalid must feel, who is willing to age a few months so that he might crawl out of his sickbed and see the sun, or a father, willing to give up a few years so that he might see his children's futures. There are too many such instances in a human life, when one doesn't live in the present but wants to vault over time into a dubious future. Everything following the ship led directly homeward. I knew full well that what awaited me was a roomful of sorrow, and yet I wanted to push on ever faster. Was this so as to have it over and done with? I hardly think so. I longed to be home, I envisioned my homecoming—riding in the public carriage from the train station, standing at the door. But never, in my imaginings, did I dare to cross the threshold. That moment I did not want to spoil by anticipation.

I grew anxious and impatient. I knew that back home they were holding up the last act for my arrival, waiting for me to ring up the curtain. The last act was unavoidable, but the whole household was awaiting my presence, loath to end the play without me. The ending was predictable, and yet I was afraid lest, God forbid, I miss a drop of what my nearest and dearest were about to experience. How long could they hold out, waiting for me to arrive? If on the ship I had strolled leisurely about the deck as if it were a long, sunny valley leading nowhere, with my memories of the past cold and remote, I was now in such a state of impatience that I didn't want to see anyone. Everything appeared as an obstacle on the way to my goal. I no longer wanted to join a world of strangers and to engage in conversations that would have consequences. All this now seemed a waste of time. I decided to see how far it was possible to restrict myself to my own company. I sensed, even though I didn't know how it would happen, that I was on the verge of some meaningful event that would open my eyes to much that was still unclear. Now that I was finally on the right road, I felt I must not stray.

The steady clack of the train's wheels calmed me somewhat, precisely because the train, speeding toward my mother, seemed to have taken on my restlessness. When I closed my eyes, I might have been traveling on the very same train that, on a certain night twenty years before, shortly after midnight, bore me away from home. It was now also just past midnight and it would have been something of a consolation had this, miraculously, happened to be the same train. But when I opened my eyes, all such sentimental thoughts vanished. There was no comparison to the train of twenty years ago. That train I would have recognized, skinned alive!

Next to me sat a priest dressed in loose robes with a wide cowl that looked warm as a blanket, and with sandals on his bare feet. He had a long, yellowish beard and his unusually large rear took up so much room that I was squeezed into a corner. The other passengers in the cheerless compartment had all nodded off. Only the priest was awake, contentedly reading a French newspaper and from time to time stroking his beard with one hand, in good Jewish fashion. The dozing passengers had all retired into themselves, as if to sleep away their troubles, as well as to avoid contact with one another. I had no choice but to close my eyes, too, though I had no desire to sleep.

I was roused from my dreams by a cold shudder that passed through my body, rattling my sleepy bones. The priest was no longer seated beside me, his place taken by a slender man of a totally opposite demeanor, with a small head and thin, pursed lips. His hands, resting on his knees as though he were sitting for a formal photograph, were so thin and transparent that one could make out every bone. When I opened my eyes, he looked at me, then quickly turned away, pursing his lips until they disappeared, as if to prevent them from uttering a single word.

It was now lighter outside and easier to make out that many in the compartment were not strangers to one another. A woman who lay stretched across a seat began giving orders to the man beside her, sitting scrunched into the narrow bit of space she had left him. Sleepily, the man was doing her bidding. On another seat, two men were asleep, propped up against one another. It was hard to tell whether they were friends, or strangers whom travel had brought into intimacy, possibly even an "Aryan" and a "non-Aryan." A woman in a far corner had one eye half-open. She was struggling to open both but didn't want to be the first to disturb the harmony of slumber that still prevailed. With great difficulty I stretched my limbs that had fallen asleep. I got up and, treading carefully, as if I were walking on sand on rubber soles, dragged my still lifeless, bloodless feet into the narrow corridor.

Dew-soaked fields, small villages nestling among rocky hills rushed past the window. The sky was overcast, with a hint of rain. Standing beside me was a short, broad-shouldered man, in his early forties. He stared out the window at the passing fields, forests, villages, all the time turning his head to me as if he wanted to tell me something, but each time looking away and again fixing his gaze on the misted window. At last he said something in German, and when he saw that I didn't answer readily, switched to broken English, carefully feeling his way through the language, asking me if I was an American. He was dressed in a suit, the very picture of propriety, his trousers so perfectly pressed that it was a miracle how he had managed this so early in the day, when everybody else was still tumbling about in a state of dishevelment. He was fair-haired, but not that arrogant German blondness which wouldn't have suited his whole, modest appearance. His dirty-blond hair was sprinkled with gray, and his large face was set off with a pair of sad, nearsighted eyes. He was a businessman, returning home from Paris, who had once done considerable business in America. "Now," he chuckled, as if wanting to make a joke, "America has stopped doing business with us. But Canada is still a good customer."

"Do you mean the American boycott?" I asked, with as much feigned indifference as I could muster.

He laughed again, seeming to take pleasure in the fact, as if it were all child's play and he the adult was watching from the sidelines. "*Ja,* boycott! Boycott!" he confirmed.

"So, how's it going?" I asked cautiously, seeking to gain his confidence.

"Not very good! Much poverty among the workers, many factories shut down. My own silk factory had to lay off half its workers."

"How will it all turn out?" I asked, growing bolder.

He shot me a look and broke out in helpless laughter, almost choking on his gasps. "We mustn't talk about this! No talking! It's better that way. No talking!"

Again exercising caution, I retreated to a more innocent line of questioning, until another opportunity to ensnare him might present itself. But he would no longer let himself be caught. When he sensed that we were on the verge of a dangerous subject, he had only one response: "No talking." He laughed some more, to indicate that he was sorry he was being so impolite, his laughter ending in a somewhat hysterical screech, the kind some people make upon hearing bad news. He explained to me that it wasn't in his nature to be impolite, but there were certain things one couldn't talk about. He even tried to pull back from his former indiscretion, that factories had gone under throwing workers into poverty. "Things will probably get better," he said.

The passengers were now waking up and the corridors starting to bustle. From all sides people appeared, wrapped in bathrobes. Outside the washrooms, passengers gathered impatiently, cursing the villains who had laid siege to the facilities and who were taking their leisurely time going about their business. In the morning light, the German's face looked even more familiar and likable, his brown eyes ever ready with a smile. His broad shoulders bespoke power, but his large face, for all its severity, had an air of gentleness.

Men and women called out in a New York–accented, Yiddish-inflected English, and the German said to me, in almost awestruck tones, "Many Americans going to Europe now."

"It would seem so," I replied.

A tall Jew in a short robe walked by, looking me straight in the eye. "You forgot your razor," a woman called after him.

"That's right," he answered and turned back, again looking me in the eye.

"What about your towel?" the same woman's voice cried out.

"Dammit!" the man said, and went back again. On his return, towel in hand, he passed by once more, and after giving me a searching look, finally said, in English, "Good morning," making it sound like a Yiddish greeting, with overtones of, "Ah, a Jew!" I returned his salutation.

We were now passing through Belgium. Mining towns whizzed by, with soot-covered houses and men going to work, carrying lunch pails. Various pieces of machinery dotted the rusty ground. The train sped on. The German stood looking out the window, mumbling to himself about Belgium's coal and iron mines, its copper and zinc, its textile industry. The conductor, sporting a neat, waxed mustache, who had been going back and forth, now stopped and beckoned to me and the German. We acceded to his mysterious invitation and followed him into another car, where he proceeded to open a window and told us to look out. The train was passing through steep cliffs, creating a gloom, like the darkest of tunnels. We looked out and saw nothing, but the conductor's face lit up with anticipation. Suddenly, he cried out, *"Le roi—* the king!"* The German and I stuck our heads out the open window, but still couldn't see to the top of the high, terrifying cliff. The train slowed down as it passed the giant wall of rocks, stained in a variety of rusty hues. Suddenly we saw, at its foot, bunches of flowers and an inscribed date, "February 17, 1934," along with some other words which we couldn't make out because the train had again picked up speed. However, I immediately realized that what we had just passed was the site where King Albert of the Belgians had ended his rock-climbing career. I was at a loss to understand what he might have been looking for in this desolate spot, except perhaps death.

The conductor kept looking back to the cliffside memorial. I craned my neck to catch a last glimpse and was seized by a shudder when the thought occurred to me that it was only a few months before that Albert had fallen to his death and lain lifeless in the place where the wreaths now lay. The conductor pulled in his head and sat down, looking spent, as if he had just undergone a horrible ordeal, like being present himself at King Albert's final moments. He gave us to understand that we were a lucky pair, having been granted the privilege of seeing what nobody else on the train saw. When we thanked him for his kindness, he countered our gratitude with a look that seemed to imply that there couldn't be thanks enough for the glowing experience he had provided.

Again, I found myself standing with the German in the corridor of our car, looking out the window, indifferently observing the green stretches of field and the isolated little houses. My companion, however, was staring intently, drinking in every detail of the passing scene, as if searching for something. Suddenly, he gave a start, raised his hand, and pointed outside. "You see?" he cried out. "All that land over there? It used to belong to us." He made a fist, as if to hold it in his hand. "They took it from us by force." His eyes filled with tears and his shaky hand seemed to caress the rich, green fields that were hurtling by. I looked on with continued indifference. I felt pity for the man, who was now completely convulsed. I sought a living connection between these particular stretches of ground, which the train was chewing up with a fury, and his tear-stained eyes. But my sympathy didn't affect my indifference. I even tried to talk myself into thinking that I envied him for feeling so personally the loss of his territory, but this was of no help either, and I didn't succeed in fooling myself. I absolutely did not envy him. Jewish cosmopolitan, Gypsy, opportunist, internationalist—I even tried hurling all the familiar charges in the anti-Semitic book at myself, for the fate that didn't allow me warm attachments to bits of land that one country had stolen from another. Typically Jewish! Suddenly I decided that I must somehow smuggle into the conversation the fact that I was a Jew. I began to feel that it was unethical on my part not to do so, for the sake of the hundreds of thousands of German Jews. How could I stand fearlessly beside this "Aryan" and not disclose myself? It was also not altogether right of me to deceive him, but out of sympathy I hesitated, because he had grief enough. Should I present him with a new problem and add to his distress by declaring my Jewishness? A demon finally pushed me over the edge. I was no longer in control of myself, and my tongue tossed off words before I had even come to a decision.

"As a Jew," I said, "I can't understand such personal attachment to a piece of ground, such fervent patriotism. I'd like to say that I appreciate and value all this, but even out of politeness I can't, because I simply don't grasp it. At most I can say that such feelings strike me as tragicomic."

Had I spoken loudly enough? Did I make clear my Jewishness, in no uncertain terms? The German stood still glued to the window, but then I noticed him looking at me out of the corner of an eye. He finally turned to me and I felt a change had come over him, even though he tried to hide it. He wanted to catch a good look at me from the side, but I looked at him full face, with open anticipation. He placed a trembling hand on my shoulder, a heavy hand it was, but he kept it there lovingly.

He soon removed it and took my right hand in both of his. "It's going to be all right," he said. "It's going to be all right. I understand your Jewish desire for revenge, it's justified, but everything's going to be fine."

I was caught in a terrible tangle from which I didn't know how to extricate myself. I felt no hatred toward him personally, and it wouldn't have bothered me at all if Germany got back its lost territories. The German, too, found himself in a quandary, telling me how deeply he felt about the wrong that had been done to his country, yet not agreeing with everything that present-day Germany was doing to foster its revival. Indeed, he was far from agreement, but as he had said earlier, "We mustn't talk about this." There were several Jewish families, he told me, living on his street, whom he didn't know personally but to whom he sent secret notes, assuring them that things would get better. Nevertheless, his Jewish neighbors went about with bowed heads and didn't let themselves be consoled. They looked ashamed. "We Germans, who were humiliated by the Treaty of Versailles, have found someone else to humiliate," he said, "but as sure as it's God's will, we mustn't talk about this."

He almost screamed out these last words as a warning to himself, because now entering our car was a group of seventeen-, eighteen-year-old blond youths, proud and high-spirited, wearing swastika armbands. Their thick, peasant faces broke out in laughter; they moved about vigorously, confidently, as if striding on solid ground. Each time we passed one another in the corridor, colliding lightly, they offered polite apologies. These members of the Hitler Youth filled all the cars, greeting each other, arms smartly upraised. At each encounter, up went the arms in mutual salute. They kept up a steady humming and buzzing, like members of an orchestra tuning up, awaiting the conductor's baton to burst into performance. They looked freshly scrubbed, as if they had just risen from sleep. Beefy conductors had also come aboard with a "Heil," but in their case this seemed merely routine, a perfunctory exercise. Clearly, we had crossed the border from Belgium into Germany.

"Aachen!" said the German, still standing beside me, his lips pressed together. Each time a hand went up before him, he automatically raised his. Everyone in the train was startled by this sudden invasion, no one said a word. All this lifting of arms looked like a religious ritual, a kind of sign of the cross to bid one another "Good morning." The German stationed himself between me and the Hitler Youth as if he wanted to shield me from the joy of the victors.

My first reaction wasn't rage but childish surprise, that what I had only read or heard about I was seeing with my own eyes. I thought of New York, where giant rallies were being held, protesting these very salutes, and here I had spanned the magical distance and come face to face with the actuality. In New York everything that I was now seeing was remote, imagined; here, it was palpably real. A foolish thought insinuated itself: So must China, Japan, and India also be real. The only wondrous thing about them is their distance. One need only travel to get to everything that one has taken on faith.

It occurred to me that I had experienced something similar when I once sat in the courtroom at a sensational murder trial and saw for myself the two defendants, who had been so deeply in love that, together, they did away with someone who had stood in their path. Until that time, I had been one of the many thousands who had only seen newspaper photos of the "beautiful" murderess. Now, in the courtroom, I saw the real face and heard the two lovers speaking in drowsy voices. The man of the pair was a short, hunched figure, with cheeks so ruddy that he looked as if he had been made up for the role. His partner in love and crime sat nearby, her face flushed, her hair disheveled. The "beautiful" murderess was well into middle age. Who would kill even a cat for her? During a recess, as she was led out of the courtroom, I noticed her tiny, dainty feet and wide hips. Only later, after leaving the courtroom, did I realize that I had seen two living corpses.

With the same realization, I now regarded the young, blond youths and their outstretched arms. At first, it was hard for me to see past the childish theatrics and to connect them to the passionate anger of the New York rallies. But I soon understood that along with everything else I had heard about, it must also be true that these young men had dragged men and women from their homes with the same theatrical joy to God knows where, tortured them, and kicked them in the face. I was now in the land of hell. I still felt no hatred, but my face began to burn, out of helplessness. Should I get up and make a speech, an impassioned speech? Shouldn't I at least interrupt the celebration and cry out: "I am a Jew"? No great courage required for that from a Jew with an American passport in his pocket! The army of swastika-decorated youth grew noisier and merrier. I sought protection in the shelter of my German, but just then I caught him with an upraised arm, responding to a "Heil."

While the train was standing in the next station, I got off in search of further instances of Nazi reality, but there were none to be seen. The small-town station looked no different from any other of its kind— porters pushing carts piled high with baggage over rattling cobblestones; conductors sitting on train steps, sunning themselves; small groups of people, talking among themselves. I searched for a Jewish face. A proud, good-looking girl, with serious eyes, so serious that they seemed almost angry and unfriendly, was walking back and forth on the platform. She appeared to be about sixteen or seventeen, yet a world of sorrows showed on her face. She walked proudly, head high, a rare blend of youth and seriousness. It was impossible to look at her with the same sheepish stare one usually casts at a young girl. She would probably return it with a disdainful sneer at your frivolity, out of eyes that looked older than yours. Yet it would be some accomplishment if you could ignite a spark of joy in those sad and clever eyes. A tall, older woman, dressed all in black, came over and took the young girl by the arm. The two walked silently back and forth. Were they Jewish?

My German was also pacing the platform. He now looked much shorter, as if he had shrunk. He was somewhat ashamed to look me in the face and followed me like a shadow. Several times he caught up with me and looked up at me with sorrowful, cowlike eyes. He wanted to see whether he and I could still talk. He shrugged his shoulders, gave a helpless wave of the hand, and furrowed his brow, as if to say, "What can a person do?" When the train started moving again, we sat together at a small table in the dining car. The train rocked. A fat, uniformed German walked up and down, carrying a huge, metal platter heaped with hot food, which he portioned out to each diner. He didn't look at all like a man, but rather like a heavyset woman; even his creased face resembled that of an old, faithful female cook. After serving everybody, he passed by again, giving out second helpings with womanly solicitude. My German and I sat across from each other. He ordered a bottle of wine and poured me some, too. I was heavy-hearted and didn't touch it. The dining car looked like a homey country restaurant, with its simple food and fat waiter. My table companion was urging me to eat and drink and, as if answering my thoughts, carried on a running commentary on the timeless things in life, which "will remain forever"— the friendly atmosphere of restaurants, the human warmth that will triumph, vanquishing all the sorrows, which will disappear. "Eat some more," he said. "Have another drink." But I felt a constriction in my throat, as if somebody had his hands around my neck, not quite choking me, but about to do so. I still felt the same way later, when my German was leaving the train and gave me a warm farewell, again declaring that everything will yet be all right. I wanted to ask how that could be if one and all were raising their arms in the Nazi salute, but I felt sorry for him. He kept repeating: "*Danke schön, danke schön. Thank you.*"

That was how I felt the whole time the train was puffing its way across German soil, as did the few other Jewish passengers, who sat playing cards, not even looking out the windows. Berlin, however, aroused some curiosity. When the train stopped there, we got off to look around, treading with cautious steps, as if we had no right of residence and we were there illegally.

Toward evening, the fat, rich, cultivated fields began to disappear, giving way to lean, neglected patches of ground, their green less green, their soil's blackness less black, their rows less orderly, their plantings scattered helter-skelter. Two thin deer, paralyzed by fear, stood gazing at the train. Only when it rushed past them did they spring away, with remarkable gracefulness, dancing on their forelegs, their hind legs seemingly suspended in air. By now night had blackened the train's windows completely, and when several slightly built, narrow-shouldered conductors put in an appearance and the first words of Polish were heard, my heart lightened. The hand that had been squeezing my throat vanished, and the strange conductors, who somehow managed to look like Shabbes-goyim, those Gentiles hired to perform tasks forbidden to Jews on the Sabbath, made me feel closer to home. Incomprehensible! A middle-aged woman, festooned with diamond earrings and bracelets, who had let me know that she was a wealthy widow on a visit to pay respects to family graves, squeezed into the seat beside me. With the appearance of night, her burning eyes looked half-crazed. She pressed one passionate leg against mine, and I could only thank God that there were other people in the compartment. Otherwise, who knows what might have happened to me with that insistent widow, there, on the border between Germany and Poland. "I'm a free spirit," she said to me, winking like a man. "When it comes to love, I don't think about the hereafter." The other passengers were now stretched out on the hard benches. I was afraid to fall asleep, because it was clear that my neighbor was lying in wait, with half-open eyes. I lay curled up in a ball, not daring to move. It took a while, but the widow finally succumbed to sleep, crashing like an old building that had strained to stay erect beyond its capacity to do so. Once down, she let herself go altogether. She began to moan and groan in old-lady fashion, then, abandoning all restraint, broke into snores, like a full orchestra. After that rousing performance, she lapsed into silent sleep, as still as a lamb. It was hard to believe that this serene old creature was the same woman who, not long before, had breathed fire and seduction.

It seems that I must have fallen asleep as well, because when I next opened my eyes, I heard the conductor calling out: "Zgersz! Zgersz!" I stood up with a start. Zgersz! For me that meant only one thing, the home of my brother Binyomin and my brother Marcus. Zgersz . . . Binyomin . . . Marcus. I ran over to the window; maybe I'd catch a glimpse of their familiar faces. The train didn't stop. I dropped back into my seat and fell under the rubber wheels of a dream that drove relentlessly over my aching bones. In my phantasmagoria, I had fallen into a deep well and lay at the bottom, drowning. I was certain that I would be saved—but who knew when? It must have been several hours before I opened my eyes.

The train raced past tumbledown huts. Peasants followed our progress with sad, sleepy eyes. Barefoot peasant women stood like madonnas, with babes in their arms, holding them up to us, as if pleading: "Here, take our children, lighten our burden." The babes in their mothers' arms had the same sad eyes as the old peasants. The wheels rolled ever faster, accompanied by the entreating looks of the peasants—"Bread!" The clacking wheels were condemned to repeat the plaintive request— "Bread-bread-bread."

Blackened chimneys . . . smoke . . . soot . . . and then the conductor's incredible call, "Warsaw!"

4

The coachman pulled on the reins, and the scraggy little horse pranced off with the shaking carriage in tow. The Warsaw streets were still half-asleep. It was already hot, unusual for so early in the day. Exhausted from my day and a half on the train, I curled up next to my bundles. The streets rolled by with uncommon strangeness. My head felt heavy and I kept lifting it up in an effort to stay awake. It seemed as if I had worn myself out these past twenty years waiting for this moment, and now that the moment had finally arrived, I was too spent to greet it properly.

The past few sleepy, rackety early morning hours on Polish soil had left me troubled and confused. My brain was awash with the sort of dream you have when, after first waking up, you fall back asleep, and return to what you were dreaming before you awakened. This time I strove, consciously, to re-create the details of the dream in all its illogical import. My brain being in the weakened state that it was, everything that had been part of the dream now, willy-nilly, assumed an unwelcome order, its bits and pieces taking on the completed aspect of a full-fledged composition. It proved too difficult to translate the hieroglyphics of the dream into understandable language, but everything that in the dream was misty and formless now, in my drowsy condition, became tangible, solid shapes with hard edges. The original dream was as lively as an anthill, but in its repeat performance, I brushed the anthill aside, and incidents from various corners of my past life came rushing in.

The undercurrent of the dream was a vague fear of impending destruction. Church bells were tolling, deep-toned Russian booms, lighter

Polish chimings, as someone with a twisted stick, like a branch, raced through the main street of the Jewish quarter, banging on all the shops to warn against desecrating the Sabbath. Businesses shut down in sleepy obedience and a fearful silence descended on the closed stores and the empty, shadowy street. In the midst of all the grand Russian Orthodox cathedrals and their less imposing Catholic neighbors stood the half-fallen Jewish prayer-study house. The street leading to this holy place was dark, and from inside its walls emerged the spirited refrains of the Friday-night hymn—"Come, my beloved, to meet the Sabbath bride." "Come . . . come" . . . the invitations scurried over the little synagogue's threshold, like frisky kittens. A tall water carrier approached with slow, heavy steps in the company of a shorter Jew. Clearly, this was the Hasidic rebbe, renowned as "the steel head" for his acuity, yet it was he who looked up reverentially at the taller man. "Rebbe," he said to the water carrier, "you know how to stop evil. Are you going to allow this punishment—allow the destroyer to obliterate this entire community of Jews?"

"Don't call me 'rebbe,'" snapped the stoop-shouldered water carrier, ordinarily a submissive soul. "Berish the water carrier will never let anybody put a rebbe's fur hat on his head. Don't try to pass your authority onto me. I won't allow it." But it was the smaller man's turn to rage. He spoke in a taut whisper. "If you play at modesty you leave ordinary Jews without a shepherd, with no one to turn to for counsel. The Destroyer is at the gates, and you amuse yourself with humility?" The water carrier's shoulders sagged, as if they had just assumed the heaviest burden of the day. He doubled up in pain and leaned against the smoking lamp post, sobbing quietly.

The lively Sabbath greetings kept issuing from the prayer house, little black and gray kittens that rolled down the darkened street. "Come, my beloved, to meet the Sabbath bride . . . come . . . come." The church bells tolled piously, and the town clock sounded the midnight hour. Then two pairs of heavy boots appeared on the muddy road leading into town. They stopped at the far side of the cemetery, just before the city gate. A sickly sun provided the watery sky with some semblance of daylight. The two were now certain that they had reached the outskirts of town and allowed themselves the pleasure of resting. The taller of the pair, a man with a flaming red beard and tiny, green eyes, sighed deeply and began tugging at his torn wadded coat. The shorter man, who reached only to his companion's belt, had a gray, strawlike beard and red cheeks, like frozen apples. He wouldn't let go of the tall man's hand, despite the latter's efforts to free himself. The tall man let out a roar, and the little one pinched his hand so hard that the giant began to bellow, until his nose ran. When I heard the wailing, I recognized who it was—Crazy Abush.

It wasn't yet fully day, but already the mischief makers were out in force, splashing barefoot in the puddles. When they caught sight of the two men leaning against the city gate, they whooped, "Crazy Abush is here," their merry shouts resounding down the length of the road. Meanwhile, a little boy with pious cheeks was on his way to heder to begin his studies for the day. He carried a warm roll spread with melted butter, a bag of sour cherries, and, in his pocket, a two-kopek coin for an after-school treat. The boy was so familiar I wanted to cry. He stopped when he saw Abush, broke off a bit of roll, and extended his hand. When Abush tried to grab hold of the offering, the boy prompted him quietly with the opening words of the High Holiday recitation: "*Ve-khoyl ma'aminim*—And all believe . . . " Abush's green eyes lit up. He began to sway to and fro, in proper prayer fashion, and through clenched lips intoned the liturgy, mixing Hebrew and Yiddish:

And all believe
That God must be served,
Must be served.
He has to be served
With joy and delight.
He redeemeth from death,
And delivereth from destruction.

The little Jew, who was Abush's father, swayed alongside. He drew comfort from the fact that his son managed to earn a living: for many years now they had been trudging through muddy towns and villages and as God the Father was witness, they made it through the week and came home Fridays, in time to welcome the Sabbath at their rebbe's synagogue. Abush had a gift for singing. The father himself could also give out with a good "Ve-khoyl ma'aminim"—but not as melodiously and without his son's soulful sigh. Parts of the father's mind were already dulled, and his words came out muffled. Without Abush the old man surely would have gone to his grave by now.

The young boy with the pious cheeks looked around to make sure that no one was watching and offered Abush another piece of his roll. "Abush," he said, "can you tell me the time?" The father closed his eyes. He knew what was coming, even though he had never agreed to such things, but he also knew that this was part of earning a living. Abush fiddled with his trousers and took out his "thing," turning his hand clumsily around the exposed part, as though he were winding a clock. The boy, who had seen this performance any number of times, let out a shriek and raced off to his heder.

The Gentile market was already bustling, filled with incoming wagons, tended by peasant women selling chickens, eggs, vegetables, fruit, and a variety of berries. Jewish housewives were haggling and examining the hens for plumpness. A peasant relieved himself alongside his wagon, leaving a huge puddle that trickled its way to the horse, which proceeded to lift its legs. Meat cutters in bloody aprons sharpened their long, pointy knives. One of them grabbed hold of a girl and lifted her high in the air. Several others jumped in and shoved their hands under the girl's skirt, which was blowing in the wind. The girl squirmed and kicked her legs, screaming, "Have you no fear of God?"

The market smelled of ripe melons, strawberries, raspberries, fresh carrots, lettuce, cucumbers, and radishes. It was a feast for the eye and nose. An old peasant woman, who looked like a witch, was milking a compliant goat. She handed a fresh glassful to a young Hasid with curly sidelocks who sipped the milk with fierce concentration, clutching his heart after each swallow, as though partaking of a miraculous cure. Mixed with the fragrance of vegetables and fruit were the animal smells of cows, chickens, dogs, and horses, particularly the latter's fresh deposits. Angry dogs with aged faces were tied to the wagons, pulling at their leashes and barking. Half-smothered hens, buried under a mountain of rags, somehow managed to poke out their heads and let out a choked cackle before collapsing into a stupor. A Gypsy woman slipped through the crowd, tugging at everyone's hands, her bracelets and necklaces jangling. Jewish housewives consulted one another, and Jewish men sniffed about, in search of bargains for the Sabbath. No one paid any attention to Crazy Dvoyre, who lifted her skirts up to her eyes and shrieked hysterically, in a childish voice, "Jews, the Messiah will come! The Messiah will come!" The day was humid and the peasants were sweating under their heavy coats. One by one, the wagons began pulling out, back to the small peasant villages, where a cool sky hung suspended over huts scattered among the thick woods.

A blind old beggar sat in the middle of the marketplace, playing a concertina and singing a hymn that everybody already knew by heart. In his hands the concertina looked like a hand mill, grinding out the same tune over and over.

I am blind, but
Jesus is good to me,
Good to me.
And Mary is good to me,
Good to me.
So, dear people, you be good to me,
Good to me.

In and out went the concertina, turning in all directions, like a slithery snake. The beggar's singing was so saccharine that it lay disagreeably on the lips. Everybody avoided him, including the dogs and horses. Even the ducks and the hens circled around, trying not to touch him with feather or foot. A consumptive-looking priest with a long, thin nose and a freckled face stopped beside the old beggar and engaged him in discourse, singing:

Good day, little grandfather,
A good day to you.
How does the light of your heart
Serve you today?

The beggar slowly wound down his playing, and answered with the words of his hymn, no longer singing, but accompanying every few words with a quiet wheeze of the concertina:

Jesus is good to me,
Good to me.
And Mary is good to me.

"That's good," said the black-clad priest, piously closing his eyes. He took out a groschen, examined the coin from all angles to make sure that it wasn't a gold piece, and dropped it into the beggar's cup. The beggar immediately resumed playing his hymn, his crouched body swaying back and forth.

The priest then went from one stall to the next, stalls hung with rosaries, statuettes of Jesus, red glasses for votive candles, thickly painted Marys in gilt frames, bleeding hearts, pictures of Jesus with a crown of thorns on his head. He touched each religious article devoutly. Peasants followed his progress, kissing his hand. He approached a young woman, who was sitting surrounded by tall, earthen pots filled with raspberries. She jumped up and, blushing, grabbed the priest's hand and pressed it to her lips. The priest helped himself to some raspberries and popped them into his mouth, smacking his lips. He held a few in the palm of his hand and inspected them closely. "Very good, a successful yield," he said as he chewed. "This year the good Lord has blessed our trees and our soil." While the priest was contemplating his palm, now stained red from the berries, the entire marketplace, from one end to another, suddenly turned somber, perhaps because darkness had descended, the darkness of a Sabbath eve.

The man with the twisted stick was still racing down the main Jewish street, banging on all the shops. At a signal of the priest's reddened palm, the Russian and Polish church bells began to ring out. But then suddenly they fell silent of their own accord, and would not resume despite the red palm's bidding. The blind beggar went on playing his concertina beside a urine-streaked wall:

I am blind, but
Jesus is good to me,
Good to me.
And Mary is good to me,
Good to me.

So, dear people, you be good to me,
Good to me.

On the train to Warsaw, I had emerged from this dream with the disagreeable taste in my gums of the old beggar's song. Now again, as I was being tossed about in the carriage, I had the same sour sensation as I had then when I emerged from my dream to see, through sleepy eyes, real Polish cities and towns rushing past the train's windows. I was grateful to my sleepy head, which had concocted such a welter of images. Thanks to my dream, I was returning home after twenty years not only with a strong sense of home, but also with its sad tonality. I now felt as if my pockets were stuffed with the homey goods of my dream which I had preserved through twenty years of estrangement. Now, at last I felt like emptying my pockets and scattering my memories over the Warsaw streets. See, I never betrayed your trust! My tongue truly cleaves to the roof of my mouth, but I have not forsaken you, O Jewish Poland, with your terrors and sad celebrations. Do not forsake my right hand as I have not forsaken you.

Early-morning Warsaw hadn't welcomed me yet, the city still slept. I was saving my passion for Lublin, the city of my dream, of my fearful Jewishness, ever seeking shelter between two sets of enemy bells, the Russian Orthodox and Polish Catholic. That I was now on my way to my aunt via New York struck me as peculiar, as if I had detoured so as to enter by a different gate and approach her house by the back door. Once upon a time, I traveled from Lublin directly to Warsaw. Now, having left Lublin for New York, it takes me a mere twenty years to return via Warsaw to Lublin.

The direct trips that I took between Lublin and Warsaw were for social visits, big-city experiences, knocking on editors' doors—and to take the entrance exams at the Krinski Business School.

A bookish Hebrew was spoken in the Krinski corridors. The classrooms were not as solid as those of the Lublin Gymnasium, the Russian high school that I had attended, but rather looked as if they had been hastily slapped together, like a flimsy sukkah for the Feast of Tabernacles. Krinski students lacked the high spirits of youth. Their brows were furrowed with practical considerations. Even the youngest among them felt rejected by the world and forced to stay within the Jewish fold. Seen in their overcoats Krinski students may have looked like those in the government business schools, but the missing brass buttons on their uniforms and caps let out the secret that these were makeshift outfits. The Krinski administrators made a heroic effort to transcend the distinctive ghetto mixture of Jewishness and worldliness, an effort as hopeless as Jewish life itself. The students hummed the Zionist hymn "Hope is not yet abandoned," but nagging at them was the common fear: What would they actually do after graduating from the Krinski Business School?

Krinski's was the destination of those with no other alternative, after the Gymnasium examiners had completed their annual dashing of Jewish hopes for advancement to a Polish school of higher education. Climbing the squeaky, unsteady stairs, you absorbed the taint of the Jewish world of trade that permeated the building and, indeed, the entire neighborhood, Simon's Arcade, with its leather and yard goods and Krinski's Business School. Business and trade . . . school . . . rags and business.

The Lublin Gymnasium was a one-story building. A few marble steps led into the forbidden temple. The wooden stairs at Krinski's creaked, ghetto style, taking you into an atmosphere of no-choice-in-the-matter Jewishness and a hothouse secularism that saw no sun and felt no rain. Its chief adornment was its director, a man with a prominent red nose and a beard so expansive it looked pasted on. Rozhdestvenski, head of the Lublin Gymnasium, could permit himself a thin, black mustache, but his Krinski counterpart Woskresenski felt that he must sport the broad, red beard of a Russian Orthodox priest. He served as Krinski's advertisement of its Christian secularity. But Rozhdestvenski's little mustache inspired more fear than Woskresenski's pan-Slavic beard, which looked more like the caricature of a Jew trying to pass for a non-Jew. Woskresenski's function was to serve as the Gentile gatekeeper of Jewish education, but his close association with the students consigned him to the same fate as theirs. He was ejected along with them from the Gentile world.

I arrived at the Krinski school with a younger student I was tutoring.

He had lively brown eyes and a stubborn lower lip. I assumed that he saw the same things I did as we traversed the hallways, but he said nothing. He, too, grew heavy-hearted, his head bent, as if ready to receive the Jewish yoke that would be placed on his shoulders in these classrooms. Our passage through the corridors felt like an exhausting climb up a mountain. I, the mature fifteen-year-old tutor, and he, the twelve-year-old pupil, were both seeking opportunity and purpose, and coming up against a blank wall.

On the other hand, the Szwienteduski hospital did bear a certain similarity to the Lublin Gymnasium, at least as far as I was concerned. Only in the corridors of the Gymnasium did I, a Jewish boy, feel the same tightening in my chest as in the hospital. Every time I had to stand for examinations, which were administered in the Lublin Gymnasium, I felt as if I were terribly ill. The teachers were surgeons, with scalpels at the ready. The walls gave off hospital coldness and the clean rooms smelled of disinfectant. The examiners flashed me a chiseled smile as they called out, "Yakov Isakovich Glyatshteyn," accentuating the last syllable. "Heh, heh," it implied. "Yakov Isakovich! A little Jew wants to share our privileges." The teachers chatted with a priest, who was present during the exams, to lend solemnity to the occasion. Once in a while he would also throw in a question. "Yakov Isakovich," he would begin. I don't believe that he expected an answer, he only wanted to dig around in me with a little knife. It was at the Szwienteduski hospital that they cut out my appendix.

The nuns of the Catholic hospital washed and bathed me and jabbed my veins tenderly, asking over and over whether we Jews had any institution like theirs, where sick little Catholic boys were so well cared for. A fellow patient, a Gentile boy who had just had his leg amputated, asked me innocently why I hadn't gone to a Jewish hospital. This was at the height of the Polish anti-Jewish boycott, and there I lay, a single Jew among thirty-six Christian hospital beds, surrounded by Christian charity. Everyone was kind to me, and everyone kept repeating how much kindness I was being shown, even though I was a Jewish boy. A man in our ward, with a black mustache and a yellowish complexion, died, with a kindly smile on his face, as if apologizing for making us feel uncomfortable. He was a train conductor who had been brought into the hospital following a train accident. He received last rites, his family standing by quietly at his bedside.

Red lamps in the corridors . . . stifled groans from the beds . . . the Russian doctor, with the good, thick hands, who took out my stitches . . . The last few nights of my stay, when I was able to walk around, I kept feeling that I, Yakov Isakovich, an ailing Jew, was walking the hallways of the Christian Lublin Gymnasium.

Weariness permeated every bone in my body. I looked out from the carriage at the Warsaw streets as if from behind a pane of glass, trying to reconstruct the past. We were now crossing the bridge to Praga. After twenty years with all the world upheavals, my aunt still lived in the same courtyard. The building manager, who often sparred with his sons and boasted about his dalliance with the cabaret singer Kavetska, must now long be dead. His eldest son, who had always threatened to convert to Christianity, was as good as his word. In the honeymoon months of restored Polish independence, he underwent conversion and became the chief of police in a small town. In good apostate tradition, he then proceeded to make life miserable for the local Jews. This I learned from the younger brother, the one who used to instruct me in manners. He, too, had converted in order to study at a Catholic seminary, but his fellow seminarians gave the new convert such a hard time that he ran off to America, where, with his mesmerizing manners, he quickly found himself an aged millionairess. Whenever we met in New York, he asked my advice, whether to marry the old woman, who was agreeable to the idea, and become an instant millionaire, or to give in to the pleadings of the old lady's daughter and run off with her.

My aunt, as it happened, had made one change in the intervening twenty years; she had moved from the right side of the building to the left. I wanted to slip into the courtyard unnoticed, but it was not to be. A little girl began running toward me, two boys grabbed each other by the hand and skipped around the courtyard like messengers, an old woman with an overgrown nose, as big as a potato, asked who I was looking for, a man with a bandaged beard started to shout across the whole courtyard, a few women appeared on their balconies. The courtyard was stirring. By the time I reached the stairs, my aunt was already halfway down, clapping her hands, her face stained with tears.

5

As yellow as her face had become, it was the only bright spot on the dark stairwell. I recognized her immediately. And as closely as she resembled my mother, there was yet enough difference so that it would take a journey of another few hours to flesh out my mother's actual image. It was like straining to recall a face and coming very close, but still missing a crucial detail. There was just enough resemblance to assure me that I was about to see Mother herself, and despite my aunt's shocking aging, I couldn't help but feel glad that I was already—almost—seeing my mother. It was like after a dream, when you open your eyes and see standing over you someone who looks familiar, but hasn't yet fully taken shape. You know that you must open your eyes wider to clear away the last wisps of dream so as to see that person in real life.

My aunt led me into the house, sobbing, "Your mother must be a great saint to have lived to see this day. She must have great merit in Heaven." For a while it seemed as if she had brought me to a wax museum. Several figures stood stock-still, staring at me. Children rolled about on an unmade bed. One child, with a snub nose like the chopped-off tail of a dog, and only a few upper teeth, made faces at me. A second child, a little older, began to cry, while a third jumped off the bed and disappeared into another room. The waxen adult faces continued staring fearfully at me.

"Don't you recognize them?" my aunt asked. "These are my daughters. This is the youngest, named after Grandmother Drezl. Don't you recognize the middle one? You've forgotten even the eldest?" Looking at the three yellowed faces, I reflected as never before on the wars, starvation, pogroms, terror, and poverty of the twenty years since my departure. Their fear affected me, they were ashamed of how mercilessly time had dealt with them. But above all, they were afraid because they had been caught unawares, because of the unmade beds, because of the child still making faces, because they were worried that I might not forgive them for wasting their lives since we had last seen each other, because I had surprised them red-handed in the process of their growing old before their time.

I felt even worse when I gradually perceived traces in them of the three mischievous little girls who used to titter, with stifled, impatient giggles, on the mornings following my late-night arrivals as a guest from Lublin. Before I awoke, they would be stretched out on an opposite bed, lying in wait for me, like kittens. My aunt would tell them to let me sleep, but they never had the patience to lie still until I awoke. They used every means to get me to sit up, and when I finally opened my eyes, they broke out in merry laughter, covering themselves with the heavy featherbed. I'd pull them out, one by one, by the hair, by a plump, bare foot, or even by an ear. Now they stood before me, petrified, and the more I began to recognize in them traces of their girlish selves, the tighter grew the constriction in my throat. One of the daughters suffered from goiter, and her eyes were glazed over. A second had lost almost all her teeth, and her bottom half was three times as wide as the top half. The third daughter, the youngest, actually had the oldest, most sorrowful-looking face of all. Two young men emerged from a side room. One, with a sullen, conspiratorial face, was introduced to me as the husband of the eldest. He took off immediately. He was an unemployed baker and was hurrying to a union meeting. The other young man was my aunt's son, born two years after my departure. Only eighteen, he already had a shiny, bald head and the features of a worried businessman.

In the kitchen I changed into fresh clothing and washed up at the rusty pump. Meat, crawling with maggots, was soaking on a window sill. It was twenty years since I had seen such creatures, and now they gave me the same fright as when I was a boy and they would nip at my toes when I stepped on them barefoot. They were creepier and slower moving than New York cockroaches. The floor, the walls, and the ceiling were the same dingy black. My aunt had never been known to keep a neat house, but now the gloom stemmed from poverty, not sloppy housekeeping. The difference was obvious. Poverty wasn't merely black but muddy black, the earthy color of things about to crumble.

When I returned from the kitchen, my uncle was already seated, sipping a glass of hot tea. He had once boasted the thick, black beard of a corpulent government functionary. Now that beard was gray and wispy, not so much unkempt as thinned. He extended an aged hand. There was no sign of the onetime vigorous meat dealer, whose face was always so ruddy that he seemed on the verge of apoplexy from an overabundance of good health. I could barely recognize him, apart from his nasal speech and the bitter smile that had always played around his moist eyes, with the warning: "You can't put anything over on me." "Let's eat something, he must be faint from hunger," my uncle said, uncertain as to whether it was permissible to address me with the familiar, singular "you." My hunger notwithstanding, I sipped my tea warily, thinking of the crawling creatures and the black stain of poverty.

A man, six feet tall, possibly a bit over, with a large head and a stomach like a kettle drum, bursting its way through the widest of trousers, entered the room. He came right over to me and stuck out a broad hand. "Welcome, welcome!" he said, and then sought confirmation from my aunt, "Mother-in-law, is this him?" My aunt hastily explained to me that this was her "Garden of Eden," her middle daughter's husband. I was truly grateful to him for bringing a change of atmosphere into the house. His brimming vitality and protruding stomach swept away all the oppressiveness. "Why is everyone so quiet, like in a house of mourning?" he demanded. "Please! A person's just arrived in Poland and already you're serving him warmed-over troubles. Are you afraid that he might miss out on something?" His huge belly bespoke great energy. I had never before seen such mercurial bulk. He darted from one place to another as lightly as a dancer. "Mother-in-law," he said, "why such a sour face? Don't you love me to pieces?" He kissed his mother-in-law, then his wife, and in the same breath invited me to his house for lunch. He then dashed out like a whirlwind to shop for provisions and make preparations.

After he and his wife left, my aunt told me his whole "history." He came from a rich family that never accepted the match. "He's a boor," said my aunt, "but the boorishness is his own creation. They tried stuffing him with learning. What didn't they push down his throat? Lessons after lessons, violin lessons, dancing lessons, gold and silver with diamonds, but he never wanted to stand out. In the first place, he fell head over heels in love with my daughter and took her just as her mother had her. They chased him with dowries of twenty thousand dollars the way a groschen chases a bagel. He has a golden trade, he's a dental technician, but he hates working. He's already spent six, seven years in Uruguay. He came back last year and now he's packing to leave again. He'd be a wonderful person, but he loves to eat and drink and —the less said the better—he even has an eye for other women. He wants everything. He has big eyes, a big stomach, and Gentile tastes, but go reason with him! He's a bit crazy, but when he starts talking, he's worth listening to."

When I later sat at his table, I was given every attention. We drank clear Polish vodka, and he tried to push more and more food on me. "Why do you eat like a bird?" he teased, immediately lapsing into the familiar form of address. "Strength comes from the pot. You'll need a lot of strength if you're going home to a sick mother." The more he ate and drank, the more talkative he became. "As I live and breathe," he said, "I grow wiser from day to day. That's because I've discovered that it's better to be a bit of a fool. Once I was a complicated young man, with problems by the bushel. I was always sick. Those were the days when I loved nothing but chamber music, you know, intimate, quiet music. And, Dostoyevsky, son of a gun!" He tossed off another drink. "I tried dieting," he continued, "but the more I dieted, the bigger my stomach became. I saw that the whole thing was a matter of vanity. Then I thought, what's so bad about opera? A little Verdi, Bizet, Halévy? And when I started going backward from chamber music to opera, it occurred to me that even opera is too grand for a simple fellow like me, so I kept going backward to popular songs. A touching Yiddish folk song suits me just fine. And when I ended up with folk songs, that was when I first began to feel satisfied, the way you do when you eat a good sour pickle, or some juicy sauerkraut. My heart was always drawn to folk songs, but there I was, dabbling with highfalutin chamber music."

The way he stuffed himself, you didn't see the likes of even in the most authentic Romanian restaurants on Allen Street. It was like attending a concert to watch the virtuosity and infectious joy with which he ate. Even his wife, who sat at the table with us, appeared happier than before. She seemed younger and her stony-frightened eyes now looked at me warmly.

"Chamber music," he wound up, "is sickliness, a refined disease, while folk song is eating, drinking, life. You have no idea what life is, hardly anyone does! The world babbles on about heroism, but heroism, in the last analysis, means death, it teaches you to love death. If I knew that I was about to drop dead, I'd lie down on the floor and scream and holler loud enough to join heaven and earth. Why should I play the hero? They can all go to hell! A man's going to leave the world one day. That's no small thing! Me, I'm afraid of death, and I'd scream like crazy, because a life's being cut off, a belly, a mouth, eyes are shutting down forever. They can all go to hell with their heroism!"

He saw me to the station and put me on the train for Lublin. He fell upon me with his massive head and kissed me goodbye, still carrying on about folk songs and living life to the hilt. "Swallow big chunks of life. Eat, drink, as much as you can, and be less of a hero," he said. "It was heroism that led to Hitlerism." He got as close to me as his paunch would allow and whispered a secret into my ear, "If you live in Poland and see all those sad Jewish faces, you lose your appetite for life. That's why I'm going back to Montevideo as soon as I can. South Americans still know something about living, and they let you live. 'Live and let live,' as the saying goes. So what if it's a cliché? Life is everything!" He squeezed my hand, jumped off the already moving train, and ran a short way after it, stomach preceding him, energetically waving a handkerchief.

6

A young man of about twenty-three or -four joined me in my empty compartment. He gave me a nod and sat down across from me by the window, which kept framing a series of moving pictures, glimpses of forest, fields, streams, and a smooth, pale-blue summer sky that offered immediate assurance of a full rainless day with no thunder or lightning. The slender young man smiled warmly, even before opening his mouth to speak. I apologized for my rusty Polish, explaining that this was the first time in twenty years that I'd had an opportunity to dust off a Polish word.

"Where are you from? Are you a stranger?"

"Not a stranger—estranged. I've come all the way from New York."

"In that case, you must put on these headphones and let our music be the first to welcome you."

He pointed to the radio headphones, and I did as he asked and stuck them into my ears. The train sped along as my ears crackled with the squawks of popular cabaret songs. Nevertheless, I was grateful for the young man's offer. The cheap Polish tunes, and their even cheaper lyrics, had their own peculiar charm and were as singular in their way as the fields and the woods rushing by. "Magnificent," I said. "The musical version of the native flora and fauna."

"That's exactly it," he beamed. "Our poverty, our joy, our sadness— our very own." He wiped his glasses and looked at me with misty, brown eyes. Without the glasses his eyes seemed somewhat harsh, but now they were smiling. Twenty years before I had seen few such young Polish faces. The Europeanized countenance across from mine was a long way from those flaxen-haired peasant boys, with their calf's eyes and pimply cheeks. The cultivated face opposite mine had grown up in, and had been nurtured by, the atmosphere of an independent land. I said this to him as delicately as I could, not omitting the detail of the peasant boys of yore. I said I was as grateful for the way he looked as I was for the musical welcome on his radio; this was something different and new. He wrinkled his forehead in apparent distress. This young man, I thought to myself, practically carried a Jewish hump on his back; we Jews were burdened by our landlessness and he, by the weight of a new land, a young polity afflicted with measles and other childhood diseases. "We're working hard to raise Poland's prestige in the world," he said, again removing his glasses and wiping them, but this time to avoid my gaze. "You're a Jew?" he asked. He used the pejorative *zhid,* but the word came out softly, without the usual snarl. "There are others among us who would drag down Poland's beautiful traditions into the ground," he said, "but they're like a fungus. We'll get rid of it." He gave me his hand, as though making a holy vow to himself. We understood one another and spoke no more of the matter.

He was an engineer, working for the government. For a while he had worked in Warsaw but was now being transferred to another city, closer to home. He said almost nothing more about himself. Instead, he bombarded me with questions about America, President Roosevelt, and my journey home after twenty years. He was also on his way home, but what a difference in our respective homecomings! As opposed to my twenty years, he had last seen his parents only a half-year before. "Twenty years!" the young man couldn't stop exclaiming. "I should shut my mouth and let you concentrate on your sacred mission. Imagine being away twenty years from your own flesh and blood, and now you've come back. What a remarkable drama!" I urged him not to stop, to go on talking.

For my part, I told him how alone I felt, going home after eight, nine days of travel over sea and land—alone and abandoned. Along the way, I had engaged with all kinds of people, and now all had vanished, I would never see them again, not even in another twenty years. There would be no reunions. "That's all well and good for traveling salesmen," I said, "who live for the moment, grab hold of it without qualms, who don't put down roots anywhere." I told him that I had met a host of fine people en route and became absorbed in their revelations. Nothing had actually happened in all that time but for their talk, and their talk was more interesting than any adventure. It was interesting even when I didn't really hear it, when life in the form of words buzzed around me, and afterward I could retreat into my own personal archive of afterthoughts. It's the dialogue, not the action, that makes the play —the turn of phrase, voice, facial expression. It may be my fault for being so self-centered, but it often seemed as if the people I met were escorting me home, and now they have abandoned me and left me to complete the journey on my own.

My young Pole was silent for a moment, which gave me opportunity to recall at least some of the faces that had crossed my path. "Yes," he said after some reflection, "everyone has his own measure of loneliness, but some lonely people manage to seem surrounded by a full jazz ensemble and others don't. Wouldn't it be strange, though"—here he threw me a smile—"if you showed up after twenty years, accompanied by the whole musical group you met on the way? Anyhow, each one of us must walk alone on his own via dolorosa." His mother, he added, wouldn't be able to hold out if he didn't get to see her at least twice a year. He was her only surviving child of the six she had borne. Two died before he was born and three afterward. "Children are the biggest uncertainty of all in the small Polish towns. Until they're ten or twelve, you can't even count them as certain members of the family."

"I also have three dead brothers," I said. "Two died before I was born. The third, my little brother, was three or four when he died. I was there when he closed his eyes." I turned my head to the window and began trudging—alone as my companion had rightly observed—down my personal via dolorosa, remembering Hertske, the little brother who had brought death into our house and how my father and a few other men had stood over his crib as his soul departed his body, my father crying out with all his might, "Hear, O Israel, the Lord our God, the Lord is One." Hertske's eyes were glazed, and my father escorted little Hertske's departing soul with his wailing prayer until the crib fell still.

It was already late at night. We had all gone to bed, only my father had stayed up, standing watch over the crib. Hertske hadn't left us yet. Each time I woke up, as if from a fever, I heard my father mumbling Psalms and sobbing quietly, so as not to awaken the household. In the early morning, I woke up to the sound of full-voiced lamentation. This was my mother, sitting over the covered crib, weeping profusely, as she did when reading aloud from her women's Bible. The words were archaic, not of the kind used in everyday speech, but taken from the sacred literature, specially compiled for women. Her patient Jewish piety had snapped, she was complaining to God, hurling accusations. I wandered around the house in pain. Everything hurt, even breathing was painful. I held my breath for as long as I could, and when I couldn't any longer, I let it out with a gasp. I begged my mother at least to let me kiss my little brother's golden head, but she said, in a crushed voice, that this was against Jewish law. However, to please me, she removed the covers. "Look, my child," she said to me, "see what's become of his angelic little face." I was overcome with grief. My mother kept hurling her accusations at God, her face turned up to the ceiling, demanding justice. "Can it be right," she moaned, "that such a young, beautiful, heaven-sent gift of joy should be cut down and laid in the grave?"

There was no reply from the ceiling. I felt that Mother hadn't sufficiently shaken the Throne of Glory and, remembering that two of my brothers had already died before I came into the world, I jumped to her assistance and reminded her that she had an even stronger reason to be angry with God. "Mother," I said, "a Jew is commanded to tithe, to offer up a tenth of his wealth to God, but God has already taken a lot more from you than a tenth. Is that just?" I thought that this was an impressive formulation and was convinced that it couldn't be ignored or dismissed with a gesture. Mother immediately grasped the validity of my charge and began to lament anew, "O Master of the Universe, a Jew is commanded to offer up a tenth of his wealth, and You have already taken a lot more than a tenth from me. Is that just?" I calmed down some, pleased with the fact that my mother, a grown-up, had seen fit to cite my point in her quarrel with God. I believed that we had bested Him and that Mother, Hertske, and I had won out. Our argument was incontrovertible. There could be no justification for the event that had occurred. God Himself must now be ashamed—a pity the damage had already been done. The waxen doll lying lifeless in its crib would never be live Hertske again. But the more Mother, parroting my words, railed at the whitewashed ceiling, the calmer I became. Our side had won and somewhere above, there was consternation, because the Heavenly Judge had no proper answer.

Shortly thereafter, a man showed up at the door, blind in one eye and with a halting walk. He carried a small casket, tied with a strap. He moved sideways, as though stealing in. Mother gave a start. The man stood helplessly by, appealing—man to man, as it were—to my father, who, wailing, brought him into the house.

I begged my companion's pardon for having wandered off in a trance for so long. "My mother is very sick," I told him, as the thought suddenly struck me: Who knows? She may no longer be alive. The fields rushing by looked parched from the burning sun. An old dog barked at the train. A small, sad-faced boy waved his hat. A thick patch of woods caught a glint of the sun, shattering the light into a thousand pieces and gilding the trees.

My companion perked up when I told him that at some point I was planning to visit the Soviet Union. "The Soviet Union?" he exclaimed, giving me a dark look. He removed his glasses, wiped them with his handkerchief, and stared at me intently. "What regards," I asked, "in the name of an intelligent, young Pole, shall I convey to the Soviet Union?"

He continued wiping his glasses. He spoke in measured words, but with oratorical fervor: "In the name of a substantial part of the Polish youth, tell them that we follow all that is happening in the Soviet Union with great curiosity. More than that I cannot say. Just be sure to emphasize that we are exceedingly curious, so curious that they have a moral obligation not to disappoint us. They must take care not to commit errors that would harm us and derail our progress. As a state bordering theirs, we'll feel the brunt of their mistakes more than the rest of the world, which is far away. We're right next door, a hand's breadth away."

Suddenly, he took out his pocket watch and his face brightened. "You have only a half hour left to go, exactly thirty-two minutes, even less," he declared, becoming increasingly excited over my imminent arrival home. "After twenty years," he said, holding out his watch, "it's now exactly thirty-one minutes to the fateful moment." He kept looking out the window with growing restlessness, all the while consulting his watch, counting off the minutes. As his excitement mounted, an image took shape in my mind, of the convict in that Chekhov tale, with the wild hair and full-grown beard. Or it may have come from some piece of Chekhov reportage, or even a legend told about Chekhov. It seemed as if we were reenacting the prisoner's story—me with my flushed face pressed against the cold window and the young Pole staring at his watch.

The convict had just been released after ten years in Siberia and was on his way home to his mother and father. The account of his long, arduous journey, buried deep in a newspaper, so captured Chekhov's imagination that he couldn't get it out of his head. He followed the convict's entire progress from city to city, studying maps and railroad timetables, until he had pinpointed the exact minute when the convict would step off the train and fall on his parents' necks. On the day that the convict was due to arrive, Chekhov was beside himself with impatient joy. He kept taking out his pocket watch . . . only four hours left . . . two hours . . . one hour . . . half an hour . . . minutes. In this way Chekhov lived through the entire drama of the convict's passage to freedom.

"Sir, you have only two or three minutes left, if that," my timekeeper announced.

The train's whistle let out a few sonorous blasts. Coming into view were, first, factory chimneys, then some isolated cottages surrounded by foliage. It was almost evening and the trim, modest dwellings reflected a sun now spent of its heat. The young Pole stood next to me in the corridor and rested a hand on my shoulder, as if seeking to lighten the gravity of the moment. There were tears in his eyes. The train began to puff more slowly. In unison with the conductor, the young Pole joyously sang out: "Lu-u-blin!"

BOOK TWO

Homecoming at Twilight

1

"Even from the gutter will I sing praises to Thee, my Lord, even from
the gutter." Supper was nearly over. A number of guests had already
left the dining room. Those who were lingering on at their tables
picked their teeth and nursed their glasses of tea. At one of the tables
every seat was still occupied. A man in a skullcap sat at the head of it.
The seven or eight other men at that table were silently listening to
him, occasionally dipping a spoon into their stewed fruit without looking at it, slowly sucking and rolling the prune pits on their tongues. It
was not the food they enjoyed, but the presence of the man in the skullcap. Never for a moment did they take their eyes off him.

"Come here. Give us your opinion." The man who was speaking
caught the arm of the proprietor, who was just going by. The latter was
very thin and nervous, and seemed always to be sniffing at something
with his long nose. He kept a sharp eye on the room, watching the
faces of his guests for the least sign of displeasure. To follow him darting about the dining room was positively dizzying. To all he would repeat as though it were a proverb: "You pay the bill; my job is to satisfy
you. That's only fair."

"Come here, Mr. Buchlerner, and give us your opinion," the man in
the skullcap repeated. "You have an intelligent-sounding name. My

friends here say I can't have another drink. They maintain I'll be drunk. Do you know what I say to that?"

The proprietor stood politely by the table, turning his head—or rather his nose—to keep tabs on the other guests in case they might require attention. He did not like to be pinned down, but the man in the skullcap was a guest, and a prominent one at that.

"Do you know what I say to that? I say that even if I did get drunk and fell in the gutter—a respectable man, with beard and skullcap—that even from the gutter I would sing praises unto Thee, my Lord, even from the gutter!"

"That's very well put, sir," Buchlerner said, nodding approval. He had just ascertained that everything was all right in the dining room. His nose stopped turning, and he gave his attention to the table. "That's very well put. A little drink can't do any harm. My grandfather, may his soul rest in peace, took a drink before his meals, drank with his meals, and after his meals. But you mustn't think he ever got drunk, God forbid. Not at all—just a bit—tipsy."

"That settles it. Let's you and I have a drink!" The man at the head of the table filled a glass and handed it over to the proprietor. Then he filled another for himself, and was about to speak when he saw that the proprietor had already drained his glass.

"Heaven bless you—you don't drink like a Jew, you drink like your grandfather!"

Buchlerner was embarrassed. He stood there with his empty glass and everyone at the table was laughing.

"No, no—we mustn't drink like that, without a toast. That's Esau's way," the man in the skullcap said jovially. He took the proprietor's glass, filled it to the brim, and handed it back to him. Buchlerner stood there helpless, since the slightest move would spill some of the drink. The man in the skullcap spoke: "The trouble with us Jews is that we do not love the Lord of the universe enough." He raised his glass very high, as if toasting someone above them. "To be sure we fear Him, we tremble with awe on Yom Kippur. But why don't we love Him every day of the year? We ought to long for Him with every fiber in our bodies, yes, love Him really, with all our hearts." Now he sniffed at the glass as if it were a snuff box, and took a tiny sip. Buchlerner, too, had raised his glass, higher than if he had been saying the *Havdalah,* but he hesitated to down it.

"All right, so I'm going to get drunk. But even from the gutter I will sing praises unto Thee, my Lord, even from the gutter."

He straightened his skullcap and began to hum quietly to himself. It was impossible at first to tell the tune, until all of a sudden it emerged, melting in its sweetness. It was a haunting melody, one to carry you away. The others at the table joined in one by one. Buchlerner's timidity was overcome. He took a sip of his drink and joined in the singing.

The song took hold of them one after the other, until it seemed to possess a momentum of its own. Only now, when they were entranced, heads aslant, eyes half-closed, did the man in the skullcap say, "To your health, my friends, to your health!" And he drained his glass.

As the singing began to die down, and the singers came out of their trance, a young man of twenty-eight or twenty-nine got up from his seat at another table and started over to them, walking with stiff, military bearing. At the same moment, a tall, sturdily built man rose at a neighboring table. He watched the young man, waiting to see what he would do. After a few resolute steps, the young man suddenly stopped, turned around and went back to his table, but did not sit down.

"Mr. Bronski!" the tall man called. But the other pretended not to hear.

Bronski bowed solemnly, standing by the table where he had been sitting alone. Then he walked back to the table where the singing had just stopped and addressed one of the group in elegant Polish. "In ancient Egypt the mummies used to make a terrible racket," he said. "The only way to calm them down was to show great kindness, unusual friendliness."

The man whom Bronski had addressed frowned, as though the words caused him intense pain. Bronski stood, waiting for a reply. His face was oddly flushed, as though with momentary embarrassment. But the flush did not go away. He had large blue eyes, but they were veiled like blue glass covered with a mist, like a sky overcast with clouds. He seemed to be looking straight at the man he had addressed, but actually his line of vision went slightly past him.

The man at the table felt ill at ease. He squirmed in his chair. His companions seemed somewhat puzzled. The man in the skullcap picked at crumbs on the table, conveying them to his mouth.

The tall man who had been watching Bronski now came up to the group. He took hold of Bronski's arm. Very firmly he turned him around to lead him out of the dining room.

"All right, I'm coming," Bronski said. He meekly let himself be guided.

"That's a real tragedy, a tragic tragedy." Buchlerner was the first to speak. He spoke at all only to relieve the embarrassment of his guests. Addressing the man to whom Bronski had spoken, and who was obviously uncomfortable, he added: "Such a pity. He is a wealthy man, but it would have been better for him if he had never been born." He raised his voice so that everyone in the room could still hear him, but he was only reassuring new guests who had been subjected to a scene. "His sister is staying here, too, and that big man never leaves him for a minute, though he wouldn't hurt a fly."

"Still, you can never be sure about a lunatic," said the man to whom Bronski had spoken. He had recovered his composure now. "They can be gentle as a lamb one minute, and then take a bite out of you the next."

"Oh, he won't do any biting, never fear. I wouldn't let him stay here for a minute if he were dangerous." The proprietor was very convincing: he was not going to lose a customer. "He has been here for six weeks, and, thank God, no one has been bitten yet."

But the other was not so easily appeased. "We were in higher regions, and then he has come barging in with his crazy talk about Egypt. Why did he have to pick on me? Lunatics shouldn't be allowed in the community, any more than the dead. When the light of reason goes out, a man is dead."

"And what about charity? Is that dead, too?" Buchlerner retorted. "If a man loses his mind, should we shoot him down like a mad dog?"

"Who said anything about shooting? I was just thinking aloud. What I mean is that it's a terrible thing. A bright light has gone out of the world."

The man in the skullcap had tried several times to get up without being noticed, but he always sat down again, aware that he was not too steady on his feet. He kept humming a little tune, although by now half his companions had left the table.

"How about it, Mr. Steinman?" said one of the group who realized that he needed help. "Shall we go now?"

"Aren't you being a bit impertinent? You're hinting that I can't walk under my own power. Well, I'll show you." He got up suddenly, stood still for a moment, and then walked to the door.

"What a man! He is truly remarkable!" said the last guest at the table. "No, Mr. Buchlerner, you don't often meet men like that. He isn't one of your invalids."

The proprietor looked off into the distance, his nose distinctly in the air. After a few moments, when he felt he had made the right impression, he put as much distaste in his voice as he dared without actually offending a guest.

"You're very much mistaken, sir," he said, "if you think this is a hotel for invalids only. I want you to know that this is a place for healthy people, for anyone looking for rest and relaxation."

The other was not to be challenged. "I have the impression that nearly all the guests in this resort are sick. I'd say nine out of ten are sick."

"That is a dreadful exaggeration. People who are a bit on edge, a bit tired, come here for a rest, and the fact is, the air here is really invigorating." Buchlerner shot out his arm in the air, closed his hand as though catching a fly. A moment later, opening his fist, he extended a bony hand as though presenting some precious stone. "Can't you feel the fresh air? I'm sure you do—after all, you're from the city. What we have here is not just ordinary air, like anywhere else. Not on your life! You have to come here to breathe air like this. Just drink it in—it's like champagne! It's not just refreshing—it revives the dead."

The two girls clearing the table were the proprietor's daughters. They moved as silently and efficiently as when they served dinner. Buchlerner occasionally said something to them, but they never as much as looked at him, and it was impossible to say whether they were following orders or ignoring him. They did not even speak to each other.

A young Gentile girl came in to help them. She was tall and slender in her bare feet, and a smile flickered in her eyes. It was difficult to guess what the smile said. There was mockery in it, arrogance, and provocation, plus a good deal of peasant shrewdness. Her feet were dirty, and though she wore no shoes, when she moved the house shook. Glasses on the tables danced, but she moved around all the more vigorously, as though enjoying the stir she created.

When I went out, I found that there was indeed a little breeze. While far from champagne, as Mr. Buchlerner had claimed, it was refreshing. Guests peacefully digesting their supper sat on a large porch that ran around the building. They had moved from the table to the porch, apparently too lazy even to walk down the few steps from the porch to the small strip of lawn. The narrow walk from the hotel to the street was lined with recently planted trees. Even that was occupied by rocking chairs—very much in action, as though agitated by the same breeze. Many of the men and women on the chairs were corpulent, and it was something of a surprise to see them rocking so delicately. A low trellised gate served as entrance to the three-story hotel from the street.

Steinman, the man who had been at the head of the table, was pacing back and forth on the porch, followed by several women. He had taken off his skullcap. His thick gray hair was mussed, but as he walked, the breeze blew it back into place. He held his head proudly, setting off his well-groomed silvery beard. His coat was thrown over his shoulder like a cape, and he carried a stick. With the women following him, he looked like a sultan. When he spoke everyone in the hotel could hear him.

"Father is letting himself go," said a stout middle-aged woman with a sad face.

The woman next to her rocked a little faster. "He is a handsome man," she said. "It's a pleasure to look at him."

"All in all he's not too healthy. He has kidney trouble, and rheumatism, too," Steinman's daughter said.

The other woman stopped rocking for a moment. "Is that so? You're supposed to be able to tell from the way they look, but he looks perfectly fine."

"He's a sick man. I have to look after him, and see that he gets his sleep. Let me tell you, I have my hands full at night, when my own back is aching too. He has to take his pills and he never wants to go to bed. If he had his own way, he'd be on his feet forty-eight hours a day."

"Oh my, he is a handsome man," the other went on. "Old people should always look like that," she added wistfully.

"Papa!" Steinman's daughter called.

"At me to go to bed already?"

"Not yet, Papa, but soon." Then, turning to her acquaintance: "He took one drink too many tonight, and he'll pay for it, too. The trouble with him is that he gives everyone else sunshine, while I get the clouds and the rain." She spoke as though to herself, with a note of reproach.

Steinman stopped in front of his daughter and raised his stick as if to strike her. "I'll use this on you, if you try to send me to bed with the chickens again. Tonight I mean to go to the park, listen to the music, and look at the pretty girls. Do you want me to spend my time with these old women?"

"That's not very chivalrous, Mr. Steinman," said the youngest female present, coquettishly.

"Papa, what's the matter with you? What are you celebrating?"

"Today's a holiday, didn't you know? Sabbath is only two days away: just think—only two days away, our 'lovely Queen.'" He turned to me. "Let's go, young man. My name is Steinman. What's yours? I think I saw you arrive about lunch time, didn't I?" He took my arm and suggested a stroll in the park, only a short walk from the hotel.

"Don't forget, Papa, I'm right here. You're not on the loose for long."

"I'll turn you over on my knee and spank you, if you try to keep your old father from talking to another person." Again, he threatened his middle-aged daughter with his stick, and then leaned down and kissed her.

He readjusted his overcoat, putting one arm into the sleeve, and wrapped the rest of it around him. His free right arm now looked younger, and the stick was given a rakish twirl. As he walked along, with me in tow, he turned his head to speak to his daughter, who was trailing us. "Let me have half an hour, Frania dear, just half an hour. Don't shadow me, like a detective."

2

People were streaming toward the park from every direction. They walked with controlled impatience, as though restrained by propriety from actually running. They were just able to keep from bumping into each other.

Past the gate, where the guard inspected us casually, we were enveloped by the wholesome smell of the thick foliage lining both sides of the paths. Most people kept to the dusty main avenue. The last colors of sunset were beginning to blur and fade away. The water in the little lake around which the main promenade divided was blue black.

From a bandstand partly hidden by the trees came the brassy music of a small but vigorous group of musicians. A card with a large number five was posted on the bandstand, indicating that the orchestra had reached that piece on the program. It was *L'Arlésienne*, and it was almost over. The newcomers, as they closed in, seemed to fall in step with the music. Even had one been obsessed with one's private thoughts, the music must surely have penetrated them. And when the music stopped, everything slipped from memory—the thoughts with the music.

People were wandering around the little lake and all over the park. Even on the other side of the lake you could hear the band. From over there the music served as a bridge, a guarantee that you were not striking out on your own, but still at one with the community.

Just opposite the leafy bandstand was a wooden structure built out of logs, but not exactly a log cabin. You went up a few steps and found yourself on a shaky floor, only a scaffolding, really, where people sat in pairs or alone, doubtless dreaming the same musical dreams—dreams that a single note of the trumpet dispels or a drumbeat frightens away. This was the outdoor café. Just to walk past was to taste the cookies. Couples sat at tables looking into each other's eyes. Around the little lake, more like a pond, were elaborate flower beds, severely patterned with respect to both color and shape. Little clumps of flowers sprung up every few steps as you walked, but they had begun to lose their vivid reds, yellows, and greens. In the twilight all colors were blending into a common color, a dormant, latent color. The flowers now looked like wildflowers, there was dew on them, and they were losing their sharp, shrill, carefully cultivated individualities. The surface of the water was settling to a jelly—a thin film over a dense darkness.

The band was playing the "Blue Danube" waltz. The electric lights in the trees were turned on, and the whole area was drenched with a brightness that made the side paths look darker still. As the waltz played on, it more than ever seemed that those who walked around were dancing. And indeed, in the café couples actually got up to dance, leaving only a few solitary drinkers at the tables. It was the end of August, and these melancholy men were probably the first to become aware, in the midst of summer pleasures, that winter was on the way.

"If I were Rothschild, do you know what I'd do?" my companion said, interrupting my private train of thought. "I'd arrange for the entire Jewish people to spend a month or two in this atmosphere. This is just what our people needs to restore its shattered nerves."

We had taken one of the side paths and come to a little bridge. Under it couples were scooping up water in tin cups and drinking.

"This is the Fountain of Love," Steinman said. "I tried the water, too, but it gave me a stomachache. I am too old, I guess; it seems to agree with the young people."

A smallish man wearing a rabbi's velvet hat came up. "Good evening, Mr. Steinman," he said.

"Good evening. How are you?"

"All goes well with me, praise the Lord. How are things in the higher spheres?"

"So-so. And there you have it in a nutshell."

The other walked away perfectly happy, as though this reply had solved all problems for him.

He was followed by a slightly taller man, also in a rabbi's hat, which, however, shone less in the artificial light. It was rather battered, in fact. A little boy the man was leading by the hand was squirming to get away from him.

"No, you don't, Zalman," the man said with feeling. "Have you forgotten what happened yesterday when you ran away and got lost?"

The boy still struggled to get free. In a hoarse voice like that of a grown-up he protested: "So what? Nothing happened, did it? Wild animals didn't tear me to pieces." He shook his head vigorously, revealing long earlocks. His little velvet cap slipped, and we could see that there was no danger he would ever go bareheaded. Under the velvet cap he was wearing a skullcap. He could have been no more than six or seven, but his face looked much older.

At some distance beyond them was another wearer of a rabbi's hat. It was hard to say how old this stroller was—he might have been seventeen, but he might also have been no more than thirteen. He was alone, and his feet were encased in white socks and patent-leather low-cut shoes. From the absorbed way he walked, you could suppose he was performing a rite, an Old Testament patriarch.

Two young women, both a little taller than average, were on the path behind him. They had shawls around their shoulders—one red, the other green. They were talking in low voices, almost whispering. Now and then one of the two craned her neck to see whether the little boy had managed to get free. "Zalman dear!" she called after him. She was quite some way behind the little boy, but from her voice it was clear that she was someone near and dear.

Behind the two women came a group of ten or twelve men, all with beards, red, black, and gray. They walked in no particular order, strung out across the whole width of the promenade, and talked in loud voices. When they had caught up to us, they seemed momentarily taken shy, and everyone of them said "Good evening, Mr. Steinman," in a very respectful voice, rather as though chanting, turning their heads toward my companion who now stood leaning the whole weight of his body on his stick.

"Did you notice them?" Steinman said after the little troop had passed. "I know the whole history of that family, better than they do themselves. I could tell you stories about their grandfathers and great-grandfathers, all the way back to Ba'al Shem, stories to make their hair stand on end. They don't begin to suspect." After a pause, he added in a mocking tone: "We're lucky the young prince didn't see us. He's a terrible bore. He likes to argue and we'd never have gotten rid of him. How about sitting down for a bit?"

He led me to a bench that stood wholly in shadow under a big tree, some way from the promenade. I reminded him that his daughter had said he must be back early. He sat down unhurriedly, made himself comfortable, and spread his coat around him like a blanket.

"Oh, I don't pay any attention to her," he said. "She doesn't run my life. I've been here for three weeks, and I'm fed up with being pushed around. I've done everything you can think of—I've taken salt baths, mud baths, sulfur baths; I've drunk waters that tasted like deadly poison; I've gone to bed with the chickens. Once in a while a man has to celebrate." He leaned over, as though to impart a secret. "The fact is, I overindulged a bit at supper tonight. When I have one drink too many, I feel it at once in my feet. My head is clear, but my feet are as though paralyzed."

"Everybody here seems to know you," I said.

"It's high time they should know me," he replied. There was a note of pride in his voice, although he did his best to conceal it. "This is the seventh year I've come to this resort for treatment of hardening of the arteries."

He went on in great detail about how "arteriosclerosis" actually has two meanings. In the medical sense, the term indicates that the arteries are calcified, that the pipes are getting rusty. But in this resort, he said, the word is used in a different sense, to signify a hardening of the brain. The people who first came here did actually suffer from hardening of the arteries, but gradually the news got around that the place was good for the nerves, and real mental cases began to come. Only the quiet kind, of course, not the violent ones. Thus here you find people in full possession of their faculties alongside madmen: kind of a microcosm of life. You never know whether you're talking to a mental case, and everyone looks at you suspiciously, too. It drives you to drink. "As for the lot that just went by, I know a bit about them," he concluded, waiting for me to ask him for details.

"Relations?"

"No," he said, waving his hand. "I come from Jews of a different kind, Jews who earned their living by the sweat of their brows. There were some great scholars in my family, but still they worked hard for a living. I am a writer myself. I write Hasidic stories for newspapers. Only in that sense are we a bit related. There was a time when there were Jews of a different mettle, really great men who truly saw themselves as the Lord's representatives on earth, and, no mistake about it, they were real prophets. They knew all the tricks of the Almighty, and He knew theirs. For years on end they wouldn't be on speaking terms with God—nothing personal, you understand, the argument was about the people of Israel. They would make up with Him on the Sabbath and on holidays. At those times, the Jews would forget all the troublesome things and make their peace with the Lord. Do you follow me? I have a Hasidic soul myself, I am a hundred percent Hasid. But there is no saintly rabbi for me to make my pilgrimage to."

He proceeded to tell me about the rabbi's family we had just seen. "The old man travels about from city to city and village to village. He works hard. He is the sole support of the entire family; none of the others lifts a finger. The old man was a fine Jew, but when you have to support such a big crowd, bless them, you have no time to pray for yourself, you're kept too busy praying for others. A man like that has no time to look at a book. He told me once that if it weren't for the dignity of his ancestors, he would feel that he was an out-and-out fraud. For what is he himself? What has he got to sell? Has he the time to take stock of himself? To intercede with the Lord that the Jews may be more prosperous? Has he the authority to give orders to those on high? How long can he depend on his grandfather's favor with God? There is a limit to everything. You can't forever hide behind your grandfather's skirts.

"The old man used to tell me all this himself. The burden of earning a living weighs heavily on his shoulders. You should see how well his family lives—like kings. But recently he has become embittered, taciturn. When I run into him, I can see that he is dying to pour his heart out to me, but he just shrugs his shoulders as though to say, 'What's it matter? My days are numbered anyway.'

"Did you notice the one who walked ahead of the others, with the elegant hat, the unkempt beard, and the rosy-red complexion? They brought him all the way from America. And he, too, is of noble descent. Did you see his wife? She was the one with the green shawl. A real beauty, though that's not her own hair—she wears a wig. She is pregnant at the moment—you see how much gossip I know?

"Shall I tell you what went on when the pampered young man came over from America? It's almost beyond my powers. It was arranged that the young people should meet in Vienna. The future bride came from Poland, her fiancé from America. They feasted their eyes on each other, and parted—she went back to Poland, and he to America. Did they like each other? That is beside the point—they had been betrothed long before this. A year later they were reunited in Poland, and the wedding was celebrated. I'll be brief, but you must have read about it in all the newspapers. Fifteen thousand Hasidim carried on for days on end in an outdoor celebration. They were lodged like gypsies in tents, there were theatrical performances every day, the masters of ceremony cracked jokes and made up funny poems. The men dressed up in women's clothes and wrapped kerchiefs around their beards. They rode horses, too—just like real Cossacks. This went on for all of two weeks. I myself attended the wedding—and, well, I've seen quite a lot, a lot of things during my lifetime, but I've never seen anything like that. There were about a thousand shnorrers—beggars—it was as though all the Jewish poor were holding a convention. The quarrels and brawls at their tables were indescribable. The waiters, the cooks, the helpers, the supervisors—you should have seen how hard they worked: they were really run ragged. And all the different orchestras, the magical violinists, the singers with their special accompanists, and the little boys whose voices hadn't changed yet, each of them with his own instrument and really God-given talent. Whole oxen were slaughtered, not to mention the chickens, the capons, the geese, and even the turkeys that were consumed. They ate and drank and danced—they danced until they dropped from exhaustion, and all this because it's a great merit before God, a sacred duty. They really did their best to observe this commandment at least—I wish I could say they were as careful about all the other 613 commandments.

"During all this, the old man wandered around looking like a ghost. He knew that he'd have to pay for it all in the end, that he was now getting another mouth to feed, and another household. None of his sons has achieved anything of the slightest importance. When one of them loses his position as rabbi in a small town, he doesn't hesitate a moment but moves back, lock, stock, and barrel, with wife and children, to his old father. More than once during the wedding celebration, the old man stopped near me and was just about to tell me what he was really thinking, but then he would sigh, make a resigned gesture, and walk away."

Suddenly we heard someone close to our park bench, panting hard. It was Steinman's daughter, out of breath. She had found us despite the dark. "You've played a trick on me, father. How could you do such a thing?"

"What's the matter? What happened?"

"I've been sending out search parties. I myself have been all over the park trying to find you. You should have been in bed two hours ago!" She dropped onto the bench, breathing heavily. "My own father is going to give me some serious condition—heart or lungs, or some other ailment. And it's all your fault," she said to me. "He behaves so long as he has no one to talk to. But the moment he makes a new acquaintance, there's no holding him."

"Frania dear," Steinman said, stroking his daughter's head. "You won't have to suffer much longer, you know—another fifty years at most."

3

"Cheep! cheep! cheep! Come, come, chickens, ducks, geese! Come and get it! Cheep! cheep!"

I opened my eyes and looked out the window. Everything was still, except for the Gentile girl of the night before who was calling the barnyard to breakfast. The little chicks, still unsteady on their feet, fought over every grain of corn. She teased them by throwing the grain as far as possible, but they were all over the yard, clucking angrily. I don't know what it was that had wakened me—the noise from the poultry yard or the quaint kind of Yiddish the hired maid spoke. She darted barefoot among the fowl, like some older sister of theirs. The pullets looked like children wearing shorts next to the fully feathered adults, but they were the most arrogant in their greediness, and no matter how much they got, they wanted more.

"Chickens! Ducks! Geese! Cheep, cheep!" The girl went on with her quaint accent, stressing the last syllable of every word. Then she noticed my head at the open window. Seeing my surprise, she proceeded to dazzle me by wishing me "a good awakening" in Yiddish, and before I could reply, she burst out laughing. Her big, slightly irregular teeth laughed more than her voice did. Then she went back to her chickens, now fluttering angrily around her, as though to reproach her for not giving them her full attention. As she nimbly threw bread crumbs to them, she sang:

There was a little shepherd
In the land of Canaan.
He sold sheep and cattle with horns,
Till he was a wealthy man . . .

She sang lustily, all the time eyeing me to observe my astonishment.

The morning was still damp with the freshness of dawn. The fowl kept running in and out of some sheds, next to which was a privy. You could see through its closed door where golden strips of light slanted, and big yellow and green flies getting in through the larger cracks, buzzing angrily a moment inside, and then coming out again. The buzzing was the only sound, apart from the servant's young voice.

The ducks stood around a big basin that held soaked bread. Buchlerner was already up and about, turning over the chairs which been piled upside down for the night.

"I see you've gotten up early your very first day here," he called, and stopped what he was doing for a moment. "Today, God willing, we're going to have really superb weather. Just look at it—a sight like this is a real treat. Look at that hill over there—it's not going to be too hot a sun today, just a nice, gentle, caressing sunshine."

On the hill he pointed to there was a little wood which, from where we stood, looked like a clump of five or six trees. It was a serene hill, and the sun was just crowning the few trees at the top with its first rays. The patch of sky immediately above glowed copper, but to left and right the sky dimmed gradually to a less brilliant light.

Buchlerner was still gazing at the rising sun. His features now looked shrunken like a mummy's. Nearly all his hair had disappeared. There was no highlight to give relief to a single feature—his face looked like some piece of fruit from which all the juice had been squeezed out. He was wearing a tattered shirt with sleeves cut short, linen trousers, and bedroom slippers.

"Since you got up with the birds, you should take a long walk to work up an appetite. You could make the tour of the village, or you might visit the hill over there. The climb will do you good. There's a little stream to cross, where people splash about all day, but there's a narrow board across it. I warn you, walk straight ahead, don't look back, because if you do, you may not turn into a pillar of salt, but you're sure to fall in. Well, nothing to worry about, the stream's very shallow, you'd only get your clothes wet. But you may not want all that exercise. After all, a hill is just for the pleasure of looking at it. Go to the park, and see what it looks like without the crowds. The grass is fresh, like in the Garden of Eden, and the flowers are beginning to open.

"I know, I know," he went on, "I've no call to give advice, don't pay any attention to me. If you've got young healthy legs, it can't hurt you to climb the hill. We really have a smaller hill, though, something between a walk and real climb. Not that it's very steep, you know—you won't even be winded. Just turn to the right when you're past the village. It's not very big, but there are historical associations. Poniatowski made a heroic stand on that hill. But why am I boring you with all this? Our shikse here knows more about it than I do."

"I've told you a thousand times, Mr. Buchlerner, that my name isn't shikse. My name is Andzia." Her Yiddish came out singsong, with a coquettish effect.

"Do you hear how well she speaks our language? Better than my daughters do—they're ashamed of speaking Yiddish, but she likes to speak nothing else, just for the heck of it. Unfortunately she is deaf—when you ask her to sit, she lies down. This *besulah*"—he used the Hebrew word for *maiden*—"is a native of the village."

"*Besulah, besulah*—phew, I hate such words!" the girl said with a grimace.

"Of course she hates to be a besulah. How long have you been fed up with being a besulah?" When he said this, I realized it was a standing joke between them, repeated for my benefit.

"Ah, Mr. Buchlerner, you're being naughty!" She shrugged her shoulders, and went back to her ducks and chickens.

In the village I passed a little shop out of which drifted odors of kerosene, herring, and tobacco. In the street, an old beggar had already taken his place, sitting against a tree. He scratched himself; and made the sign of the cross, while his old jaws chomped away. He would break off a small piece from a very dry larger piece of bread that lay in the lap of his tattered short overcoat. When he chewed, he made such dreadful faces that his poverty and blindness were much more affecting than normally. Each time he had softened up a piece of bread and swallowed it, he would open his mouth and yawn, as though to celebrate the achievement. When he yawned, you could see that he had not a single tooth left. After all this hard work, he would start to beg, holding out a palsied hand, but then he would change his mind and go back to another chomping session, tearing off another bit of dry bread from the piece in his lap.

The hill stood in the center of the village. I climbed up the narrow path that ran around it. From the top there was a view out over sparsely wooded orchards, among which a surprising number of summer cottages were hidden away.

I lay down on the grass. The sun was getting warmer by the minute, and I imagined that it was I who communicated my warmth to it.

4

I was conscious only of a hazy glow behind my closed eyelids, and I felt that everything around me was drenched in sunlight. This is the place, I thought, where I would rest up from my weeks in Poland before returning to the United States. For twenty years I had been looking forward to this visit, and now I lay there, my bones aching, half-asleep.

Now and then I could not resist the temptation to open my eyes. There was a tree on my right, from which hung a brass image of some saint. The saint had a long beard and a severe, anguished expression. I admired the marvelous workmanship of the icon; it would be easy, I thought, to steal it. But then the silly idea occurred to me that all the church bells would instantly begin to ring, alerted by some secret alarm, should I so much as touch it. It was foolish, but I was afraid even to touch the saint who was watching me with eyes that seemed very much alive. I noticed with pleasure that the old man was a true product of the New Testament. Although he was, in one sense, as much of a patriarch as Jacob, still he came out of another world entirely—perhaps he had been born a Jew but then had been baptized. I wondered what human hand had managed to suggest all this with a few lines on metal. The old saint looked down at me with shrewd eyes.

Looking back at him, I recalled that not so long ago I had been made to play a part in a real Old Testament drama. It had been an exhausting experience, and it was because of it that I was lying here as I was, longing for sleep, long days and nights of sleep.

The Old Testament drama had been set in the building which housed the offices of the Jewish community. On the walls hung portraits of the elders, men whom I had known as a child, but who were long since dead and buried. I had been formally summoned to appear —a messenger was dispatched to say that I, "the American son," was wanted at the community offices.

At a long bare table, on a long worn bench, sat a row of men with heroic faces. When I came in, all stood, bowed to me, and sat down again without a word.

"What can I do for you, gentlemen?" I asked.

The men who answered my question were modern Jews in the city of Lublin, but they seemed to have stepped out of the pages of the Bible. They were the sons of Heth. One of them, a man with a long, gray, pointed beard, told me that the piece of ground the community was giving me for my mother's grave would be a bargain at one thousand dollars, but considering that my mother had been a saintly woman, and that I was a guest, and that they did not want to take advantage of a guest, I would not have to pay any more than five hundred dollars. "Five hundred dollars, what is that betwixt me and thee? Bury therefore thy dead," this Hittite said, like Ephron. "Today is Friday," he added. "Your mother was a woman of great merit, to have died on Sabbath eve: this means that she will be admitted to Paradise without delay."

"There is no time to lose," another Hittite said. "You're getting the plot practically for a song. You'll see for yourself, it's right next to the rabbi's tomb. There is the tomb"—he pointed to an imaginary plan on the table—"and there is the plot we're giving you for almost nothing, so that nobody can say we've taken advantage of you. Your mother surely deserves that you should act toward her as a faithful son."

Ita Rachel had lived some seventy years, according to her Russian birth certificate. I was mentally unrolling my own Bible and saying to myself, "These were the years of the life of Rachel." Ita Rachel was standing impatiently before the open gates of Paradise. There is a death notice with big black letters on her house, but I have still to conclude my deal with the children of Heth, and buy the cave of Machpelah, just a few steps from the rabbi's tomb.

I got up from my seat and bowed deeply. "I am a stranger, but I am a native of your city. Here I was brought up, and here I came to bury my dead."

"You're getting the choicest plot in the cemetery, because she was a pious woman," a broad-shouldered Hittite said.

I took out the papers, I weighed out the Polish silver to Ephron, and the pact was concluded. The Hittites got up from their bench and bowed deeply to me. "The funeral will take place in half an hour!"

Soon the streets were black with people, and the shops closed their shutters. They would reopen again once the hearse had made its mournful journey across the ill-paved streets, humped like camels.

The sun now weighed heavily on my lids. I knew that the hushed street, and the charity box with its rattling coins, and the advancing carriage, and the men and women following the cortège, and the broken cry that hung in midair—I knew now that none of these things was real, that the movements and noises were only an illusion, that actually they had come to full stop, an absolute stop, that each and all of them had fallen silent for all eternity, and that there was no way of changing this, not by a single hair, that it was the end. . . . And now that it was all over I wanted to go back to the beginning, to what came first. What did come first? When does the first become the second, the third, the seventieth? Is the first really the first? Who was "first"—could it be the little boy in a dark blue suit and cap, the little boy I now suddenly saw before me in my waking dream?

A little boy wearing a dark blue suit and a cap with visor was skipping along. His mother had buttoned his shoes with a buttonhook, and they squeaked. Now he had put the town far behind him, and his shoes were covered with dust. The houses grew smaller and smaller, until there were no houses at all. Instead, orchards appeared, with all sorts of fruit trees. The pears were just beginning to grow red, and the green apples made your teeth tingle just to look at them. The cherries were big and fat. Flowers were crowding against the iron bars confining them. On a meadow with yellow daisies a cow was lying down, as though too lazy to stand.

The little boy was intoxicated by the smells and colors and began to run. His shoes picked up more dust than before.

"Stop! Don't run, you'll get lost!" The woman who scolded him was his Aunt Etka. She was holding a basket in one hand, and with the other was trying to keep a firm grip on him.

Aunt Etka had to squint, walking into the sun. The little boy teased his aunt, and at one moment he succeeded in wrenching free from her, and skipped ahead pretending that he was riding a horse. Then he heard a dog barking and he ran back to his aunt for protection.

"Stop! Don't bump the basket! You'll spill the broth, and father won't have anything to eat."

By then the boy was wondering whether any broth would be left for his father. The overladen basket was already wet, and the drops of soup made a little path in the sand behind them.

Aunt Etka sat down on a rock and wiped her perspiring face. "It's quite hot," she said. "Don't sit down, you'll get dirty, you'll ruin your new pants."

The basket was still warm although they had walked quite a distance from their home near the Castle. The boy felt fine and was making sounds like "oo-oo-oo." Suddenly he asked, "Is it still a long way to the barracks?"

"I don't know. There's still quite a stretch. It's so hot!"

"Is it true that father is in the army?"

Aunt Etka was still wiping her face. "Of course he is. Poor man, they gave him no choice."

"Who are 'they'?"

"The Russkis."

The little boy could just see a big fellow, with a big Russki nose, standing over his father, ordering him to aim a gun and make it go bang, bang! Father had often showed him with a stick how this was done.

"What does it mean 'to serve,' Auntie?"

"To serve is to be a soldier."

"What is it 'to be a soldier'?"

Aunt Etka had gotten up and walked carefully with her basket. She did not speak, for the boy had asked his last question casually.

"What's a soldier?" the boy asked again, this time earnestly. He kicked at the ground and raised a cloud of dust.

"I don't know, my word, I don't know."

"You do too know! Tell me, tell me!" The boy was insistent. Now he began to make a noise like crying, but without tears, because he felt so good, because the orchards smelled so good, because the sun was so warm, and because the dogs had stopped barking.

Every day his aunt carried lunch to his father, who had been called up for three weeks' duty. That way he didn't have to eat the tsar's garbage. Today the boy had made up his mind that he would go along with her, and there had been no way of holding him back. He wanted to see his father wearing his military cap, he wanted to see his uniform.

"Army service!" the aunt said with distaste.

The boy began to gallop away from her on his imaginary horse, shouting, "Service, service!"

"Stop! Don't, you wild thing!"

Aunt Etka rarely laughed. Her expression always seemed to the boy like a dripping candle. Every year a bit more dripped off it, every year her face shrank and became less firm in outline. But this time, when they walked together to the barracks, her face still had all its original seductiveness. The dripping off had just begun.

His mother stayed at home. She had warm hands when she stroked his head or combed his hair. Somewhere far away his father was doing his term of duty, living in barracks, and now he was walking with his aunt from where his mother was to where his father was.

"Don't forget to kiss your father's hand," his aunt reminded him.

He walked and walked. No one walked behind him or in front of him, no one looked at him, no one was there except for his aunt—and perhaps also a young man, a thin, emaciated young man, watching the boy.

He truly did not take his eyes off the boy or the aunt, as he walked on and on, all by himself in the bustling crowd. And now the young man was by himself once more, without his aunt, in a foreign city, elbowing his way through the others and keeping a bit apart from them. Had he not kept himself apart, in later years, no one would ever have known him as the same little boy who once wore a dark blue suit and a cap with visor.

Now, in the foreign city, he could smell the red watermelons and slightly decayed tomatoes on the squeaky pushcarts. A penny apiece, ladies, only a penny apiece, come and get them, a bargain at six for a nickel!

The air had a cool, clear fragrance. The lights in the windows, the little lanterns on top of the pushcarts, the warm coolness, the signs on the movie houses, the man on the wagon with the watermelons, the Jews leaving the synagogues after evening prayers—all this seemed far away and foreign—more than that, in some other world. For some unknown reason, the most ordinary things had an aura of extraordinary strangeness, of fairy-tale remoteness. This had something to do with the nights and how light it was at night, with the way the colors shimmered at night. It had something to do with the way the nights penetrated your pores, settled around your heart, and even got under your fingernails, the better to sing in every finger.

It was a foreign world, but in the familiar friendly East Side which had just sent Meyer London, one of its own sons, to Congress. He could still see London's noble features, twinkling eyes, thin sensitive nose. He remembered being in the crowd which had just elected one of its own to Congress, in that foreign world, that foreign city where he was alone, even in the crowd, and walked and walked and was perhaps no more than a pair of eyes still watching the little boy and his aunt carrying the basket.

In the midst of all the delights of the foreign city, the eye of the young man never lost sight of the little boy, kept track of mother at home and father in the barracks, and strained to glimpse again the earliest memory of father and mother, the little boy standing on some sort of precarious bridge between them. Had he ever allowed the little boy to fall out of his sight, the young man would have become no more than an eye that looks ahead, forward, forward, as he makes his way through the enormous bustling crowds—a man apart.

Had this young man not kept his eye on that past, thinking back and always struggling to know where he had come from, no one at all would have seen the little boy with his aunt. Their image on that road would have evaporated like smoke. They would have arrived at the army barracks where the little boy could see his father in the military cap. He would have been too surprised to remember to kiss his father's hand. His father would have shown him around, the shiny clean guns with their gleaming bayonets, stacked neatly in threes, each three held by a clasp. The black-mustachioed officer would have picked him up and taken him for a ride on his shoulders, the little boy afraid to cry.

Father's cap would have made him look somewhat of a stranger, and the boy standing at a distance would have watched his father wipe his plate with a piece of bread while he chattered at Aunt Etka, who sat peculiarly still outside the barracks, eyes lowered, as though dazzled by the sight of so many soldiers' boots. "Etka, tell Ita Rocheshe from me that may God give her as much pleasure as she has given me. I could kiss her hands."

Mother's hands knead little crescent cakes full of raisins and cinnamon. When she takes them out of the oven, their fragrance fills the house. Mother kneads them with her own hands, so that afterwards her hands smell of cinnamon and warmth and butter cookies.

All this would have taken place in any event. The little boy would have walked back by the same road, past the orchards, the flower gardens, the barking dogs, under a somewhat cooler sun. But no one would have seen him, had not that lonely eye on the East Side excavated him out of the faraway past, out of the remote origin of a first, unsteady, childhood step.

The eyes of the young man later searched out the image because he felt that he was at a new point of origin, taking a new first step, that he might become one of the crowd and be swallowed up forever, did not someone seize this image and hold it fast—someone who walked at his side step by step through the East Side, redolent of warm togetherness—fruits, peddlers, girls going to the movies, the cool night air, the flashing lights, the foreign sights and sounds and smells, tangy and invigorating.

And so, now the searching eyes of the thin young man had followed the little boy, followed him back home, where, one day, he found for the first time an adult self-assurance at the sight of another little boy crawling around on all fours like a kitten with a large human head.

Then came glimpses of frost-covered windows, long winter nights oddly discrete in time, shutters shut fast, and then rain and the mud with the coming of milder days.

It was warm at home. Father was back now. No one even remembered when he had not been there. As she worked on her embroidery, Mother sang an old lullaby, "*In dem beys hamikdesh, in a vinkele kheder,*" the widow Zion sits in a corner of the ruined Temple, alone. Little brother no longer crawled on all fours but walked and fell down and got a bloody nose. Grandfather stood by the tile stove warming his hands. And there were now other people living downstairs. That was Sheindele, the whore, who blessed the candles every Friday evening, then put them out, and went to meet her soldiers. The little boy must have grown by then, for the older people were careful about what they said in front of him; yet certain words reached his ears and stayed there like cobwebs.

Sheindele's daughter, who had red pigtails, enticed him up to the attic and played with him. She spoke Polish. It was dark and suffocatingly hot in the attic, and it was fun when she clapped her hands and sang a song he did not understand. It was ticklish, warm, and dark, like the attic.

The young man who was looking back took the boy and his aunt and built a courtyard around them. There was a house, and a meadow in the distance. There were aunts and uncles, and there was even a synagogue. Now the boy was no longer suspended somewhere between his father and mother but was surrounded by a host of friends in the yard, and there were many grown-ups, and acrobats who turned somersaults, men who swallowed swords, strong men who held up heavy doors, balancing them on their teeth, and blind singers led by barefoot boys with old eyes.

Aie, have you hea-eard, dear friends,
What occurred in Pe-ters-burg.
Aie, a building burned to the ground,
Aie, it was a great misfortune,
Three poor children burned to death.

But this was much later, long after the walk to the barracks. This was weeks, months, perhaps years after the first recollection. Many summers and winters had gone by, not just one seasonal alternation—from the cold and dark to the warm and bright. There were the seasons of sunlight, always ushered in at Passover, and there were the seasons of cold and wind always ushered in at Sukkot.

At this point the distinctions begin to blur. It is not quite clear whether the little boy was swallowed up and lost in the eyes watching him, the eyes of the thin stranger, or whether the young man prowling the East Side had become the little boy, and slept with him through a summer, a winter, a summer, a winter, very often sixteen hours a day.

An alarm clock roused the grown-ups every morning. They would scratch themselves, mutter, and grumble as they dressed, flushing the toilet again and again. When they had gone, a faint smell pervaded the rooms where they had performed their hasty morning ablutions. A quarter of an hour later the same faint smells were being exuded through the pores of their skins as legs pressed against legs, buttocks against buttocks, in the crowded subways, rickety elevated trains, and overcrowded trolley cars. To the rumble and clank of the morning traffic, to the screech of brakes, he went right on sleeping.

Because the two had merged, the young boy suddenly found himself in New York. He walked about, looking up at everything. True, now he was no longer accompanied by his aunt. His aunt's tallow face had by this time lost nearly all its shape. First she married a capmaker who had a daughter by a previous marriage. After she divorced him—he had maltreated her—she married an elderly widower, and this marriage, too, ended in divorce. All these marriages and divorces had so disturbed her that she moved in to keep house for her older sister. She had become even more shriveled up, still tinier, and she spoke less and less often.

The little boy walked about New York by himself and was surprised that he could understand everything he saw. He smiled to himself and never wanted to grow up. The foreign language felt good in his mouth, and he was perfectly happy to make a fresh start all on his own.

He attended a precollege cramming school, where he made a brave show of being grown up. The other young men held down jobs, earned their own living, and the girls kept crossing their legs to make him restless until he felt the legs were around his neck, tickling and choking him. But he was well aware that he was still little, that he had not grown up and was very much underweight. He weighed very little more than he had the day he went to visit his father at the army barracks.

And while the little boy walked about the streets of New York, the grotesquely puny East Side youth, no more than skin and bones, and homesick to boot—little more than a pair of prying eyes—began to play tricks. At will, he could transport himself back to Lublin, every recollection of which he would savor, collect, build into a monument. Or he would use it to invent a whole separate slice of life, with a beginning, a middle, and an end, leaving out no detail of the weather, the time of day, the exact quality of the pinpoint of sunshine piercing the clouds.

The little boy pretending to be an adult attended the school on the East Side, where tired tailors, shirtmakers, and pocketbook stitchers poured their last ounces of strength into the dream of one day making their way out of the dark sweatshops and climbing one rung higher up the ladder. The gloomy shop itself was in the process of renovation, with added windows, shorter working hours, and a proud, demanding workforce. Next on the ladder stood the podiatrist who removed your corns, and he in turn was looked down upon by the not unkindly pharmacist just above him, while from still higher smiled with yet more assured superiority the dentist, the lawyer, and the doctor.

Rather off to one side of the ladder where the angels climb, stepping on the corns of the first professional with his little clippers and nail files—angels climbing down while they imagine they are climbing up—stood one teacher with a fat Mephistophelian face who, when he laughed, laughed until his eyes shrank, growing smaller and smaller.

Afflicted with a Jewish accent, this teacher could not get a job in the city schools. In reaction to this great misfortune, he deliberately exaggerated his accent, vaudevillized it into a kind of Galician–German–English–East Side idiom. He would stand there chanting his Yiddish-English in front of all the ambitious get-aheads, mocking their hopes, their ambitious plans, their careful calculations. Like a very efficient, experienced baker, he would pop a garment worker into the oven, brown him a bit, and then pull him out a pharmacist. He had to move quickly, for time was short, the sweatshop used up your strength, and the years addled your brains. But while he was waiting for his recipe to achieve its work, before the finished product appeared—a man transformed, a new chapter opened in his life—he would stand there and laugh until you thought he would burst, and the whole class would burst out laughing with him. His malice was kindhearted. He would never have gone to the trouble of hurting anyone, though when his students clustered around him, begging for it, his hatred of them was a purely passive hatred.

He would often speak in rhymed couplets, until the walls of the classroom echoed in rhythm. He taught English history and literature in the singsong chant of a reading from the Hebrew Bible. He really knew English literature, and his clowning helped a great deal to make his lessons stick—to impress them upon the slowest students. Some funny tag made every single bit of information memorable. He made fun of Shakespeare's heroes, of their loves, passions, and murders; he ridiculed the heroes of history.

"Did Shylock go to the synagogue and say his prayers before he set out to cut off his pound of flesh?" he would ask his class. It would answer him as one man, "No! No!"

"Have you ever seen a Jew eating a steak cut out from a living goy?"

"No!" the class would thunder.

"Was Shakespeare a great poet?"

"Yes, sir!" they all answered dutifully.

"Was Shakespeare a great anti-Semite?"

"Yes, he was!" the class would answer, shaking with laughter.

The teacher enjoyed all this as much as his pupils. His eyes grew very tiny when he recounted how one of the Kings Charles cried out to his mother on some historic occasion or other: "Mother! Hand me my rattle, I'm going off to battle!"

His wife was a homely woman, and in his spare time he wrote ardent erotic poems which were published in obscure Greenwich Village magazines. His more innocent poems were posted on the school bulletin board. The principal was enough of a businessman to advertise the talents of his teachers, to stress how far out of the ordinary they were. One poem addressed to a girl began: "You are the horse, I am the rider —You are the wave, I am the rower who wields the oar."

"What do you want to spend all your time on this for," he would mock us. "Open a candy store, or sell kiddie clothes! Get married, wear a vest with a watch and a gold chain, make your wife grow a respectable behind."

When the bell rang for recess, he would stuff his mouth with chocolate and refuse to answer questions. "I am a strict union man," he would say, "I don't work overtime." And he would go right on chewing, cheeks distended like a child's.

Everyone envied him and would have laid money he was going to live two hundred years. They all lost their bets the day he died on the elevated, on his way to school to give us more lessons in laughter.

At about that time the little boy had a more personal encounter with death; he looked at it sideways so as not to look it straight in the eyes. There was a perpetually tired young man with dark eyes who had flunked his geometry exam five times, but in the end managed to get into college. Perhaps the examiner had felt sorry for him and helped him to get a foot on the next rung of the ladder. They had spent the whole evening walking—the young man and the little boy. The young man planned the life now opening up to him, in the closest detail. He showed his sweetheart's picture, told how much money he had in the bank. The money would last for exactly two and a half years, and then his sweetheart would help out with her savings. A few days later he was dead of pneumonia. The little boy could not forget his dark eyes, intense with hope. Later he once caught sight of the dead young man's sweetheart in the street. She was alone, and paced back and forth. He hesitated, wanting to go up to her and tell her he understood how all her planning had come to nothing; he wanted her know that he knew about the bank book and how everything was fixed for two and a half years. But he was afraid to speak to her. Obscurely, he felt that she was in love with death.

Death even knocked at the thin wall of his tiny furnished room. It was Patsy's hand on the other side of the wall. Patsy was the imaginary name of a man he never saw. The boy had to imagine a face, a figure, for someone who lived so close to him. He could hear him on the other side of the wall, had heard him sing and moan on his creaking bed. Between his bed and the stranger's bed stood a wall, a poor wall with the paint peeling off, a hopeless wall like all the walls of all dingy furnished rooms.

The boy could hear him groan at night, hear him talk in his sleep, but he never laid eyes on him. Perhaps the man was speaking to him through the wall, in the strange terrifying language of the night, when every creaking noise holds myriad terrors and every human cry seems a scream for help.

One night the man groaned so heartrendingly, and tossed about so wildly on his bed, that the boy was unable to sink back into his own nightmare territory, which all airless, musty furnished rooms turn into when the lights are out. The next morning the whole house was in an uproar. The boy's neighbor had "taken gas." He had stopped up every crack, plugged up the keyhole, and stuffed rags around the windows so that no one would smell gas and stop him.

The policemen slapped his cheeks and pounded him on the back. Their attempts to discover his identity were unsuccessful. The old landlady did not even remember his name.

"Patsy! Patsy!" The policemen tried to rouse him from the death he had so carefully arranged, inventing a name as soft as his dead cheeks and as hairy as the hairy chest they were kneading. "Get up, Patsy, hurry, or you'll be late!"

Patsy, the imaginary man who sang on the other side of the wall and had given up the ghost groaning and tossing on the creaky bed, made no sound. Maybe it was because "Patsy" was not his name, or maybe there had been some secret purpose in his taking his life, and he was resolved not to be called back.

The coolly deliberate death of the unknown man, the abrupt end of the young man who had worked so hard at his geometry in order to make a new start in life (he was a buttonhole maker), and the sudden stifling of the teacher's sardonic laughter—all these deaths had gripped the boy mightily, as though to pull him forcibly out of himself and to put some kind of foundation under his feet. He needed a foundation after all—if only one of sadness—for how much longer could he wander around phlegmatically with that original wonderment as if his destination were still the army barracks with his father wearing a soldier's cap?

But a dark cloud descended over the world. The little boy decided to postpone his efforts to get ahead in New York, even to postpone adulthood, until his alter ego—the thin young man who had come to America and lately traded perspectives with his younger self—had done with his homesick excursions to Lublin and learned why there had been no letters and how his father and mother, brothers, and little sister were doing.

He sat in Doctor Tenenbaum's office and looked into the doctor's old eyes. How long ago had it been when the doctor had come back from the Russo-Japanese war, a young man with a clipped blond beard and earnest desires to be a healer of the poor? How many years had it been since he had come to our house, looking wistfully out the windows over the yellow-green meadows that spread for miles in every direction? "Air! Air!" he had said on that visit, putting into it all the hunger of children condemned to live in stuffy basements. "You are to be envied. You don't know how much you are to be envied." Doctor Tenenbaum had visions so vast that he could not see what was under his nose. He never noticed that before the meadows started his eyes had been offered the spectacle of poor, draughty, rain-soaked rooms, and one privy in the backyard for the entire household.

But Doctor Tenenbaum had been young then, and now he was old. He sat there in a patched-up coat and comically short trousers, which must have had the cuffs trimmed several times. He was a tiny man, but he looked even tinier when he was sitting down—his feet did not reach the floor. It was said that people in the city had stopped going to him, that rumors about him had been spread so systematically and cruelly that a few months earlier he had been evicted from his apartment. Soon he lost his entire practice. He sat all day long playing chess with retired doctors in a club. Father still consulted him out of loyalty to that other man, the doctor he remembered coming back from the Russo-

Japanese war, out of loyalty to the years when Father's beard had been blond, too, and the doctor took care of the children. Mother had always suffered from one complaint or another, but she rarely paid attention to her own troubles; as for Father, he was sure that there was no illness that could not be sweated out in the bathhouse.

Now the doctor was sitting on a rickety chair in his shabby office, swinging his short legs, and was saying that there was no hope for her. You could touch it with your hand—a tumor as big as a walnut. By now anyone could feel it, it didn't take a doctor.

There was no hope! Not for himself, not for Mother, not for the whole generation of men whose beards had been blond during the Russo-Japanese war; not for any of the mothers in labor at that moment, or bringing up their children.

No hope—that was the diagnosis of the whole generation. His own wife had died a few years earlier. It was as though he was marching at the head of his army of patients, leading them resolutely down, down, down.

"You see, your mother is not really suffering from any illness. She is sick with the disease of death. Death is the very opposite of life." When he said it, he gave his little child's legs with their tiny shoes a swing.

The doctor was not saying this to the little boy nor to his alter ego, the East Side companion, but to a third party, one who could scarcely extricate himself from their tangle. He could recognize this third embodiment of himself only in occasional flashes. For instance, whenever he remembered the teacher who had died suddenly on his way to school, what he saw was the figure of Richard Corey. But Richard Corey did not belong, he was sure of it, in the storehouse of the boy's memories, nor did the young man on the prowl ever notice him in his wandering between Lublin and the East Side. Richard Corey was part of the dream baggage of a third party that had become entangled with the other two precisely because of his efforts to disentangle himself from them—grasping at every straw that would help him achieve clarity.

It was obvious that the man the doctor had been speaking to was the same man who had just been riding in a droshky, and who could not keep from screwing up his eyes, even though the dusk was darkening.

It was like a dream come true. It was just a short ride from the railroad station to his father's house, but the street was as though paved with miracles. Every stone, every rock, whole mountains and valleys cried out to be noticed, so that it had seemed the drive would never end. But it had lasted only a moment, and he had not captured it all. The sky had indeed been rent open, but his eyes had been closed. Now he was traveling on the other side of his dream. His mother had died on the first side, old friends had come up and spoken to him, the old houses had given him a message, but the droshky went no farther—it had stopped for a greeting, a wink of the eye, a smile, a sad memory, a forgetting—and now it was already leaving again.

And if he had had the strength, if he could be sure he would be obeyed, he would have begged the driver to take pity, he would have cried with his last strength, "Let me out! Let me out! Stop!"

The droshky and the driver's indifferent back were leaving everything behind. A dream may last a whole twenty years, and the moment of fulfillment be only a moment, barely caught hold of, barely glimpsed in the impetuous onrush of time. Now he was already weaving around himself the strands of a new dream, one that devours time and flesh and bones so greedily that it scarcely matters whether you wake up or just keep on sleeping. The dream will dream itself on and on, and gradually your own children, your own grandchildren, one by one will appear in the dream.

5

A little rabbit paused, one leg slightly raised. It scratched itself, listening intently for the least sound of danger. I lay flat on my back, careful not to frighten the creature. For its sake I broke off the thread of my memories. It was warm in the sunshine. Suddenly I heard footsteps, and the rabbit, startled, scampered away.

Steinman was standing there. He had caught sight of me in the grass the moment he got to the top of the hill. "How have you already discovered my hill?" he exclaimed. "I come here every morning to enjoy the view. What do you mean coming here without my permission?" He sat down on a bench, and I pretended to apologize.

"Well, the fact is I don't resent your being on this hill as much as your having gotten up early and come here ahead of me. Usually, I am the first here. I make it up here slowly, groaning and cursing like Balaam, but the moment I've gotten to the top and look out on all this, I bless what I see. I look around at all the little hotels the Jews have built here, and I am overcome, I sing out loud, 'How goodly are thy tents, O Jacob!'

"Over there, to the left, is an old monastery with an old graveyard. A great deal of blood has been shed on this hill, and not only way back in the days of Poniatowski. In the Great War the hill was an important strategic spot. It changed hands several times. The Russians fought like lions, driving back the Austrians time and again. There weren't any Jews here until just a few years ago, and no Jew would have dared climb the hill. Now most of the Gentiles have moved away. Do you see the tents? 'How goodly are thy tents, O Jacob!'—may they stay here for years to come."

I glanced at him sidewise and could see that he had not had enough sleep. He half-closed his eyes when he spoke, but his voice was all the warmer. Time and again he would lose the thread of what he was saying, then pick it up again, lightly. His tone was wistful.

"I don't think you slept well?"

"When you're as old as I am, young man, you won't sleep well either," he said. It was almost a rebuke. His eyes closed but he forced them open again, and he shook his head several times to drive away his sleepiness. Then he went on, talking in the tone of someone who has been interrupted in a long speech:

"I've been a widower for twenty years now. My daughter is all I have left. It's because of me she never married; she nurses her old father instead. Believe it or not, but the older I get the more I understand the importance of having male heirs. The Oriental longing for a son, an heir—how well I understand it now. I too am looking for an heir, though if you ask me what I have to bequeath, I would find it hard to reply. Very often I sit and think, and—a flash of lightning, thunder, hocus pocus—and I see my son and heir standing there. But what have I got to give him? It's a difficult problem. My father reached the ripe old age of ninety-nine. He just fell asleep in his chair. Once I believed I'd live as long, but my heart tells me that isn't to be. Well, if I am asked to go, I have no choice. By the time father died, I was myself a father, I already had gray hair. I turned gray at an early age. I know, your generation is a generation of skeptics. You'll want to know what I have to pass on to you. I often think to myself that I'd like to adjure you to hold something dear, but what it is I haven't found out yet. And time is moving on."

He spread his coat on the grass and lay flat on his back beside me. The words that came out of him were like soap bubbles, rising and bursting in the air. He closed his eyes and hummed a little tune.

"Even as a little boy I knew I was not alone, though I want you to know that the word *alone* fits me perfectly. I was raised by an uncle of mine, in a Polish woods where he was forester. Have you any idea what a Polish woods was like in 1860? Just close your eyes and try to imagine.

"However, being alone never bothered me. I knew all about my ancestors. Oh, what saints and scholars! On my father's side I descend from Maharam Tiktin, on my mother's from Magen Abraham. I knew that I was descended from nineteen generations of rabbis. The continuity was broken in the woods. But with such prominent ancestors, how can anyone be alone, even in the woods? Note also that my uncle was a fiery scholar, and that he had written my father, asking that I should come and stay with him, so he could study with me. He had a license to be a rabbi. But he was obliged to work, and work hard, for a living."

He again began to hum a little tune, his sleepy voice growing still sleepier. "Ah, a tune. A tune solves everything, even the toughest problems. There were among the rabbis inarticulate souls who couldn't speak to God through the Torah, so they spoke to Him through melody."

Unexpectedly he sat up, pressed his hands hard against his eyes, and wiped the lids, as though to squeeze all his weariness out of them. When he reopened his eyes he actually did look refreshed.

"A little nap like this, talking in my sleep, rests me more than a night in bed. In bed my tired old bones have a hundred complaints. Well, let's go back, you surely must have worked up an appetite by now. Buchlerner's herring is one of the marvels of the world. You have to be a connoisseur to appreciate it. It is reddish, it does smell a bit, and it looks a bit rotten, but for gourmets that's the thing. It has a tonic effect."

We walked leisurely down the hill, and he led me to the hotel by another route. "Think over what I've told you," he said to me on the way. "A man cannot calmly close his eyes for eternity if there's no heir waiting for him, ready to take over his father's riches. My father in his old age used positively to long for death, the way a pious Jew longs to do some new good deed. Needless to say, his shroud had been ready for him for many years. He often took it out and looked at it. To him a Jewish funeral was one of the good things every Jew is entitled to. But I walk alone, as the Bible says, and who shall be my heir?"

In front of the hotel several dozen guests were waiting impatiently. As we came up the walk, the hotel owner came out and began impassively to summon his guests by ringing a not very loud hand bell. He shook it in all directions like a lulav, but on seeing us he began to ring it more cheerfully. He raised the bell higher and walked toward us, as though to make a special welcome for Steinman.

Steinman understood the gesture. He walked a little faster, pleased by the special attention, and held himself more erect to give himself dignity. Not until he had gone into the hotel did the rest of the guests surge forward.

♦♦♦ *Chapter 2*

1

After the meal, when Steinman was on his way out of the dining room, his daughter brought him a pill and a glass of water. He popped the pill into his mouth and washed it down with a swallow of water, not even turning around to look at his daughter. The pill interrupted him while he was speaking, at the very moment that he was carefully analyzing an idea.

He had been talking to a man in a light-colored cap with checks. The man was shorter than Steinman, and his considerable paunch made him look even shorter than he was. Tufts of curly hair stuck out here and there from under the cap. Even with his head covered, you could tell this was all the hair he had left. Indeed, the tufts might almost have been part of the cap.

Steinman introduced me to the man, who asked me a number of questions, then suddenly cut off my attempts to reply. "That's fine, I know who you are now, no need to go to the trouble of telling me. And now I want to tell you something. You missed being my son only by a hair.

"Ah, I see you're surprised. Well, I was strongly urged to marry your mother, and the match was well under way, but your mother just as strongly objected to my background. I liked her very much. I wish she had felt the same. On top of it all, I was a poor boy and couldn't make her forget my humble origins by a show of wealth. Anyhow, we had almost reached the point of celebrating our wedding when suddenly the whole thing was called off. You see, Mr. Steinman, he is almost my son."

I was about to tell him that the girl he once wanted to marry had recently died, but he did not give me the chance. He was too carried away at discovering that I was a sort of relative of his.

On the floor of the porch, a woman lay sprawled, smoking a cigarette. Several plush-covered cushions shielded her bulky figure from the wooden hardness. She had a big head topped by a towering coiffure which called to mind the treasure cities the Jews built for Pharaoh. Looking at her, with her back against the wall, you could not miss her broad bosom, and her legs were stretched out in front of her so that no one could get by. People who got as far as those legs turned back: no one wanted to take the responsibility of disturbing her. She looked like a big but precariously balanced building: were she made to move, the elaborate coiffure would tumble down, the bosom would fall to the floor with a thud—it would be a disaster. But for all that she looked so comfortable, she was managing to make her long earrings jangle noisily as she disposed of the ash from her cigarette with masculine neatness. At closer quarters she looked like a gray-haired gypsy.

"Roza," my new acquaintance said to her, "I want you to meet this gentleman—he might have been our son. I'm sorry, I meant to say my son." He still could not get over it. He looked at me tenderly, as though I really were related to him, and he told the whole story all over again. She went right on smoking, an expression of studied boredom on her face.

"Now, Mister Finkel, Mister Finkel," she said in a mocking tone and gave him a look as though he ought to know better than tell her such things. Not only he but I too was taken aback by her attitude. He looked at me helplessly.

"My second wife," he said in a scarcely audible whisper, with a wink, as though this explained everything. "My second wife." I must understand his position, and see for myself there was no arguing with her.

He made a slight show of character, nonetheless, affectionately linking his arm with mine, as if to show that nothing had come between our kinship, no matter what his wife might think. He resumed his favorite topic.

"No," he said, "your father may be a fine man, but speaking from a practical point of view, your mother didn't make the right choice. I am known in Lublin as a wealthy man. I own several big apartment houses, one right next to the Saxon Garden. Do you know what property is worth in that neighborhood? And people think that I am worth" —here I expected him to drop a big figure like a bomb, but he softened the shock, "People think that I am worth about five times as much as I am."

Steinman was getting restless, just a bit irritated that no one was paying any attention to him. He turned away, but my Lublin acquaintance caught him by the sleeve. "God bless you, Mr. Steinman, you can't just stop in the middle of your story and walk out on me."

Steinman was not appeased. He walked over to a chair and sat down with the air of a man who wants to be alone. But when we drew up rocking chairs next to his, he became friendly again.

"You didn't interrupt me at all," he said modestly. "After that enormous meal, I was remembering how we used to eat fifty or sixty years ago. Food is an important matter. We speak of national eating habits. And it is true that food has a character all its own. When I think back to when I was a child, I always remember a slice of bread rubbed with garlic. I can see the bread and smell the garlic, and see my mother's hand holding it out to me. It is part of my childhood. But I've come a long way since then—I must have been about four. Now I eat pills."

"May you live long, Mr. Steinman, I wouldn't want to miss anything you say," Finkel said warmly. "You explain everything so clearly that it's a pleasure to hear you talk. As a young boy I once happened to go to Galicia, and whenever I remember the food there, everything comes back—the sights, the smells—and all my senses are reawakened." Finkel was very pleased with his eloquence. "Take a word like *beans,* which we call *bonen.* In Lublin some call them *boyne,* others say *bob* or *fasolyes.* But when I use the Galician term, I can at once see the water carrier leaving the Saturday services. His clothes are shabby and ragged, but on his head is a worn fur cap, which makes him look like a poor rabbi. That was Galicia."

A tall army officer came up the front walk through the trellised gate. He came right up the steps and walked straight up to a man sitting by himself. The officer beckoned to him with one finger, and the other rose and followed him as though hypnotized. It looked like some unusually important occasion, but without a word they sat down at a table nearby, set up some chess pieces, and in a moment were deeply engrossed in a game.

"I remember the barrels with pickles," Finkel went on—and Steinman gave him a friendly smile. He enjoyed this kind of light conversation after breakfast. "I remember the sauerkraut, and an apple that was dug up from the cold barrel, an apple that could have brought the dead back to life. Chopped onions with eggs was a royal dish. We also used to eat something which I can call only the semblance of a soup. Once in a while there was a bit of meat in it, and you had to fish for it with your spoon—yes, really, we had to fish for it in the soup. Just imagine—this Galician family of six trying to divide half a pound of meat, a rare treat for them. Ah, the poverty was terrible!"

Warming up to his subject, he took off his cap and wiped the sweat off his ruddy hairless head. His skin had large yellow spots. The strands of dead hair stood out wildly around the bald pate.

"You couldn't complain about the bread. The dough was mixed on Thursday, and Friday at daybreak bread was baked for the whole week. We also had pancakes with milk, or kasha with milk. Beans and meat were served with a spoon, but on Saturdays we had *cholent* and one meal with fish which, even when it was stuffed, tasted like inferior herring. Also peas, and noodle pudding with fat. On weekdays we had fish once in a while too but this was a different kind of fish, with lots of bones. You had only to taste it to know it was just an ordinary day of the week. And then the little rolls, and the potatoes baked like chestnuts, which had a special taste when eaten with sour cream. A slice of bread with chicken fat and salt was a great treat. And all this poverty and misery was washed down with a chicory brew black as ink, with a muddy foam. Ah, it was grand to be alive!" Finkel was almost out of breath just thinking about it, and he put his cap back on. "I was then a boy of fourteen. Galicia!"

"Excellent! I didn't want to interrupt you," Steinman encouraged him. "It was excellent."

"Thank you for letting me pour out my heart. When I try to tell my wife about my childhood, or about food, she makes a sour face and she purses her lips like a little bird. It bores her. She is my second wife, you see," he added by way of excuse. But he looked in her direction to make sure that she couldn't hear him.

He pointed at a guest who was just going by, and asked me whether I knew who it was. "See if you can't remember," he kept saying, holding up one finger as though he were putting me to some test.

The man did look familiar, as a matter of fact, but I couldn't remember who he was.

"I'll give you a hint. He is a feldsher from Lublin."

"Berl the Medic!" I exclaimed.

Finkel laughed so hard he almost fell off his chair.

"Berl, indeed! Berl the Medic has been in his grave for about twenty years. He was in his eighties even in your time. This one is Szpak—he too is about eighty. But look how straight he walks, like a sergeant. He is deaf as a post. He can't hear a thing." He beckoned the old man over and performed introductions. Szpak stood rigid, without saying a word, and left us a moment later.

"He walked away," Finkel explained, "not because he thinks he is important but because he has entirely lost his sense of hearing. He doesn't even bother trying; he knows he has been deaf for the last twenty years, so why should he make a fool of himself? And since he can't hear others, he is too proud to let them hear what he has to say." Finkel laughed again. "That's a good one—Berl the Medic! This one gives you quinine for fever, and charges you all of forty pennies, while Berl never asked more than a gulden and used to say with a frankness that could really be touching—are you listening?—he would say, 'I haven't the slightest idea what's the matter with the child.' Then a woman would come in who could say the formula against the evil eye, she would have the patient urinate on some freshly stewed prunes, and he'd get well in no time at all."

He looked back in the direction of his wife to make sure she could not hear him reminiscing. She had just lit another cigarette and leaned more heavily against the wall.

"Well, hurry up, it's your turn!" the officer urged his partner. "Come on, make a mo-o-ove!" he chanted.

His partner said that if he wasn't allowed to think he'd quit at once. He hated to be hurried, he said, he had to figure things out. After all, chess wasn't marbles!

"All right, all right," the officer said, patting him on the shoulder. He was humming a little tune, and it was obvious that he was pleased at having driven the Jew into a corner. But when his Jewish partner calmed down, the officer began to chant again, aping the singsong of Talmud students. "What's the matter? Make a move, Mister! You can rest on the Sabbath."

By now his partner was deeply absorbed in figuring out his next move. He was holding a chess piece and took up the singsong tone himself. "Rest up on the Sabbath, rest up on the Sabbath! Make a move, make a mo—o-ove. All right, a move I'll make," he intoned. The officer too became absorbed, and soon both were chanting like a duet of sleepwalkers, adding little squeaks to punctuate the silly chant.

"Make a move, make a move!" Then the Jew suddenly switched to a deep bass voice: "Some Sabbath that is, some Sabbath!"

"These chess players are both slightly deranged," Steinman said. "The Jew is crazier than the army officer, but the officer has an insane hatred for Jews. It's his misfortune that he is a passionate chess player, and can't do without Jews. No Jew dares refuse him a game. This man here out of fear sometimes plays ten games on end, and is so exhausted when he is through that he can hardly walk. The officer is a better player, but you should see him when something goes wrong and he loses a game. He turns into a maniac, a murderer, a pogromist, and calls the whole Jewish nation a bunch of cheats and swindlers."

"It doesn't take much to turn them into pogromists," Finkel said in a low voice. "Just look at him—you can see he is out to murder. But psst—he can understand Yiddish."

"A great-uncle of mine was obliged to play chess with the landowner from whom he leased his farm. He had to be careful never to win,"

Steinman said. "Every time he lost a game the landlord abused him, calling him a bungler, an idiot, but once my uncle was careless and won a game. The landlord beat him with a stick so badly that he was in bed for three weeks."

"They are pogromists by instinct," Finkel said. "They'd be happy to bathe in our blood." Now he was speaking in a louder voice, "It started with Pharaoh who bathed in the blood of Jewish children. Why, oh why, why do we deserve this, Mr. Steinman? What do they have against us, Mr. Steinman?"

"Ah, you're raising fundamental questions," Steinman said. He had become grave. "You want to go to the root of things. Well, I'll tell you: they want to destroy us, nothing less. Yes, to destroy us. For instance, take me—I am a patriotic Pole. And yet they'd destroy me too. They want to exterminate us, purely and simply. Yes, exterminate us. May they not live to see the day!"

"But why, why?" Finkel asked with dismay. "After all, there must be a reason. When I was poor they hated me. Now I am a rich man, God be praised, and they begrudge me that too. My father, may he have a bright life in paradise, was a pious Jew, and they hated him. But my son, my only son, is a trefniak, he eats pork and lobster, and never goes near a synagogue—yet they hate him too. Sometimes this thought oppresses me so much that I feel like screaming in the street—why, why?"

"Why? For the Sabbath. What a question! Do you want me to start from the beginning and explain why Cain killed Abel? Cain is their ancestor, they're the descendants of Cain. They hate us for observing the Sabbath, and they hate us for violating the Sabbath. They hate pious Jews, and they hate freethinkers who eat lobster. They hate our capitalists and they hate our beggars, they hate our reactionaries and they hate our radicals, those who earn their bread and those who die three times a day from starvation. They invent beautiful names for all this, economic causes. Sometimes the ringleader is called Pharaoh, sometimes Torquemada, and sometimes Hitler, may he be accursed, but—

"You know what?" Steinman suddenly switched to another tack. "I witnessed the famous pogrom in Kalisz personally. It is usually called the first pogrom in Poland, though I can't guarantee that our Gentile friends never went on a murderous binge before that. But since that is the opinion of the historians, and since I am a historian too, I am obliged to stick with the others and call it the first—after all, there always has to be a first time for everything. So we'll assume this was the first one, though the truth is that anti-Jewish pogroms have no beginning and no end. And the pretext for this first pogrom was the wire marking the Sabbath zone—the eruv. The Gentiles spread the rumor that this wire was a secret Jewish telegraph. This happened fifty-five years ago. Jewish blood ran in streams. I was saved by a miracle, hiding in the synagogue in a book closet. All around me the synagogue was being made a shambles, the hoodlums smashed everything, plundered, stole, tore to shreds, desecrated scrolls of the Torah, they didn't even spare the famous Torah scroll of Rabbi Yehudah ben Nissan. I suppose you never heard of that relic, but just to give you an idea, there is a legend recorded that when this scroll was written, sparks flew from every letter. And this precious scroll fell into the hands of the wicked ones. Fortunately, the hoodlums didn't catch sight of me. It was pure luck. A book from that closet where I hid is still in my possession. It is a frayed section of the Talmud, the Book of Baba Bathra. I shall never let go of it as long as I live."

Finkel's eyes filled with tears. He looked at Steinman with awe—Steinman who had survived the pogrom in the synagogue. Finkel mentally re-created the scene, and his mouth seemed to be saying the gomel blessing, praising the Lord for rescuing Steinman from mortal danger. "I don't know whether you're much older than I," he finally said, "but there is a difference between one old man and another. When I tell stories, they're about eating, but when you talk it's as if someone were reading me a storybook."

2

A few more men joined us. By now Steinman was in the center of a group of seven or eight rocking chairs.

"The yeshiva where I studied was moved to Bzhezin because of the pogrom. A short time later, Dr. Israel Hildesheimer came to Poland. He went to Łódź to collect funds for his rabbinical seminary in Berlin.

Ostensibly, the purpose of his trip was to enroll students in the seminary.

"Now, this Hildesheimer—it's easy to say the name, but it's a long jump back into the past for an old man! Hildesheimer is a chapter in himself, more than a chapter, a whole book." Steinman paused for a moment, then went on to recount what a stir the German Jew's arrival caused in Poland.

"People flocked to hear his sermons. He dressed like a real German, but he was strict about religious observances, to the point of mania. He was stately, you couldn't take your eyes off him. To see such a face at that time was like seeing a member of the Lost Tribes. And then, the eloquent sermons he preached in the synagogues! They were something! The people couldn't get over this newfangled preacher, who did not threaten them with the barrels of pitch in hell, but instead talked about the Jew's higher duties to the Creator of the Universe.

"Needless to say, he elevated God into Master of the Universe, *ribono shel olam*. The Polish Jews did not have much confidence in this Germanized God, but they loved the sermons, which Hildesheimer delivered in real German, not a Germanized Yiddish. His sermons always built up to a big climax, and then there was a summary. Even before he got to the end, the people felt that he had gotten the last drop out of the well. It was the first time the Polish Jews had ever heard the Jewish God discussed in a foreign language they only half understood. This God was not the kindly Father to whom the Berdichev Rabbi poured out his heart; this one was aloof, remote, spiffed up, thoroughly Germanized. Young people began to play with the idea of a secular God, and Doctor Hildesheimer talked to them about "the philosophy of religion." In their section of the synagogue, the women did not understand a word of all this, but they wept at his words as they did at Kol Nidre. As a rule, they burst out sobbing at the first word they could pick out from the surging tide of German. It might be some perfectly innocent word, but the women clutched at it as if it were some distant relative who had been lost a long time among the Germans.

"Dr. Israel Hildesheimer's well-sounding name was on everyone's lips. Everyone knew that he had come to enroll pupils in his seminary.

"Well, the upshot of all this was that I registered along with several of my friends to study at his seminary," Steinman went on. "By that time, my mind had been poisoned by the literature of the Enlightenment. I had absorbed the *Sages of Israel, Chronicles of Creation,* the *Sins of the Samaritans, The Hypocrite,* and the gentle pastoral novel *Love for Zion.* I was nursing a dream that sounded very important—no more or less than to reform the spiritual life of Polish Jewry." Steinman paused. The new arrivals were drinking in his every word.

"Believe it or not," he said, "but we all went to Berlin on foot. We walked filled with the most beautiful, the purest hopes, longing to drink at the fountainhead of knowledge. But the welcome we received when we got there was something else again.

"Whether because Doctor Hildesheimer's mission to Poland had ended in failure, or because by temperament he hated Polish Jews, the fact is that when at last we arrived in Berlin, ready to drink at the famous spring, he didn't pay the slightest attention to us. He just ignored the boys from Poland. So there we were in a foreign city, penniless. We had to beg for bread. The Jewish community was ashamed of our caftans and wanted to get rid of us as soon as possible.

"The weaker among us let themselves be persuaded and made the trip back home. But the stubborn ones, and I was among the latter, stayed on, to the dismay of the German Jews. We lived on charity, and all of us passionately studied German. I devoured books on literature, geography, history. I managed to get permission to attend courses at the university without matriculating. Some Gentile professors took pity on our honest thirst for knowledge and enrolled us without fee, and from their high chairs talked down to us because they knew that we drank in every word they said.

"I don't know what we'd have done without the Jewish servant girls and cooks from Galicia—may they be blessed. It was the food they gave us that kept our bodies going, while the Christian professors tended to our spiritual needs. The Jewish cooks, with their warm hearts, looked after us. In their eyes we were yeshiva students. They found places for us to stay in Jewish homes. They slipped us the word when it was safe to sneak into the kitchen for a hot meal. Many of them had thoughts of marriage; and some of our boys were lucky enough to arouse interest in the young ladies of the house themselves—those boys really did well for themselves. In no time at all they were fat and had nice red cheeks. Yes, those chaps lived in clover. Not only did they have board and lodgings, they even got pocket money.

"As for myself, I confess that I was unlucky as can be." Here Steinman stopped and looked at us with his young eyes. "No servant girl fell in love with me, let alone a lady of the house. You may take my word for it that I was a handsome young man, but I was so skinny that no one could see this. I impressed only ugly old cooks, who, while feeding me, looked at me with such mooncalf eyes and uttered such heartrending sighs that I felt that my bread was buttered with the hopes of old maids. Such bread was not to my liking, it stuck in my throat.

"At that time I had not entirely given up the idea of becoming a rabbi, although the Christian kind of Jewishness they taught in Germany repelled me. Hunger finally drove me from Berlin. I went to Breslau hoping to fare better there. Professor Graetz was in Breslau at that time, and I made an effort to see him. It was not easy. To achieve that honor took some time and many letters of introduction, until finally the professor relented and asked me to come to his house. He too hated Polish Jews, like a real anti-Semite: The term *Polnischer Jude* was for him synonymous with *Lump* and *Schacherjude*. It was odd to hear such lovely compliments from old Graetz, who wore a skullcap and observed all the Jewish rites. He liked to have two men to dinner every Friday night so as to have the requisite quorum for the blessings. When he recited the Kiddush he made the most of it, chanting every word and pronouncing the Hebrew in the German manner. He chided me for reciting the blessings too fast, explaining that the Kiddush was a solemn rite, and that it must be recited with great deliberation, not the way the Polish Jews did it. The Polish Jews had no feeling for ceremonial, he said, they were either obscurantist, superstitious, dirty Hasidim—to Graetz the Hasidim were the lowest of the low—or heretics and atheists who deny the divine Providence.

"After the Kiddush the professor never failed to mention that his silver goblet had been given him by old Moses Montefiore in person. He cherished this goblet, and when he showed it around, he always managed to keep a finger or two on it, to make sure it wouldn't evaporate in someone else's hands.

"Very often Professor Graetz invited a Christian clergyman to his house on Friday night. The clergyman knew a few Hebrew words, which he pronounced with a distinct Christian accent. The conversation usually led to an argument, and there were comparisons among the various religions, a la *Nathan the Wise*. The clergyman usually called the professor 'Nathan the Wise,' but the old man was not impressed by such compliments. His eyes would blaze whenever he suspected that the clergyman was criticizing Judaism. At such moments Graetz would launch into a lofty speech about the sublimity of Jewish ethics, about our moral mission, about the 'Thou shalt not kill,' which was proclaimed on Mount Sinai to a heathen world.

"He was a fine Jew and a great scholar, Professor Graetz. His instruction to me, as a future rabbi, emphasized that I was to implant the Jewish faith not in people's hearts, he insisted, but in their minds. The heart can be easily converted, he said, but the head is higher than the heart, and the clear Jewish religion spoke to the head.

"I was ashamed of my poverty in front of the professor, and whenever he questioned me as to my means of support, reminding me of the saying that a man who doesn't eat can't study, I gave evasive answers. Often he would slip a few coins in my coat pocket. But this verging on hunger turned out to be my dumb luck. I clung to the shriveling religion that was beginning to turn more primitive and coarse. What remained was an apprehensive Jewishness, so I supported myself by selling wall hangings of Psalms that were supposed to ward off the evil eye from women in childbirth. I removed crumbs of leavened bread in Jewish homes on the eve of Passover, and I shook the lulav for family after family during the Feast of Tabernacles. Even if they never went to synagogue services, still they were afraid to begin the meal without 'shaking the lulav.' German Jews had lost all inner understanding of Judaism; all that remained was the hardened crust of ritual and the old Jewish fears.

"On the eve of Yom Kippur, I was particularly busy. The long caftan I wore was bulging because underneath it I held a cock and a hen. I went from house to house performing the rite of atonement. Before I went into a house, I always made sure that my birds who earned my bread for me were still alive, that they hadn't choked to death. Even Gentile servants wouldn't let me go before I had whirled a squawking fowl around their heads. I performed the rite of redeeming the firstborn after circumcision. I supplied willow branches for the Hoshana Raba festival, observed anniversaries of death. I could usually be found in the synagogue, and my customers would look me up there. 'Herr Prediger, Mr. Preacher, they would say, tomorrow is the anniversary of my mother's death, so please come to recite the prayer. And they would squeeze a few coins into my hand. Incidentally, many German Jews were so poorly informed about Jewish rites that they also observed their parents' birthdays in this manner; I was paid for saying the commemorative prayers for mothers who were still alive before I realized this. And on Rosh Hashanah, your Herr Prediger visited women in confinement to blow the shofar for them.

"For a short period, I got along so well that I even had a roof over my head, a little attic room at Jozefa Kubi's." Steinman smiled broadly, and it was like a gentle breeze that brought smiles on the faces of all his listeners.

"Jozefa Kubi was a Hungarian Jewess. She must have been in her nineties. She hired me not to do housework, God forbid, but to tell her a story every night before she fell asleep. Jozefa's husband, who had died several years earlier, in his lifetime earned his bread as a *shames,* a sexton, in a synagogue. His widow still kept the concession in the synagogue, and every new shames had to pay her a percentage on his earnings, including his fees for blessing the ethrog, anniversary prayers, and so on. The office was hers for life, and she lived quite a long time. In fact she survived several shameses.

"Out of my daily earnings I made enough to buy myself a salt roll, which cost fifteen pfennigs, and then nervously set out for my attic room. On the way I had to think up a good story for Jozefa.

"The old woman was difficult to please. The stories I was to tell her, she had made clear, must invariably depict the scene in Paradise when she is reunited with her husband, who is impatiently waiting for her. But before getting to this invariable climax, the story must go through a number of complications. Jozefa Kubi had a phenomenal memory. If I ever happened to repeat a detail from a previous story, she would

scream at me, denouncing me for trying to sell her secondhand merchandise for new.

"I really wore myself out inventing those stories. When I got to the
end, she was usually ready to fall asleep, and for having so vividly pictured the corner in Paradise where she was sure to be, she would sigh
with pleasure, then I was rewarded with a *yarmush,* a soup made of
flour and water with salt and garlic. When Jozefa Kubi had fallen asleep
on her four pillows—she slept in an almost sitting position—I at last
had a chance to chew my salt roll and sip the yarmush. I really earned
it, too, for I had to wrack my brain to the point of exhaustion to manage those stories. And my tears fell into the soup bowl.

"Often the old hag would make me go to bed hungry when she didn't
like the story. On one occasion I was led to tell a story that was the exact
opposite of what she wanted. You remember, every story had to evoke
her shames; apart from that, I was free to embroider as I liked. But
that night I happened to glance at the sour face of the Hungarian witch,
and instead of a husband I gave her a pain in the neck. She repaid me
in kind, giving me a pain in the neck instead of the thin yarmush. I
was ravenous, but I took some comfort from my show of independence, saying to myself that after all I had not sold my soul altogether
so long as I would rather starve than give Jozefa Kubi her licorice-sweet
shames pining for her in the hereafter."

3

Suddenly we heard a thin little voice, gentle as a May wind, but to all
of us, for some unknown reason, as piercing as a knife. In fact, the
voice was not unmelodious, but somehow it had a quality of sharpness,
an unpleasant edge.

"Mr. Finkel, Mr. Fin-kel!"

All of us had been transported by Steinman to other worlds, and now
this little voice dragged us back. We suddenly looked at Steinman—we
had not really been looking at him, only listening—and the more
clearly we saw him, the more distinctly we heard the shrill little voice
that seemed intent on making us get up. "Mr. Finkel! Mr. Fin-kel!"

When we came back to ourselves, we realized that the voice was that of Finkel's wife, who was still sitting against the wall, smoking. The piercing call had a note of panic in it, as though she were in need of help immediately, if only to get up. Then it was clear that there was a good deal of affectation in that voice, even malice. Surprisingly enough, Mr. Finkel did not budge. He did not say a word. To emphasize his utter unconcern, he turned his cap to one side, like some young tough, so that the visor was over his right ear. Moreover, he began to rock comfortably, demonstrating that he did not give a hoot for this musical summons.

"Mr. Finkel, you're wanted," one of us finally had the courage to say. Steinman was looking at him, as though begging him not to make a spectacle of himself and to put an end to the cry that was growing more panicky by the minute.

"And suppose she divorced me—would I move a finger?" Finkel said with murderous calm. "Is there anything in the world that can make me move from where I am? Have I or haven't I the right to be a man and listen to a Jewish word?"

Finkel, who only a short while before had been so submissive to his second wife, now looked like a fierce revolutionary. His calm disappeared, and he spoke loudly, so that she could hear him.

"Mr. Finkel! Mr. Fin-kel!" she kept on chanting, without raising her voice. It was the constant repetition that was so maddening. Now a real duet began. After every "Mr. Finkel!" he would roar, "And suppose she divorced me—would I move a finger?"

This hostile exchange went on for several minutes. All of us sat there frozen. Suddenly Mrs. Finkel, who had looked so helpless sprawled on the porch floor, gathered her strength like a female Samson making one last effort to shake the pillars of the temple, and got to her feet. She looked colossal as she ran past us, saying in a voice softer than before, as though whispering a secret, "Mr. Finkel!"

She did not stop, and Finkel straightened his cap so composedly that it was clear the revolution had been crushed. He smiled meaningfully and said, addressing all of us, "My second wife!"

He seemed to expect us to say something, but we were too embarrassed to look at him. He got up quietly and went after his wife. Both vanished from sight. The empty chair kept a little of Finkel's rebellious spirit, rocking gently, but it stopped finally, a symbol of defeated manliness. The episode dejected us. Nobody had anything to say.

"He is a decent old fool, you can't help feeling sorry for him," Steinman said finally, starting to get up from his chair.

"Is it our fault?" one of us said. "Mr. Steinman, you're not going to punish us because of that nitwit?"

"Heavens, no. There's no question of punishing anyone. But it's time to go. Even the most beautiful story has to end."

"Now, listen to me, Mr. Steinman," one man said calmly, taking his watch from his pocket. "You can see for yourself: We have a good two hours before lunch. It's hot outside, and here we are sitting in an Eden-like shade. And it's to Paradise you have just taken us—now you're not going to break off your story like that, are you?"

"Now, now, you mustn't be greedy—you want to eat up everything at once. Why don't you leave some of it for tomorrow?" Steinman was resisting, but it was obvious that he would let himself be persuaded.

"All because of that shrew?" One of Steinman's listeners who had been silent so far threw that in.

"That's right!" the others exclaimed. "You've found the right word for her!"

"The word is apt indeed," Steinman said. "A troublemaker if I've ever seen one. Xanthippe was a gentle lamb in comparison." He burst out laughing, and this laughter served him as a transition to resuming his story.

"Well, let's see," he said reflectively. "I believe we've gotten to the point of Jozefa Kubi's yarmush. I was getting thinner and thinner on her marvelous soup, and she wasn't getting any closer to her husband in Paradise. Finally I decided I'd had enough."

4

Steinman was gradually rocking himself back into his previous mood, and we were admiring how he tuned up his voice like a violin. Finkel was suddenly back in his chair, though no one had seen him come back. He looked more dead than alive, and the tufts of hair stuck out from under his cap more wildly than ever. Out of pity we pretended not to see him, and Steinman almost deliberately kept his eyes off him as he resumed his narrative.

"I was starving but I got back to Poland somehow. Now I was a man with experience, and I began to earn a living teaching children Hebrew and German. I could rattle off Hebrew quite decently, and I became known as 'the German teacher.'

"Later I got a job as agent with the German consul. I was also unofficial legal adviser, interpreter, and writer for the German newspaper in Łódź. With all these jobs I managed to eke out a living.

"At about that time there began to be talk about a new movement among the Jews, which was likened to the movement of that False Messiah, Sabbatai Zvi. In the synagogues it was discussed fearfully and referred to as a new sect. Elderly Jews whispered about it among themselves so that the young people shouldn't get wind of it. The sect had been founded in Russia, and the news cast a cloud of fear over Polish Jewry.

"And who do you think was the founder of this movement? Jacob Gordin. Gordin's physical appearance was a movement in itself—part Russian peasant, part rabbi. He was cut out for the religion which aimed at reconciling Judaism and Christianity—needless to say, at the expense of Judaism. His 'Brotherhood' or 'Biblical Brotherhood' preached complete assimilation, not only political but also religious assimilation.

"Gordin was a half-baked scholar, a man full of energy, a real volcano. I met him often on my trips to Russia as a young newspaper correspondent, and I can certify that he had no idea of what he was trying to do. His program could even be defended, but I am so angry at him that I won't lift a finger to justify him. He was a Christianized Jew, a Russian who wanted to turn Jews into illiterate peasants by preaching to them to go back to the soil. I don't have to tell you that many Jewish reformers still look upon this as the panacea to cure all Jewish troubles. It's an empty dream. When there is a pogrom, the hooligans find out easily enough where the Jewish peasants live, and they aren't spared. Unless what the reformers really have in mind are Jewish peasants who have stopped being Jewish, who are indistinguishable from their neighbors, and go to church with them every Sunday. Because if the Jewish peasant adheres to his faith and looks for a prayer quorum, a *minyan*, on Saturday, he won't be spared during a pogrom. Don't fall for such silly theories." Steinman spoke as though debating heatedly with some imaginary opponent.

"Gordin was a Tolstoyan. He wanted to keep the ethical teachings of the Torah and throw all the rest overboard. He thought he would extract a few moral rules from the Book of Books. You may well imagine what this extract looked like. He aimed at a new moral doctrine, somehow connected with work on the soil. Gordin tirelessly preached this bloodless new Judaism.

"The way the Jews saw it was much simpler. To them the sect was a first step toward complete conversion. They absolutely refused to argue about it, and whenever the name of Gordin was mentioned they spat in disgust. Jacob Gordin had several helpers with resounding names— Priluki, Yelisov, Portugalev, and one Jew with a name as common as Joseph Rabinovich. A Jewish historian who has since become famous was also quite interested in the movement—and the term *interested* is a gross understatement!

"Among the people there were stories that this Jewish-Christian sect observed the Christian New Year's Day, but blew the shofar on that day. They wore prayer shawls at the services of the Brotherhood, but over them they wore a cross on a chain. Needless to say, Jesus was recognized as a Jewish prophet. Those were the stories told about the Brotherhood in Poland. Jacob Gordin did everything he could to bring Jews and Christians together.

"I ridiculed the movement as much as I could in my writings. I shot the most poisonous arrows at Gordin. To no avail: the movement was gathering strength. But what I could not achieve with my pen, one terrible Russian pogrom did achieve. A bloody pogrom made a mockery of the Brotherhood. Afterward Gordin tried to reassemble the remnants of his organization, but in vain. Somehow Jews no longer wanted to fraternize with Christians after the pogrom. He even tried to do some agricultural work himself, and thus achieve salvation for himself, but he realized there was no future in it, and he went to America.

"In America his reforming zeal was reawakened. First he tried to reconcile trash and literature and then, once again, Judaism and Christianity. His Jews were Gentiles, and his Gentiles Jews. The plays he wrote were just like the prayer shawls with crosses on them. May he rest in peace, but he was a mediocre writer.

"Jewish life in the 1880s was a sorry spectacle. Jewish life in Poland had become greatly impoverished—well, how shall I express it?" Steinman paused, then his eyes lit up suddenly and he cried out: "Stupid man that I am. Here I'm looking for a metaphor to illustrate Jewish poverty at that time, but the fact is, the situation was exactly what it is today, not a bit different. Poverty exuded from every Jewish caftan, just as it does today. The time was ripe for a big vision. I supposed that for the very reason everything was so miserable, a shining miracle must be coming about. I plunged into Jewish lore. I wrote many stories about the Khazars, the fantastic Jewish hope for a Jewish kingdom on the Caspian Sea. Many of my friends had left for America. I was left alone, and I warmed my heart recalling the figures of Eldad Hadani, the Jewish traveler who is wandering to this day spreading unfounded hopes, of the wealthy Jew Hasdai Ibn Shaprut, who addressed an epistle to the Khazars, but whose letter took so much time traveling that by the time it reached its destination, the Jewish kingdom was no more than a legend.

"At that time I also took upon my weak shoulders the heavy task of defending the Jewish community of Amsterdam against the accusations leveled at it by the Spinozists. Why did the Jews excommunicate one of their own, and why did they have to strike at him so ruthlessly? This was a great, fundamental question. Spinoza had a sharp mind, but he was not harmless. He nourished a dream like Jacob Gordin's, he wanted to make peace between Judaism and Christianity. Until then, all we knew about Spinoza came from Christian sources; I undertook to portray him on the basis of Jewish texts.

"Then, suddenly, a new light dawned in our exile. A new peacemaker appeared—not another cockeyed Jew who reads the Bible with one roving eye on the New Testament. This one was a peacemaker of an entirely new kind. We heard the call: 'It's up to you to transform the myth into reality.' It was like when a composer of genius creates a new melody, one that has never before existed but that instantly everyone wants to hear over and over again. Well, when the Jews pronounced the name of Dr. Theodor Herzl—the new peacemaker—it was the same sort of thing.

"A new ray of light had appeared in Jewish life. The formula in the prayer book that we had been repeating mechanically for many centuries took on real weight and substance. I am referring of course to the formula 'Next year in Jerusalem'—next year, which will spell the end of our troubles.

"Only now did we realize that we had quietly become renegades to our faith, that our prayers and lamentations had grown stale and their meaning blurred. With the name of Herzl our prayers came to life again—Zion was close to us, within our reach. 'Next year in Jerusalem' was a goal to be attained in our own lifetimes, not in the Beyond.

"All this meant an enormous amount of work. We Polish Jews had become diffident after the experience of so many False Messiahs. We had to give the Messianic idea a rational basis. The traditional Messiah is associated with the Resurrection of the Dead, and his appearance is heralded by various signs. We had to find a middle course between faith and deeds. We had to transform allegory into logical theory, a poetic image into reality.

"Herzl was a poet, but he was a realist in politics. We young men sensed this at once. We undertook to familiarize the public with the seemingly utopian idea of building a Jewish state in our own era.

"The vague aspirations of Dr. Leon Pinsker's 'Back to Zion' movement were transferred to the new movement, and this one was less of a leaky vessel.

"When it comes to miracles, most people either shrug their shoulders or express frank incredulity. But I saw the great miracle with my own eyes. Jewish backs straightened up again. This was the ray of light in our exile. We were proud to be Jews, we began to take practical steps toward realizing the great dream.

"Yes, my friends, I attended the first Zionist Congress in 1897. I had the great privilege of standing close to him, where I could look right into his eyes. It was the biggest moment of my life. I burst into tears when I was face to face with him. I'm not ashamed to admit that I kissed his hand—not the way one kisses a priest's hand but the way I used to kiss my father's hand when he came back from the synagogue glowing with saintliness.

"Herzl was only a year or two older than I was. But this young man embodied a great legend. He organized the will of us all. He was like a great painter who creates a figure in which all the dreams of an enslaved nation are embodied. Doctor Herzl's face was the noble image of a people which henceforward will never give up hope.

"Doctor Herzl spoke to me in his native Viennese German, which I did not quite understand. When he spoke, he seemed to become more human, more Jewish. He even spoke with a nasal twang. From the platform, too, he spoke with this twang, and it made him sound perfectly natural, the very opposite of oratorical.

"But though not an orator, he spoke with fiery warmth that we do not encounter today. It was not mere eloquence but came from a deep inner faith. He never tried to persuade. Other speakers are always selling you something, but you trusted Doctor Herzl at once. Even when he discussed facts and figures, he made them seem to float in the air like cabalistic signs. His dry figures, I might say, were poems. The millions that, according to the petty ideas of the time, would be the cost of redemption seemed formidable enough, but when Doctor Herzl mentioned such sums, I would have sworn he already had them in his pocket.

"At the Zionist Congresses I also used to run into a little man with a paunch—a real diplomat's paunch—whose cutaway looked as though it had been molded on him. No, he had no lion's voice. Any peddler has a lion's voice. His was more like a bear's. He was a tremendous speaker, and he wielded the weapon of satire like a master. Doctor Herzl rarely indulged in wisecracks or funny stories, but Dr. Max Nordau's wit had the crack of the whip. He was the child prodigy of Europe and was looked upon as the greatest living public speaker. Doctor Nordau's face was so intelligent that at first I could not imagine how such a man had ever gotten caught up in a dream. But scholar that he was, he could soar to great heights and take the public with him. He made you laugh, but he could sing, too, and he developed his arguments the way a great architect constructs a building. When he had finished speaking, I had the impression that his speech stood there right next to him, four-square, and that both he and I were admiring it.

"I served as courier for the Congress. I was entrusted with urgent and important letters to Herzl. When he finished reading the messages I brought, his pale sallow face would take on a bit of color. At such moments he looked as though he were tanned by the sun. He would at once write down his replies to the other leaders who were consulting him on tactical questions. I was just the mailman who delivered the sacred messages. Yes, I had the privilege of being Doctor Herzl's personal errand boy who was entrusted with confidential messages.

"Don't imagine that we Polish delegates traveled at the time as comfortably—indeed, luxuriously—as the Zionist delegates of today. Far from it. We starved on the trip to Basel. We would take along a few loaves of bread, a jar of butter, and a piece of cheese that had gotten moldy by the time we arrived. We traveled on those hard benches in the third-class coaches of that time, and we had had to work hard to get enough money together for our fares. It was worse than walking there on foot would have been. Many of us were unable to collect even so small a sum as the fare required and traveled without tickets.

"At the Congresses we kept quiet. None of us was ever given the opportunity to take the floor. Had anyone called on us to speak, we would surely have fainted from terror. We raised our hands when a vote was taken. Otherwise we were satisfied to have only walk-on parts in the great drama. But for all that we said nothing, our hearts were nonetheless eloquent with joy, and you could hear them pounding.

"But the moment we who were tongue-tied at the Congresses got back to our little towns, we became so eloquent that no power on earth could have silenced us. Miraculously, in the towns and villages we were the great awakeners. The silent joy we had stored up at the Congresses now burst out in thunderous speeches, our tongues miraculously untied. We shouted out our joy and enthusiasm in the synagogues and the houses of study. We translated the abstruse speeches we had heard into plain Yiddish and thereby made them accessible and understandable. We were the popularizers of the great idea.

"We preached Zionism in the synagogues, but we had our greatest successes in the tailors' and shoemakers' synagogues. These good men at once caught the idea that our purpose was not to hasten our redemption but drag it out of the swamp in which it had gotten bogged down. The plain artisans gave us new strength and faith. They were the first to be won over, and not long after them the bastions of the middle class began to come over to us, too.

"They crumbled before our onslaught like the walls of Jericho. True, it took more than a blast of trumpets; it took a great deal of hard work and education. We had to create dozens of different styles of approach —for the pious Jew, for the skeptic, for the agnostic, for the Jew who believed that after his death his body would roll to the Holy Land under its own power. And then there were those who knew all about the signs by which the coming of the Messiah could be recognized. We had to persuade old men, young men, businessmen, and dreamers.

"We turned into poets, statisticians, financial wizards, lay preachers, religious preachers. To each group we had to speak its own language, until even the most pious rabbis began to understand. They were the most difficult group to persuade. They regarded us with the greatest distrust. They, the patient, healthy Jews, had plenty of time to wait for the Messiah. But they finally came to realize that the people was at the end of its tether. They decided that Zionism was, after all, the trumpet signaling the coming of the Messiah. After all, the Messiah could just as well come after the Jews had returned to their homeland."

Steinman stopped, and his eyes took in the group around him. He looked at each of us in turn, silently. His eyes were sober—or, more accurately, sobered.

"Ah, ah, little children, little birdies, close your eyes," he said, imitating the tone of someone telling a story to put a child to sleep. "You're rocking on your chairs like infants in their cradles, and you're about to doze off. I suppose you're waiting for the end of my story, but even if I kept talking for a thousand and one days, the story wouldn't be finished."

"Well, we understand why that Hungarian witch was happy to give you soup for telling her stories," one of Steinman's listeners said. "You're a real healer of the sick. My word, you could cure the hardened arteries of a thousand Jews with your stories."

Steinman's daughter came up and without a word put a pill in her father's mouth and made him wash it down with a glass of water. Stein-man made a face as though he had swallowed something bitter. "Have you seen the pill? That's the end of the story. It's a good thing you reminded me of Jozefa Kubi. This pill takes me straight to Para-dise, where Jozefa is enjoying the pleasure of her husband's company." "Don't say such foolish things," Finkel burst out. "I won't let you talk like that. We'll be visiting this place for many, many years, and you'll keep on telling us your stories."

"I suppose you can guarantee that?" Steinman asked with good-natured mockery.

"I promise you," Finkel said, jumping up from his chair. "Just a minute, I'll tell you something. A pious Jew in Galicia once made a wish that whatever my fated life span might be, I should live ten years in addition. Well, I'll share this gift with you. I declare before all these witnesses that I'm giving you five years."

"Who else wants to give me a present?" Steinman asked. "Five years is nothing to sneeze at. If everybody here were as generous, I might yet live to be as old as Methuselah."

"Come, come," one of the group said to Finkel. "This pious Jew didn't take your wife into account. She'll shorten your life by ten years."

"That's a silly thing to say," Finkel retorted, embarrassed. "But just to set your mind at peace, I'll tell you that my pious Jew did foresee that eventuality. He promised me that my wife would not survive me."

"Why didn't you say so to begin with? No wonder you can stand your wife. You have something to live for."

Everybody laughed at this and there was a general movement of get-ting up and stretching. At this moment Buchlerner appeared. "Don't scatter like the chickens," he said. "We're about to ring for lunch."

"We have to take a little walk, at least—we need some fresh air and exercise," Steinman objected.

"All right, you can have a quarter of an hour. That will give you time to walk all over the village, from one end to the other," Buchlerner said. "While the tables are being set, you can work up an appetite. I warn you that there's lots to eat, and as you know, I insist that you eat up what I put on your plates."

Steinman walked out, followed by his listeners. At first they let him walk ahead, but they surrounded him from all sides, so that people were walking at his right and left, in front and in the back. Suddenly he stopped and said: "If you don't mind, my friends, if you really don't mind, let me walk alone with my thoughts. What I told you today brought back so many memories that I must spend some time with them alone."

"Ah, of course, of course, we understand perfectly," all of them cried out in one voice. And they walked away, each by himself. Only Finkel stood still and followed Steinman with wistful eyes. He looked like a big bird craning his neck.

"Ah, that's a real man, a real Jew," he said. "May he live forever!" His eyes were full of tears.

♦♦♦ *Chapter 3*

1

That afternoon and the whole next day Steinman avoided my company. I could see that he was simply running away from me. He was positively hiding. Whenever he saw me walk toward him, he turned away. I was surprised, then I realized that it might be just as well. This man was like good wine, and I shouldn't overdo our intimacy. Perhaps he had some such idea, too, and wanted to give me a rest from his good company, so as not to overwhelm me with attention.

In the meantime a young woman who said she was a cousin of mine looked me up. She had found out that I was here and made up her mind to visit me. What right she had to call herself a cousin of mine I did not quite see. Actually, the only basis she had for considering me a relative was that a cousin of hers, a man, had married into my family.

Her name was Saba, she said, short for Sabina, and she recognized me although she had never seen me before. That was because, she said, she was intuitive. This was not the first time she had recognized someone whom she had never seen before. Having told me all this, she walked silently by my side, keeping very close to me. After about ten minutes of this, she began to splatter me with words like confetti. She was young and sad, and there was about her an aura of oversophistication. She was full of aphorisms, about how beautiful it is to be young, about how happiness blooms only to fade away and die, and about how silence is really the graveyard of buried words.

We walked up a hill. When I sat down, she seated herself a bit lower than me, and looked up at me in silence for a while.

Then she said suddenly: "You know, if my husband caught me here with you, he'd beat the hell out of both of us. I'd get the worst of it, but he wouldn't spare you either."

Involuntarily, I edged away and was about to get up.

"My husband is very strong," she said soothingly, "but after all it wouldn't do you any harm to act a bit more heroic."

I told her that to be a hero was never one of my ambitions. If I were to be beaten up on her account, I would have done nothing to deserve it—such blows are the hardest to bear. She then told me that her husband was far away at the moment, though he had the habit of dropping in on her unexpectedly. He was very jealous of her, and he was always investigating to find out where she went and whom she saw. He even questioned their little boy, who was only five.

"And is he faithful himself?"

"You're joking! He betrays me right and left!"

To begin with, she said, she must tell me what he looked like. He was twenty years older than she, he had a big bald head and a thick neck with suety folds. He was short but broad-shouldered, and he had disproportionately short legs, even for his height. Those legs of his seemed mere appendages for walking, stuck on to the torso without relation to the rest of his body. He had heavy hands, and when they hit anyone, they hurt. He beat her up regularly, though he pulled his punches. He always made it clear that he could have hit much harder. He looked intelligent, but his features were spoiled by anger. He had keen eyes and a fleshy nose, thick rather than long.

"He comes from a distinguished family of scholars and businessmen. I too come from a good family, but mine was very poor. He took me as I was, without a dowry, and everyone said I made a good marriage, for the whole town knew I had had lovers. He has never reproached me for this, although it is obvious that this is the cause of his constant suspicions. He is driving me crazy. My maid spies on me and my child spies on me. But, my dear hero, you mustn't be scared. I have sent both on a little trip, and they won't be back till tonight."

By now I was a trifle more interested. "And how are you making out?" I asked her. "Who is winning—the spies, or you?"

She did not answer at once. She lit a cigarette very slowly. "May I have as many thousands of złotys as the number of men the spies have missed," she said. "It's a kind of game to me. Who'll get whom? When you're bored, it's not a bad game. Everything becomes a matter of strategy, and I'm keen on that."

"Well, has he ever caught you?"

She shuddered. "Bite your tongue off! God forbid! That would really be my funeral. Many times he has almost caught me, but it's a long way from almost to catch. He slaps me around quite often, but in the end it's always he who turns out to have been wrong. His conscience bothers him when he beats me on mere suspicion."

"How long has this game been going on?"

"About six years. We've been married eight years, but the first year I made a real effort to be a good, faithful wife. The second year I learned to outsmart him."

"How do you know," I said, "that I don't belong to your husband's staff of detectives?"

She laughed. "That would be a good joke on me. It would mean I had gone out of my way to get into trouble." After a pause she added: "Do you know something? It has often occurred to me as I play this game that I'd like to lose once in a while. I am getting quite tired of it, really." And she went on to say that she slipped most often when she was sad at heart. "And do you know why I speak so openly with you? Because I know nothing is going to happen between us. I have nothing to worry about."

Her husband, she said, must now be sweating with worry at his cigarette factory. No matter how hard he works, she went on, it's nothing in comparison with how he works his employees. A really tough character, her husband. "But I have no right to complain. He showers me with presents—dresses and jewels, and entertainment and pleasure trips, the best candy, the most luxurious furs. I take everything. I'm sure I'm a bad woman."

It was in Warsaw, she said, that she had first gotten into trouble. For a year she attended courses at the university. She shared a room with a musician, a girl who played the piano. The girl had had many friends —poets and painters, actors and musicians. She was a wild girl, a real glutton for pleasure, who wanted to try everything once. "And I was a stupid little goose. I fell in love with every man I met, and every man taught me to fall out of love. I was in the harness and out of the harness. To artists love is a pretty casual business. As soon as my heart was torn to pieces, they would get free of me with the greatest of ease. Only one clung to me and was quite serious, but there was a drawback—he was a Gentile, and I couldn't bring myself to disgrace my parents. To this day he puts my initials in the dedications of his poems. He is a well-known poet. I often remember him, and it helps me to keep my sanity. He was a profound man, and a sad one. He never laughed. What he saw in me I have no idea. I'm empty-headed, I have no mind at all. All I possess is an inborn sadness. Maybe he loved me because of my sadness. He wrote many poems addressed to 'the sad girl,' to his 'melancholy joy.' He liked to play with words, but it is true that the joys of youth are melancholy."

She tore out a handful of grass and put it to her nose, smelling it as though it were flowers. "I like the smell of the earth," she said. "At first it's unpleasant, but it becomes as familiar as your own sweat. Do you hear the way I talk? When I was younger, painters and writers talked to me a lot, and now all they said oozes out of me. I wish I could get to the point when I have something to say of my own.

"Yes, I believe it was that gang that spoiled me. They're wonderful boys, but they're always on the run and they ran over me. It was too heady an experience for me—too high an altitude. Their talk, their movements, their interests—it wasn't good for me. Strange thing, with each of them I felt perfectly whole, but the moment they dropped me and I was on my own, I went to pieces. I was a lamp without a light, or worse—a discarded handkerchief. It was all too much for me, I had to develop a protective shield of flippancy if I wasn't to commit suicide. Oh, I thought of that often. That was when I took everything seriously, but everything becomes a mockery when you're made to feel like a fool.

"Sometimes, when I become absorbed in my own thoughts, it seems to me that I am looking for a man who'd make me whole again. I'll never find one."

She said she had "something very interesting" to tell me. About a year ago, she met a man she thought she could love. How could she tell? Because he made her think about herself, about what she could give him. When she had such thoughts, she usually kept quiet, she explained, for fear that someone else's voice would come out of her mouth. Whenever words came easily, she was afraid that they were just odds and ends from all the chatter she had heard as a young girl—artists are good talkers.

A year ago she thought that she had actually found the man who would be her life's companion—she had met him right here in this resort—the man who would take her away from the money, the jewels, and the rest. She had never supposed she'd actually meet such a man, but she'd always kept herself ready for him. In fact, even today she was playing with the idea of being poor again, but she still hadn't made up her mind whether her child was part of the alien life which had been forced upon her, or whether she must stay with him, rich or poor, happy or not.

The man who had brought a ray of light into her life was a graduate chemist—which for a Jew in Poland meant certain unemployment in his chosen field. He was from an assimilated family, but at the university he began to do some soul searching, partly no doubt because of the way he was abused by his Gentile fellow students. He became a pious Jew, and when she met him at this resort he was among the followers of the rabbi who comes here every year. His skullcap and his pious manner did not deceive her: the moment she saw him she knew she must get to know him. It wasn't easy, but one day she managed to strike up acquaintance with him when he had gone for a walk by himself.

"He was a real comforter, a professional comfort giver. When I met him he was somewhat confused. He had made up his mind that the Jews were going through a terrible period. Not only were they persecuted but there was no one to console them. So he took upon himself the mission of going from town to town, from village to village, in order to spread the good word, to be a preacher of joy, as he put it. He was a handsome man whose blond beard stubbornly refused to be Hasidic. He still looked like a student. His blue eyes glowed with his faith, and his mouth was warmed by his voice. He knew all the words that gave comfort, and his name had become famous in Jewish communities. When he appeared on a Saturday in a village synagogue, he gave the poor Jewish people a joy they had never known before."

At the time she met him he was going through a period of doubt. He wondered whether he was not doing the wrong thing, whether, instead of comforting the Jewish people as a whole, it was not his duty to go from door to door, to comfort the people individually rather than en masse in the synagogues. It was a long time before he told her that, and more generally, before he began to share his thoughts with her. She had to work hard. It was a game to her, but different from the one she played with her husband. That game she was sure she would always win. This time she knew she would lose.

"For four months I struggled with him and with myself. All that time I also had to keep an eye on my husband. I suspected that he was suspecting me. My bookkeeping became so complicated that I almost lost my mind. On top of all this I felt that somehow there was a little devil inside me who was making fun of me, laughing himself sick at my expense. I imagined that I was reenacting the story of Joseph and Potiphar's wife. As luck would have it, his name too was Joseph, and in my eyes he was every bit as handsome.

"There is a little woods outside the village where it's cool and quiet. Dead leaves lie scattered everywhere and crackle under your feet. The leaves are slippery and the ground is moldy. There are many dead trees in that woods. It was there that we most often sat and talked. He never got close to me, never looked me in the face. I had almost talked myself hoarse before he agreed to so much as sit and talk with me in the woods. I campaigned as if I were a whole army, and he a city under siege. I ambushed him, pursued him, tormented him. At the same time, I felt sorry for him. But I had to do it because I was even sorrier for myself. 'Saba,' he would beg me, 'Saba, I'm afraid of you, you have such hungry eyes, such a hungry mouth, even the words you say are hungry.'"

He often talked to her about the inherent poetry of Judaism, and this opened up a whole new world to her. She had long been surrounded by prosaic, tired people whose lives were anything but poetic. Her brothers were just ordinary Jews, who wore Jewish caps and slippers. Her father had died when she was a little girl. The only bit of poetry in her parental home was heard when her mother blessed the candles Friday evenings, and the words she pronounced were bright and warm. Not so Joseph—he was in love with Judaism, and he spoke about it with such ardor that she understood why he could set the hearts of others ablaze, why he was a comforter.

On one occasion he confided to her that he'd like to go to Germany, that if he could only smuggle himself across the border, he'd go, for it was there that he was really needed. At the same time, he confessed to her that he was filled with such pride when he told himself that he had power to give comfort that he became frightened and tried to punish himself by going without food and sleep, to humble his pride. At such moments she felt that he was a Christianized Jew, that he had too many problems for a Jew. She once told him so, and the next day he told her that her remark had caused him a great deal of pain, that he had been thinking it over and decided that she was right, that he was perhaps an outsider after all, cut off from his own people.

"One day he was very nervous. This is the only pleasant memory I have kept of the whole affair, and it doesn't amount to much. He was restless, could not sit still, paced back and forth, and finally stammered out that he was about to get married, so as to be more at peace with himself. I understood his restlessness. I felt just like a mother, I understood exactly what was bothering the child, and this gave me a kind of satisfaction. When I saw him so restless, something inside me alternately laughed and wept. 'Goodbye, Joseph,' I said to him, 'goodbye,' and I spoke to him more tenderly than I had ever dared before. But now I was sure that I had lost him, and that I had lost someone very close to me. He looked at me bewildered. It wasn't nice of me to be so much more reasonable than he was at this moment. He was as green as the woods around us.

"He left me, and three weeks later he was married. I was as happy as if I had married off my own son. He married a Jewish woman of good family, who brought him a handsome dowry. I am glad that a man like him will not be obliged to work for his daily bread.

"Later I took to going to the woods all by myself and sat in the same place. I scrawled hieroglyphs on the moist ground, and I dreamed that I was getting smaller and smaller, that I was shrinking, so that I took up hardly any space, like when I was a child. I often dreamed this way, too, that I was taking up less and less space in God's world. I liked to stare at small closed newspaper kiosks and imagine that I lived inside them, or in a tiny cell, all alone. My friend the poet once told me that such thoughts reflect a longing for the mother's womb. This may be true. Very often I pull the blinds on sunny days and lie in my little boy's crib. It is small, but I am alone and so close to myself that I can dream the most wonderful dreams.

"In this way I both lose myself and pursue myself, entirely detached from the ordinary daily round. I perform my duties to my husband and child with the little bit of life remaining, like a sleepwalker. My only real contact with myself is my friend the pianist, who used to be as restless as I have become. But today she is very respectable, poised, reserved, and a good housewife. She married money too. She often comes to see me and sits wrapped in a shawl printed with flowers, as though shielding her body from some barbarian assault. She sits with her head on one side, as though she were afraid of something. Her limbs are sharp and bony, like a child's. She has an open face; I don't know how it strikes others, but to me it is a map on which I can read all the sinful pleasures of her youth. She sometimes falls asleep in the shawl, and then she looks like a young grandmother, and she smiles in her sleep.

"When I ask her whether she loves her husband and whether she is happy, she becomes impatient with me and says that people don't speak about such things. She has calmed down, she says, and she tries to convert me to her point of view. You too, she says, should be happy. To have a husband, a child of one's own—if I only knew how much that means, she keeps telling me, how perfectly sufficient that is to make a life.

"But when she gets up and takes off her shawl of resignation, when she walks about the room, I recognize her old self. As she walks, her elegant legs dance in front of her in the old provocative way, proclaiming with quivers of joy that here is a woman, ready to take and be taken. That is the art of walking—a prelude to the art of lying back.

"Occasionally she speaks of the harmonious life. She has got a brand new idea—the Jewish female, she says, must control herself. Once we perform the rite and take the oath, we must be true wives. Whatever we may have done before, once our husbands accept us, it's all over and done with. Once we're married, we must remember that the Jewish home has a firm foundation—one God and one man. Of all people, it's she who talks that way, she who had so many lovers. 'I should put you across my knee and give you a good spanking,' she says, or 'I should scratch your face,' and then she becomes as affectionate as a kitten. She takes me in her arms and strokes my hair. I like to tell her at such moments that I am a sick woman. All women are sick, she replies, but when they lead a healthy life they become healthy. The wifely estate is a new source of strength, a new reservoir of youth. 'You pay attention to what I'm telling you, you little bitch,' she chides me, 'If I could settle down, so can you!'"

Finally Saba left me, asking me not to walk her back to the village. I watched her walk down the hill; it had occurred to me to see her home. When she had left I thought about Joseph's observation that her words were "hungry."

I had forgotten to ask her who Joseph was. Was he real or had she invented him while lying on her little child's bed? A starved woman can invent hundreds of things and poison her life with her own imaginings.

And the smaller she grew as she walked down the hill, she seemed also to move more and more clumsily, as though she were walking backward in time, pulling me along with her into some miniature childish world, a frozen wax world prior to speech, a world where yellowed memories were painted bright red.

Then I recalled my first love, Yochevet, or Yochtche, as she was called. She must have been all of six years old when I fell in love with her, and I was much younger. She had pigtails and big black eyes, and always sat on the doorstep of her house, daydreaming. For a long time she refused to take notice of me. I prayed God to make me an acrobat so that I could perform some trick that would force her to look at me, but at that time I found it hard even to stand on my head with the help of a wall to lean on.

I finally conquered her. It was during the Passover holidays: I bribed her with half a *chremzel*, that succulent matzo pastry. After that we would sit together on the stone steps in front of her house, and she told me stories. The things she told me were so implausible that even at that time I realized she was making them up as she went along, although she always swore the most solemn oaths that everything she told me had happened to her personally.

Her stories were of lions, tigers, and bears, about gypsies who steal Jewish children, about devils who play the violin and pull out your soul through a little hole, just like you suck an egg by making a hole in the shell with a pin.

Yochtche also liked to hide with me in a dark cellar where she would always choose the darkest, farthest corner, and tell me the scariest tales. She asked me to put my hand on her heart so I could feel it pounding while she was telling me these stories. It was very agreeable to be scared in the dark with Yochtche beside me. We would emerge from the cellar sleepy-eyed, and we would see many little specks swaying on tiny threads suspended in the air.

2

Specks were beginning to swarm before my eyes, and I saw that a man was standing next to me on the hill. His face was composed of several recognizable traits. When he turned his glassy eyes on me, he looked like Buchlerner, but in a moment when he stood still his features were those of the girl who fed the chickens and the ducks every morning, speaking Yiddish to them. This composite figure was wearing a caftan, which did not surprise me. I even found it natural that he should be stamping his feet and crying, "ai-ai,"—those particular sounds and no others: "ai-ai!"

I knew why he was wailing like that, poor man, He was assaulting high heaven for the great wrong he had suffered. Weisgelt had starved his youth away, studying the violin. No sacrifice was too much for his father, a military tailor, who spent everything he possessed to get his son the best teachers. And finally the day came when he began to play in public, started the long climb to musical eminence. God was good to him, and his name, Abrasha Weisgelt, began to be seen in the announcements of musical events. Abrasha is to play at the Craftsmen's Hall, for the Office Workers' Union, and the Professional Men's Club —finally, Abrasha is to play with the Philharmonic. He actually made it that far, our own Jewish fiddler, Abrasha the violinist, our Jewish virtuoso. Then, suddenly, just when he had reached the top of the heap, his hands and feet were stricken with paralysis. For ten years he had been lying like that, neither dead nor alive, an affliction to his parents.

Was this not a monstrous injustice, if there ever was one, a case for smashing the windows of Heaven? What mockery, to have climbed onward and upward, while all the time paralysis was following him like his own shadow. And then, at just the right moment, at the very moment the world was within his grasp, it was the shadow that took over, and rendered him a martyr.

After such misfortune, what is there to say? The poor man just stood there, nothing but "Ai-ai, ai-ai" escaping from between his tight-closed lips. It is a great wrong, and you should be ashamed of yourself, Lord God. What kind of a way to act is that? Don't raise me up just to hurl me down!

"Ai-ai," he kept muttering there on the hilltop, and none of it surprised me. But then I noticed his feet. I suppose I expected a pair of strongly built, mud-spattered feet, perfectly white under the mud. But what I saw was a pair of calves' feet, the kind mother used to give us on Friday nights—pickled calves' feet. This man was standing there, jiggling, on feet which had been cooked and pickled. I began to feel quite uneasy.

I made up my mind I must get up. I pulled on my socks, but I could not find my shoes. I was wearing my dark blue suit, but how could I go around dressed like that in my stocking feet? But no matter how hard I looked for my shoes, I couldn't find them. There was only one thing to do: I set out in my stocking feet. A number of couples were strolling around, paying no attention to me, but I knew that their indifference was a pretense, and this made me dash about wildly. Somehow I was sure that right around here in the dark I had left one of my shoes. Yes, it was the left one—I grabbed it and put it on, but as I did so my right sock fell off the other foot. Now as I dashed and hopped about, one of my feet was bare and the other shod.

Then it flashed through my mind that I might just well resign myself to the ridiculousness of the situation, because all that was happening was just a dream.

It was about time I realized this—for the same dream had come to me many times before. Never in my life had I ever run around barefoot, nor been obliged to do so for lack of shoes, and yet this dream recurrently disturbed my sleep. The moment I realized I was dreaming, I began to walk more slowly. It was still embarrassing to be wearing my good suit with one foot bare, but I was no longer so upset about it.

Suddenly I came into a dark place. There were many doors, and all of them, but one, were closed. Through the one open door a column of light streamed in. There was a mighty wind blowing through, but though the light wavered, it stayed bright. I concentrated on that light with every ounce of my strength, as my salvation from terror. All at once, to my enormous relief, I heard voices coming through the open door.

I stared, fascinated. A stage had been set up diagonally across one corner of the room, rather than in the usual place. I could tell that the play being performed was not the Purim play which I had written at the age of eight, and which I, dressed in mother's best clothes, performed for my friends who paid a penny each to see me. Nor was it *The Manhunters,* a play our local amateur theater group had presented in the "Rusalka," a real theater, before a real public. I had been the prompter for that production, and from the prompter's box I shouted the cues so loudly that I could be heard in the gallery. I had been given a baton, and it was with that I was supposed to signal the orchestra to begin playing, at the point where a friend of mine, in the part of an unhappy lover, victim of the manhunters, breaks quavering into song,

The sun goes down in flames,
The sun we can scarcely see.

Nor were they performing *The Vow,* another play we had put on at the "Rusalka," with Esther Rachel Kaminska in the leading role. We had had red posters made to inform the public that Esther Rachel

Kaminska was giving a guest performance, and all of Lublin flocked to see it, even though it wasn't a comedy, and had no songs or dances.

I ruined that great occasion. Once again I was the designated prompter—devil knows why, but my friends in the theater group would never give me so much as a walk-on—and this time I became so engrossed in Kaminska's heartrending performance that I forgot to give the cues. Poor Kaminska—she was playing the part of Ronia the postmistress—kept inching down to the prompter's box and kicking it, to remind me of my duties. She would hiss at me, "Give me the lines, you fool!" and when she walked past the prompter's box, she would aim a kick at my head or at least manage to step on my hand. The other actors, too, kept banging against the prompter's box to make me give them their lines, but I was in a trance. I forgot completely that I was prompter and simply turned into one more enraptured member of the audience. Gradually the whole performance slowed down and stopped like a clock that has not been wound. There wasn't a single tick more out of the actors, and the stage fell shockingly still. On his deathbed, Ronia's husband forgot to ask for her solemn vow, and she forgot to give it. They had to bring the curtain down to break the spell and wake me up.

No, it was not *The Vow* that was being performed on the oddly placed stage just visible through the open door. I could make out some of my own words in the play, but I had never seen the actors before. As each actor spoke in turn, he would glare at me savagely.

We were all sitting on long wooden benches; behind me sat my father with my mother next to him, but they were seated in armchairs, as though in a private box. Mother was all dressed up and radiant with joy at being off her feet and away from the kitchen and the dining room for once. Father was taking it all in critically, as from a great distance. He might have been saying, "Well, it'll be pretty bad, I expect, like so much of this fuzzy new Yiddish writing. Why can't he write so that his own father can understand it, at least?"

I was annoyed—I felt that to please my mother they should have given a performance of Goldfaden's adored operetta *The Witch*, with a rendition of the song "Hot Cakes." Suddenly a cat ran across the stage, the sure sign that this must be Goldfaden's other classic, *Shu-*

lamith. Would its hero, Absalom, appear, too, I wondered hopefully, would Mother after all have an opportunity to hear its lullaby that mothers have been singing ever since, *"In beys hamikdesh, in a vinkl-kheyder . . . ?"*

Saba was sitting next to me, chattering steadily, keeping up a continual stream of critical remarks. "You call this a drama? Where is the conflict?" A drama, she said, must have a plot, complications, counterplots; only Chekhov was a good enough writer to do without all that. She had me on the ropes, and she quoted great critics from memory. One said this and the other said that, and when you put them all together they spelled out the fact that I wasn't a playwright. Her every well-turned aphorism was a warning to me to give it up. I was holding her hands in the dark, and they were hot. She talked so much that the people around us began to shout, "Shuddup! Shuddup! Shut your trap!" The vulgarity of the expression shocked me. How would anyone call so pretty, so eloquent a little mouth, a trap? I was ready to take them all on, but she went right on chattering. "I pay no attention to them," she said, "their yellow press and their shuddup! This is Europe!"

After this things seemed to go better. The actors, God knows why, kept looking at me angrily. Often they vanished completely and the performance seemed to go on without them, following my script exactly, not missing a single stage direction, a single line or emphasis.

BASIA: After all, I'm just a poor Jewish woman, heavy-hearted, but if it's no sin to say so, God works in mysterious ways. To one he gives too much, to another a pain in the belly. As my grandmother, rest her soul, used to say—it doesn't add up.

GNENDL: You didn't go to the synagogue?

BASIA: No, I stayed away on purpose. When I'm at odds with God I can't go to His house and wish Him a merry Sabbath. Right now, if I may say so, I'm good and angry with Him.

GNENDL (*her mind elsewhere*): With whom?

BASIA: With whom? With God in person.

GNENDL (*taken aback*): May the punishment fall on my enemies! Honestly, Basia, it's a sin a talk like that. You don't sound like a Jew.

BASIA: I've kept quiet long enough. Itche Scab and his saintly wife, the whore who sleeps with every soldier, wriggling her fat you-know-what—they get the places of honor at the east wall of the synagogue, and I have to go scrounging for a bit of food for the Sabbath. (*wiping her eyes*) Why should I keep quiet? Because God might strike me with a thunderbolt? For all the pleasure I get out of life, I should care!

"You know, for an amateur she plays very well, that Basia," Saba said pressing closer to me.

GNENDL (*with animation*): I bought a pike today, you've never seen anything like it. Maybe you'll take a few pieces of fish? My word, it's too big for me. Who is going to eat it at my house anyway? The children I don't have? And as for my Nahman, he nibbles like a bird.

BASIA: My husband has stopped eating altogether. He sits all day with his red-rimmed eyes, digging away at the Talmud—he'll end up putting a hole through it. He sits like that day and night, studying and thinking, and between one thought and another he makes me children. A big help!

(*Sound of bells from a Catholic church, echoed shortly afterward by the heavy Orthodox bells. Through the open door the chants of the worshipers mingle with the chiming bells.*)

BASIA: They're ringing in honor of the Christian God. They even begrudge us our Sabbath. Just listen to the awful noise they're making.

GNENDL: As for me, whenever I hear church bells, a shudder runs through me.

BASIA: The young priests bleat. They sit by their stained-glass windows and stick out their tongues, like little devils, when Jews go by on their way to the synagogue. They're having a good time with the Yoshke we gave them.

GNENDL (*sadly*): May God forgive me for saying so, but on Saturdays and holidays my heart tightens with anxiety. It's all right the rest of the time. The Sundays and the Mondays pass quickly, but the Saturdays and the holidays drag on and on, and the candles throw shadows on the walls.

(The church bells grow louder, drowning out the chanting in the synagogue.)

BASIA: Jewish life is sad. It scrapes on and on like a fiddle at a poor man's wedding.

GNENDL: Sometimes when I'm all by myself at home I dance and sing like the untouched girl I once was. My dress feels ablaze and my blood is on fire—and then my Nahman shows up on the doorstep unexpectedly, and makes me feel ashamed of myself.

BASIA: That's the way it is. A shikse stays a shikse till the day she dies, but once a Jewish girl puts on her bridal veil she takes on the whole burden of Jewishness.

GNENDL: No wonder they used to call me the Jewish shikse in Tarnow. My steps danced like flames when I was a girl, but now I've become a matron.

(Enter Nahman with a dinner guest.)

NAHMAN: Good shabes.

GUEST: Good shabes.

BASIA: O my goodness, here I've been standing talking . . .

(Gnendl runs after her with a few pieces of fish on a plate and comes right back.)

GUEST: *(reciting the traditional song of Sabbath greeting)* Sholem Aleichem, ministering angels, messengers of the Most High! *(pointing to Gnendl.)* Your wife? Lovely!

NAHMAN: My "woman of valor," may she be safe from the evil eye.

GUEST: *(looks at Gnendl)* A real fortune of gold, silver, diamonds.

(Gnendl, embarrassed, moves more quietly as she sets the table.)

(Nahman strokes his wife's head while the guest wanders around, turning frequently to bow to his hosts.)

GUEST: What's your name, young man?

NAHMAN: Nahman.

GUEST: You listen to me, Nahman. The Rizhin rabbi once recited, "*sholem aleichem,*" and at once angels and seraphim appeared in the room so that the ceiling took fire and burned until the Rizhin rabbi escorted them out personally. And I, sinful mortal that I am, as I greet my hosts here, I feel that angels are at rest in every comer. It's a great thing, the peace of the Sabbath.

GNENDL (*shuddering with fear*): One shouldn't speak of the angels.

GUEST (*stopping*): What's the matter with you, silly woman, what are you frightened of? (*to Nahman*) That's right, young man, stroke her head—ai! ai! Gold and silver and diamonds, a real treasure.

(*Guest says the Kiddush with fervor, Nahman mutters it quickly and pours Gnendl a bit of wine. They wash their hands. The guest uncovers the hallah, cuts off a piece and eats calmly as though not really hungry.*)

GUEST: How are the Jews doing in this village, are they getting by all right?

NAHMAN: It's a poor village. Everybody's penniless, we barely keep alive. The Gentiles even begrudge us our poverty—they think we're all Rothschilds.

GUEST: That so! And what do you do, young man?

NAHMAN: I trade a bit, I work part-time as a goldsmith. I fix broken springs, locks, I make gold crosses, we somehow manage. When there's a fair we're always afraid the Gentiles will get out of hand, but at least it brings in a few złotys. All in all, there's great poverty here, ai, real misery! I can tell you, it tears your heart.

GUEST (*with emotion*): Is that so?!

GNENDL: Now take that Basia who was just here, the poor thing is badly off. The way she was talking! Such language should never be heard in a Jewish house.

GUEST: What do you mean?

GNENDL: About God—she was speaking against God! May her words be scattered to the empty fields!

GUEST: A Jewish woman who dares such things! Is that so! Is that so!

NAHMAN: The poor woman is having a very hard time. They're very simple people, not a piece of bread in the house, so the words just spill out. And what is your business?

GUEST (*snapping awake*): You mean me? I'm a traveler. I travel from place to place—I'm not to be envied. A lonely widower, my wife died ten years ago, she was childless, and I was left all alone like a stone. Thank God I'm not a beggar, but I'm penniless, no money at all.

NAHMAN: And what's new in the world?

GUEST: Oh, nothing much. (*eats slowly, speaks carefully, measuring his words, as if weighing the risk*) Jews aren't too happy. The young people are looking for God. It's sort of a new fashion they have—searching for God.

NAHMAN: Not very Jewish, that. That's the Gentile way. Jews should never reason too much about God. We know there's a Creator of the Universe, and that's that.

GUEST: I see you're a sensible young man. That's my opinion, too. But the searching for God isn't the worst. There's also subversive politics. Secret meetings, boys and girls together.

GNENDL: Oy! That's very bad, very bad!

GUEST: It certainly is! What business have we got meddling in their affairs? They can worry themselves to death. Not to mention that Judaism itself is being threatened, let alone true piety.

NAHMAN: Too bad the situation of Jews is so miserable. I think it's high time for the Messiah to come and redeem us. We're at the end of our tether.

GUEST: True, true! (*chews calmly*) There are Jews who behave like Gentiles, and others, may their names he cursed, who baptize themselves and their children. They run away from the Jewish flock. (*glances at Gnendl*) But you're a very lucky man to have a pearl like that in the house. She spreads warmth into every comer. (*Gnendl walks softly, bringing in and removing plates.*) Just look at her, how gently she walks, such dear, lovely legs, may God pity me, a poor wandering soul.

"The part of the guest is very well done," Saba said, huddling up to me. "Who is the amateur playing him?"

"Some amateur! Just listen to that violin voice—that's Alexander Moissi!"

(*Enter Yankel Satan.*)

YANKEL: Good shabes, good shabes, kiss the old *babbes*.

GUEST: What an extraordinary creature!

NAHMAN: He is my apprentice—a merry Andrew, an agnostic, but a good worker and an honest fellow.

YANKEL: I just ran into Goddam Devilsfilth. He's coming here tonight. He sighs for Gnendl, he flies to Gnendl, ay chiri-bach chach-chach, ay chiri-bach chach chach.

GNENDL: You've got a big mouth, Yankel. You should swallow a dose of silence.

YANKEL: Good idea—why not?

NAHMAN (*laughing heartily*): Do you hear, Mr. Guest, how they have a share in my wife? It's bad to have a pretty wife. The whole town covets her.

YANKEL: Why not? So now it's forbidden even to look at her? And yet she's faithful to her Nahman, so faithful it's a pain in the neck.

GNENDL: Have you been getting drunk? Tell me the truth!

YANKEL: Gnendele, I love you more than life. As soon as Nahman has given up the ghost . . .

GNENDL: Shame on you! Yankel Satan with his tricks!

GUEST: Some card! He's a real boor!

NAHMAN: Oh he's a good boy, a real treasure. He just doesn't believe in anything—no more than a dog. But it's none of my business, I won't burn in hell because of him.

GUEST: Oh certainly not. I'm not afraid of atheists. Why, I even like to have discussions with them.

(*The church bells ring, first thin Catholic bells, then the heavy Orthodox ones.*)

GUEST: Just listen to them quarreling among themselves. The

Catholic church says bim-bim and the Orthodox church says bom-bom. A real debate.

YANKEL (*with pretended seriousness*): Quite a debate. It's almost like a theological disputation between two great rabbis.

GUEST: Still, there's a distinction between these spheres—they're worlds apart.

NAHMAN: Don't expect Yankel Satan to recognize any distinctions! Kasha and beets are all the same to him.

YANKEL: Which is the kasha and which are the beets? I'm taking you up on this. Maybe you used your measuring tape to find out which is the kasha and which are the beets? Go ahead, prove it to me.

GNENDL: If you sang instead of talking, Yankel, no one would find out what a fool you are. You really believe that the world is a clock and that it's your job to break it.

YANKEL: It's out of order as it is. Just listen to this, if you please. My grandmother left brooches to everyone else in the family, but all she gave me was a Jewish face. So I walk around proudly with my Jewish looks, and any no-good Gentile can spit straight in my face. I wipe off the spit, and—what a lucky break!—I still have my pride. I'm a Jew, *ein Jüde*, an *Israélite*, a believer in the Old Testament, a Hebrew. O joy, O rapture.

GUEST: It's a great thing to be a Jew. After all, there must be something to it. Just think—the nations of the world really hate one another, but they all get together to hate the Jew. There must be something to it. (*chants a Sabbath prayer, extolling the Lord of the Universe*)

YANKEL: Can you really explain what that something is, that something we're supposed to be so proud of—that has given us such a fine reputation with all nations that they hate us?

(*Nahman takes a seat close to Gnendl and strokes her head. She lowers her eyes modestly.*)

GUEST: Because they all are afraid of us. (*He picks crumbs from the table and throws them into his mouth.*) They're afraid of our—(*taps his head with his hand*)

YANKEL (*sarcastic*): Some proof. Something to write home about, what we've accomplished with our brains. Well, listen to what I have to say to that: if we had really been smart, it's like the Lithuanian skeptic puts it, "If my grandfather had any brains, he'd have become a Christian and today I'd be a carefree goy."

NAHMAN (*laughs*): You think that would have helped you to get a wife? Why, even a shikse wouldn't touch you with a ten-foot pole.

GUEST: Still unmarried, this noble specimen? (*points at Yankel*)

GNENDL: No, no, Yankel will find a wife. A Jewish girl will live with this scoundrel.

YANKEL: As I am a Jew, Gnendele, you love me, but you're ashamed to admit it.

Oy it's me you miss
Oy it's me you'd like to kiss
Oy it's me you're yearning for
Ay, chiri-bach-chiri, ay chiri-chiri
Bach chiri-chiri- (*dances a few steps*).

GNENDL: Sure, it's you I miss, I'm being driven crazy missing you.

NAHMAN: Ah Yankel, you devil, if you're after my wife, you're playing with fire. Gnendl will let you have it, and she has a sturdy little hand.

GNENDL (*laughing*): What am I, a bully, God forbid?

YANKEL: You see, Nahman, she has a Jewish heart.

GUEST: A real comedian. Now you leave that Jewish daughter alone —such a jewel!

(*Door opens, enter Goddam Devilsfilth. He is tall and thin, with sinister green eyes, set in a hawklike face. He moves jerkily; his gestures are mockingly courteous.*)

GODDAM: Good evening. Begging your pardon, good shabes.

YANKEL: Kiss the old babbes, and when you're kissing, don't pull your punches, make the most of it.

GODDAM: Ah, Yankel (*He pronounces the name with the accent on the last syllable, like a Gentile.*), you and your cracks.

NAHMAN: We got rid of the dogs.

GODDAM: Got rid of my dogs! They keep me enslaved, I've barely managed to escape. It's always iti-miti, in and out!

YANKEL: Listen to that line! Iti-miti, in and out!

GUEST: What's that about? Maybe you're a dog catcher?

GODDAM: No, my dear gentleman, God forbid.

(*Nahman and Gnendl laugh.*)

YANKEL: No, he is a beaten dog himself. That is, he has about thirty dogs, and he is happy and so are we.

GUEST: Is that so? And he is a Jew?

YANKEL: Of course. Isn't it obvious? A rabbinic authority! You'll hear his version of the Midnight Lamentations—you can hear the barking and howling when he runs back and forth with the dogs, inside his house and all over the village.

GODDAM: Ay, what a joker. And how is Gnendele, my little chickadee, my little Gnendl-chick? Ha? (*with a strange flash in his eyes and impudent gestures*)

GNENDL (*a bit uneasy*): I'm fine, thank God.

GODDAM (*falls at her feet*): I'm at your feet, Gnendele, my dear, have pity on me! Just one friendly look, one smile, something, alms for a beggar. (*gets up*) Iti-miti, in and out.

YANKEL: Where did you get that phrase of yours? Some witticism, that. He winds up everything with "iti-miti, in and out."

(*Guest, somewhat embarrassed, groans, wriggles on his chair, takes up his prayer chant again.*)

NAHMAN: Don't be scared of this joker. He's a strange sort of Jew, but he does a lot for the Jews. He's on good terms with the priest and the landowners; they treat him as one of their pack.

GUEST: Scared? Who's scared? I've seen worse—I once fell into the hands of thieves, may no one have to undergo that.

(*Knocks are heard at the door, gradually growing stronger. The door opens. Enter two Gentile youths. They are drunk.*)

FIRST YOUTH: Don't be afraid, gentlemen, we've just dropped in for a moment. (*general surprise, expressions of fear*) I've come to show him (*gives the other youth a push in the back*) a Jewish princess. Here she is, the Jewish princess. (*points silently to Gnendl and moves closer to her*)

YANKEL: What are we waiting for? Give him a punch in the jaw that'll knock him out or sober him up!

(*Second youth smiles stupidly.*)

FIRST YOUTH: She always sits by the window there and caresses every passerby with her eyes. No, she does more than caress them, she kisses, kisses them. Jewish princess, Don't be scared. Give me a kiss, and I'll shoot myself for joy. By the Holy Mother of God, I'll shoot myself in the head.

(*Gnendl draws back in fear. Nahman moves between her and the youths. Goddam moves closer to the first youth.*)

GODDAM: You snotnose, I'll tell your father on you. (*Pushes him out of the house, the other youth runs after him, bangs the door shut. Noises of a scuffle and quarrel outside, then silence.*)

GODDAM: That's the innkeeper's son, a rascal, a clown.

YANKEL: You should have punched him in the nose.

GUEST: Better not, with people like that it's better to use the gentle approach.

GODDAM: Sure, sure, the gentle way is the best. You just saw, didn't you, iti-miti, in and out.

(*Gnendl is still upset and frightened. Nahman bends over her affectionately.*)

NAHMAN: What's the matter, Gnendl, are you scared?

YANKEL: It's time for her to go to bed. That was a dirty trick to play on her. I still think you should have punched him in the nose.

GODDAM: Well, good night!

YANKEL: Good—Gnendl, go to bed, you'll feel better in the morning. (*exit with Goddam*)

(Guest, still seated, drums with his fingers on the table. The candles are about to go out. He chants softly.)

NAHMAN *(leads Gnendl to the bedroom, then comes back, addresses the guest)*: I hope you don't mind—you can sleep here on the sofa. *(stands helplessly)*

GUEST: I have no choice, have I? And as for you, go join your wife. *(smiles)* Don't worry, I'll manage to make my own bed. Go on in, to your treasure. *(hums the same melody as before)*

(Nahman still stands helpless in the doorway to his wife's bedroom.)

GUEST: You see I'm alone, all alone, I never sleep in the same place, I'm a poor neglected widower. Well, of course *(yawns)*, I'll make my bed on the sofa.

(Exit Nahman. Guest remains seated in dimmed room, singing softly.)

CURTAIN

Father and mother were gone now. Throughout the performance the audience had kept changing. All sat with their mouths open wide, staring at the lighted corner—at Nahman's bedroom. Gnendl was lying in bed, one foot sticking out from under the featherbed. Suddenly I no longer could feel Saba's hot little hands in mine. Astonishingly, she had left her seat and was now playing the part of Gnendl. I wanted to tell her that she was not suitable for the part, that she would spoil it with her temperament, but now something happened that really made me hold my breath. I got up from my seat and began to walk through the audience heading straight for the stage. I limped a bit, trying to distract attention from the fact that I had only one shoe, and then I felt like Nahman. A moment later I was playing the part of Nahman, standing beside Saba-Gnendl's bed. A small lamp burned with a low flame throwing light on her tired features. Spectators were watching the scene with binoculars. Their heartbeats made an audible pounding, like a concrete mixer.

"Joseph," she said, stretching both hands toward me.

I bent over her and whispered that in the drama my name is Nahman, but she seemed not to hear and kept calling me "Joseph, Joseph," her arms still stretched out to me.

I played my part with passion. It was just as well my parents had left. Only the presence of the guest worried me a bit. I was sure he was spying on us through the keyhole. But since my parents were not watching, I began to play without restraint.

NAHMAN: I love you so much, Gnendl, my dearest, I can think of nothing but you. We'll run away from here together. I'll have my beard cut, and I'll look like a goy. I swear to you, Gnendl, I'll be a goy with a clean-shaven face, and I'll play you like a fiddle at the country fairs—let it rip!!—and when my beard is gone, all the Sabbath candles will go out and the night candle too, and there will be darkness without shame.

GNENDL: Joseph, Joseph, be kind to me, be unkind to me, be cruel, beat me, beat me hard, Joseph, Joseph.

Suddenly she began to scream hysterically, and her features shriveled up, and she looked very old. I ran off the stage, to the accompaniment of yelling from all sides: "Cheats! Swindlers! We want our money back!"

I ran on and on, my unshod foot dragging, until I fell into the ditch of half-waking restlessness that heralds complete awakening. I felt as if I were drowning and was barely able to keep my head and hands above the water.

3

I lay like that for several minutes, hot and drained of energy. The sun was beating down on my head. Saba's screams rang in my ears. Finally I sat up, but could not shake off my drunken sleepiness. Around me the grass, the woods in the distance, and the sun heading away from the zenith were sharp and vivid. All along the river, at the foot of the miniature hill, there was a miniature life stirring, and within me the action of the dream had not quite stopped. My eyes still mirrored sleep, and my ears were attuned to distant sounds, not to the ones close by.

From where I was I could see people splashing about in the river below. The red, green, and yellow bathing suits looked like big flowers blown about in the distance. I could hear the noise of the bathers, but the sounds had lost their intensity by the time they reached me. Each individual shout came through meaningless to me, but it was clear that these were joyful cries, cries of delight.

Closer than these cries was the appeal in my ears of the porter, which I still could hear as clearly as when I saw him several weeks before. He was sending me a message for his brother in America. I was to tell him, "May you be choked to death with all your family!"

The porter's gruff cry was the voice of a whole class. The sound came from the depths, stained with blood. It was as moving as the bellow of a cow after her calf. He stood with one finger stuck in the rope around his waist which served as belt and cursed: "If you see my brother, who is ashamed of his own flesh and blood, tell him that I hope he falls from the highest cliff."

His face was covered with wrinkles. It was the face of a child that had grown old without ever having passed through youth or maturity.

"He is ashamed of his own brother. It doesn't matter to him that I have nothing to eat. May he and his family drop dead. May God slap his face as he slapped my face, in front of everyone. Just because he has become respectable, a tailor, does that give him the right to be ashamed of his brother who is just a laborer?"

His voice grew more agreeable from minute to minute. He seemed to be reciting his invectives from a prayer book. He stood in the middle of the market place, cursing. "It's all right, don't be ashamed to tell him. Say that this is what his own brother said to tell him, the brother whose blood he shed, whose sorrows he refused to hear. May he turn deaf and dumb. May he have to chew stale bread like me."

I could still hear his singsong chant, so much louder in its grief than the joy along the river, where I could hear the splashing of the bathers. I clung to the accents of the poor snubbed brother, so I could carry them back just as they sounded, to the tailor in a distant land who had made his way up the social ladder. I wanted to memorize the voice, the face, everything about that burly man with the rope around his waist, who stood in the market place, and railed at fate.

He spoke like a man condemned by generations of forebears to speak the language of the earth. He spoke the way a condemned man was supposed to speak, but his voice took on luminosity and liturgical sweetness. It resembled the moaning of a mother in front of the Holy Ark praying for a child suddenly stricken, but with added male dignity and grit.

The porter's lament was the deepest of all the expressions of Jewish misery I heard. For there had been others, too, one after the other, some of them embarrassed, some demanding. I witnessed a parade of beggars. All the community of the poor came to see me, their hands extended—not to me personally, but to me as the messenger holding out the promise of the mythical bread.

i

There came a neatly dressed Jew, a tall man with a high forehead, a dignified thatch of gray hair and black beard. He had brought a prepared speech, a complete essay, which he carefully took out of its case like an etrog from its box. He spoke of the poverty that dogs the poor man's every step, about the commandment that a man should find a husband for his daughter, and about Sabbaths when to produce even an illusion of gaiety you have to pinch your own cheeks.

The story was like this. His daughter was a beauty. So long as she was young the young men chased her, but later on they were concerned only for making their living, and his daughter had been left high and dry. One by one the suitors had fallen away. Now they were all married men, and his daughter, poor thing, never complained, but the sight of her cut her father's heart like a knife.

The story was like this. He had formerly been quite well off, he had dealt in timber, but he had gradually lost everything, and now he was at the bottom. But God had mixed the medicine before He sent the affliction: his wife's brother had been taken to America while still a little boy. Well, to say that he had been "taken" is only a manner of speaking. What really happened was this. He was a wild boy, and his wife's parents were respectable people. One day the boy did something that disgraced the parents, so his father decided to teach him a lesson. He spoke to the janitor of his apartment house, and asked him to give the boy a good beating. Would you believe it? The janitor was an infidel and took the request literally, beating the boy so hard that the child could not sit down. "Are there Jews with goyish hearts? May I live as many years as there are!"

Next day the boy vanished as completely as though he had been swallowed up. There were rumors that he had himself baptized, out of revenge. His parents turned gray before their time. This was their only son. Besides him, there was one daughter, who is herself now the mother of an only daughter; these were the only children.

The boy's mother wanted to divorce her husband for his cruel deed, but friends interceded. Many years went by, then the parents heard in a roundabout way that the boy was in America. They were overjoyed and wrote to him, but he had never forgiven them, and he replied that as far as he was concerned, so help him, they were all dead.

"But now his family is really dead, except for his sister. Several years ago, when we had lost everything we had, she wrote him a letter that would have moved the heart of a Gentile god. And it must have moved him deeply, for within the month we received a whole hundred dollars. From then on the hundred-dollar bills came regularly, and this meant more to us than you can imagine. My wife had kidney trouble, and the money saved her life. We were able to put something aside as a dowry for our daughter. My daughter's eyes glowed with hope, like burning candles. She is our only one, the apple of our eye.

"But just as the bills had started to come without any warning, like birds of good omen, they suddenly stopped coming. My wife has worn out her fingers writing, and how many tears went into every letter, alas! And how many of my daughter's tears went into every line, alas! But it has been like talking to a wall. No answer at all. We began to worry, wondering how we had offended him. But my wife has kept on writing, and I always add blessings in Hebrew to each letter.

"So this is the story. You see before you a man still living, the father of a daughter, but if you don't help me find my brother-in-law and ask him why, after filling our hearts with joy, he is now letting us die of hunger—why he kindled our hopes only to snuff them out again, why his heart has become as cold as stone—it will turn out badly. Do ask him this, but hurry, there is not much time. I swear to you, I am going to put a rope around my neck."

ii

There came a Jew with a tittering laugh. "Tee-hee, you don't remember me," he said. "Once you had a reputation for cleverness, but on the other hand, you've got so much else on your mind, and the passage of time counts for something, too.

"Tee-hee." Even as I was trying to visualize what he looked like without gray hair and wrinkles and the other changes of age, he burst into tears and buried his head and beard in his hands on the table. Then I remembered: he had been a well-to-do man, a dealer in flour, and had enjoyed the respect of the community. His seat in the synagogue used to be next to ours. It was when I imagined him in a silver-trimmed prayer shawl with purple threads that I remembered who he was.

Now, he told me, he was all alone in the world. The Lord had taken his wife, but had refused to take him too, and so he was doomed to a lonely old age. Two of his three children were dead, and the other one gone to America. Although he had had news of him indirectly, the son never wrote to his father.

"Here is his address. Look him up. And tell him that may God forgive him for letting his father starve. That's what I want you to tell him —I pray God continually that he will be forgiven for that. Tell him, too, that on the anniversary of his mother's death, he should sometimes say the Kaddish. Maybe he will be forgiven."

iii

The town cantor came, a man in his late seventies who boasted that he could still roar like a lion. It was true: he could be heard from one end of the synagogue to the other. Formerly he was a well-to-do merchant and served as cantor only for the honor of it. Now, however, he had become a mere synagogue functionary. So long as he performed the office without demanding payment, the town took him for granted. Now they wouldn't save him if he were drowning in a teaspoonful of water.

His trousers were simply patches held together with thread—though with gaping holes between some of the patches, and several important buttons missing. His alpaca coat was in tatters, and his arms were out at the elbows. His earnings had to go to support his daughter: Her husband, poor man, was bedridden. Yes, he was living with his daughter, and—why should he lie about it?—there was not so much as a piece of bread in the house. That, despite all the work he did, the anniversaries of deaths commemorated at the cemetery and funerals as well as the regular services. In the old days he could count on a Sabbath meal at his brother's; he had always gone by for the Kiddush—a glass of aquavit with a piece of cake; and then he would wash his hands and enjoy a piece of fish. But one day his brother told him bluntly that while he was welcome for the Kiddush, if he was counting on a full meal every time he'd better drop the Sabbath visit altogether. "You don't give me a chance to miss you," his brother had told him.

"So my own brother took away my Kiddush and my piece of fish— I should mention that he has no children. When Cain murdered Abel, he didn't behave any worse.

But how can I complain about my brother when my own son—he lives only a few hours away from here, and I spent a fortune on him so he could go to the conservatory and become a composer, which he is today—when my own son pretends he doesn't know that his father is starving?

"So what can you do for me? My wife, rest her soul, has a large family in New York; one of them lives like a king there, he is swimming in money. Occasionally he sends me a few dollars, without even enclosing a letter, and saves my life. Here is his address. I don't have to tell you what to say—you'll know yourself. Tell him"—he pointed to his neck—"that I am fed up, up to here."

iv

My old teacher of the Talmud. He had not changed a bit. He sidled in, as though carrying something important under his coat, something he was anxious not to lose. It is said about him that he carries a lot of money on him, his life savings. He is said to have gold pieces, old ones, dating back to Nicolas I and several hundred złotys besides. It is all this that he is supposed to be carrying around on him.

He began by pointing out that he had hammered the Torah into my head, and if people were telling the truth, he hadn't labored in vain. It seems to have been very useful to me. So he felt he could take the liberty of asking me a favor. After all, a pupil owes his teacher something. Even a teacher who spanks you, let alone one who was never impatient, who made learning a game—such a teacher has earned the right to ask a favor.

Did I remember his wife? She died. Did I remember his only son, the one with the red beard who used to chop wood in front of the house, the crazy one? Well, with God's help, he finally acquired some sense and now has become quite respectable. For the past several years he has been in America. At first he wrote regularly—nothing special, but at least his father could be sure that he was alive and in good health. Occasionally a few złotys were enclosed for a holiday. But for some years there had been no word.

"I have his address, so do me a favor and tell that son of mine that even if he is crazy he ought to have a thought for his old father. You mustn't believe the gossip about my being a rich man. I just wish the souls of these who speak like that would be gnawed with envy as I am gnawed by hunger. And it wouldn't do you any harm to give your old teacher a few złotys. The lessons I taught you deserve something in the way of return. But the main thing is, don't forget to look up my crazy son. If he yells at you, yell back at him, and you have my permission to slap him. I used to hit him even when he was a young man in his twenties. A slap in the face sometimes does no-goods like him a world of good. Don't waste words on him. Just tell him: Father, bread, eat, eat!"

V

A woman had brought her three children along so that I could appreciate the full extent of her predicament. Her husband had played a dirty trick on her. When she said this, her eyes blazed with anger, and she peered around at the ceiling of the room.

He made a real mess of her life. All in all, there had been no more than two happy years with him. He married her, but all he gave her was poverty. There was enough to eat during the week, but there was never enough for the Sabbath. For the Sabbath she had to toil hard. I shouldn't ask her how she managed "to make a Sabbath"—she accomplished it by brute force, so to speak, dragging it into her house by the ears.

She was an unfortunate woman. Already twice divorced, now this last husband of hers, what had he done? He had made her a widow. A dirty trick. And once again she flashed her eyes angrily, looking suspiciously at the upper corners of the room.

Here she was with three small orphans to support. That had been his legacy to her—these three tiny tots were all she possessed. She was childless herself, the children were his, but what could she do? She pitied the poor little things, it broke her heart to look at them.

"A brother of his lives in America. He is a heartless man, a real scoundrel. I have his address. Now, do a good deed, not for the sake of a poor widow, but for the children. They are as good as your own children—for if they aren't yours, they aren't mine either. Tell him that if I have no news from him, I'll do him a favor, I'll put the three children on a ship and send them straight to New York."

At that, the children, two boys and a girl, burst into tears.

"Shush, be quiet, I just say that to scare your uncle. Ah, what a dirty trick your father played on me! Some provider he was!" And she studied the ceiling carefully as she got up to go, as though her dead husband might be hiding there.

vi

His breath was foul, with the stench of hunger. Apparently he knew it, for he would quickly cover his mouth with his hand after every few sentences. Then he would look at me in silence for several minutes.

He was just my age and had gotten exactly nowhere in life. Fortunately he was a bachelor. It's easier to starve when you have no family.

Gradually his speech grew more literate—polysyllabic words such as you see only in books began to appear in his conversation.

Taking into consideration the material conditions of the collectivity as a whole, he said, and the circumstances of social existence as such, the conclusion is unavoidable that the individual is of no importance. It may even be argued that the collectivity, in the last analysis, consists of individuals who embody specific attributes of the mass at the climax of its development. On the other hand, among backward people, at the lowest level of evolution, the social physiognomy is more pronounced —and there was a great deal more like this.

He rattled off all these complicated sentences with extraordinary facility, making proper transitions, constructing logical pyramids of discourse. He confided to me that for all his uncompromising atheism, he always fasted Mondays and Thursdays, for his sad circumstances left no alternative. His face was longer than broad, with waxen features that recalled a candle gradually being consumed. He was a pitiful sight, but the moment he began to talk he sounded as though he were issuing a petition to the authorities.

"The intellectual drive that has characterized my tribe from time immemorial has driven me into the arms of education. Lacking the minimal prospects of material security, and despite the insignificance of education in the ghetto, I looked forward to the eventuality of some unforeseen development."

His story turned out to be as follows. Twenty-some years ago he had completed six years of his preuniversity training, but when he attempted to obtain Polish credits for it, the Polish educational authorities refused to honor his accomplishment. So he sat down and began his course of study all over again, from the beginning, at home. By this time he had gotten as far as the seventh grade of secondary school, with only one more year to go to obtain his bachelor's degree. But he is at the end of his tether, he has no strength to finish, for he has had nothing to eat. He has a bit of roof over his head—his married brother gave him a cot in a dark little room. His uncle could be his salvation—that is to say, his mother's uncle who lives in America. But his situation must be put to his uncle solely in terms of education.

"In spite of the hopeless situation of the Jewish people and that of the educated youth in particular, education is an end in itself, which is transcendental and practical in its very impracticality," he said as he rose to leave.

vii

A middle-aged man with two or three flecks of gray in his not very full black beard walked in.

From his pocket he carefully drew a paper yellowed with age, which had been mounted very cleverly on a piece of cardboard. It folded in four. "This speaks for itself," he said extending it to me. He chewed on a strand of his beard, looking at me expectantly.

"And what does it say?" he asked suddenly, with a very solemn air, as though putting me to some kind of test.

It was a letter signed by President Hoover, thanking him for having written him and conveying the president's warm personal regards.

"You do know English," he said after a moment, perking up at this.

"There are Jews, you know, I think you call them 'bluffers,' who have been to America but don't know a word of English. Several years ago I sent a message of greeting to the president of the United States. It was in Hebrew, a beautiful message, such as I know how to write. Why did I do it all of a sudden? Well, cast thy bread upon the waters. . . . It's good to have dealings with a president. It can't do any harm. And he replied at once with a personal letter of thanks, as you can see for yourself. I can't read it—how could I? But people have read it to me several times, and each time it gives me great pleasure.

"When I was earning a living, I sort of forgot about the president. But now that I have lost my rabbinical post and can't get another one, and am reduced to begging for my bread, I got out the president's letter and here I am, ready to go. The only question is, who is to pay my fare? Then I recalled that I have a well-to-do brother-in-law over there. I want you to tell him that I'll pay him back in full, just as soon as I get to America. It shouldn't be hard to get in there with a letter like that. The gates will open for me, and I'll be given a generous welcome, don't you think?"

There was a triumphant gleam in his eyes as he gave a confident little laugh: it had been clever of him to provide himself with so valuable a document.

"I wouldn't trade this piece of paper for a hundred passports! Once I've gotten to America, I'll show them that I'm a real rabbi, not—what do you call it over there?—not a 'bluffer'! That's a real document, isn't it? It was nothing less than divine inspiration on my part to send that beautiful message of greeting!"

viii

Her heels were so high that she teetered on them, and I got up and ran to help her when she came in the door, for I was afraid she would slip and fall.

The only question that bothered her was whether I'd recognize her; if not, it was all to the good, for she was embarrassed to come. In fact, she said, she only took the risk of coming to see me because she had decided that I would not recognize her. Years ago, when she had known me, it never occurred to her that she would not be married already, by this time, but that was the way it had turned out. And now here she was singing the well-known song—a widower or an elderly man.

I must not suppose that she was eager to get married at any cost. Not at all. She simply couldn't bear the social stigma of being an old maid. And anyway she couldn't go on like this, being a burden to her old father. She was well read, familiar with Yiddish literature and with the classics. She would be willing to marry the very worst sort of man: She'd suffer in silence.

In the town where she lived she was what was known as "a literary supplement." She knew that people talked about her behind her back. She hadn't minded it, when she was younger, that people had it in for her. She had felt compensated by friendships with writers and the more educated sort of theater people. But now younger "literary supplements" were coming along—a whole new generation of them—and she found herself left high and dry with her memories. And such silly memories! She wondered if they would not choke her in the end.

Now she has the choice between two men—one is fifty-five or so, and the other is a hunchback, but it is an intelligent hump, not too conspicuous. Neither man, however, will marry her without a dowry.

"I can assure you I have enough reason to be willing to pay my dues. I didn't spend my youth saying prayers. Here is my brother's address."

ix

He took a chair and rested his head on the silver knob of his stick. He looked up at me with one eye, smiling.

God be praised, he owned a stocking factory, and there were several thousand złotys in the bank. All his children had been to college. One became an oculist, the other a dentist. Both were making good livings and had married well. His wife is able to visit watering places to enjoy the hot springs. He himself had become a Zionist—in more general terms, an enlightened man, a rationalist. He kept up with all that goes on in the world.

He was aware that I had been here for several days, but he hadn't wanted to bother me until now. Finally he just couldn't stand it any more and so here he was. What he wanted to tell me—here he suddenly raised his head from the silver-headed cane—was that he looks down his nose at America.

He looked quite fierce when this came out. He had long wanted to advertise his scorn to the world. And now, what he wanted me to do was to pass the word along to the important people, that he, a Jew, a rationalist, had been able to get through life without American help. He had brought up his children, and brought them up well—would that all Jewish children might be so lucky! Would I do him the favor of telling those concerned that he, a Polish Jew, didn't give a tinker's damn about America—no matter what America may think of that? It would be doing him a great favor, for by nature he detested boasters, and the trouble with America was its conceit. Why, it was a great thing, something for the whole Jewish nation to be proud of, that he had worked his way up to wealth without any assistance whatever from big, rich, arrogant America!

x

A man of dour features came in and sat down without a word. His lips seemed sealed. For a long while he just sat there, shaking his head, as though accusing someone. Then suddenly he took a deep breath and began to speak.

He couldn't understand, he said, what things were coming to. Whatever he tried his hand at turns out to be against the law. There was a jinx on him: the moment he earned a little money he was in trouble with the law. What he had done might be perfectly legal—the most legal occupation imaginable—but the moment he got involved in it, it never failed: He got in trouble with the authorities. On the surface everything always seemed fine. Thanks to his work others were able to make their living. He had a wife and children, and he too was obliged to earn a living, but in his case something always went wrong. Take bankruptcy, for example. Hundreds of people do very well for themselves going bankrupt, but the moment he tried it he wound up in prison. The simplest thing had a way of becoming complicated the moment he touched it. Whether it had to do with him, or with the fact that Polish law was too complex for him, every enterprise he engaged in simply turned out to be illegal. And yet it would be sheer slander to say that he involved himself in risky enterprises. Something simply went wrong in the process, and he found himself again in the hands of the law.

How long would this go on, and how would it end? Now it was down to a question of bread and salt—no longer of furnishing a luxurious apartment. Things had reached the point where he was ashamed in front of his wife of being such a *schlimazl,* such a sucker as always to be the one that gets caught.

"In short, what I want is an affidavit. Here is my brother's address. You must tell him to take pity on me. I'm speaking to you as I would to my own brother, I have no more strength left to struggle against the law. Let him send for me, and if he really wants to, he can do it. After all, America is different, the laws there aren't the same as here. I mean, it can't go on like this. Or even, do you know what, I'm ready to make an agreement with you. Let my brother send me enough money to live on, and I won't insist on going to America. Nor will I ask for much— all I want is enough for bread, for my wife, my children, and myself. Bread! bread! bread!" By this time, he was pacing back and forth across the room. He chanted the word *bread* as if tinkling a gold coin, and he would stop as if to listen to the precious sound.

Hunger had often paraded in front of me in that room, and spoken without reserve. And yet after each hungry man I always thought back to the first of them, haunted with the memory of the porter who so roundly cursed his brother in America: "May he and his family drop dead!"

Once upon a time there had been two little brothers. They had played games together, free of care, stared up at the sky together, and caught flies. Together they had put the flies in a little hole in the ground, and covered the hole with a piece of glass through which they could watch the little creatures struggling to get free. Later one of the little boys went away to America, and the other stayed behind, a sorrowing brother, lying in a ditch he had dug for himself.

xi

"Do you know what a brother is?" I was asked by a man who had been regarded as unusually bright when he was a child. Though he was only a few years older than I, he had occasionally taught me some Talmud.

"A wife is cut from a rib, but a brother is part of your mother's heart.

When we were boys we both clutched at her apron asking for bread, and now one of these brothers is asking the other for bread. And the other does not even answer his letters. How can such a thing be? I don't care about much any more, but this problem torments me. You lie with your little brother under the same torn blanket, and you tell each other stories. You share father's attention, mother's smiles, you have such a marvelous, divine partnership. Then one goes away, and the two begin to live separate lives. I get the shivers. You know, I could never understand it even in the case of cats and dogs, but when I see two human brothers living for themselves, I begin to question many things."

Even more pathetic than the hunger was the hope. In all this despair there was an obstinate faith that salvation would certainly come from across the ocean. And I, who had seen the other side of the certainty, I found my mind turning from the sad faces of Lublin in front of me, to those other faces far away across the sea: the clean-shaven faces of the Lubliners who had escaped to become cigar makers, shirtmakers, buttonhole makers, pocketbook makers, one and all of them rich American Jews.

I recalled the big white loaves of bread, and the more fragrant dark loaves. When I was little, the white bread had always stood for silver to me, and the dark bread for gold. But who at that time could have grasped what was true in my childish insight, when mother sent me out into the Jewish street to buy bread?

xii

The Jewish people is merely being pauperized, not proletarianized, Glaichbaum explained to me with a sour smile. We constitute a very special stratum of the population. Among all other peoples, lice and starvation go hand in hand with stunted minds, but not so with our people. Their minds work just as hard as the rest of them. They keep a lamp burning to verify that they are indeed in darkness.

Glaichbaum, who had taught me Polish years before, had turned many an intellectual somersault in his life. He came from an assimilated family, and his father's heart melted with joy when he saw him in his green college uniform. He had many Gentile friends. He was blond, and had a shrunken yellow face. But his manners were truly Polish: his skinny figure made all the proper bows and inclinations. He was a good dancer, and he was very popular with the Gentile girls for his elegance—or perhaps for the very reason that he was not handsome. He had no trace of those specifically Jewish good looks that our Gentile neighbors find so unattractive.

Then one day Glaichbaum almost gave his father a heart attack: he purchased phylacteries and announced that he was henceforward a pious Jew. His father, when he recovered from the shock, laughed at him; his mother fainted; his younger brother and his sisters said he should be thrown out of the house. But nothing deterred him. Glaichbaum—he was then eighteen—got himself a private tutor who taught him the Hebrew language and Jewish ritual. Every morning he would get up early and hurry to the synagogue before going to his class at the commercial college he attended. He even went back for evening service and took every possible occasion to linger in the synagogue and pick up crumbs of sacred learning. There he would sit in his uniform with its gold buttons, wearing the cap with its shiny visor. He got special permission from the school authorities that he would not be obliged to write on the Sabbath. Then, all of a sudden, with less than a year to go before graduation, he dropped out of college entirely. He became estranged from his former friends, and his supple dancer's body now was kept bending gracefully at the various prayers in the synagogue.

There followed in time a number of other intellectual enthusiasms: Zionism, Socialism, the Polish Socialist Party, and the Labor Bund. He became a leader and was elected municipal councilor. Jews were proud of his ability to defend Jewish honor with the ardor of a true Jewish preacher, in excellent and eloquent Polish.

Still later he became something which in Poland no one even dared to call by name: he became a Communist or, as is more euphemistically referred to, a Marxist. Then he abandoned that, too—just why, he did not have the inner strength to analyze, he told me. It had happened only a short while ago, and he wanted to keep quiet about it for a few years, to be alone with himself.

"I know," he said, "that all this will end up with my going back to the synagogue. Inside me sits the soul of an ancestor who summons me back. There is no other explanation for it. My brother and my sisters have all been baptized. I am the black sheep." He had a sour little laugh. "But before I go back to the synagogue, I have to conquer my cynicism. When you jump from one cause to another, you become a bit of a cynic. I can't go to the synagogue with that hump on my back."

He gazed at me with his yellow eyes, which had over the years become so Jewish that no Gentile could possibly have mistaken them.

"Please, take a look at the address. It's some sort of cousin, I think, just an idea. If you see him, you may tell him, if he remembers me, that I'm not doing too well. But I must tell you at once not to take too much trouble about it. It's just an idea of mine, and probably nothing will come of it at all."

4

The sound of footsteps roused me from my half-slumber. By my side stood a young man whom I recognized by his clothes as a member of the rabbi's retinue I had seen in the park during my walk with Steinman. He had walked alone, behind the others. He was now wearing the same slippers and white stockings; he had had a hard time getting up the hill in this footwear. He was about to go past me when he changed his mind and stopped.

"I know you're an American," he said, sitting down near me. "I've seen you with Steinman, that man who writes stories of no great consequence. How are the Jews getting along in America? But to tell the truth I don't have to ask you, I know the answer myself. I can see everything with my imagination. There are things about America I know better than you do, because you merely saw them while I imagine them. Not a bad thought, don't you agree?

"Well, I can tell you how the country is ruled, who is the boss, how the Jews behave there. Once I accompanied my father on a visit to a small town, and before we got there I imagined what the town and the first Jew we met there would look like. You won't believe it—but everything was exactly as I had imagined it in advance. Do you suppose that's a miracle? Not at all, I can supply perfectly natural causes for it.

"This is how I can prove it to you. Man lives threescore and ten years. But what does that amount to? Not even a drop in the bucket. It is a millionth of a millionth of a millionth part of the time it takes God to bat His eyelashes. Man, the crown of the creation, felt embarrassed that his life span was so insignificant, and he devised a kind of apparatus that stretches it like a rubber band, to make it seem a considerable length of time.

"See what I mean? It's not easy to get it. When a man is born, his grave is open, ready to receive him, but between birth and death many things occur in rapid succession. You can't imagine how swiftly they flash by. But the apparatus man invented works well and stretches out each event. Even the most trivial events are assigned a place. Occasionally you run ahead of your apparatus, and you arrive at an event that is scheduled to happen only several years later. You think something will happen to you in five years, but actually it is happening right now, or perhaps has already happened. You get the idea? You outsmart your apparatus and you discover what time really is, measured against the brevity of human life.

"It's rather hard to grasp all this. If you want me to, I'll go over it again for you from the beginning. I've been thinking about this for four or five years, and when I finally understood the whole thing, it was like a flash of light inside my head."

"How old are you?" I asked.

"Sixteen. But this isn't the only idea I've had. You must understand that every rabbinical family is distinguished by a special talent. We are the philosophers and the rhetoricians among the rabbis. We like to speculate. It's a marvelous game, but it's also an ordeal. It's like walking on a narrow bridge. One false step, and you fall into heresy. But if the Lord is with you, if you don't stumble and can keep your Jewishness intact, you cherish your idea doubly, because it achieves union with the Creator who sent it into the world.

"An idea that does not lead back to God but wanders at random is a bastard idea, it has no father. I wrote an essay in which I developed my theory. It's a wonderful piece of writing.

"I like to take walks by myself and think about Hasidism. Faithful to my theory, I try to grasp ideas that will occur to me years later. That's why my eyes look so much older than I really am. I want to discover things. I don't like my grandfather's way and I don't like my father's. I don't like the way of my older brothers. I told Father that I was not too satisfied with his way. Yes, I told him that, for all my respect for him I had the courage to tell him. Then he confided in me that he was even less satisfied than I.

"I have read all of Jewish literature, I know everybody and everything. But what is there except rhetoric? Peretz's Hasidic stories are anecdotes with a moral. He looks at things through a keyhole and then blows them up. I want to see things from within. I want to renew Jewish thought. To begin with, you understand, we must do away with Gentile forms. A Jewish creation must be everything—poetry, prose, philosophy, drama, psychology, astronomy, epigrams—everything. We have no use for neat little compartments. We must be a creative encyclopedia—do you hear me?—an encyclopedia, but a creative one. Do you grasp what this means? It's tremendous. Have you ever read a story by the rabbi of Bratzlav? There is my hero among the Hasidim. I am in love with him, I think about him all day long. He was an innovator and he loved Yiddish. Do you know what Yiddish is? What a marvelous language it is?"

He went on to say that he was troubled by one thing: he couldn't understand why the Bratzlaver was so proud. Believe it or not, he said, it took him two years before he finally understood. Now he could explain the rabbi's pride perfectly.

"He was always a sickly man, a broken vessel. If he had been more modest, no one would have taken him seriously. He knew he would die young and he wanted to accomplish something during the few short years he was granted.

"That is why he praised his own wares so much. He didn't do this for his own sake. Everybody knew that he loved poverty and privation. He swam in misery like a fish in water. But he had things to sell, and he advertised them so that people would buy them. He praised himself because he wanted people to listen to God's word. I am sure that he laughed at himself when no outsider could hear him, but his scribe, Rabbi Nathan, kept his secret faithfully.

"That is one possibility, but I have another idea, namely, that a rabbi must never be modest. A modest rabbi diminishes the majesty of God. It's his duty to give the people some notion of God's greatness. Since his task is to relate God's great miracles, he must also play the role of a great man in his own life. There is a vast difference between greatness and pride. The Bratzlaver was a great man, but he associated with the great and the small alike, with both the rich and the poor. Now, just think: if such a great man was willing to make friends with the humblest people, how could a plain ordinary Hasid strut about like a peacock?

"Some day I'll read you some of my new ideas, and you'll see for yourself that they are simply extraordinary. But don't think I get them from my own little brain. After I fast on a Monday, a Thursday, and then the following Monday, I begin to shed all my unworthy husk of materiality. I walk in the woods, all by myself. When night falls, and my hunger expects to be stilled, I keep on walking and thumb my nose at the flesh. So you think, I say to my hunger, it's all right to break the fast now? Not at all. I won't be rushed.

"Then something happens to me, I become faint, a sweet weakness spreads over all my body. My limbs want to shout, but all they do is to peep like little birds, the poor things haven't got the strength. They sing softly. At such moments I hear a voice.

"Here I must stop for a bit. I must tell you that I could describe this voice to you, but I am forbidden to do so because the voice speaks to me in a sacred solitude. It would be uncouth of me to reveal something so intimate. But he who has never heard such a voice gropes like a blind man when he speaks of God.

"Usually I feel weak and drowsy just before I hear the voice. Everything around me fills me with awe. I fall on my face and I call out: Speak to me, Father in Heaven! I am ready!

"When I get up again from the ground, I am never without having gained something—a thought, an idea, a metaphor—and I feel that these are not my own but have dropped on me like ripe pears from a tree. Sometimes I get up with a whole poem. Listen to this, for instance:

Brigand, brigand, against whom do you lift your ax?
Against whom do you lift your ax?

I lift my ax against my own desires,
My own evil desires.
God of Abraham, hear my song:
Ai, chiri-biri-biri, glory to God;
Ai, ai, glory to Thee.

"I have a tune for that one, sweet as sugar.

Cossack, little Cossack,
Against whom, tell me, do you raise your sword?
I raise my sword against my lust for evil,
My lust for evil,
My wicked desires.
God of Abraham, hear my song!

"And here it goes with greater brio, more passionately:

Ai, chiri-biri-biri, glory to God,
Ai, ai, glory to Thee.

"Sometimes I trick Satan and stick out my tongue at him. For instance:

I lust
For the breast
Of righteousness.
I fondle, I kiss
The Divine Presence.

"See how I trick Satan? Just when he thinks he has me in his net, he gets a punch in the jaw.

"It's time for me to go. But I must warn you: you haven't gotten rid of me yet. When I begin to talk there is something to hear. There are so many things to say. So I want to make an appointment with you, and next time I see you I'll give you a hint how faith and heresy can be reconciled, how heresy can be made to burn with such fire that it will soar and weep before the Throne of Glory. It will weep there with all its figures and formulas and questions and doubts. Never fear—God, blessed be He, can bear up with it. I'll also tell you a secret—how the modem Hasid can find his way to Jewish life."

He began to go back down the hill. Little pebbles rolled after him. I remained sitting where I was, completely baffled. His last words had been "Jewish life," and these words were suddenly so vivid to me that I saw meaning in them as never before. They even seemed to express something corporeal.

I felt a will to life stirring around me. The hungry mouth that had just been clamoring to me in various voices also had a head, a fiery head. That hunger had a will to live and to think.

It was now getting cool up on the hill, and I got up and started back. Halfway down the hill I found the sixteen-year-old thinker waiting for me.

"I couldn't stop myself," he said, "I thought I must tell you about a curious encounter I had recently." He smiled, as if reexperiencing the event.

"I had just recited evening prayers," he went on. "I enjoyed every breath of air I took in. Usually I walk with my head down to facilitate meditation. Suddenly I felt that instead of air I was breathing an inconceivable fragrance. It made me think of the sweet smell of a baby's hands or feet, it was both earthy and not earthy, it was as though earth had not yet had time to become completely earthy.

"This filled me with wonder. I raised my head and looked about me. I saw at once that I had lost my way. The trees looked like trees in a dream, the sky was like a very thick crust, it was as if a last film had been removed from it, I could see the most marvelous things. I heard birds fluttering and twittering, but I could not see them. Dusk had fallen, but it was not very dark yet—the light was pink, not a bit frightening.

"On a bench two men sat talking. I could see very well that they were talking, I could see their lips moving, I could even hear what they were saying, but each word just flickered and faded out at once, like a falling star.

"One of the men had a royal appearance. In the twilight it was hard to say what clothes he had on, but there was an air of royal dignity about him. The other man too looked like one of the great, though of a lower rank. It is hard to say how I distinguished between the two—the light above the second man was almost the same as that above the first, but with something a little more common, less rich, about it.

"I was devoured by curiosity. I began to weep aloud, but the two men did not even look over at me. I came up closer and closer to them, until I was right in front of them, and then I passed through them as if they were nothing but thin air.

"Suddenly a veil dropped from before my eyes, and things took on firmer outlines. The dusk had lost its pink glow, it was darker now, but this didn't bother me. In fact I could see much more clearly than before.

"There was still another change. Instead of one bench I now saw two benches. Each of the men sat on a separate bench, silent, as if waiting for me. I bowed deeply before the royal figure of higher rank. I clearly saw his sad face and I knew everything.

"'Sabbatai Zvi,' I said to him, 'what are you trying to tell me? What is the vision you have granted me?'

"'It is not I who granted you the vision,' he said. 'It is you who came upon it when you lost your way. Well, so be it, it's your choice. May it be to your benefit.'

"'Sabbatai Zvi,' I cried, 'you false Messiah! Is this the world of deception in which you are living?'

"He looked at me with so much genuine sorrow that I realized at once there could be no question of deception. I became confused.

"'And are not the true Messiahs also false?' he asked, smiling sadly. 'For what have all of us accomplished? Just because we dreamed, do we deserve to be branded as false and stoned? And it is you of all people who say such things, you who know so well how we hoped, how stubbornly we hoped, desperately bent upon bringing about at least one hour of happiness. Even the truest Messiah would have become false if he really sought redemption. Indeed, the true Messiahs are those who do nothing but wait patiently. Or should they be called the wise and practical Messiahs, whereas we should be called foolish Messiahs, failures? But *false* Messiahs? How can you of all people say that?'

"In my sorrow I turned to the other man. 'Jacob Frank,' I said. His eyes were so sad that it was painful to look at him.

"'I have spent a long time in sorrowful silence,' he said, sighing.

'What's the use of talking? Occasionally I talk to Sabbatai because we understand each other easily, but . . . '

"I interrupted him. 'All I want to know,' I said, 'is why you changed gods. I wanted to ask Sabbatai the same question, but the other had at least a kind of excuse—Ishmael, our kin, the Crescent. But what possible excuse is there for the Cross?'

"At this moment a little Jew came running up to me as though brought by a wind. The two benches were now wrapped in complete darkness, but the silvery beard of the little Jew gleamed and glistened. 'What's the idea of hassling these two men?' he said to me. 'What business is it of yours to make them give account of themselves? For God's sake, don't you see that these two Jews, for all their falseness, served the cause of truth? They wanted to make the truth so irrefutable that they turned it inside out. They went into the very abyss of Sheol, just to show whither untruth can lead—and you call them to account?'

"He smiled then and gave me a friendly pat on the back. 'Ah,' he said, 'let's recite late-evening prayers and forget all this!'

"I was about to pray with fervor when I realized that the little man was reciting a weird set of prayers: 'Greetings, dear Father, I have come in to your vestibule to bid you good evening. This is an ordinary Wednesday, Jews are toiling and trading, not for themselves, God forbid, but for their wives and children, for their families. They are up to their necks in all kinds of worries and troubles, yet all the same they take time off to say their evening prayers, to turn their faces to the east, to raise their eyes to You, God our Father. So I ask You, dear God, is it fair that You should always be throwing it up to us that You have chosen us as Your people? Whom else could You have chosen? Whom? Do You know of a better people?'

"He vanished as suddenly as he had come. I realized that I was in a dark alley, and I set out looking for the main road. I ran into my older brother and I was about to tell him what I had just seen, but then I decided I wouldn't—I know him well, he likes to argue, a real Litvak. But I told it to you since we've been talking anyway. You're a stranger here, you'll go away soon, across the ocean. You will think that a confused young boy has been talking to you. But don't be too sure. You might take another look at the whole thing. For even if I had a thousand heads on my shoulders, I couldn't invent such a thing. And anyhow inventions aren't as difficult as all that. Why should I make up stories when real life is so full of wonders?"

5

"Know what? Come and pay us a visit. For once, obey your virtuous impulse. No one will harm you at our house." He added, "I will show you some essays I have written, which no other living soul has seen. I have a fiery pen, and I teem with ideas. You're sure to be rewarded for your trouble. Only it's a pity my father is away. It's too bad because he is a remarkable man. It would be a shame to miss meeting him, for there won't be many more like him."

I walked with him across the narrow board over the little stream. The board bent under our feet, as if it were made of rubber. No one was anywhere around. From down there the hill looked as though it had been stored away, but just for the night. My companion led the way, turning around frequently to make sure that I was following.

We passed through a garden, and he led me quietly to his room, as if he were sneaking me in. He closed the door and lit a small lamp in addition to the large chandelier. The small lamp was like a searchlight —I felt that it must be used to discover things undiscoverable with the help of the large lamp alone.

"What do you prefer—to have things read to you or to read them yourself? Naturally it depends on whether your eyes or your ears are the sharper. But it also depends on the things I will show you. Some of them are for the eye, others for the ear."

He handed me some long, thin strips of paper. I realized that the manuscripts, written in a tiny hand and full of blots and erasures, were not something I'd care to puzzle out myself. The ink was watery and the strips of paper looked like unrolled mezuzahs with letters missing.

"I hope you'll forgive me, but I must say a few words to introduce each piece I'll read to you. First I'll treat you to a letter. Letters are important. You take a sheet of paper and you write to someone because you can't see him and speak to him face to face. A letter must be short and to the point. I composed a dozen letters as models for a modern book on how to write good letters.

Dear Mr. Nightingale,
Enclosed you will find two worlds, the world of here and now and the world of beyond. You may choose between them, it's up to you. The world of here and now is limited—one hand suffices to take its breadth, and one foot to pace off its length. The world beyond is of a purity that cannot be described. The world of here and now knows only pleasure that shrinks and shrivels, gets old, and turns to dust. The world of beyond consists of eternal joy, which brings you ever closer to a great decision. I am very truly yours, who wishes you a happy choice.

"And now I'll show you a sample of a prayer. You must realize, prayers have to be recreated in each generation. But a prayer must also have an old-fashioned quality, if it is to be agreeable to recite.

Thy house stands firm on the mountain
Thy house stands high on the mountain
I climb toward Thee a wanderer exhausted with wandering
I have sinned by taking wrong paths
I have played the fool by asking questions
I have grown solitary, possessed of all kinds of doubts
Extend Thy shining hand to me
Light my way to Thee
Let me not stray from the path that leads to Thee.

"I have written countless poems, but I am not satisfied with them. My poems seem empty vessels. They sit there like carafes, with long embarrassed necks, waiting to be filled. But I'll read you a short one, for a sample:

The golden peacock from the golden land
Speaks to the son of man, who does not understand.
My sealed up muteness has dulled your hearing
As my eyes think their way to the mind's hushed clearing . . .

"If you care for that sort of thing. But the fact is I am strongest in discursive thought. At that I am hard to beat. I'll let you hear an excerpt from one of my essays.

Inventions are concretized miracles. In former times, when people had faith in miracles, they needed no inventions. And when people had faith in miracles, they also had a strong will. That's why, in former times they could dispense with magic, whereas today magic has to be rationalized and made to produce inventions. Inventions seem to mediate between a degenerate people and the grandeur of miracle. When you press a button on the wall, you imagine you have accomplished something, but if you study the science of electricity, you realize that the button is no less incomprehensible than the miracles of old, and that you have invented the button to make it easier for benighted minds to believe. But the truth is, standing right next to the light switch you can still say, Let there be light, and there will actually be light—though we don't see this, we don't understand or believe this, and so, fools that we are we have invented the light switch to make it more comprehensible. The invention does for us what our own will and our own faith should be able to accomplish. We come back to the miracle by the roundabout way of doubting, our doubts finally giving birth to magic buttons.

"Well, what do you think of it? Did you grasp my point? I develop the argument further, and I prove that our inventions rebel against us and make their own way back to the miracle, to the primeval mystery. The human hand must learn to regain wonder directly, without taking the long way around so-called invention. I don't expect you to grasp that at once. It is an idea that requires a lot of reflection.

"It is my opinion," he went on, eyes flashing, "that we do indeed have to learn the seven sciences and the seventy languages, but that they must all be raised to a higher power. The sciences, too, are bodies, are concrete things. When someone speaks French to a Frenchman, he merely uses a means to make himself understood by the Frenchman. He is applying knowledge which he has acquired, but between him and the Frenchman the French language is no longer a language, it is a spiritual affinity. They are no longer speaking a language, they *speak*. The same is true of mathematics. If a man were to walk around constantly keeping in mind the full content of the art of calculation, he'd be a fool. Calculation must vanish and be transformed into pure wisdom. From this it follows that there must be a point where all the sciences meet, where they dissolve and become like one another. There, in some no man's land of human sublimity, all the sciences flow together to become a unified wisdom, which is no more than one infinitely tiny flicker of light from the Great Source. A man must not flaunt his knowledge. When we know what knowledge is, we see that it is no more than imitation. It is only when the various sciences meet and become spiritual, that knowledge becomes a reality. Until that occurs, it is a deadweight that drags you down and drowns you.

"What I've just been saying has come to me all of a sudden." He picked up a pencil and began to write. "I must note it down, for this is a golden thought. Such a thing mustn't get lost."

When we went into the other room, there were people sitting, almost as though waiting for us. There were things to eat on the table, and I was touched by the warm glow that shone in everyone's eyes.

The American son-in-law, who was wearing a skullcap, smiled at us, as though putting a question mark after everything I had just heard. He asked me, "Well, how do you like my little brother-in-law? He's got a lively head on his shoulders, hasn't he? Don't worry about him, he'll get somewhere."

"Well, I don't think so highly of my little brother." The man who said this had a broad face with large fleshy lips and a fleshy nose; even his eyes and his large rectangular beard looked fleshy. He too sat there as if waiting for me and the chance to get in a word. "No, I don't. The American thinks he is very original, but I stick to my belief that a man must know how to control his thoughts, to bring them to a halt before they run away with him. Ideas must have system, order, a beginning and an end. I do believe that horses think, that all the dumb animals think, but in a confused way, without order. I think that's why they don't produce thoughts that can be understood. My brother's mind is like a coiled spring. When you wind it up it thinks, but in the end it goes right back to the same position it was in before."

"I could answer you, but what I'd say would not be for your systematic ears," the thinker said heatedly. "I'll let it go."

The American brother-in-law burst into a little fit of laughter, but there were tears in his eyes. "Ah, brothers, brothers," he finally said. "Why must you always quarrel?"

"I? Quarrel with him?" the older brother said. "Why, he never even gets in my way. All I want to do is to give him guidance, but he won't let me."

"Some guidance. What he wants to do is to put blinkers on my mind."

"You're pigheaded," the older brother said good-naturedly. "I want to teach you some notion of human order, but you think you're above all that." Then, turning to me: "What's wrong with him? He thinks he has it, but he still hasn't got it. Do you see what I mean? He hasn't got it yet."

Two women sat in armchairs. One was doing some embroidering, the other sat as though waiting for an opportunity to join in the conversation. I recognized them at once as the two women in the colorful shawls I had seen in the park, walking in the rabbi's retinue. The one who was embroidering looked up frequently, revealing an oval face with a pointed chin. Her lips moved as though she were conversing quietly so as not to disturb anyone, and she seemed to get satisfaction from it. The other had a chubby face, little-girl features, and large laughing blue eyes. She got up at one point and passed me the tray with fruit, which made a very rich impression in the room. Somehow, bananas looked more banana-like on this tray.

"He's just envious," the younger brother said excitedly. "Didn't I catch you red-handed? It wasn't so long ago in the synagogue that I heard you chewing over an idea of mine in one of your sermons."

"What!" The older brother was so indignant that he stood up. "Do you really think I'm so hard up that I have to borrow your ideas?"

"Not at all. Quite to the contrary. You're rich, but you can never get enough. Whenever you see a good thing, you grab hold of it."

The American brother-in-law laughed a great deal at this, tossing his head around as though it were not quite firmly attached to his body.

"You're very naughty," the woman with the chubby face said, pouting. "The poor boys are having a serious argument, and you're making fun of them."

"But darling, don't say that. It's marvelous, it's amusing, it's colossal!" And he again choked with laughter.

She passed me the chocolates, and then a tray with pastry. "Do have some, you need to keep your strength up with these people." When she moved around in the room, it was clear that she was pregnant. It made her look younger, strong and energetic. She appeared to be in her early twenties.

"I cannot permit you to treat a quarrel between my brothers as a vaudeville entertainment." But her eyes were laughing when she said it.

"But my dearest, you're not being fair. You're slandering me." The American was serious now.

The lady who had been embroidering lifted her face from her work and whispered to herself. Then, lowering her eyes again, she said more audibly: "There is a poem, by Leopardi . . . "

All the others fell silent immediately. She kept her eyes down as she talked and did not interrupt her work. She mentioned Bergson, quoted Verlaine in French, recited excerpts from Słowacki in Polish, and referred to the most recent developments in German poetry—all this in connection with the quarrel between the two brothers. The quarrel, she said, was actually a higher type of love—each of them went his own way but both were searching for the truth, and they long for each other with a sad longing.

Her voice was pleasant to listen to. She was generous with quotations, but her manner altogether modest. Coming from her, with her slightly aged face, the lines of poetry sounded like sleigh bells tinkling somewhere in the distance along a snowy road. She suddenly stopped. The others thought it was only a pause and waited for her to go on, but it was as if she had switched off a light around her.

"You must come and see us again," the younger woman said when she saw me getting ready to go.

"Why should he come? Now that he has been exposed to my little brother's crazy ideas . . . "

"Now, now, don't get started again," she said, bringing her hands together with a smart slap.

"Let him, let him. Anyone can see he is envious."

The American son-in-law once again shook with laughter to the point of tears.

"Wait a minute, don't go just yet. It's pitch dark outside, you won't see the stairs that go down to the garden." The younger woman took a lamp from the table and walked ahead of me out the door. The lamp cut the green trees with bands of light. "Watch out. There are three steps there, and the first one is quite high." She extended her left hand to me. "You must come and see us again. It was very pleasant."

When I got safely down the steps, I felt ashamed for having sat there with my head uncovered. I felt even more ashamed when I realized how tactful they had all been not to notice it.

6

When I got back to the hotel, Buchlerner was loud with reproach. "You played a very naughty trick on me. You went out this afternoon and you didn't appear at supper. Your chair stood vacant like Prophet Elijah's chair at the seder, and I sent out a search party for you. Have you forgotten that I am responsible for every single one of my guests? However, I'll make an exception for you just this once," he said, and his face grew less stern. "Take your seat, and I'll wait on you myself. But do be quick, please, for we have to get ready for tomorrow morning's breakfast."

After scolding me for eating like a bird, he sat down with me over a glass of tea.

"Well, I've gotten over it. Here I've been nagging at you so much I'd better try to make up with you. I have such a lot of work to do around here I scarcely know where to begin. It would seem I have a couple of fine daughters and a strong Gentile girl to help out, too, but without me nothing goes right. I have to organize everything. If only my wife, may she rest in peace, were still alive, I'd be much better off. She really looked after me, as well as though I were a son-in-law boarding with us, or a woman in confinement. But God took her young. It was heartbreaking to see so young a woman go so soon."

Two other guests had lingered on in the dining room, at another table—a young woman who looked to be about thirty and a man of the same age. They sat opposite one another but never looked at each other. The woman ate rapidly, as though someone or something were driving her, but the man, who was wearing dark glasses, ate very deliberately, constantly picking at the food in the plate. I told the hotel owner that apparently I wasn't the only guest late for supper.

Buchlerner's voice dropped to almost a whisper. "So you don't know yet who they are. Though, come to think of it, how could you? I have, thank God, some eighty guests here at the moment—a real army. Well, those two aren't really late for supper. They aren't quite right in the head—cases of arteriosclerosis in the broader sense of the word. This is their second supper. A couple of hours after supper they complain that they're starving, and I have to set the table for them again. You see what a hotel owner has to put up with? I have to be a psychologist along with everything else. For instance, I got these two together—I mean to say, I put them at the same table. I have to judge from a guest's looks whom I can seat him with. As you see, they don't have a word to say to each other, but at least they sit still this way. Any other arrangement won't work. The one or the other gets up in the middle of the meal and walks out. I really have to be a psychologist, to figure out which guests are compatible. As soon as a guest arrives, I take one good look at him, and I know with whom to seat him."

He said that the young woman lost her mind when her child died. She had sat by the empty cradle for a whole week—it was her first child, and no one could persuade her to stop singing lullabies and rocking the empty cradle. May God protect us from such misfortune! She was an educated person, too, Buchlerner assured me, she knew Hebrew and often quoted verses from the Bible. Her husband, thank God, was wealthy and could afford to have someone look after her. This was necessary, to see to it that she was washed and dressed; otherwise, she'd let herself go completely.

"Once she came into the dining room in such a state that I wished the floor would open and swallow me up. When I scolded her for looking like that, she said she just didn't care about making a good impression on people. The only thing that keeps her going is her appetite. God bless her, she gobbles up two breakfasts, two dinners, and two suppers. Her husband pays me double the usual board, but I'm sure I lose money on her even so. And I really don't begrudge her the food. Poor thing, she's a fine person. She never bothers anyone, and her conversation usually makes perfectly good sense. She has one delusion—that somewhere in a little town near Warsaw there is a prince with such beautiful eyes that if she could only once look into those eyes of his, she would be perfectly well again. She thinks it is her husband who, out of jealousy, keeps her from going to see the prince. Her husband is an extremely busy man—he owns a sugar factory. When he comes here weekends she gives him a rough time. 'Shaia,' she says accusingly, 'When are you taking me to the castle, to see the prince?'"

The man having supper with her, Buchlerner went on, was another sad case. He was a teacher of Hebrew, one of the really good, the prominent ones. A bachelor and an only son, when his mother died he grieved so much that finally he had a nervous breakdown. The doctors say that the muscles of his eyes have become so weak that he cannot keep his eyes open, and that it requires enormous effort on his part to focus on things around him.

Buchlerner got up. "Well, there is no lack of troubles in this world," he said. "People are poor things at best, and some people break down under the slightest trouble. They just can't bear the burden. Oh—I nearly forgot to tell you—there is someone waiting to see you. I told him to wait because I thought you should have your supper first. If he's got bad news for you, it's important you should eat first to have the strength to take it. And if he's brought you good news, it won't be any less good after supper—an extra dessert. That's how I think about these things, anyhow—of course, I may be all wrong, and you can probably find fault with my reasoning."

◆ ◆ ◆ *Chapter 4*

1

In the main lounge, where a few chess games were in progress, a man with a pointed beard was sitting on a bench. He wore thick eyeglasses. When the proprietor led me to him, he took off his glasses and wiped them carefully with a handkerchief. Only after he put his glasses back on, and carefully folded his handkerchief and put it away, did he take a good look at me.

"I must say I don't recognize you, but I want to bid you welcome anyway. This is a small town. When several persons told me you were here, I had no reason to doubt their word. I assume that this is really you, and you must assume that I am really I. We must take each other on trust, so to speak."

My impatience to know who he was left him unruffled. "Don't try to guess, don't make the slightest effort. Even if you stand on your head, you won't guess who I am."

When he finally identified himself as Goldblat, my old teacher of Hebrew, I was angry with myself for not recognizing him. There were still a few strands of yellow in his pointed gray beard. I should have recognized him not only by the beard but also by the shape of his head, the thin nose ending in a stubby bulge, and the reddish nearsighted eyes which had peered at me in just the same way through thick glasses thirty years ago.

"I am furious at not having recognized you," I said. "I can't forgive myself."

"Oh, come now, who can hope to escape the effects of the passing years? When you last saw me, my dear friend, I was about thirty years old, and now I am sixty. When you knew me I was just getting ready to divorce my wife, and now it is five years since I found the courage to do it, and finally got rid of that pain in the neck. As you know, I have no children. In those days I was a teacher of some reputation, and now I am a flop. When people used to say, 'Goldblat the teacher'—well, they were talking about a fine Hebraist, an enlightened Jew, a man who wrote letters to Nahum Sokolow and to whom Sokolow wrote back that his Hebrew was as clear as daylight. Yes, that's what he wrote me! I still have the letter. Today, when they say 'Goldblat the teacher,' what are they thinking? The name has an empty sound, and it doesn't evoke anything—not anything at all.

"Thank God, my old reputation isn't totally extinct, though I am ashamed to say how I do manage to earn a kind of living. You must remember Hillel Tuchman, who had the brick factory. He is a rich man, he swims in money—may we have the leavings from his table. Did you ever meet his father, by any chance? Well, he is still alive, and may he live forever, for if he ever died God forbid, it would be goodbye to my job. Reb Zalman Tuchman his name is, close to a hundred years old, maybe even a year or two over it. He is blind, and so his son pays me to pray and study the Talmud with him. The old man is also hard of hearing, so I have to scream my lessons to him. The old man has a wonderful memory, and when I read a chapter of the Bible with him, he can often recite it by heart better than I can read it aloud, looking at the text. But the trouble is, he falls asleep between one sentence and the next, and when he wakes up he has forgotten the place, and then he quarrels with me. It's hard to earn a living in the city, too, and here at least I am my own master. The old man's son rented a fine house for him here, and I live with him. Often I have a young man to replace me, paying him almost nothing, and the old man never notices the difference. Then I walk in the park and meditate on higher things. So now you know what has become of Goldblat the teacher. You can see how low I have fallen when I pray that the old man, already a centenarian, should survive me—for what would I do without him?

"Do you know what?" he said suddenly. "Order a drink—but don't take it literally, you may treat me to couple of drinks. It'll be easier to talk then, easier to recall the old days."

Actually I should have been able to recognize him by the frock coat he was wearing. It might have been the same coat he wore thirty years ago when he came to our house to give me a lesson. It was worn and shiny, of the same greenish black material. In those days, that coat and his rabbinical hat used to inspire me with great respect. It was a great change from the *cheder,* when he appeared in our house. He would usually take off his hat, leaving on a little silk skullcap. In those days Goldblat always overestimated my capacities. Besides teaching me Bible, with the more difficult commentaries, he had me read Peretz Smolenskin's didactic novel *Hatoeh bedarkhe hahayim,* and even tried to get me started on a treatise on logic. All this confused me quite a bit, but Goldblat would reassure my father, saying that I'd get it all in time because I had a good head. He taught me some German, also, and read me Heine's poems. "You can't be an educated man without German," he explained to my father. But my grandfather looked askance at him, and told my father that once a man had learned German he would be pretty sure to stop praying. So long as you don't know German, he said, there is some chance you will remain interested in Judaism; German was incompatible with being a Jew.

I was no more than about ten years of age at the time, and the treatise on logic as well as German Gothic script were supplementary to my lessons in the Talmud. For the latter I had a special teacher. I did seem to take everything in, but only two-dimensionally, so to speak, as if it were no more than paper wisdom. The things I learned wove together in my mind, but my knowledge seemed to me composed of scraps of paper. I found the treatise on logic complicated and overelaborated, and I could scarcely distinguish one letter of the Gothic script from another. I thought of these subjects less as intellectual challenges than as paper fortresses to be stormed. I would look at all this as through lighted windows, windows so bright that you could not see what was inside. For me there was no "inside," and I did not so much as suspect that things could have an inner meaning.

However, I was always an eager student, and never more so than after my classes at the cheder, because I was held spellbound by Goldblat's frock coat, his persuasive voice, and the gold frames of his eyeglasses. I felt sure that the cheder was merely an antechamber to the hall of learning, where everyone spoke as softly and gently as Goldblat did to me, and bowed as politely and elegantly as he did when he came to our house.

Only on one occasion did my respect for him suffer a blow. I happened to he passing the apartment house where he lived. Taking my courage in my hands, I started to climb the stairs to his flat, but even before I reached it, I could hear voices raised in anger, screaming abuse such as one never hears in a decent home. Goldblat stood there in his waistcoat, a cheap skullcap on his head, waving his hands. Facing him stood a woman in a red wig. She had hold of him by his hair, and he was yelling at her that he would give her such a kick in the belly that she would see her dead grandmother.

I ran out of the building before he could catch sight of me. What shocked me was not the language of abuse, not even his sorry predicament, nor the coarse tone of voice devoid of the expressive nuances I heard in it when he read Heine's poems. What shocked me was the waistcoat. Without his frock coat he looked naked, utterly irrelevant to the Gothic "V" or the elaborate *epsilon*. He was more like a lowly Hebrew *aleph* torn out of a battered, poorly printed prayer book. For a long time I was haunted by that sight of Goldblat without his frock coat, having a row with his wife in the intimacy of his home.

Goldblat was not my first secular teacher, but he was the first to take me strolling, as it were, on the walkway of Jewishness, and he proceeded calmly, with dignity, his hands behind his back. He never tried to diminish what I was learning at the cheder, he merely added to it. He was like Peter the Great was to Russia—opening a window onto the wide world, showing me what could be done with biblical words when they were transposed into a modern context. It had never occurred to me before that you could take the words of Jacob and Esau and Joseph and apply them to the contemporary world. I remember an occasion when father asked him how his wife was; he just shrugged his shoulders, and said, "I have despaired of my life," sighing prosaically, seemingly unaware that the phrase had behind it a history of Bible readings that went back hundreds, perhaps thousands of years, back to the very Creation.

I liked the uselessness of everything I studied with him. At home everyone always talked about what I was going to do when I grew up. Grandfather thought I should be a rabbi, and my mother gave him some timid support. Other relatives felt I would become a bookkeeper, or perhaps a scribe, and Father talked about sending me on to the Russian gymnasium. Goldblat's lessons had no relation whatever to plans for a career. They had no purpose at all. There was about them the air of luxurious relaxation that a wealthy household exudes on a Sabbath afternoon.

They reminded me of Freitag, a rich man to whose house I had been admitted several times when Father called on him to request a favor. The maid would lead us through quiet rooms furnished with comfortable upholstered armchairs, and in one of the rooms there would be Mr. Freitag wearing a long dressing gown, napping in a chair. He had a friendly, sleepy face and he always turned down Father's requests with dreamy friendliness. By the time we were shown out through another door, I always had the impression that I had just made a trip through some enchanted orchard where the trees were all asleep and the fruit could not be eaten.

Goldblat's teaching had no beginning and no end. He would ask questions in a very quiet tone of voice and I would answer in the same tone. As the lesson progressed I would often find my eyes closing. I would sit opposite him, and the gold-framed glasses and the little silk cap would grow misty and faint. The Bible lying between us was like a half-finished glass of wine, the liquid barely stirring in the red glass, when my mother walked softly through the room, as though careful not to disturb our slumber.

2

All the teachers I knew before Goldblat had been bent on teaching me useful knowledge. Uncle Feivel, who was more often called Feivel the

Scribe—a tall man with a gray beard which stubbornly refused to grow long—taught me to write with flourishes so that I would seem a practiced writer. In our family he had the reputation of being a real doctor, and he was said to be composing a medical book based on Maimonides. When a child fell ill, Uncle Feivel was the first to be called. If he sighed, a doctor would be summoned, but if he pinched the child's cheek, everyone knew it was nothing serious. He warned me never to drink water after eating the Sabbath cholent: this might give me diarrhea, for fat and water he said do not mix well.

But there came a moment when Uncle Feivel's learning ran out. When he brought me to the point where I knew the difference between the masculine, the feminine, and the neuter genders, he sighed deeply, which meant that the case required a doctor.

This time the doctor was his own son, a teacher in the municipal school. Joseph was the exact opposite of his father: he was short and stocky, and he had a luxuriant black beard which I thought of as a Zionist beard, perhaps because it reminded me of Theodor Herzl's. Joseph wore the uniform of a Russian functionary, and his pupils were Gentile boys. They tormented him a good deal, scribbling the various nicknames they had for him on the walls of the school building, but the nickname that stuck was "Phew Marai." Just what it meant was never clear—perhaps it alluded to his dislike of inkblots on compositions (*marat* is Russian for "daub"). Joseph was a pious Jew, and I remember that I often found him wearing a prayer shawl and phylacteries over his Gentile uniform when he was at home. At the time I regarded this as a sign of attachment to the faith every bit as heroic as that of the Spanish Marranos. Every time he kissed the phylacteries, I could imagine the uniform warring against the prayer shawl and Joseph repulsing the infidel, keeping the cloak of Judaism fast over it.

It was Father's idea that I should take lessons with the *monopolnichka*, the woman who ran the licensed government liquor shop. He wanted me to acquire a decent Russian accent. The monopolnichka was a tall spinster of about forty years of age, who wore thick eyeglasses over large, warm black eyes. She was not a bony old maid, but on the contrary, quite running to flesh, with long fat arms and long legs. She liked me to sit in her lap for my lessons, so we could both use the same book. I don't recall any unpleasant feeling associated with this. Her black hair tickled me, and her breath was warm on my neck. I usually had to wait for her before our lessons could start. I entered through the shop itself, where the green-labeled bottles of vodka were neatly arranged on shelves. The shop was as clean as a pharmacy, and I could hardly believe that in a place like this was sold the terrible stuff responsible for our janitor being found so often lying dead drunk on a heap of refuse.

When the monopolnichka emerged from behind her bottles, I would take off my cap, kiss her hand, and bow, saying *zdravstvuite*. Then I would pass on to a room in the back of the store, where there were always three or four clocks ticking away. Here I had to wait sometimes quite a long while. From an adjoining room would come a rattling of dishes and the scraping of forks and spoons. The cooked food gave off a smell that nauseated me—I was sure that only the most treif of all unkosher foods—only pork—could smell like that.

While I sat there all alone, my heart became another clock ticking away in that room where the heavy curtains were always drawn. A kerosene lamp burned on a large table. From time to time a big dog would come in and sniff at me. While I did not much care for this, it was an old dog, and he was not too interested in me.

When the monopolnichka finally came in, wearing a long black dress, she always looked so clean that I could scarcely believe she had just been eating that vile-smelling food. Even before she came up to the table, I was filled with eagerness to get close to her black hair and to feel her warm Russian words breathing down my neck. Often she would sit down at the piano first, play some romantic reverie, and then weep. Even through the tears she would keep on playing, humming softly to herself. A few tears would remain and fall down my collar once I had clambered into her lap and we were bending over the textbook together. She was quite nearsighted.

Later on, I had a number of "practical" teachers. I attended a private school run by the Zankos, a Ukrainian family which consisted of an old man with a short, well-groomed beard and a big wart on his nose, an old woman with a yellow face and distinguished manners, and a tall son with a prominent Adam's apple. The son smelled perpetually of vodka, the old man of tobacco, and the old woman of freshly laundered linen.

In their school I was the only Jew among fifteen or so Russian, Polish, and German students. There was a large, sunny courtyard where we played between classes. Old Zanko had a friendly, smiling manner when he taught us. The son was nervous and gloomy, and the old woman took us in with gray, serious eyes. Quite often Madame Zanko would disappear into the kitchen and come back bringing small plates with the same smelly food as the monopolnichka used to cook. The other students licked the plates clean, and considered they had had a great treat. Madame Zanko did not even offer any of this to me. Her husband on such occasions would give me a friendly smile and whisper to me, "Ah, well, you can't help it, it's treif!" He would pat me on the head to make me feel at ease, and would usually fetch me a red apple from the kitchen. The only remark ever passed was by the German student who sat next to me and was two heads taller than I. He told me that I was a fool not to go ahead and eat like the others. During these feasts, for all old Zanko's friendliness, I felt I did not belong and was more than ever aware of the icons that hung in every corner.

Zanko's brother was on the administrative staff at the Lublin gymnasium, and I thought that it would be easy to pass from Zanko's school to there. But as it turned out, to have been a pupil of Zanko's was of no help.

Nor did it help me to have studied for a time with no less a person than the daughter of Kurbas, the gymnasium inspector. Every time I arrived for my lesson with her, Kurbas would be dining alone at a richly set table, with a spotless white napkin tucked under his chin and broad black beard. He was a fat, barrel-shaped man, with short legs. As I went by him, he always gave me a hearty good morning, in a booming voice like several bells of the cathedral striking at once and echoing off the walls of the spacious dining room. After his greeting he would laugh heartily and childishly and go back to his meal. Kurbas taught Latin at the gymnasium, and Latin proverbs hung everywhere in his dining room.

His daughter could not have been more than seventeen, but she was very tall and thin. She had extraordinarily thin legs, an oval-shaped face, and she wore her hair in two long plaits. Hers was a timid expression, and she had little freckles. To my eyes she was endowed with all the charms of the heroines of every Russian novel I had so far read. I was fourteen at this time, and we were embarrassed when we were alone with each other. When I took a book from her cold, bony hand, I blushed.

My French teacher had a pockmarked complexion further ruined by red, green, and black cosmetic preparation. She lived alone in a five-room apartment overflowing with all kinds of feminine gear—tiny shoes with high heels, silk dresses, underwear, miniature handkerchiefs of every color, corsets, bottles with scented waters. When I would finally get to the innermost room where we had our lesson, there she would be sitting, a shriveled old woman covered with wrinkles, the veins standing out dark on her yellow hands. She seemed pieced together of all the things scattered around the apartment—the silk dresses, the lace handkerchiefs, the corsets, the improbably tiny shoes, and the scented waters, the combined effect of them all giving off a sharp, sweaty, sweetish smell. Her face could almost have been tattooed, the areas of makeup were so distinct on it. No matter how often I saw her, I was always amazed all over again. Moving through the apartment with its colorful feminine clutter, I always hoped that in the innermost room I would find Kurbas's daughter waiting for me, with her lovely freckles, long legs, and little feet. But as I got closer, even before I entered it, I could already smell the sweetish emanation of scents and lotions which failed to cover up the smell of age.

3

Another worldly teacher who helped to expand my perspectives of Judaism was less a teacher than an examiner, and less an examiner than a brilliant talker. His tactic was to trap me into agreeing or disagreeing with some short maxim, and then, as we discussed the few terms involved, this scanty intellectual fare built up to a banquet of several hours. He might begin with a verse from the Bible and adorn it with so many commentaries, questions, answers, comparisons that the verse in the end took on so many multiple senses and set off so many trains of thought that it seemed to provide wisdom for a whole generation. You could imagine being born, growing up, getting married, and attending the weddings of your children, all the while feeding on the wisdom of that single profound verse. This teacher infused it with such music and such magic that the words composing it became so many sirens luring one on and on into ever more impenetrable deeps of knowledge and wisdom.

That was what could happen to a few words after Reb Levi had gotten through with them. One verse would remind him of fifteen related verses, each of them with a number of various interpretations, and these in turn led to commentaries, to Greek proverbs, to the discoveries of Ibn Ezra, and to the secular sciences—astronomy, anatomy, botany, and philosophy.

Reb Levi suffered from an incurable disease. He was bedridden and received me sitting up, his head resting against pillows piled up high. He always wore a velvet skullcap. His face was yellow, but it glowed like a wax candle. His yellow beard was short and thick and untidy from neglect—but even in the untidiness there was a certain restraint, a proportion appropriate to his features. It was a modest, honest beard, which gave nobility to the face. His nightshirt was always as spotlessly clean as a high priest's robe. Very often he closed his eyes while speaking, and then he looked to me like a high priest on his deathbed, laid out in his sacred garments and ready to meet his Maker. His arms rested on the down quilt like the motionless branches of a still tree.

In the city everyone knew that Reb Levi was dying, and people spoke of him with lowered voices, reverently, as one speaks about a great saint.

Everyone knew that the wealthy Simon Berger had been struck a terrible blow. He was about to lose the jewel in his crown. Simon had had many children, but none of them turned out successfully by the standards which then obtained in Lublin. This pious rich man, it was thought, whose piety and learning were a byword, deserved better children. One of his sons was a wastrel who chased Gentile girls and worked as a traveling salesman for a candy factory. A second son had gone off to Switzerland to study chemistry and had come back a complete goy, with a green student's cap that looked as if it were made of glass. His only daughter was a cripple—the poor girl was paralyzed in one hand. His pride and joy was Reb Levi, the one son who devoted his days and nights to serious study.

At this time there were many scholars in Lublin. It was not thought too unusual that Levi should obtain his rabbinical license at an early age. This was admirable, but not extraordinary. At one point he had gone off to live in a small town, where he had married a girl much taller and sturdier than he was. He had tall, gawky children by her who, when they stood up, looked as if they were bending in a heavy wind. Then Levi fell ill, and people began to say that the rheumatism from which he always suffered had reached his heart. He was brought back from the small town to his father's house and put to bed, in one of the most comfortable, lightest rooms of Reb Simon's house.

Reb Simon occupied the whole building. Downstairs he had his textile business, with living quarters above it. Downstairs was the physical, the prosaic side of his life, where doglike he chased after every penny, now more than ever needed, as his son required the attentions of the best doctors and specialists. Simon never gave up hope that somehow they would save his son—the soul of his being—but upstairs, Levi's strength and health were slowly ebbing away, like a lingering Sabbath afternoon.

It was not until Simon's son was bedridden that the people of our city began to grasp what an unusual man he was. His own father and mother had not realized what a treasure had been entrusted to them for a little while. Levi was no more than thirty-eight years old at this time.

People began to show up at Simon's house who had never been there before, who had never been to Lublin before. There came great rabbis, scholars, men whose very names filled Jews with luminous hopes. Among the visitors were saintly mystics, Gentile scholars, university professors, famous writers. Simon and his wife would exchange silent glances, weeping with belated joy. "You see whom we are losing!"

Only now did it become known that Levi, while he lived in the small town, had conducted correspondence with these rabbis and scholars, and that these great men addressed him as Master. The Gentile scholars were saying that he was one of the greatest philosophers of our generation. The people of Lublin now said that Reb Levi was one of the greatest saints, perhaps one of the thirty-six just men who by their unpublicized merits keep the turbulent and insecure world in existence. It was also said that he had written works that truly enlighten, works that reveal the most arduous mysteries.

I had the privilege of sitting on a little stool next to his bed. There were usually two rabbis in the room who put their questions to Reb Levi in a businesslike manner, as if he were not a gravely ill man. He would answer them briefly and matter-of-factly, but now and then his gray eyes would light up, his yellow face would glow, and his voice would become a song. Then the rabbis would fall silent and sit very still, fearing to make the slightest move. They had deliberately stimulated Reb Levi to rise above his suffering, they had led him on to where he could get the full light of the sun on his face. His face now glowed so brightly that some of the light was reflected in the faces of the rabbis. Meanwhile I, a little boy who had been told that Reb Levi was dying, gazed at him, trying to discover the secret of a dying man's last words as well as the secret of fear.

When the rabbis left him, they would tell his weeping mother outside, after they had kissed the mezuzah on the doorpost, that the ears which had heard her son's words were blessed, that she mustn't cry, that God would help him, and that his own parents should be filled with great joy and pride.

Only once, I recall, did one rabbi lose control of himself. Reb Levi had ventured into the deepest caverns of thought and had emerged safe and sound, and then ventured again, and again reemerged to daylight with a shining face, when suddenly the rabbi burst out in sobs: "Rabbi, Rabbi, Reb Levi, who will ever take your place when you have left us!"

At this moment Levi's father and mother came in and began to mourn him as though he were already dead. His mother wept passionately, as though she had long been waiting for permission to weep, a permission she had never dared to ask for.

Having wept themselves dry (if I am not mistaken, I too wept—a childish accompaniment), they were ashamed. They were ashamed because Reb Levi's glowing face was smiling. And when they had all subsided, Levi spoke about the years he had spent in the small town, where he could not properly fulfill his duty to honor his parents. He spoke about the rare virtue, which is a joyous duty—the sole duty that raises the human species above the beasts, because only in the human species is there a permanent bond linking father and son, mother and child, until the child himself becomes a father.

The real meaning of the term *Karet,* or excision, Reb Levi went on, was precisely this—to be cut off from one's living parents, from the joy of fulfilling the duty to honor them; and that is also why God gives long years of life to those who honor their parents.

After they had all left, the wrinkles in Levi's face became smoothed out. Perl, the maid, fed him a few spoonfuls of oatmeal. His face was serene, as if his illness had been only a pretext, an excuse to get away from his tall wife, his grown children, the outside world in general, as if his illness had given him the repose all restless people pray for.

"How is your father? Is he still working in the store downstairs? Come closer, don't be afraid. What are you studying now? Jeremiah?" And soon a verse would flash out like a brightly painted boat on the water. He would take me aboard and steer it this way and that. I was afraid to sail with him too far, for I could see his dead hands, and I feared that he was calling me with them. Nevertheless I went along with him on these trips, my heart pounding.

At the very moment Reb Levi lay in his father's house against the white pillows, another man of about his age was lying in a shed in the courtyard of the apartment house we lived in, near the Castle. This shed looked like a dog's kennel, pieced together of old boards. In the courtyard stood the privies—also wooden sheds—and across from the privies, separated from them by an ill-smelling garbage box and a yard that was freely used by children and even grown-ups who were too lazy to use the dark privies at night, stood the low shed. Formerly it had been used as a place to throw old clothes which even the rag picker had rejected.

One day when we were just getting up, we heard wild screams coming from that shed. We found a man there, lying on the floor, roaring like an ox. The man's legs were crippled. He could not raise his hands either, but only thrash about in the straw that someone had put under him. He had a jet-black beard and black eyes, which reminded one of the eyes of a cow. His disheveled hair seemed to cover his entire forehead. Around him pieces of bread were strewn, and next to him stood a bowl of water to which he often rolled himself to take a swallow. This freak was chained to one of the boards in the shed. He rolled back and forth uttering terrible screams, all the more terrible because they were not ordinary human cries but the desperate efforts of a mute to speak.

No one knew where this wretched cripple had come from. At all events we children never learned who had rented the shed to its strange occupant. Many of the children threw stones at the shed, and this drove the cripple to utter blood-curdling screams. We somehow learned that his name was Zelig, and the children mockingly called him Reb Zelig. We also knew that a woman had undertaken to perform the good deed of washing him and changing his shirt once a month. She also provided Reb Zelig with bread every other day or so.

I often heard his cries at night. I knew that he was lying all alone in the dark shed, in that ill-smelling courtyard. Eventually, the shed itself emanated such a stench that even we children, ordinarily insensitive beasts, would not go near it. Reb Zelig's screams grew so unbearable that Yankele the tailor, who lived on the ground floor, and Getzl the baker, who lived in the basement, looked for a way of getting rid of the cripple.

I often looked through the open door and saw him lying there on the ground. He was so weak now that his roar had become a mere bleat, and his unkempt face looked drained of blood. At such moments I imagined that he was about to open his mouth and speak to me in a familiar language, perhaps even to offer a commentary on the Torah, like Reb Levi when he lay in his nice, clean bed piled high with pillows.

Several women consoled the unhappy tenants of our apartment house with the thought that there was no point making a fuss, since the poor man's sufferings were obviously nearing an end.

I remember both these dying men—the one who was mockingly called Reb Zelig, and the one who was tenderly called Reb Levi—as being with me for days on end. I watched and heard them die, the one in the shed near the privies and the other in his comfortable bed. The one went in silence, the other with luminous words on his lips.

Two days before Reb Zelig was found lying silent, curled up like an animal, the woman who had looked after him went into the shed and washed him. Lying there helpless, when his face had been washed, he did not look so different from Reb Levi, or any less serene—this body could have been that of the soul which lay in the house of Simon the rich man.

Reb Levi died the same day as Reb Zelig was found dead. It was clear to me that there was some connection between the mute animal body that had suffered all the tortures of the damned in the dark, stench-filled shed, and the soul which passed on in immaculate surroundings, with words on his lips that were repeated over and over in our city for a long time thereafter.

Some time after Reb Levi's death, Father one day brought home one of the essays the great man had left behind. It was written in tiny characters, hardly bigger than pinpricks. Several rabbis came to our house to read it, but afterward they declared with a sigh that instead of illuminating dark caverns, the essay only made the darkness thicker. They feared that Reb Levi had taken with him to his grave the radiance of his spoken words. His writings were no more than the intellectual body of his words; they failed to convey his spirit and his light. "That's what we always think—that now bright light will at last illumine us and disclose the mystery. But each generation is left in the lurch." Such was the verdict of a young rabbi with a long, thin nose, a few scraggly whiskers on his chin, and so nearsighted that he had to hold the manuscript up close to his glasses. The hand that held the essay did not tremble, but his head moved right and left with the regularity of a pendulum, racing back and forth over the obscure lines.

4

Goldblat was reminiscing about his pupils—those he had set on the right road and who had made good. He ticked them off on the fingers of his right hand, finger by finger. One was a lawyer, the second an oculist, the third had made a fortune, and the fourth was elected deputy to the Diet. When he got to the thumb, he said, well, the thumb had grown up to be a coarse, boorish fellow. Goldblat was ashamed of him.

He owned several apartment houses with such miserable, damp basements that God preserve us from ever having to stay in one. It was basements like that he rented out to families of nine or even ten people. Really they should be paid themselves to live in such miserable quarters where the damp cold was penetrating, summer or winter. And then the stench, the crowding, the lifeless eyes that seemed to turn on rusty springs, eyes that never sparkled, and the coughing and the wheezing, the complexions as withered as the skin of a smoked herring. Such poverty—it could darken the most beautiful day in May: were it ever to crawl out of these cellars, it would infect the day with all kinds of disease.

Whenever you passed one of these buildings, you saw people who had just been evicted. They lay there on the sidewalks looking like rags, the rags they wore indistinguishable from the people. You couldn't tell whether this bundle of rags was a child or whether this child simply looked like a rag. And the laments and the curses of the evicted! If only one percent of those curses came true, the landlord would be a goner, too. He had so many evictions that it seemed as though this evil man had gathered together all the poor people of Warsaw in his cellars, just in order to be able to turn them out again, one by one. He was a shark, a usurer, and incapable of begetting children.

"For whom are you working so hard?" Goldblat had asked him one day, gently, when he happened to run into him. All the scoundrel did was to sigh deeply. "Can you believe it? It was a sigh, I'm telling you, that could have moved the stones to weep. Gangsters like that, for all their thick skins, can still shake their heads and sigh. 'Isn't it perfectly clear, Mr. Goldblat?' he said to me. 'God has punished me, I am alone in the world.' I took the occasion to suggest that if he cut down the number of his evictions, God might help him. 'Ah,' he said, 'a progressive like you, Mr. Goldblat, you should know better than to say such superstitious things!' You see, it pays him to believe that God is punishing him, and it simply doesn't pay him to believe that anything can be done about it!"

The man's money, Goldblat went on about this former student, had not come from a very pure source. Goldblat didn't go in for gossip, but everyone knew that his wife had earned all that money, and not in a decent way, either. During the First World War, when the Austrians held Lublin for a time, people made fortunes by obtaining a permit from the authorities to import a carload of merchandise without having to pass customs. His wife was the one who obtained the permits. She managed to make her way up to high-ranking officers, including one general. While her husband stayed at home, she dolled herself up and brought back the permits. The fact is she was a beauty, a very luscious piece. It is said that the officers enjoyed her company a great deal.

"Even if I spent all night and the next day with you," Goldblat said, getting up from his chair, "I couldn't tell you all that has happened to my pupils. For instance, one got himself baptized and became a censor. One day he asked me to come to see him, and I went. I had no choice, though I am afraid of converts. He asked me to translate some difficult Hebrew sentences. He is so dutiful a public servant that he is seized with a panic at the thought that he might let pass something that would displease the Polish government. Of course, he wanted me to believe that his real purpose was to defend Jewish honor, to save Jews from trouble. Perhaps, he said, he was like the famous Daniel Khvolson, who was destined to become a Christian in order to champion Jewish causes all the more effectively.

"On one occasion when he was drunk, the censor confided to me that he had become a convert out of revenge against Jewish girls. One girl after the other rejected him, complaining that they could not stand the smell of his feet. You can imagine what sensitive noses the pampered daughters of the Jews must have had. The censor complained that they could smell his feet through the shoe leather. So he married a Gentile girl, a quiet creature who never complains. She has given him five children, and not once has she complained about his feet— damn it.

"Tell you about my pupils? Well, I wouldn't know where to begin and where to stop. So I'd better not begin at all. But one thing I must tell you. I am no longer what I once was. I shall not deny it, I have become an ignoramus. The little I did know has become fusty, and I haven't acquired any new knowledge. I am amid strangers, so to speak. All around me people are discussing their problems, forming parties, and so on, but I don't share any of it or want to. Even my Hebrew has become outdated. Recently I glanced through a Hebrew newspaper, and I thought my eyes were playing tricks on me, it was like some sort of hieroglyphics, totally incomprehensible. I wiped my glasses again and again, to no avail. And as for the bit of German I inherited from my father, it was never much. Believe me, when I study now with my hundred-year-old pupil, we understand each other, but the new generation I don't even begin to understand."

Goldblat took off his glasses and began to wipe them. He looked at me with myopic eyes which, without the glasses, seemed to stare in opposite directions.

"I am too severe with myself," he said. "That's my trouble. I am simply poisoning my life, making myself unhappy. I often feel that the bit of useless knowledge I had, I gave it all away to my pupils, and that I have been left with nothing at all. I feel as though I were walking around naked like Adam. Moreover I can't stop asking *why* to everything. No matter what happens, even the most trivial thing, I am bound to ask *why*. The world is topsy-turvy. I can't make out the pattern at all. Take poverty. Every time I see it, it's as though somebody had punched me in the jaw. I feel ashamed of being a man. And what do I mean by poverty? Well, I suppose, just knowing that there are people in the world who are dreaming of a bit of cooked food, a warm meal, a crust of bread. I know this has been going on from time immemorial, and the sun rises and sets, and the world marches on and makes a noise, and people fuss about. But it's unbelievable! A fine world this is, that has not abolished hunger, and yet has the nerve to take itself seriously!

"You know what," he said, digging into his beard with two fingers to scratch his chin. "I'll say good night now. I've bored you enough. Tomorrow is another day, and anyhow we aren't going to change the world in a minute."

5

It was quite late. The Buchlerner hotel was asleep. I walked on tiptoe up the carpeted stairs and tried to find my room in the half darkness. In this way I startled what looked like a two-headed creature. But the creature divided into a man and a girl. The man was the sturdy Gentile who looked after Bronski, the mad student who raved about Egyptian mummies. The girl was the one who helped clear up in the dining room and fed the ducks and the chickens every morning. The man did not run away, but stood there, chin jutting forward, very much the chivalrous male ready to face the music. Or was he merely embarrassed, ashamed of himself? His attitude could even mean that he was ready to fight. As for the girl, she ran barefoot down the corridor, the carpeting muffling her footsteps. She did not sway as she ran, but ran like a boy, briskly, lifting her legs high.

Then I saw that I was a floor below the one where my room was, the top floor. When I finally got to my door and put the key in the lock, a shadowy figure in slippers came out from another door on the landing. It was wearing something on its head—an old cap, a woman's bonnet, or a skullcap. The shadow sneaked into my room after me and shut the door. Then he snapped the switch and the room filled with a jaundiced light. My guest and I found ourselves staring at each other in a long greenish mirror covered with fly specks. I recognized the proprietor.

"You aren't asleep yet?" I stammered, vaguely frightened.

"I can't sleep until my last guest has turned in," he said. "I'm responsible for the lot of you, you know. That's the kind of job it is."

"Have I kept you up?"

"Yes and no. I mean you are the last guest to come upstairs but I shall not sleep until everything downstairs quiets down."

I listened intently. I couldn't hear a sound. Did he mean the serving girl and the Gentile? No, I thought, after all it was I who had startled them—and they hadn't been making a sound.

"Whom do I have in mind?" Buchlerner went on. "I can guess what you're thinking. The girl is none of my business. She doesn't work for me at night. If she wants to have some fun, it's her own affair. As for the Gentile, what can he do?" He spread his hands in a gesture of helplessness. "No, it's neither the girl nor the Gentile, but the door that the Gentile is supposed to be watching, that's the room that's keeping me up.

"You see, this is Tuesday, and Tuesday night I always have to keep awake. The mad student has to have a lover once a week. A lover—that's his elegant way of putting it. But whether she is or isn't a lover, the man looking after him knows what he means and finds something for him in the village.

"You must realize it's hard to find a girl who is willing to spend the night with a madman. The whole village knows who he is, and people are simply afraid. So far nothing bad has happened. The Gentile smuggles a girl into his room late at night and watches the door like a dog. If he has a bit of fun in the meanwhile, it doesn't hurt anyone.

"But think of my position in all this. To be sure, he always gets her out by dawn. You're a friend, so it doesn't matter, but if other people staying here were to learn of this, I might just as well cut my throat. Just put yourself in my place. Nothing bad has happened so far, but who can tell with a madman? The Gentile guard says that he will be responsible. But he doesn't own this hotel, so what does he care? He only has to slip up once—and what could I do, sue him? In short, Tuesday nights I worry myself to death, and wish I'd never seen the hotel. I pace up and down all night. After a while I feel as though the man downstairs isn't mad at all, on the contrary, he is perfectly healthy—it's I who am mad, missing my sleep, listening for every creak and squeak.

"Good night, sleep well," he said, "and don't give any of this another thought. After all, you can sleep in peace. You don't own a hotel with mad guests. Oh God in heaven, how I wish I didn't have to earn my bread in the last years of my life!"

He tiptoed out of the room, soundlessly closing the door behind him.

◆ ◆ ◆ *Chapter 5*

1

"Are you looking for a male or female?"

I had been so sure I was all alone that for a moment I thought the solitude was jeering at me, I was flabbergasted to see it was Steinman. He was the last person I should ever have expected to run into along this dark wooded hillside, which sloped precipitately upward on the one side and fell off sharply to a ravine on the other.

Steinman was wearing galoshes that flopped noisily as he picked his way over the damp ground. It sounded as if he were walking through puddles. On his head was a formidably broad black hat, and he wore his overcoat like a cape. He carried a gnarled stick with a carved head.

"If you're looking for female company, I can't help you. But if it's a man you're looking for, you won't find a better one. Not in this neighborhood, at least," he added with a smile.

"I must confess that this last remark is not original with me. That's what the old rabbi of Trisk used to say. He would take his long beard in his hand and exclaim, 'Oh Lord of the universe, what art Thou waiting for to redeem us? I swear by my beard and earlocks, Thou wilt never have a finer Jew than I am. So why not send us the Messiah right now?'"

He glanced at my mud-spattered shoes and burst out laughing. "You have optimistic shoes, I see. Apparently you're unfamiliar with our soggy countryside. There have been swamps here since the creation of the world."

I felt guilty about Steinman, for I had not looked him up since I first met him. It must seem as though I had been avoiding him. I began to apologize, when he interrupted me. "Now, now, set your mind at rest. Actually, I've been afraid you were sore at me for avoiding you. Lately, I've been busy putting my papers in order—my poor bit of immortality. When my time comes and I am called to meet my Maker, I want my papers to be in order."

He began to walk faster, keeping a few steps ahead of me, and from time to time turning around to look at me with the expression of a boy proud of walking faster than a grown-up.

"If you made your way to our mountain pass all by yourself, you must have the soul of an explorer," he said. "It is possible to stay here for months on end without suspecting the existence of these hidden valleys. Some of them are real wonders—chunks of the primeval world.

"If my daughter knew that I was wandering about like this, she'd come for me with a net and drag me back to the hotel by my ears," he said, looking around him. "If you think that all this dampness is good for my health, you're very much mistaken. And yet right after lunch I sneaked away. I suppose they've sent out search parties for me. Everyone wants to take care of me."

All night, he said, he had had no more than a few minutes' sleep. When he did drop off, dreams beset him in battalions—some of them so stupid, he might have been a ten-year-old boy. "Yes, I even dreamed of a naked woman. Just imagine. Do you know how long since I saw a naked woman? It seems centuries ago. And now, at my age, to have Lilith with me! And how about you? Did you sleep well?"

I assured him that this had been my best night of sleep in the hotel, a night of deep dreamless slumber. I told him that Goldblat, my old teacher, had evoked so much I had forgotten from the past that I scarcely turned over for ten hours.

There was a glitter in his eyes. "You do well to get your sleep, young man. All that good sleep will serve you well when you reach my age. Most people think that old people do nothing but sleep. If that were only true. The sleep of the old is a broken kind of sleep, it doesn't do you any good at all. To begin with, your bones ache. You feel as though you were fainting with exhaustion—a foretaste of death—or else you just get a kind of light nap. It's as though someone were holding a drug-soaked cloth over your face, lifting it up every few minutes.

"And the dozing is a time of self-reproach. You should have made this move, you should have held back that one. You go over the whole game, and the terrible thing is that the game is already over—that you can't play it over again and get it right this time.

"What I regret most is having neglected to tend my own vineyard. Much too early I became a Jewish drawer of water and chopper of wood. I became too busy, too much engrossed in public matters. And now, when I began to go over my precious writings—I was horrified by how little I had accomplished, mortified and ashamed."

He drew an old newspaper out of his overcoat pocket and spread it over a rock so covered with moss that it looked rotten. He sat down on it, uttering a little groan which he tried to stylize so as to eliminate any suggestion of old age or fatigue. He asked me to sit down, too.

"I am a very ambitious man, but I never became a real writer—at best a teller of little stories about Hasidic courts and dynasties of rabbis. This is not self-deprecation. We are the sons of a poor nation and we must do our duty. In my own modest way I did help too. You must understand that for the time being we have no room for a so-called great literature. Do you know why? Because a great literature is a literature dealing with trifles—little pleasures, little cares, little everyday happenings, little folks with little worries, little hatreds, little loves, little wives and little children, how they work and what they do in their spare time. We have never known the peace necessary to create such a literature. We are simply not settled enough—constantly on the move, driven from one place to another. Ours is a history of heroes and martyrs, and heroes are not people. Ours is a heroic literature on the grand scale and with heavily dramatic effects—perfect for the Sabbath, to read about in books, but not a very healthy literature.

"Maybe, on second thought, I'm just rationalizing my own colossal failure. For I must admit, I've often resented our more pretentious men of letters, those who write as though we were a public of Frenchmen or Norwegians. I used to belong to some of their organizations, but I always felt like yesterday's man. It was like being in a chilly church. Their concerns seemed remote from our living people, as if Jews were some tribe in Hotzeplotz. What our people needs is a warm, popular literature, full of moral tales, like in olden times. Because the moment we turn an illiterate into a reader, he moves on to Gentile culture. Those who come to us are starved for popular literature; what they need is a word to warm their bones, to move them to tears.

"Still, I went too far in the direction of popularizing or vulgarizing, of giving the Jewish reader prechewed, softened, easily digestible spiritual food. I had a natural talent for history. The Polish government recognized my abilities and my contributions in the field of ancient Polish history. But I squandered that too, settling for much less grand achievement. And do you know why? Because the Jewish people breaks my heart. It can have the shirt off my back any time—it engages me body and soul. How can I set myself the goal of a personal career when the career of my people is so desperate? It would be asking them to carry me on their shoulders were I to become famous at their expense. How could I ask to be honored and respected, when I know that they need bread, milk, health, and a roof over their heads for at least a few generations? Not books about bread and milk, but actual bread and milk, to eat and to drink. How could I strut about like a peacock among them, saying what a great writer I am!"

Steinman gave a deep sigh, not attempting to conceal it this time. "Believe me, our people arouses infinite compassion in me. I am not exaggerating things—our people really deserves compassion, it is truly a tragic people. Every time it has been about to recover strength, to catch its breath, the Almighty has dealt it so much punishment that not all the hundreds of millions of Chinese or Hindus could have endured it. We too often forget that we are a small people, without much strength."

He took off his black hat and wiped his forehead with a handkerchief.

"I'm beginning to get out of breath—these steep hills are closing in on me. Let's get away from here. Maybe we'll stop and look at the royal palace. I know every corner of it. It's a fine bit of Polish history studded with beautiful episodes. Very few people realize that we can learn a lot from Polish history, with its winged dreams of freedom and democracy, and its aristocratic closeness to the people. But the finest Poles, who have been so marvelously humane, forgot to leave heirs. Only the bullies have been fruitful and multiplied, and they have such a deep-rooted hatred of the Jews that nothing will ever knock it out of their heads."

He was now walking quite slowly, although it was clear that he wanted to get away from the damp woods. Now and then he would stop still, but without interrupting the flow of talk.

"Do you know what? I didn't mean to imply that I compare myself with our great ancestors, but now that I am approaching the end of my allotted years—for I am just approaching threescore and ten—I can see the past, the present, and even the future spread out in front of me like a green field. I can see our whole people—the aged, the young, and the children. I can see them class by class, the rich and the poor, those who stick to the national ways and those who become assimilated, the intelligent and the foolish—it's a colorful crew. I feel like Jacob on his deathbed. I should like to gather them all around my bed so I could tell them many things, so I could admonish them. I'm talking about real people. Writers tend to imagine a people, to dream up the characters of a people of their own invention; it is easier to write for an imaginary public. But I see real people face to face every day. I see their confusion, the chaos and uncertainty, the deterioration of the stalwart man of faith with his marvelous powers of endurance.

"I don't mean to say that he has wholly disappeared. He is still to he found, both among pious Jews and among the radicals. There is a great spirit of self-sacrifice in the Jewish Labor Bund, it has organizational energy, and it has done marvelous things for the working class. And among the Communist zealots there are fanatics who risk their lives daily, quite aware that they may end up in the torture chambers of Kartuz-Bereza. They live holed up like mice, they keep 'under cover,' as we say. Nor should we overlook the virtuous Jew whose heart is generous and whose door is always open to the poor. But at the same time, you cannot ignore the erosion of the 'image of God,' the stampeding assimilation, the panicky flight from Judaism. I see also the masses of poor, whose children still burn with the eternal flame—for education, knowledge, enlightenment. I should like to gather them all around my bed, just as Jacob gathered the tribes, and here is what I would say to them . . .

"What actually would I say to them? Now, don't rush me, here, as the expression goes, is where the dog lies buried. . . . Obviously, the same language won't do for all tribes. But perhaps I could explain to them an old-fashioned notion: that the beauty of the Jewish people lies in its capacity for martyrdom. Yes, yes, I know, it sounds outmoded, obsolete, the same old story. But don't rush me. By *martyrdom* I want to suggest a single term descriptive of the great many different burdens we carry on our shoulders. Socialism, for example, which I think premature as a reform program, but nonetheless something for which we are tortured. Zionism, for example, the rallying point of a people eager to stand again on its own soil, together as one people. Religious piety too, purity of soul, and generosity—the challenge to look after every household, every hungry mouth.

"I don't care what kind of burden a Jew chooses to bear all his life, but he should never be without one. We ought to amaze our neighbors by the purity of our lives. It would be truly marvelous if we never went in pursuit of great wealth. The Rothschilds and their ilk haven't done much for us in any case. Yes, it would be marvelous if we could get along on so little that there would be nothing to take away from us!"

We had by now reached the regular highway. My muddy shoes looked grotesque in the afternoon sunshine on the dry road—no less grotesque than Steinman's heavy galoshes. We sat down on a bench in front of a little house.

"Stefan Żeromski, the famous Polish writer, spent many summers in this house," Steinman informed me. "And over there"—he pointed —"is a monument to his son who died young. Are you in the mood for more? Żeromski has helped me collect my thoughts again. The sense of our mission must be reflected in our literature—our writing should be obsessed with it. Our literature ought to be purer and more elevated than other literatures. Actually, Gentile peoples have been fertilized by the Bible and produced literary giants as a result, whereas we Jews have turned our backs on the Book of Books.

"Just think a minute, and you'll see my point. What is the glory of our past? The prophet, the pure man, the fiery chastiser, the man of conscience unable to tolerate wrongdoing. Well, this is the secret of our existence going forward. We must recover the spirit of the prophets—prophets, mind you, not profits! Since it is our fate to be a gadfly to the world, we must protest every injustice, not just wrongs against ourselves. We ought to speak up for every living creature. When all is said and done, it isn't a bad specialty—conscience. That is the word to be inscribed on our banner. There must a party above all parties—a party of modern prophets who seize every occasion to sing out or, rather, to shout, into the ears of the world, unafraid of anything.

"But to give substance to our protests and warnings, every Jew—from the highest to the lowest, from the richest to the poorest—must become a high priest. The others invented one Christ on one cross, but we who have been crucified for centuries, we can and must become the embodiment of the highest purity, so that we may conquer them by sheer moral strength, without rifles, artillery, or airplanes, by the resurrected voice of our eternal prophets."

He was speaking more calmly now, as though he had caught his breath. "Without moral strength we are on the same footing as any Wojtek or Staszek—but unlike us, Wojtek and Staszek have something to stand on, a country and legal rights, while all we have is pieces of paper, promissory notes forever due, and we can only complain that we have been maltreated.

"And there is something else I'd like to say to the assembled tribes. Every generation must reformulate Judaism in accordance with its own ideas and needs. This was what the writers of the Mishna did, and the Amoraim, and the Gaonim, and that was what the Rambam and the Ba'al Shem tried to do. That should form also the very core of our literature. It must become a mirror of our own idea of Judaism. If you will assess our literature from this point of view, you'll come to some interesting conclusions."

A woman who walked by waved a cheerful greeting to Steinman. She went by so fast that I did not catch a glimpse of her face. Steinman gallantly raised his hat. His eyes lit up.

"Do you know who she is? She is a famous Polish Jewish historian. Several of her monographs caused a stir among Polish historians. Shall I tell you how I made her acquaintance? One day I was strolling around in the old Jewish cemetery—yes, the one in Lublin—copying inscriptions from old tombs. Suddenly I saw this woman lying there next to a grave, but in highly unhistorical circumstances. She was not lying there alone, but with a young man, and in a very intimate pose at that. Of all places, she had chosen the old cemetery, with all its evocations of the dead centuries, for some most lively behavior. If I'm not mistaken, she married the same young man. As a matter of fact he is excessively thin—a real skeleton, while she herself is as ugly as sin. To care for her, real historical lust would be needed, and to gratify it in a cemetery would be highly appropriate." He laughed loudly, like a boy.

"This is all very well, but I have a daughter—may she live a hundred years—a dear child, but she's out to destroy me. Let's see whether I can manage to slip into the hotel by the side door. Then I'll pretend that I've been looking for her."

He set off, walking on tiptoes in his galoshes, as though on his way to commit a burglary. "You'd better get back now, too. It's almost supper time," he said, looking back with a friendly glint in his eyes.

2

Immediately after supper they got busy in the main lounge moving tables and chairs. The women all disappeared, to come back one by one, freshly rouged, their hair twisted into various fantastic structures, and with all visible areas of flesh freshly powdered.

When the men saw that the women were taking this thing seriously, they too did what they could under the circumstances. They changed, combed their hair, and some even went so far as to shave again. The latter could be recognized by their bluish faces when they came downstairs—it looked as though they had tried to shave down to the bone.

The hotel guests were assembling for a "dancing," as they called it.

The women pronounced the English word as though some more elegant category than a mere dance were involved. The term derived from some imperfectly grasped usage in American movies.

Buchlerner was hopping about in a pair of slippers, made by cutting the uppers off a pair of high shoes, and with a skullcap on the back of his head. Nobody paid any attention to his incessant orders. In the confusion of tables and chairs being moved about, his appearance gave one the impression that an old-fashioned Jewish wedding was about to take place.

Finkel came down in a frock coat, his double chin wedged behind a stiff collar. He walked about gingerly, hands behind his back, testing the floor to see whether it was too slippery. He gave out advice and suggestions in an imperious Polish, addressed to the Gentiles who were working on an improvised stage and did not even turn around to look at him. Other men were putting colored shades over the electric light bulbs, to make them look like paper lanterns.

Finkel was so firmly caught up in the Polish language that he even spoke Polish to the few old ladies who, exuding a scent of eau de cologne, grouped themselves around him. Finkel was bragging about his dancing exploits as a young man. Whenever the waltz was performed, at all the entertainments, he had always been the leader. He had been a master of the dance—one, two, three, one, two, three, he chanted as he briskly performed the traditional steps of the waltz. Gradually the waltzes and three-steps gave way to a *kozatzke*. Half-squatting, he held up the ends of his frock coat like black wings and demonstrated how many times he could still kick up his heels in the strenuous position.

The officer who had been sitting in a remote dark corner of the lobby working on a chess problem suddenly got up and joined Finkel in his Cossack dance. Several women marked time by clapping their hands, and Finkel hopped on like a demon. Even when the officer stopped, Finkel went right on kicking out his short legs, which by now were getting tangled in his coattails. When he saw Steinman and me, he came up to us. "I've been recalling my exploits as a young man," he said, stammering with embarrassment at having been caught by us in so ridiculous a pose. "It's a good thing my wife didn't see me."

He was panting, wiping the perspiration off his face, and straight-ening the sparse clumps of hair around his shining bald dome. Then, picking up some courage, "Well, how about it, Mr. Steinman," he said. "Shall we join the young people today and dance a bit?"

"What young people? Those girls over there?" Steinman asked, pointing to the group of old women. "No, Mr. Finkel, I'm through with dancing. I'm willing to leave it to the younger generation"—again pointing to the old women—"they can have it."

The room was filling up. Guests from neighboring hotels appeared. Three violinists mounted the little stage, tuned their instruments, strummed the opening bars of a familiar fox-trot, and then stopped abruptly.

Steinman walked toward one corner of the room, and I followed him there. The younger men and women were flexing their muscles, moving about now as though tuning up their bodies, getting ready to slip into the dance at any moment. The colorful shades on the electric lamps threw grotesque shadows on the ceiling, like shadows of imaginary creatures, and spread a colorful half-light through the room. The air was tense with the impending dance.

One of the violinists, who had an unusually long, drooping mustache, kept tuning his violin, tightening the pegs and shaking his head —he was still unsatisfied. Now and then he would draw the bow across the strings very delicately, as though cutting the throat of a tiny chick. Suddenly he clapped his hands. The couples stopped moving about, tense but gracefully attentive. Then the music began.

Bronski, the mental case, came in, immaculately and elegantly got up. He swayed in anticipation of finding a partner, tapping the time with his leather pumps. Before we had time to turn away, he found a young lady, and danced off with her cradled in his arms, his eyes closed. He danced as if he were walking in his sleep.

Next to him danced the sturdy Gentile, his guard, with Buchlerner's maidservant. She was wearing shoes tonight, and a large black cross hung dangling on her neck. Apparently we were to understand that although she spoke Yiddish and worked here taking care of the chickens and washing dishes, she was not to be taken for just another of Buchlerner's guests. Her partner looked preoccupied—besides attending to his girl, he had to keep an eye on Mr. Bronski.

The musicians gave the dancers no respite. The moment the couples were ready to leave the floor, a new tune would strike up and bring them right back. The musicians played as mechanically as a hurdy-gurdy. Finkel time and again danced by with his wife, who bore him swooning on her trustworthy bosom. At one point they dropped out and went to one side of the floor. Finkel bent down to one knee and tied one of his wife's shoelaces that had come untied.

Steinman's daughter separated herself from her partner for a moment and ran over to us. "I think you forgot to take your pill today," she said to her father.

"So I'll owe you one pill," he replied testily. "Just pretend that I'm bankrupt and that I can't pay my debts. Why don't you for once forget about your father and have some fun?"

"Say something to me," Steinman asked me a little later, in a sleepy voice, as if he too had fallen into the mood of the dance. "I like to hear people talk against the strains of music. I don't want to exploit you, God forbid, but after all I've bored you enough with my talk, and now is your golden opportunity to get even."

All that came to mind at that moment were matters of such triviality that I was ashamed to speak of them. Of all things, I suddenly recalled the exceptionally tiny shoes a friend of my youth had been wearing when I went to see him. His feet had simply not grown but stayed tiny, like the bound feet of Chinese women in former times. He had received me with mincing little steps in his beautiful apartment and kept trying to impress me. First it was his wife's photograph. Such a pity, he told me, that she should be staying in the country for the summer. "Just look at that lovely complexion," he said. "She is a gift from God." His shining black eyes filled with tears and his red lips were moist when he showed me his wife's picture. From his wife he switched without transition to showing off his apartment. "Completely modern, the very latest things, just as you have them in America." He kept flushing the toilet to show me how well it worked. Each time I got up from my chair, he had another gadget to show me. "Remember how we used to squat in those outdoor privies like acrobats? This is more like civilization!" And he would play with the flush-tank again, unable to leave it alone.

Another foolish recollection that came to mind was a waxen hand that kept screwing a monocle to one eye in a waxen face, the better to survey the theater, three-quarters empty, where the man's rhymed extravaganzas were playing. "We're doomed," he said during an intermission, waving his hand over the empty seats. "You can see there is no hope for us."

And I remembered another writer, a tall, slim man, smoking his pipe phlegmatically, stylishly, in a café favored by literary men. He ran down the occupants of all the other tables and grumbled about the lack of recognition that—may I be forgiven for saying so—adorned his head like a crown of thorns.

What I finally told Steinman about was my visit to the Jewish children's sanatorium, set in lovely green fields. I told him how devoted were the men and women teachers, with their sad Jewish eyes, and how keenly they felt their great responsibility. The children there, badly undernourished and low in vitality, many with fear in their eyes, would one day become a people with healthy lungs, strong bones, and powers of resistance.

I had watched the pathetically thin children, boys and girls, doing calisthenics outdoors, where the air was filled with the smell of new-mown hay. Meanwhile a number of Jewish doctors (who were neglecting their own practice to volunteer their services here) were supervising the preparation of big pots of hot beef soup and tasty baked potatoes. The doctors made encouraging comments about the progress of individual children and took pleasure in their neat athletic uniforms.

A Gentile doctor, one of the most notorious anti-Semites in Poland, paid a visit to this sanatorium in his professional capacity. There he forgot all about politics and was full of admiration for the work of his Jewish colleagues.

It was with this same Gentile doctor that I had visited the sanatorium. We were the first visitors ever permitted. Our inspection started by sampling the piping hot potatoes. Then we were given wooden spoons and ate the soup from a common bowl. Our spoons moved swiftly from bowl to mouth, pausing only long enough to savor the marvelous borsht, before plunging into the bowl again with scant regard for manners. Two friendly Jewish women who had cooked the soup stood nearby and awaited our verdict. The doctor and I smiled at them with gratitude, and we looked over admiringly at the teachers and the children, then back at each other with a feeling of closeness that grew with each swallow of the savory soup. Unexpectedly, the anti-Semitic doctor gripped my hand on the other side of the bowl and gave it a strong brotherly squeeze. "Science will triumph over everything," he said as though to comfort me. "It will triumph over all diseases."

Once again we took our spoons out of our mouths and plunged them into the common bowl, in the blood-red liquid ritually affirming our brotherhood.

Now the musicians suddenly stopped playing for a few moments. When the violins struck up again, they played a frenetic number in the course of which the dancers flung their partners and caught them again. It was an American number with Polish trimmings. Steinman had been deeply moved by what I told him, and his big eyes glistened in the dark.

"The Jewish children, may God bless them. And the Jewish doctors, too, who work without remuneration. Ah, they're a fine group!" he said with tears in his eyes. "Sooner or later the day must come when men will be united in a covenant of eternal friendship. The resurrection of the dead? I don't know anything about it, but I shouldn't mind it after lying in the ground a long time. It would be grand to have someone come whisper in my dead ears and give me the glad tidings that the great day of a perfected humanity has dawned."

A woman with sad, bulging eyes set in a face like a slightly bruised, frozen apple came over to our table. Only after Steinman had gotten up from his seat and politely offered it to her did I recognize her—she was the elder of the rabbi's daughters-in-law.

"Oh don't get up, please," she said, "unless you want to dance with me."

"I dance to a quite different kind of music," Steinman said.

"And my music requires a different kind of dance," she replied. "So you see, we're very much alike. But occasionally I feel like having a bit of fun, though dancing always makes me sad."

Her intelligent face, her tall, slender figure, and her becoming dress made her stand out in that roomful of people.

"And you, don't you dance either?" she asked, bending over me. I felt the warm breath of her perfume as she did so. Her eyes had the trembling glow of experienced middle age.

"Well, that's my luck when I try being adventurous," she said pensively. "There is a good Pushkin quotation to illustrate this, but here in Poland, if you quote a Russian author, you prove not so much your education as your age—you prove that you were at school before Poland recovered its independence."

She had barely finished when Bronski took her under his arm and led her away elegantly, to join the dancers.

"Her husband is a very honest man, but unfortunately he has no common sense in practical matters, and everything he undertakes fails," Steinman observed. "He isn't fit to be a rabbi even today. And the poor girl is attracted to people like a moth to a flame. She is a bit older than her husband. Though you might not believe it, she was once a regal beauty. She is to be pitied, but I'm sure I'm the last man who could help her." And with that he gave me an equivocal pat on the shoulder.

After a few turns around the floor with Mr. Bronski, she slipped away from him and came back over to us.

"I didn't realize what kind of partner fell to my lot," she said with a laugh that contained a hint of hysteria. "That'll teach me a lesson. Madness! It was indeed madness on my part to come here. Why is someone like that allowed to dance freely with the others?" she asked resentfully.

"What guarantee have you that the others are sound of mind?" Steinman said to comfort her. "All of us here have to cope with this kind of world."

She gave us a hasty goodbye and left the lounge.

"Neither of us was very gallant," Steinman said to me. "We should have asked her either to stay with us or to let us take her home. She has a long way to go in the dark."

The three violinists began to pack up their instruments. Several dancers were protesting against Buchlerner's stinginess; it was mockery, they said, to organize a party that ended almost as soon as it had started. Some others said they would take up a collection to pay for another hour or so of music. But for all these protests it was clear that the dancers were tired. The young people still whirled around a bit, but the others went outside to get a breath of fresh air.

"You should thank me, Father, for having let you stay up so late, carrying on and all. Say good night to me now."

Steinman stood up and pinched his daughter on the cheek. "You bad girl, I'll . . . " He kissed her and said goodbye to me.

"When Daddy does what I tell him, I love him dearly," she said as she led him out.

"So you have no use for such silly things, hm?" Buchlerner had come up beside me without my noticing. "Vanity of vanities, isn't it? But I have to give them a 'dancing' once a week, or they'd tear me to bits like a herring. Let me suggest that you take a little walk before you turn in. It's a beautiful night, every star as big as your fist. God created a great big world with many little worlds inside it. Go out and have a look. Tonight He is displaying all His treasures."

3

A knock at the door awakened me. It had been one of those nights of memorable sleep, the kind all the money in the world can't buy. I glanced at the clock: I had been in bed only four hours. So I wrapped myself tight in my blanket and turned over, sure that someone had knocked at my door by mistake. But after several more knocks I realized I had to get out of bed. The knocks were stubborn and patient, as if saying: We're not in a hurry, we'll get you whether you like it or not.

When I opened the door an untidily dressed man stood before me. He held his cap in one hand and a carriage whip in the other.

He said good morning to me in a sepulchral, hoarse voice that came through many layers of phlegm. When he finally cleared his throat, his good morning was more normal.

He was shorter than average, but he had the look of a man once taller and stronger, beaten down by life. The lost height had gone to fill him out in the other dimension, and yet he was still not so sturdy a figure that a few more good kicks might not beat the rest of him down.

He put his cap back on. It was so shabby that instead of making him look taller, it seemed to cut off some of his height. He gave a little crack with the carriage whip and said that his vehicle was waiting for me downstairs. Then, seeing my bewilderment, he grinned, displaying a row of tobacco-stained teeth.

"You've overslept, but may I remind you that you ordered my carriage to take you to Kazimierz this morning? I'm punctual, as you see."

I told him that I had ordered no carriage, that I knew nothing about it, and that he had awakened me for nothing.

He studied me carefully to see whether I was not trying to deceive him. "Woe is me," he said finally. "I'm afraid you're right. Forgive me."

A quarter of an hour later, when it seemed that I was finally about to get back to sleep—for the theme of a dream was just beginning to announce itself, the surest sign that one is falling asleep—I once again heard knocks at the door. This time the man with the cap and whip looked about ready to burst into tears. "Forgive me," he said, "but perhaps you'd like to drive to Kazimierz anyway? After all, it won't do you any harm to make a little excursion to Kazimierz."

He went on to say that he had just had a piece of bad luck. The first time he had such a misfortune in all his years as a driver. Some sort of devils or goblins, may God preserve us from evil spirits, were intent on harrying him. Actually, he said, he had had three surefire passengers to Kazimierz.

"One was a young woman, another a priest, and the third was you— I mean the young man whom I mistook for you. It turned out that the young woman was a man, who abused me roundly when I came for him, so that I had to run for my life. The priest said that he was suffering from diarrhea and had to cancel his trip. As for my third passenger, the young man, he has simply vanished. I woke up about a dozen guests here without finding him. He must be staying at some other hotel. But one man whom I woke took pity on me: He said that he couldn't get back to sleep anyway, so he might as well make a trip with me. That's when I wondered if maybe you'd care to do the same. Take my advice, get dressed. While you're dressing, you'll think, 'Why the devil am I going to Kazimierz?' But once you're in my carriage, you'll realize it wasn't such a bad idea. With two passengers the trip won't be a total loss to me. In any case, I'll give you a very cheap rate."

I tried to protest, but the man had an answer to all my objections. He assured me that I'd be able to nap a little in his carriage, for the highway was straight and smooth. It would be like riding on butter, he said.

A few minutes later, I was on my way downstairs to the waiting vehicle. A door opened on the second floor, and a silvery head stuck out from it. "Why are you making so much noise, waking everybody up? Don't you know people are still asleep?" The door opened a bit wider, and I saw it was Steinman grinning at me.

His face was sallow and dried out, as if he had been fighting death all night and conquered it, but at a heavy cost. Only his smile seemed alive.

When I told him how I happened to be going to Kazimierz, he laughed heartily. "You see, it's fate. A man has to visit Kazimierz sooner or later, so what difference does it make when you go? When you come back, we'll talk about the place for three days and three nights running."

He had something more to say, but his face became clouded. He kissed me on both cheeks in a very formal, fatherly way. Standing there in the doorway he bore a strong resemblance to portraits of Anatole France. His features were a trifle livelier than before. He looked like a man who had to generate his own energy to get through the day because his natural organisms would not suffice to carry him through.

The driver gave a smart crack of his whip when he saw me. I got into the carriage and the horse set off at a trot.

My fellow passenger seemed a very cheerful type. He kept looking at me and smiling. He was about forty, with a pockmarked face, but this did not give him an unpleasant appearance. He was dark, sturdy, and broad. He took up about three-quarters of the carriage, but he was aware of his bulk and saw to it that I was comfortable.

"I imagine that you are not going to Kazimierz of your own free will any more than I am," he said, holding out his hand.

He had a warm handshake and said that his name was Neifeld.

The road led through a little woods, after which we came out on a highway with open fields on both sides. The sky was not too clear, and the air was damp.

"If only it doesn't rain," Neifeld said, "this may turn out to have been a good idea. The driver thinks he took me in, but it was really I who took him in. I've been to Kazimierz more than a dozen times, and if you woke me up any morning and said 'Kazimierz,' I'd be ready to go again. How many times have you been there?"

When he learned that this was to be my first visit to his beloved little town, he said that he envied me. To be sure, he went on, Kazimierz is always Kazimierz, but there's nothing like the first time. That's an unforgettable experience. It's a physical sensation, something you feel in the marrow of your bones. "But I shall not go on raving about it because if I overdo it you'll be disappointed."

When he learned that I was a foreigner, he showered me with questions. How did I like Poland? What were my impressions of Polish Jewry?

"You understand, politically speaking you've come at a peculiar moment," he said. "Polish Jewry is still rubbing its cheek, thanking God that it wasn't really slapped. Not so long ago there was real danger of serious trouble—pogroms were very much in the air. When the prime minister was shot, the Endeks immediately started agitating against the Jews as responsible for the assassination plot. The government lost its head, and there was great fear among the Jews. Then it was discovered that the murderer was a Ukrainian, and the Jews were safe again. But it makes every Jew wonder what would have happened if the slander had not been disproven. It's not always easy to dispose of slander so quickly. When will the next time be?"

Neifeld said that he was a lawyer—or rather, that he had been a lawyer. He had made quite enough money, he said, out of Jewish troubles, Jewish fears, and Jewish helplessness. He was retired now. Though only forty-three, he was well enough off to live quite well, he said. So he had given up his practice.

"Believe it or not, I was once an ardent Polish patriot. In fact there was a time when all the Jewish youth was patriotic. When Poland gained its independence, we became confident and held our heads high. The Polish soil of our grandfathers and great-grandfathers seemed doubly dear to us. But we soon saw our mistake. We began to be persecuted at every step, pushed and kicked around, hard enough to make us realize that Poland was not freed for us, that Polish independence did not include ours. Equality before the law turned out to be no more than a paper promise. But I scarcely have to tell you all this, the facts are well known. We are being impoverished here in body and spirit—and Polish Jewry has spirit. It is a burning bush.

"What makes it so bad is that our children have no future here. The conditions are such that they simply cannot get ahead, but the reason they are doomed is that love has died out among them. Our young people are becoming terribly unromantic and practical, it's almost frightening. The dowry system is going to destroy Polish Jewry in the end. We are chained, fettered, bound, and tied. Since the young people have no future, material security comes before everything else. The young men set a price on themselves, sell themselves for so many złotys. And you can't blame them: they have no choice. With a bit of money it is at least possible to get started in a business—never mind that most such businesses end up bankrupt. But to try to make a start without money condemns a man, and his wife and children as well, to starvation. As a result people are afraid to fall in love. No young man makes close friends with a girl unless he knows in advance what her dowry will amount to. To be sure, the very young ones still play the silly boy-and-girl game, but in just a few years they have learned to demand of love that it be profitable.

"That's the situation. We are becoming stunted because there is no love among us. There is adultery and fornication, and the sacredness of the family is no longer absolute. Real love, love beyond price, which is the foundation of a healthy people, is dying among us. The institution of the dowry is an old one among the Jews, but we were not afraid of poverty in the past. Today we have been so terrorized by all sorts of persecution, and our economic life has been so undermined by every kind of official and unofficial discrimination, by boycotts both open and hidden, that our youth is haunted by the specter of poverty as never before. In the end, dowry or no dowry, they end up poor, but now without even having known the marvelous comfort and compensation of love.

"So what's it all come to? To this: that many a poor girl embraces the Christian religion. Rather than become old maids, they throw themselves into the arms of a Gentile. Gentile young men enjoy greater material security, for they can always become government officials at least. Also, Gentiles don't put so much emphasis on the dowry.

"The epidemic of conversions today is the more alarming because people are getting used to it, taking it for granted. Indifference on this score saps our vital strength. It isn't generally realized that we are too poor and weak to afford the luxury of tolerating converts."

Our driver turned around, smiling and yawning at the same time. "Didn't I tell you that once you were riding with me, you couldn't be sorry you were going to Kazimierz?" he said. "To the contrary, you'll like it." He yawned again.

"The problem of conversion is quite interesting," Neifeld went on. "In the course of my practice I ran into many people who had changed their faith. They were ambitious to get ahead, to climb, to obtain posts as judges. Many embraced Christianity even after they had been appointed judges, merely because their friends urged them to do so, with an encouraging tap on the shoulder, 'Why don't you do it and get it over with?' This is good-natured social pressure. Others were pushed to it by their wives. Women can be more ambitious than men, and they know that once you've been sprinkled with a bit of holy water, advancement is much easier. Such women become devout Catholics, having soberly calculated that they want their children to be integrated people, and integration, for them, is inseparable from the Church.

"There are converts who are very unhappy afterward, and they dream only of getting back to the fold. In some rare cases they move to a new town and give up their new religion. Poland is theoretically a free country, and you can go back to Judaism if you like. But this doesn't happen very often. As a rule such converts put off returning to the fold until it is too late. And once you've given up the ghost, you get a funeral with all the Catholic trappings. At such funerals you will find a brother of the deceased who has not yet become a convert, an enlightened uncle, so enlightened, indeed, that he doesn't care whether he is a Jew or not, and an aunt who has become a Catholic and married a Gentile. The priest may well have a Jewish nose for all that he sounds as though Latin were his mother tongue. Believe me, if the dead man only could, he'd get up and run! For although a convert may get used to living with Gentiles, the thought of having to lie next to dead Gentiles forever after terrifies him. It's an alien world, and their cemeteries are alien too. My guess is that every convert comes to his senses when he realizes that he is stuck with the alien company of his fellow dead. But then it's too late.

"I must warn you, however, to discount what I say on this matter of converts. I have a morbid prejudice against the whole tribe. In the exercise of my profession I occasionally had to deal with them, and after all you've got to be civilized, but God knows it was a strain for me. To me, a convert's hand is always dirty. I'd keep telling myself that I mustn't be unfair, that I must respect other people's convictions, but it didn't work. The whole business of passing over to another flock has always been hard for me to understand. Often I'd find myself investigating the circumstances of a given conversion, trying to discover why a man had made up his mind to change his faith, and whether it had been easy for him. I would go into the circumstances of childhood, the kind of parents and grandparents, trying to find out why people take such a step.

"Many so-called 'progressives' are motivated by love for their children. They are eager for their children to make their way in the world and don't want them to suffer as Jews. So they sacrifice themselves for their children and cross over. Many fathers of this type keep up their Jewish contacts, eat in Jewish restaurants, and still buy kosher meat (for they couldn't touch any other), but they do it secretly. What sustains them is the thought that they have provided for their children.

"I know a grandfather of that kind, whose Gentile grandsons and granddaughters love him dearly, but as soon as he opens his mouth and talks Polish with a Lithuanian Jewish accent, they beg him to stop. They love their grandfather as long as he keeps quiet and they can call him by the anti-Semitic pet names. No, the grandfather hasn't become a Christian, but he is happy at the thought that his offspring will not have to bear the Jewish burden.

"Nowadays there are too many contacts between the renegades and the Jews. Much of this may be explained, on the part of the Jews, as awareness that converts could be dangerous if not watched, for after all, what is a convert if not a rotten Jew? Poland is a Catholic country, and the Jews fear that should they boycott the converts or show them hostility, they'd be charged with offenses against the state religion. This is why many people keep quiet. And in many Jewish restaurants you'd be sitting next to Jews eating real Jewish dishes—stuffed chicken necks, gefilte fish, cholent—and discussing Jewish problems, with all the usual sighs and jokes and puns, but these same Jews have Gentile wives and Gentile children at home. They themselves live entirely among Jews, all their business is with Jews, and all their friends are Jews. They haven't even begun to enter the alien world.

"I once knew a convert who even flaunted his Yiddish. He let himself be baptized in order to marry a Gentile girl, but his wife left him a year after the marriage because she was an anti-Semite and her husband was still too Jewish for her. She had thought that baptism would change his appearance, his gestures, his habits. But when he went to church with his wife, he liked to hum tunes from the Jewish liturgy, as though he were bent on spiting himself.

"He was a failure, but after his conversion he got a minor government post. He worked among Gentiles, but his best friend was a Gentile who spoke Yiddish fluently. And what a Yiddish—rich, with the most genuine idioms and intonations. This Gentile was a drunkard, and the convert too took to drinking. They often sat in Jewish restaurants and sang 'God and His judgment are just.' The Gentile had inherited his Yiddish from his mother, who blessed the candles every Friday and was quite capable of reciting the Saturday evening prayer from memory. She would often beg her son's friend, the converted Jew, to go back to his old faith lest he lose both this world and the next. When he was drunk, he often thought about this threat. 'You know,' he would say to his Gentile friend, 'your mother is one hell of a clever woman. She says I'm neither fish nor fowl and she's right.' Recently he began to worry a great deal about the sufferings of the Jews. When the Jews are prosperous, he told me, you don't mind being a convert, but when the Jews are in trouble, you feel rotten about having left them. He told his Gentile friend that the sufferings of the Jews would drive him to his grave. Well, a few weeks ago he jumped off a roof into the street and died instantly. He had come back to the flock those last few months at least."

The sky had cleared. A peasant driving his cart in the opposite direction exchanged yawns with our driver. The road was not as smooth and level as he had promised. There were a good number of hills, and quite often I felt as if I had better put my hand over my heart so as not to have it jostled out of my body when the carriage bumped over holes in the road, stones, and deep puddles. But there were many good stretches. These were dirt roads. The fields on either side were monotonous and haphazard in their layout, but nonetheless a joy to look at. The pleasantest moments were when we drove down narrow, well-trodden lanes through woods fragrant with the vintage wine of fermented leaves.

"Take deep breaths," Neifeld said. "Polish woods can cure the sickest heart."

The morning was well advanced, but the woods were cool and quiet. One felt that in them the light and stillness were constant over the days and the years, as if the woods were some ancient dynasty intent upon preserving a traditional amount of light and stillness appropriate to them. Somewhere a bird was testing its voice.

Neifeld quietly ordered the driver to stop. "I want to hear this," he said, "this is the real thing."

"What is it?" I asked.

"What else but the world-famous nightingale! Ssh . . . "

Crisply it gave us a few short trills, repeated as though the singer wanted to stress the theme, but soon it went on to elaborate on the theme in lengthy embellishments. I was struck by the utterly unsentimental quality of the song. How did so cerebral an artist ever come to be praised by sentimental poets? The song of this nightingale was a recitative with many rests; each phrase was longer and more complicated than the previous one, and after each phrase the singer stopped to catch its musical breath or, perhaps, to study the impression it had just made. While the nightingale was singing, the surrounding stillness seemed more intense; the hushed silence seemed to form a guard around the precious bit of song. The singing itself was part of the primeval light and stillness of the forest, it was as if the mossy stillness had begun to speak its own language, as if the bird were giving voice to the awesome silence of the forest. There was no trace of degrading sweetness in the nightingale's song, no concession to debased popular taste. To the contrary, this was the perfection of musical expression. It was outrageous to think that this bird should have the reputation of a "sweet" singer when its musical language was so intellectual, so sophisticated.

The nightingale repeated two phrases, but on repetition the second had pointedly become a question. After this, the bird stopped abruptly, waiting for an answer. No answer came, and the singer fell silent.

"This is a late bird," Neifeld said quietly. "Usually they sing until the middle of June, and mostly at night. We have had the privilege of hearing a rare exception."

"It was a nice song of praise to the Creator of the world," the driver said curtly. "Giddy up!" He maneuvered the reins, and the horse set off at a brisk trot as though filled with new strength.

"Maybe it was a song in your honor," Neifeld said to me, smiling.

I said that in America we had no nightingales but other, far more sentimental birds. Neifeld was pleased that like him I had perceived the absence of sentimentality in the nightingale's song.

"That rusty-brown bird is as far as you can get from the pathetic in music," he observed. "Very often when I listen to it I have the feeling that its songs have been written on a special typewriter. Only the coloratura touches seem to come from a vibration of the wings. The short, abrupt notes suggest that it ponders each of them and chooses the melody very carefully. Only the trills have the charm of a genuine impromptu."

The driver cracked his whip when we came out of the forest. Under the influence of the private concert we had just heard, he honored us with a cantorial selection, imitating all the voices in the choir, from the bass to the little boy with a piercing treble.

"Believe it or not," he said turning his head around, "but years ago we had a cantor whose name was Slowik—Polish for nightingale. Well, the bird we've just heard was just good enough to shine that man Slowik's shoes. I was just a little boy then, and the cantor is long since dead and buried, but I'll never forget the way he sang his showpiece on Rosh Hashanah. That cantor had a throat that was like a flute. He came to us from Lithuania, and it all ended sadly—he was caught with a married woman, and he vanished, swallowed up without a trace. You never hear anyone like him today—unless you mistake today's cantors with their priests' voices for singers."

He tried the Rosh Hashanah piece for himself, beating time with his whip, but he sang it quietly, as though hesitating to let strangers share his childhood memory. When he turned to us to say that in half an hour we'd be in Kazimierz, there were tears in his eyes, his own singing had moved him so.

Neifeld was silent. His sallow face was covered with a thin film of seriousness, a momentary cloud over a wistful smile. Whether because he had talked so much before, or because he was caught up in private thoughts, he did not utter a word. Perhaps he was solemnly preparing himself for the entry into Kazimierz.

Along the road we began to encounter Jews with visored caps, which looked like specially chosen Jewish crowns of thorns. Their whole pride and nobility seemed to lie in their finely combed beards. Impoverished kings must, unfortunately, try to make a living. They followed us with sad eyes, which probed our carriage deeply to discover who we might be and what might be expected from us. They walked at a leisurely gait —their whole manner seemed to say that neither their poverty nor their great opportunities would run away. The shepherds of the Bible must have walked like that when they went to the well to draw water for their camels.

"These are our spinners of gold, our international bankers," Neifeld said when he noticed that I was looking at them. "Here are the Rothschilds of farm and dairy, coming to town to sell a cheese, perhaps, or maybe aiming still higher—perhaps two or three are pooling their resources to buy a calf in common. The Poles are after their wealth too. They are systematically driven from the villages, not by laws but by terrorist acts. Their ramshackle houses are set on fire, in the hope that they will go up in smoke. Agitators inflame the peasants against them, and sometimes these quiet Jews are set upon with sticks and stones. Where can they run to? Only to the bigger cities, where opportunity waits to welcome great capitalists like them. Even the territories for begging are already staked out—there is no room left for newcomers.

"The fact is that a real war is being waged against us, a war of attrition," Neifeld went on passionately. "There's no escaping it: all the countries have imposed a siege and try to starve us out by all kinds of restrictions. Here in Poland records are kept, so they can tell just how many Jewish businesses have been taken over by Poles, just how many Jewish mouths have had the bread snatched out of them. Believe me, the Poles are much cleverer than Hitler. They don't rant and rave, they just pass over our bodies with a steamroller and drive us right into the ground. A war of attrition is supposedly a slow process, but for all its slowness it nevertheless causes real suffering. Tens of thousands of Jews go through the agonies of starvation with their wives and children. Formerly you could escape by emigrating, and American relatives would send you the fare. Today our people are staring death in the eyes.

"Meanwhile the Jews of Poland have been given a bad name all over the world. What is needed is to sound the alarm, to explain to the world that Polish Jews have passion, have faith, have a treasure of faith beyond anything the world dreams. We are intelligent children, we still have a God in our hearts, and we have faith, a marvelous optimistic faith—not just a religious faith, but a faith that nourishes the soul and sustains it even in a starved, emaciated body. The Polish Jews have been slandered before the world, and we have become undesirable emigrants everywhere. The German Jews who preserved only an anemic Judaism are lucky. This is not the time to berate them. Of course they must be rescued now. But how can they be compared with the Polish Jews, whose warmth and spirituality uphold the divine image of Jewishness?"

The driver turned around as though to say something, but Neifeld waved to him vigorously to be silent. He probably feared that the driver would spoil or simplify his argument. He leaned forward and began to look around us.

"My dear friend," Neifeld said in a voice full of tenderness. "We are now in Kazimierz."

4

Neifeld was smiling as though his most beautiful dream had come true when the carriage turned off the road and stopped near a water pump.

Neifeld's smile communicated itself to me and to the driver as he climbed down and gave a hitch to his trousers.

Through this trio of smiles I looked at the old houses lining a very ordinary main street, a street that could have been somewhere in the Catskills. Our smiles, I hoped, would provide the necessary light to illuminate the odd shape of each house separately. They all looked as though they were holding each other up, the centripetal stresses all converging toward the pump which stood in the middle of them like some old weathered sundial—though whether it was recording twelve forty-five, or thirteen hundred years, who could say or possibly care?

Had it not been for the water pump, the old houses would surely have collapsed and fallen to pieces. The pump looked like the fundamental force that held the street together. Neifeld had a little suggestion: since it was so early, why not go somewhere for a bite to eat. Afterward, he would not bother me, I would go my way and he would go his.

The driver liked the suggestion very much. He was starving, he said, and was much too weak to go on without having something to eat. Of course, he added, we should get something light, and what can be lighter than a drink of vodka on an empty stomach?

He led us up a twisted staircase, to a dark door situated halfway up. We entered a room full of children, boys and girls, who scattered like chickens at our entrance. A man with a narrow, longish, black and gray beard and a serious rabbinical face welcomed us and at once set the table. He put a bottle on it, and the driver said a blessing with a pious face and quickly drank two glasses, one after the other.

He cleared his throat and suggested that two glasses are a well-tested recipe used by experienced drinkers, because the second helps get the first one down.

"If you'll let me advise you, gentlemen," the man with the rabbinical manners said, "you couldn't do better than to have a piece of roast duck with your vodka."

"How about a bit of herring with onion?" the driver asked.

"Now, really," the man said with a frown. "If I had herring here, don't you think I'd have it in front of you by now? I'll tell you the truth, last night I was raided by a dozen heavy eaters who cleaned me out of everything like a swarm of locusts. Please don't say you don't want roast duck, gentlemen, because that's all I have left."

"But bread?" the driver asked fearfully.

"*Skolko ugodno,* as much as you want," the other answered with a smile. "We're never short of bread. It's our light eternal."

The driver took up a pitcher of water from the table, opened the door, and washed himself on the stairs. A woman came out, protesting: "What do you mean flooding the staircase like this? Somebody will break his neck on these puddles!"

"Don't worry," the driver said to her. "Pretend you mopped the stairs for once."

When the time came to pay, the rabbinical-looking man vanished, and his wife appeared to take our money. Neifeld insisted that we were his guests. When the woman told us how much we owed, the driver cried out: "You're almost giving me a heart attack! What are these, wartime prices? How dare you gouge us for a duck that was nothing but skin and bones?"

"Now, now," the woman said, restraining her irritation with a pretense of surprise. "What do you care? Is the money coming out of your pocket? It isn't your treat, is it?"

"You're no honest woman, you're a highway robber! Where's your husband? I won't let anybody pay that much. It's because of you that little children starve to death. I want to speak to your husband."

"My husband has nothing to do with money matters."

"He wouldn't know the difference between one coin and another," the driver said, mocking her. Neifeld had his money out, but was in no hurry to pay: he was enjoying the scene and wanted it to last as long as possible. "Call in the poor thing, I bet he knows the value of money."

"He'll pour swill on you," the woman screamed, "if you don't shut your mouth. I hope it twists into a knot! You're not worth my husband's piss. Just imagine, this one here thinks he can tell me how much I am to charge for my duck!"

"Breindele Cossack, I'll teach you a lesson. Next time I'll bring you a plague, not customers. I can find my way to the place across the street, you know."

The woman softened and at once reduced her price by half a złoty.

"When you speak like a human being, that's different," she said with a face suddenly transformed from anger to smiles.

The driver took the bottle and poured himself another glass. Then he said: "This is my tip. And what you are wishing me now, please God, may at least half of it happen to you. Here's to you, gentlemen. To life! *L'chaim.*"

When we walked out, I arranged with the driver that he should take us back before sunset. I told Neifeld that if he had no special plans I'd be glad if he accompanied me. He was very touched by my invitation.

I realized suddenly that the low houses and the whole huddling street drew the glance downward. For the first time I raised my eyes and saw a hill, and on the hill what looked to be the ruins of a large house whose entire interior had been burned out. A little higher on the hill stood two other tall structures, but these were more like the unfinished foundations of a castle. The hill was much more cheerful than the houses below. With its green woods and ruins it looked as though it represented some younger civilization than the little houses among which we were standing.

"In my opinion, before climbing up to see Esther's castle, we should make a tour of the lower town. We'll go up the hill later."

He said the words "Esther's castle" with such indifference that I suspected him of trying to test its effect on me. And the fact is that my heart was struck as though by a golden arrow. The legend atop that hill had captivated me through the folk song of the golden peacock that flew to faraway lands.

King Casimir wore the paper crown of Purim and had a silken beard. He looked a bit obtuse and in some ways resembled King Ahasuerus in the biblical story. But he was a fiery lover and he carried the Jewish girl up the hill in his own arms, higher and higher, up to where the Spanish castles had just been completed. Below stood Mordecai scratching his head in his helplessness. What an idea to carry her so high! Why, one could get all out of breath climbing like that. Esther herself said nothing but lay swooning in the king's arms as fragrant with perfumes as a casket with spices. It seems that she was naked, or rather, three-quarters naked, for King Casimir had wanted to remove the last of her clothes with his own trembling hands. And during the long days when the king reigned somewhere far away, Esther looked down longingly at the pump, at the grimy houses where her brothers lived. At night she would let down her tresses and sing, "Were I to go out on the porch and look at the town." During one such sad moment, while she waited for the king with the silken beard, she tied a letter to the tail of a golden peacock. The letter was addressed to the Jewish people for whom she yearned from afar. But the king's magician conjured up a terrible storm with thunder and lightning to blanket the whole country roundabout. In the bad weather the golden peacock could not find its way to the Jewish people, and the letter got detached from its tail and was lost.

Later that day we stood in a dark apartment and looked at what purported to be the letter which Esther had addressed to her people. An old Jew carefully opened a cabinet and took out of it several Torah-scroll adornments—embroidered mantles, crowns, and silver pointers—which the Jewish maiden who had either left home or been abducted had sent back home. The old man told us that he had inherited the concession from his father, and his father had gotten it from his grandfather. The precious objects belonged to the community, but the community recognized his right to house the historical relics. He showed me lettering on the mantles embroidered in gold and silver, and told me that a famous Jewish writer used to stay in his house for days at a time, unable to tear himself away from the relics. The writer loved them so much—to be honest about it—he had to watch his hands lest he make off with something. He wasn't a thief, it was just that he was possessed of a kind of passion—what do you call it, "sticky fingers"—and, indeed, how could anyone not feel tempted when he held in his own hands a mantle that Esther herself had touched with her royal fingers?

When I gave him a few złotys, he said that he was not yet through with us. He led us across several courtyards and took us into a synagogue that was older even than Esther. King Casimir had gone to this synagogue countless times—might we have as many thousands of złotys! Our guide apparently wanted us to be rich. He took us into the special room where the rites of circumcision used to be performed and showed us the oversized chair reserved for the man who had the privilege of holding the baby during the ceremony.

The main thing I mustn't forget, our guide said, is that his father, who had also been the *shames* of the synagogue, was a famous man. The Jewish writer who had stayed here knew him well, often called on him and got him to tell him many stories, which he later published in newspapers, to the delectation of all. Had our guide read the stories? we asked. God forbid, he replied—he had a head full of worries, "and this is one of my greatest worries," he added, as a girl with modest black eyes and short hair joined us.

"Father, may I have the key?" she said. "There are a few visitors who want to see the antiques."

The shames stopped and slapped his trouser pocket melodramatically, as if he wanted the important key to be lost and create a commotion. But he found it at once and handed it to his daughter. "Open the cabinet, I'll be back in a moment," he said. "You can start showing them in the meantime."

She left quietly. The father stood motionless a while then gave a sigh that came from the depths where are stored all the unrealized prayers of the Days of Awe.

"You have seen her—she is just as beautiful as Esther was," he said. "And she has golden hands. I should show you her work—it's as good as all the embroidered mantles. Occasionally, just to get another judgment, I throw in a piece she has embroidered among the relics, and it is admired more than the rest of the treasure. But it's the other girls who get husbands, and why? Because she is too choosey. She has a bee in her bonnet. You would swear she was waiting for some king to come along and make her his concubine."

Neifeld drew me away then and unexpectedly led me into a cobbler's shop. The cobbler's bench stood empty, and the shop was permeated with the smell of leather. From the back room emerged a man with a little brown beard and deep-set eyes. He had a proud bearing and replied to Neifeld's greeting like an equal.

"Do you have any work at the moment?" Neifeld asked him.

"No, thank God," the man answered with a smile.

Five children—three girls and two boys, roughly between the ages of three and ten—came over and stood around him. To an astonishing degree they looked like the man who stood there in the midst of them, the largest tree in the orchard.

"These children are all I've got to show for my work," the shoemaker said, holding out his work-worn hands, with their stained fingers and black nails. "May they be preserved from the evil eye."

"And what's new in the art department, Reb Shmuel?"

"I can't complain, thank God," he replied, holding his noble head still higher.

He glanced at the silent Neifeld and without a word turned around and went into the back room. We followed him, I with curiosity greatly stirred. He dusted off several neatly stacked paintings, and the dim room lit up with misty sunrises and red-blue sunsets, curving streets and old brick facades, painted the colors that are only to be seen on very old houses in Europe—subdued yellows, watery pinks, and a gray that is the color of cobweb—houses that look to have been buried and dug up again many times. The quiet colors always seem darker just before it is going to rain.

He unrolled other pictures for us, painted on poor paper, of Jews with faces like old bricks. I had the impression of looking at some film documenting a bygone past. Where had I seen all this before? Had I really seen it? Yes and no. All the houses and all the people looked familiar, but they were not the houses I had been walking among and seeing with my ordinary eyes—they were the people and houses I had long ago looked at with the eyes of childhood. These were the same muddy walls seen in the waking sleep of a child who could hear songs even in the alleys perpetually damp and smelling of urine, only God knows for how many generations before.

The cobbler had seen and painted all this, but he had not lost the wonder of childhood vision. My mind began to run off into reflections on art and childhood, on the value of preserving one's childhood vision as long as possible, and on art as the essence of the living present —anchored in memory, to be sure, a realistic art, clear and obvious but permeated by the melancholy longing for an eternally youthful past. It is this longing which can make of reality a miracle. Happy the man who sees reality as sad, not as a boring sadness, but as a childish sadness; it is the child who knows this optimistic sadness, capable for all its terror of death of moving forward proudly into the years of life ahead.

That was what Reb Shmuel's paintings were saying to me. He himself now told us how he had become something like the second wonder of Kazimierz. The Polish newspapers had written dozens of articles about him, Shmuel the cobbler, painter of the ghetto. People had flocked to see the curiosity, judging him to be a very good artist for a cobbler, but buying very little from him. Mostly they left him their shoes to repair. On one occasion a Gentile became interested in him and supported him for a year, but God called the Gentile to Himself, and now his only hope was Palestine. There, he thought, a Jewish artist would not be abandoned, and might even be raised up from the mire and exalted.

The cobbler went back into the shop with us. He put on his apron, sat down on his bench, and began to drive nails into a sole. He did this with the air of someone trying to show us how low an artist can fall.

"God, may His name be blessed, will help me," he said with a sigh. "Isn't that so, Yankel?" he asked one of his children.

This one seemed to be the oldest, about ten. He closed his eyes and, sighing like an old man, spoke: "We have a God in heaven." The sigh and the words had all the virtuosity of a child prodigy playing a Stradivarius.

"That's what I say, too," the cobbler said approvingly. "This is my eldest, may he live and prosper. I trust in the Lord."

He put a few nails between his lips and kept them there for a while. Then, taking them out one by one, he drove each of them into the sole with two neat taps of the hammer.

"I must confess that I am a pious Jew," he said. He pondered a while and then went on: "I shall also confess that I am pious out of fear. Not out of fear of the Lord but—I hope what I say is not sinful—but out of fear that I may cease being an artist. I feel that piety and art are one and the same thing. Were I to lose my piety, I should lose my art. The fact that I wield a brush has a great deal to do with my piety. Had I been an unbeliever, I'd never have been anything but a cobbler. My ability to paint is nourished by my faith in a Creator of the World, in a Providence, in the fact that the world is not chaos and accident. If I ever thought that the world is not ruled by its Maker, I shouldn't be able to paint, should I, Yankel?"

"My father is right," the son said, with a virtuoso frown.

When we left the shop, Neifeld said that we had already seen a good deal of Kazimierz. "Whenever I feel I must come back to this interesting little town," he went on, "I don't know whether it is that I am longing to see the town itself again or the few people here who are themselves legendary, who have absorbed in themselves the great miracle. This grimy street, with its little shops and its few just men, embodies the longing for the top of the hill where the legend itself stands naked, as though shivering from the cold. I'll try to say it differently: up there it is always Sabbath, while down here it is a perpetual Friday evening, and the dark holiness is always just about to fall across the shutters of the shops, the lighted windows, the eyes of frightened little boys. Here one is always waiting for the blessing of the candles, here it is always Sabbath eve. There are many who have spent their whole lives here without ever climbing the hill. Let me suggest a banal allegory: up there stand the ruins of the Realized Ideal, while down here a dark yearning wanders about. Up there is the completed five- or seven-year plan, while down here the people are still whispering the mysterious word, 'Revolution.'

"Take the cobbler, Reb Shmuel," Neifeld went on. Is he not the embodiment of his yearning for the heights? A cobbler, saddled with a wife, children, and a talent for painting—absurd contrasts. And he does his duty as only a Jew can. No Bohemianism makes him desert his family for his art. He cobbles and paints and trusts in the Lord, like the anonymous just men who bear the weekdays on their shoulders with all their cares, yet go on longing for a miracle to save the people of Israel.

"For what has really gone on here in Kazimierz? I think I can help you to understand. The Jew had his own poor world, and the Gentile led his own separate life. We always walked as far as the city gates, beyond which death lies—a great cemetery full of ancestors. In other words, walk no farther than the gates and turn right back, for you can see only too clearly what lies in store. The grave. But the people created a legend in defiance of the limitations of this life, according to which one of our own daughters gets together with one of the others, a king, no less. There is not so much as a mention of marriage. Did Esther, the

Jewish girl, marry the king, or did he possess her without the sacred vows? No Jew will touch upon the moral aspect directly. It is enough that we Jews have created the sense of its being possible somehow to become related to them, to the others—yet not with some ordinary Pole merely, but with the king, who, needless to say, thereby becomes a lover of Jews. We have given up a daughter, sent her out into the world like an ambassador, and we ask no questions. Really pious Jews are not at all eager to look into these matters thoroughly. It is enough for them that here in the valley is to be found the legend of a Jewish girl and a Polish king."

5

As Neifeld led me out of the main street, I noticed that our horse was still standing by the water pump. The driver, installed on an overturned barrel, was talking with a water carrier, who stood there with his pole and pails filled to the brim. The streets which led away from the planetary system of the pump had no trace of squalor, although they were narrow and wound their way downward. Yet no matter how low-lying the streets actually were, the hill above them seemed part of the valley. Its cheerful greenness flooded the area below it with patches of sun and shadow on the graceful little houses and the gardens where tables were set and gay couples sat eating.

"It's very beautiful here," I said to Neifeld—the simplest thing I could have said.

"I'm afraid to keep on talking like this, lest I bore you like a professional guide, but I must tell you that I have traveled abroad and seen many summer resorts much more beautiful than this, and mountains both taller and more striking looking, but—well, here we have a different kind of beauty."

Dozens of young men and women were passing up and down in the middle of the street, talking loudly. Several girls were smoking cigarettes expertly, like men. All of them carried bundles, but they walked briskly, as if it were easier to walk when carrying something.

"These are our artist pilgrims," said Neifeld. "They come from all over Poland. Every painter in Poland, no matter what remote corner he hails from, comes to Kazimierz in the summer. Kazimierz can be painted from a thousand spots."

After walking a stretch we saw a young man in his twenties with a well-groomed beard, a beret, and fashionable broad trousers, standing at an easel in the middle of the street. He was just starting a landscape, having chosen a tree that looked old and had sparse leaves. Gigantic branches were twisted like the arms of an arthritic woman. Next to him sat two girls on folding chairs. They silently followed the painter's every brushstroke, smoking and spitting.

We next came out on a broad open space, dazzling in the sunshine.

"With this view of Queen Vistula, our excursion into the lower town comes to an end," said Neifeld. "Now we are ready to climb up the hill. But there is no need to hurry, you may rest a while. The Vistula this year has not behaved as it should. As you may know we just had the greatest flood in a hundred years; it was in all the newspapers. You can still see traces of it. The regular banks are invisible, because everything has been flooded. The downpours caused great damage. The Vistula carried away houses, cattle, and even some people. Look where trees are sticking out above the water—you might think the Vistula always looked like this, but a great deal of land is still flooded and won't emerge again for several days. In the meantime it isn't safe to get too close to the river."

Near us a number of people sat warming themselves in the sun.

"If you look carefully," Neifeld went on, "you'll see the flooded benches. They stood on the river bank and were entirely covered, but now the river is beginning to recede."

In the middle of the stream, trees, boards, and patches of grass floated by as peacefully as ducks. Who could tell what the debris meant in terms of personal loss to some poor peasant farther upstream?

The river glinted like molten steel. On the other side we could see the green and yellow edges of the woods that formed part of the hill. On top the dizzily pitched ruins of Esther's castle looked as though they must at any moment slip down into the Vistula, obviously quite capable of swallowing up the last remains of a legend along with so much else.

The hill was cool and green, but the river glistened with the midday sun. Dazzling reflections extended as far as the eye could see. Even the floating boards and trees glistened in the sunlight.

"Let's stop a moment at the halfway point," I said to Neifeld. "It's too much. Let's find an outdoor restaurant and have a cool drink."

"It's all right with me. There's no need to rush, we must digest everything bit by bit. Apropos, have you digested the roast duck?"

I looked at him. He was smiling.

"I'll tell you the truth," he said, "if you won't think me a glutton. The fact is I could really eat a bite." He took out his watch. "Though it's only a quarter to twelve. This time we'll not ask the driver to be our guide. Follow me, we'll find an outdoor restaurant and eat a homemade Jewish meal, with soup, and a piece of herring for appetizer, perhaps even marinated herring. If we are lucky, we may get a hot cabbage borsht. There is a woman here who makes an excellent borsht with marrow bones. She is also famous for her rich desserts. The dishes she serves taste like paradise. We'll sit in a garden somewhere, and enjoy God's world. How about it?"

I told him that the more he talked, the hungrier I was getting and that if he didn't lead me at once to the woman who made the borsht, I'd drop in my tracks.

"Now that's the way I like to hear a man talk," he said. This burly fellow grabbed me by the hand and dragged me off at a run, like a boy.

He stopped suddenly and said with a worried expression: "I must warn you that I'm not sure that there will be cabbage borsht today. It's a matter of luck. Sometimes the woman has it, at other times she says we should have come the day before. It depends on the day." He raised his hands to heaven as if expecting a miracle. "Is it clear? I haven't promised you borsht, so don't hold me to it."

His brown pockmarked face was laughing. At that moment I felt as close to him as to a brother. "My word, if you don't find me something to eat pretty soon—I don't care what—I'll kill you."

"That's the kind of talk I like to hear," he said, and once again grabbed my hand and ran.

The woman had two warts on her nose, one with hair. Neifeld insisted that the warts were charming; they were not, he said, the practical kind of wart that sprouts in later life so that one's eyeglasses may be held up by something. This woman's warts were on either side of a thick nose, and gave it the look of some curious growth. Her hands, however, were the hands of the proverbial "woman of valor"—good, motherly hands that could cook, bake, clean floors, scour every corner of the house, hands that could sweep out the weekday and carry in the Sabbath, that could plait pigtails, wash dishes, and tend children down with measles, smallpox, or scarlet fever. The half-naked arms were fat but strong, the hands those of a mother rather than a wife; they had a cheerful mobility and aroused confidence in the menu she recited.

We ordered pot roast because, as it happened, she had no borsht. When did she make borsht? This was hard to tell, because she had no system, she made borsht only when it occurred to her that her family were hankering for it. If she complied with every wish of her family and cooked only what they wanted her to cook, they would by now have grown tired of her best dishes. "To tell the truth," she added, "I often don't make borsht because of my husband. He has a real passion for it and eats so much of it that at night I have to give him a hot water bottle to ease his stomachache."

At another table sat a man of whom I could see only the side of his face. But it was a profile I was sure I recognized, even if I couldn't put a name to it. It would be fun to make the identification without having seen him head on, merely from the profile—that half-blind eye, that long chin, and cauliflower ear—I knew I knew them intimately. In memory I leafed through thousands, tens of thousands of profiles and then stopped triumphantly. I snapped my fingers.

"Do you see that man, with his profile to us? The last time I saw him was twenty years ago. He is a painter, a friend of my youth. His name is Farshtand."

"Farshtand? Farshtand? Yes, he has some reputation as a Jewish painter," Neifeld said, dunking a piece of white bread in the pot roast. "It makes sense that he should be a painter: every third man here is one. Since you're not a painter, nor I, he surely must be one."

Now the man turned his face to us. He had white eyebrows and white eyelashes, which looked as though made of pig's bristles. His left eye was smaller than the other, which somehow could not open.

"Well, it would be no credit to me to recognize him now," I said to Neifeld. I got up and asked the man at the other table if he would join us. He rose apathetically from the chair. He looked like someone sleepy after a heavy meal.

"So you too had the pot roast?" Neifeld asked, wiping his plate with white bread.

"Is that all you wanted to know?" the heavyset man said, apparently ready to go back to his own table. To stop him, I quickly asked whether his name was Farshtand, and whether he was a painter. This interested him a bit more. "That's what I figured," he said, and sat down, though without much enthusiasm. The expression on his face suggested that if we bored him, he'd get up and leave.

I reminded him of common friends, I gave him my name, mentioned America, and even recalled the scene when he said goodbye to me many years before, and I asked him whether he remembered the letter he had written me before the outbreak of the war. As I told him, the war had dropped a curtain over everything that had gone before, and the ocean had become a river of fire, like the legendary Sambatyon.

I must have talked with animation, for I grew emotional recalling the days when we all used to walk together in the Saxon Garden.

He said, "yes, yes" to everything, but his eyes were cold, unconvinced. When he realized that his "yeses" sounded mechanical, he replaced them with "sure, sure," but it was obvious that he did not remember me, and that my warm reminders made not the slightest impression on him. When I was through, he looked exhausted, and his "sure, sure, of course" hung in the air between us. He did not recognize any real link with my childhood memories.

I told him that I had recently seen an exhibition of his work in the home of a wealthy man who had gone down in the world. He had bought Farshtand's paintings when he was prosperous; and now his home had become a private restaurant for businessmen when their wives were staying in the country. I didn't tell him that his paintings looked overfinished, that the colors were shrill, the grass too grassy, and that the flesh of the nudes recalled illustrations in out-of-date editions of the Arabian Nights—an olive skin tone which tended to turn black.

The only thing that did interest him was the fact that I had come from America. He assured me that he had many paintings in his studio, and would like to show them to me. Several Americans had bought his paintings. Once he uttered the word *bought*, he became more animated than I. He told me he did not work in Kazimierz—let the others paint here, he came here to sit and think and look around. But back home he painted the whole winter. He hated Kazimierz. Formerly he had come here to paint like all the others, but now he came only to get this place out of his system. He had been to Paris, he said, and had barely escaped alive. Paris was full of great painters and great failures, and he had been unable to decide to which of these categories he belonged, so he didn't stay. He had been in Warsaw too, but he found life there impossible. The Poles detested Jewish artists and killed them by ignoring them, coldbloodedly. The Jews in Warsaw were just as bad, because the moment you professed to be a Jewish artist, they feted and banqueted you and killed you with all the nationalist whoop-de-do. Once you began to play the part of a Jewish artist, you were a dead duck.

Again he mentioned that he had some paintings and would sell them at fair prices.

Neifeld sat by himself, absorbed in something between sleep and reverie. His sallow face was even darker now, and his pockmarks seemed larger, as if they were breathing in his sleep. The glint of a smile peeped through his half-closed eyes. He seemed to be laughing at me, at my embarrassment, at my warmed-up childhood recollections to which Farshtand had reacted so coldly.

The painter walked with us as far as the path that led up the hill. He walked away quickly, as though glad to get rid of us. Neifeld asked that we walk slowly, unhurriedly, because there'd be plenty of time. On our way we ran into many vacationers, women in shorts, men in unbuttoned shirts. For a moment I thought I was somewhere in the Catskills. Young men carried elaborate shepherds' crooks, as though they were climbing mountains in operettas, with a song on their lips. And some of them were actually singing songs in Yiddish, Polish, and Hebrew.

We reached the first ruin of Esther's castle. Neifeld touched and caressed the walls. We went inside. Through the apertures that had once been windows we could see the whole town below, with the tranquil Vistula, which looked so much smaller and more sluggish, almost ice-bound from up here. The tranquility of the river below, its silver immobility, added to the dignity of the ruin in which we stood and made it seem much more like a castle.

"It was here every morning that Esther delighted in the Vistula," Neifeld observed, still caressing the peeling walls. Here and there were flecks of paint, perhaps the remnants of murals washed away by rains.

Suddenly we heard someone panting behind us, and in a moment Farshtand came up to me. "I've come to apologize," he said. "I'm stupid—it was only after I left you that I recalled who you were. That woman serves too big meals. I was all fogged out. How stupid of me to have forgotten . . .," and he evoked several incidents of our former friendship. "No, I'll never forgive myself—how could I—I'm disgusted with myself."

He glanced down at the river below and said that he must get back down, for up here he was subject to a peculiar impulse—the moment he was on top of the hill he was seized with a desire to dash down again, at top speed. Since there were so many people around during the day, he could do this only at night, and when he did, he felt like King Casimir in person. As he turned to go, he begged me to visit him in his studio.

At the ruins farther up the hill, children were climbing up and down the shaky stairs. We kept going still higher, passing peasant houses now packed full with vacationers. Finally Neifeld discovered a pleasant spot on a slope in the woods overlooking the Vistula. We sat down on the rough leaves. He took off his shirt and undershirt. "Go on and take off your shirt and get some of the Kazimierz sun. The sun, the coolness of the Vistula, the woods—you'll have something to remember."

I reminded him that we had to think of getting back to the driver and the return home. He drew out his watch and put it back in his pocket, then he stretched out his bare torso on the leaves, rolling happily like a little boy.

"Never mind, we can have one more hour of paradise, and I am allowing one hour for the trip back down."

◆ ◆ ◆ *Chapter 6*

1

We had reached the water pump and were about to get into the carriage when Neifeld suddenly changed his mind. He was going to stay over another day in Kazimierz. He asked me not to take this amiss, but he realized he would not have the opportunity to visit the place again soon, and he'd better take advantage of the fact that he was there. He could afford it; in fact he might stay over a couple of days. After all, there was no compelling reason not to stay on. If he knew that I had plenty of time and no other plans, it would have been pleasant to travel with me, and we could have gone to other places together.

"However, since you are soon leaving the country, we'd just have to say goodbye in a day or two anyway. Why not today? What's the use of my pouring out another bushel of words? This way I'll know you're still somewhere around and that we might have spent more time together. I'd have run out of topics, anyway, in another day or two. So it's better that I say goodbye to you now."

He held out his hand. His dark face now was lit up by the glow of the Kazimierz sunshine he loved so much, and a restless glitter appeared in his eye.

"Given the present uncertainty of Jewish life, you can never tell. It may very well happen that we'll meet in New York one day. You'll be walking down some street full of millions of people—at least they seem so crowded in American films—and I'll walk up to you and put my hand on your shoulder. And just to make it easier for you to recognize me at once, I'll say, 'Kazimierz!'"

The driver merely flicked his horse with the whip, and it set off at an unexpectedly fast trot.

"This horse is a real pearl! He understands the slightest touch of the whip!" the driver said affectionately. "Of course, he has had a good rest, he drank and ate his fill. But I'm sorry we had to leave your companion in Kazimierz. It isn't the money, I'll get paid all right, he won't get away from me, but that's a very fine young man. He doesn't look like a boor—to the contrary, he looks anything but a boor."

The horse began to slow down, and the driver once again caressed it with the whip, this time along the legs.

"This horse is a real pleasure," he said. "I hate to be on the road late at night. Not that I am a coward, I'm not afraid of robbers, and if it's necessary to punch someone in the jaw, you can rely on me. I can take on anyone."

The stillness of the evening was setting down over the black dirt of the road. It seemed that our carriage was catching up with a greater and darker stillness than appeared at any given moment from a distance. The western sky was turning fiery with strident reds and glittering yellows over patches of blue so subtle that it seemed to have been purged of dross, and only the very purest essence remained. On a hilltop a clump of trees still held a bit of gold reflected from the sun we could no longer see.

The driver talked on, but I heard him only as in a dream. It seemed as if the front part of the carriage, where he sat and the horse trotted, had gone on ahead, and I was left alone. I remembered a Spanish book I had once read. The author, Ramón del Valle-Inclán, divided the book into four "movements" corresponding to the four seasons. In the first part, the hero, a knight, is full with spring; in summer he is consumed with success like a Casanova; in fall his decline sets in; and in winter we find him lying with one hand shot off, waiting for the end. The four movements pictured a single human life posed against a barometer of time: time of sun, time of rain, time of snow, time of twilight, time of night.

I had the impression that my half of the carriage, at least, was moving into its autumnal phase. A shiver went through my body when the trees on the hilltop grew as still as the earth over which the carriage was rolling and when the red patch in the sky gradually grew paler and dissolved.

I began to understand why Neifeld had suddenly said goodbye to me. Only now did I realize that I would never see him again, that the carriage had left him behind forever, along with the day in Kazimierz. It was another part of the autumn which was invading my heart, like a premonition or perhaps an aftereffect. It was a great impertinence on my part, but I felt that I was living an allegory, and that the carriage was traveling downward rather than over flat ground. It seemed to me now, in the twilight, that I had reached the autumn of my life. The whole day, the encounter with Neifeld, and even my mother's death seemed to coincide oddly with the downward movement of my own life, and all this was in step with Jewish life as a whole, maybe even with the twilight now settling down over the whole world.

After all, I had come back to Poland to learn something. All this might be a dark omen, just like the dark ground ahead that the carriage would soon catch up with and that would be darker and more soaked with silence when we reached it.

All of us—myself and everything I remembered, and everything I forgot—would very soon arrive at winter with a hand shot off. That would be the hand which, I had vowed, I would let wither if I forgot you, and you, and everything that had ever imprinted itself on my eyes and mind.

The carriage became whole again with its horse and driver, who was now singing a Hasidic song. This was in honor of the nightingale that had performed for us in the morning, at this same spot in the woods. The driver had heard the song from his father, who literally bought it for hard cash from the Rabbi of Radzin.

"Yes, it's just as I said, he bought it. He went to the fair and came back penniless because he had stayed with the rabbi and brought back a song. Mother asked him whether the song could supply milk in her breasts. She had just given birth to my younger brother. And what do you think my father replied to her? If such is God's will, he said, a song will do just that! Yes, that was the kind of man my father was. Of course, he wasn't a driver. He knew his way around the Scriptures and the Mishna as well as I know my way about the woods. But the song is a real treasure. You relish its real savor on Simhat Torah, when Jews put their hands on one another's shoulders and dance to glorify the Lord."

The melancholy twilight spread over my whole body and was losing some of its sharpness, although I still felt a heaviness in all my limbs.

"You aren't going to believe me, but we are back home."

The horse fairly flew as though set upon winning a race. I began to recognize the hotels. We were on the sand-covered drive that led up to Buchlerner's boarding house.

2

In front of the hotel stood a group of people. This was not the usual after-supper crowd slowly digesting its meal. When I alighted I saw several unfamiliar faces. The first person that walked up to me was the younger son of the rabbi whose retinue I had seen in the park. A little farther away I noticed his brother. The American son-in-law too was among the crowd. He was asking anxiously, "When? When did it happen?"

"Just a few minutes ago. After supper he said that he wasn't feeling well."

"Woe is me!" moaned Finkel, wringing his hands. "At table tonight he was inspired, he was telling stories, making jokes, he sang, he was full of fire. Woe is me, I can't bear it, such a splendor, such a marvelous man. What does the doctor say?"

"What do you expect him to say?" a woman said with the dry, indifferent voice of someone used to such things. "He's in a bad way, very bad, he needs his forefathers to intercede for him in heaven."

"What is it—his liver?"

"Well, the angel of death will always find a pretext," an old woman interjected. "According to some, it's the kidneys, then he's also a bit diabetic, or maybe it's the heart. Probably a bit of everything, as happens in old age. What is man, after all?"

"Is he really in a bad way?" another woman asked.

"Bad way, good way," said the woman with the dry voice. "Everything is in Those hands, and mine are not clean enough to say Whose hands I mean."

I was sure they were talking about Steinman, but I addressed a questioning glance to the rabbi's youngest son.

"Of course, who else? No one is allowed to see him. He is in his room, and specialists have been called in for a consultation."

Buchlerner caught sight of me in the darkness. "Well, what do you say to our misfortune? Ha, could you have anticipated anything like this? It was he who told me you had gone to Kazimierz. What a misfortune! You should have seen him at the table only an hour or two ago. He looked like an emperor, so help me. I never tired of looking at that glowing face."

He stepped closer and whispered: "Are you hungry by any chance? You know, the one thing has nothing to do with the other. The sinful flesh must have its due."

I assured him that I had no desire to eat.

"No wonder!" he said, in a louder voice. "Such news! How could anyone sit down to a meal? Believe me, I didn't eat all day, expecting to make up for it tonight. But now I couldn't eat if you paid me. A man would have to be heartless to sit down to a meal at a time like this."

"Is no one allowed to see him?" I asked.

"What do you mean? The doctors have been in there for almost an hour."

The crowd began to gather around Buchlerner.

"What can I tell you? How can you learn anything standing outside the door? His daughter is with him. Ah, who can envy her now? It breaks your heart!"

"So you're saying that it's really that bad?" Finkel asked, sobbing rather than speaking.

"It couldn't be worse, I assure you. Look, there is nothing to lose by it, we might as well put all embarrassment aside and recite some

Psalms. What harm can it do?" He addressed this question to himself, with the air of someone trying the ultimate remedy.

"What do you mean, can't do harm?" the rabbi's older son said sullenly. "To the contrary, it can help a lot. What could help him more than that?" His upturned hands punctuated the question.

"Do we need a minyan?" Finkel asked.

"A minyan is certainly a good thing, but even if we didn't get ten men together . . . " The rabbi's son scanned the crowd. The women moved away to make it easier to count the men. "We have more than enough men," he said. "I'll tell you what Psalms are to be recited. But it's a waste of time if we don't recite with true ardor, with concentration on the meaning, in the true Hasidic manner."

The rabbi's younger son was the only one of the crowd to remain behind when the rest went into the hotel to recite Psalms. "I see you're not a reciter of Psalms either," he said to me with a smile.

I told him that I wouldn't have separated from the others but that I was still stunned by the news. I always react like that when I see what a fragile vessel man is. The here-today, gone-tomorrow leaves me with a wound that takes long to heal.

"As for me, I just don't believe in disturbing the Lord for nothing. If it were a child, I'd pierce heaven with my complaints, but when it's a man who has lived his allotted span, what good can it do to obtain from God a few more years for him? It's not right to bargain with the Almighty. And believe me, if I made up my mind to do something, I wouldn't just recite Psalms. Don't you think the Lord has heard Psalms before? And now my brother wants to impress the Lord, blessed be His name, with a chaplet of Psalms, as though it were something brand new. Well, he is very foolish. Who said that the inner source of prayers has been sealed up once and for all? Am I obliged to wear secondhand clothes? The man who wrote the old prayers was going through agonies of grief, but my grief is different, and I must find my own path to the Lord. After all, if I were sick, I wouldn't use the remedy prescribed for someone else's sickness. King David certainly didn't suffer the same way I do, and so I must find my own words when I want to knock at the gates of Mercy. The traditional prayers are made for busy people, people with no minds of their own, people who are inarticulate, that's why they use borrowed words. It's just as if I were to put on a pair of someone else's glasses. Anyhow, as you know, we Hasidim do not attach much importance to formal praying. But I go further. If people took my advice, I'd assemble a minyan of silent men. They would sit still and meditate."

We could hear the voices of the men reciting the Psalms. We could distinguish the voice of Buchlerner and that of Finkel, whose wail almost drowned out everyone else. Dominating all the voices, however, was that of the rabbi's older son, who savored every word. Even out where we were standing his voice was like a great warming light.

"It must be granted that my brother has a fine talent for chanting. He imagines he'll persuade the Lord with that voice of his. Well, I don't interfere—if he is heard in heaven, so much to the good!"

I mechanically walked up the stairs and without knowing why opened the door to the room where the patient was lying. One of the two doctors, a young Gentile, grabbed me angrily by one arm and was about to lead me out of the room, but at that moment Steinman opened his eyes and waved weakly with his left hand. This wave of the hand had an immediate effect: It was as if the patient had given an order, though he had not uttered a word. This wave of the hand was a Jewish gesture, as if to say, nothing mattered any more. In addition, the merest hint of a smile played around Steinman's mouth, a smile which even suggested mockery. It was the antidote to the tenseness that prevailed in the room. Perhaps it was this ironic smile that made the wave with the hand so eloquent. The doctor who was about to throw me out was embarrassed, as if the hint of mockery had been for him. As for myself, I was astonished at my own boldness, bursting into a sickroom like that.

Steinman could scarcely keep his eyes open. He beckoned to me to come closer to the bed. Next to it sat the second doctor, and a little farther away, on a rocking chair, Steinman's daughter, who now was also smiling. Her smile expressed the frank admiration of a mother for her child. I don't know whether she realized that her father was dying, but it was clear that had she known it, she would have been proud of him —perhaps because he looked beautiful even at this moment, because he conducted himself as he did, because everything he had accumulated in life now served him well. It was with him now in the bed, and it was a pleasure to see him so tactful, so wise, so serene. Even now he was in full possession of his faculties, and his calm seemed visibly to pervade every corner of the room. Had it not been for the presence of the doctors, there would have been no indication that he was sick. He seemed much thinner than this morning when I had last seen him, but he also looked younger. His daughter began to cry, tears running down her face without a sound, but the smile remained like a rainbow appearing before the storm has abated.

The patient moved his hand again, beckoning to me. He moved his lips, and I bent over him and listened as he struggled to form words, although only disjointed syllables were audible. Throughout he kept his patience, his expression seeming to say, "Ever seen anything like it? A strange business, isn't it?" He made no complaint, and when he failed in his attempt to communicate, he merely gave a helpless smile. All I managed to catch was that his right eye was paralyzed, and that I should stand at his left.

"It's dark in here," he said. I went to the left side of the bed. He could not turn his head, but his left eye followed me. He was content.

Suddenly the doorway was filled with faces—some curious, some timid, some weeping. The young doctor jumped up again, but he looked to his older colleague, as if waiting for an order.

Steinman stirred feebly. The room was thronged with people, but they halted a few steps from the bed, as if separated from it by an expanse of water that could not be crossed. All of them together looked as if they had come to do something for Steinman, to carry him, to raise him in the air, to accomplish something that required a common effort, like lifting some large, heavy mass.

Seeing that the doctors did not forbid them, they grew bolder and moved a bit closer to the bed. Several women appeared in the doorway. Steinman's daughter remained motionless where she sat, her eyes never leaving her father.

The men felt less constrained. They felt they had a right to be here, that they had just recited Psalms on his behalf, and that they were entitled to see whether their prayers had any effect. They all came over to the side of the bed where I was standing.

The older doctor said quietly, as though to himself, but imperiously: "He has no air. It's too crowded."

The men began to move back, but Steinman had already seen them. Buchlerner and Finkel were the first to realize that Steinman had noticed them. They blushed like children calling on a rich uncle. They were overjoyed that he recognized them, that they were seeing him for themselves; it was as if he had just come back from a long journey and they were greeting him. But they were embarrassed at the thought that Steinman had seen them visiting him when he was in so sorry a state. They sensed that there was something improper in crowding around him in his bed like this.

Steinman began to move his lips again, and I bent over him. He spoke more distinctly than before but almost voicelessly, as though the words were shadows on the tip of his tongue.

He wanted us to sing something, a Hasidic song, a cheerful song. I couldn't believe my ears. I leaned closer. He saw my surprise and repeated, "A song, a cheerful one."

I transmitted the message to the others, as if what I had to say was beyond comprehension, some text laboriously translated from a long-forgotten language. They looked at me with hostile eyes. Was I making fun of the sick old man? Or had I thought this up to make fun of them?

But now everyone could see for himself that Steinman's face had changed. His brow was knitted in concentration, his lips were twisted, and he was making faces. With a chill, I realized that he was singing to himself, though not a sound was audible. My spine turned into ice.

Not only I but everyone else in the room saw Steinman sing. His face was like a sheet of music. Everyone stared at his twisting features as if they were listening to a song. We could make out only a muffled wailing, such as people lost in the woods might make to signal their presence to each other. The muffled cry grew more distinct, and the faces of all present grew grave, in keeping with the rhythm of the song, with the depth of the song. It was not only Steinman who was making faces now; it was a chorus.

Who was the first to snap his fingers in rhythm is hard to tell. Judging by Finkel's half-swooning expression, it might have been he, or perhaps it was the rabbi's American son-in-law. The singing was so quiet that in spite of the light in the room they all seemed to be singing in the dark. I realized that they were singing the same song Steinman had sung my first night here, when he sat at the head of the table.

His daughter's head followed the rhythm marked out by the rabbi's older son. Steinman's seeing eye beckoned to me. I bent over him again and heard him singing in my ear: "A *rikudl* . . . dance . . . dance . . . " I stood there for a while helplessly leaning over him. "A rikudl, a rikudl," he kept whispering, like a stubborn child. But the moment I announced this, the effect was just the opposite of what I had expected. The crowd suddenly sobered up. The humming stopped, and each of them stood there embarrassed, as though he had done something adults must never do—and now all that was lacking was a rikudl, a noisy, lively Hasidic stomping.

They had not sung for more than a minute or two, perhaps only as long as it was possible for any one of them to suppose that only the other had broken into song or that only he had behaved in a silly manner. The men looked at each other as if trying to discover whether anyone had noticed them singing.

The older doctor sat by the bed, taking the patient's pulse. Steinman lay still with his eyes closed, a single tear rolling down from one eye. The tear was alive, and it was clear that this man who looked asleep was wide awake, alert, and possibly weeping with joy at the way the song had soared to the very heights, beyond which no song could go.

Suddenly the doctor signaled for us all to leave. We filed out of the room and closed the door gently.

"I'm going to stay all night by this door," Finkel said. "I'll lie here like a dog. Even my wife won't take me away from here." And turning to me: "I ask you, are there many such Jews? Are there many young people who'll grow up to be like him?"

He burst into tears, and he covered his face with his hands so that his sobs would not be heard in the corridor. The woman with the dry voice gave him a sneering look. She inspected him from top to toe as if to convince herself that this grown man was actually weeping. And then, to show that she, a woman, did not indulge in such silliness, she said with a voice so unemotional that there was not the slightest tremor in it: "He won't last the night. The angel of death is already there, by his pillow."

3

The rabbi's youngest son, who had been pacing back and forth in the lounge, saw me come down. When I told him that Steinman was in full possession of his faculties though very ill, his face lit up.

"Some day I'm going to look into this matter," he said. "After all, a man's rational faculties are the most substantial part of his soul. For the soul, too, has a material part. Yes, before you get to the soul, you have to break through a number of thick skins. However, when a man is granted the privilege of preserving his reason to the last moment, he thereby is given a divine opportunity to see his own pure soul, because he can contemplate himself in the intermediate realm, where the visible passes over into the invisible. May I make a suggestion? Let us walk in the park for a while. It's empty now, and the orchestra is no longer playing. Right now is the best time to walk there."

"I'm afraid I should get started packing. Tomorrow morning I begin my trip back home."

"Is that so? Tomorrow you'll be gone. Well, then we ought certainly to take a walk in the park, as a farewell." He said nothing for a few moments, standing where he was. "Home—if you only knew how proud that word sounds! How I wish all Jews had a home like yours! Tell me, are you taking anything back with you—I mean something that has given you food for thought?"

He became pensive, and we began to walk slowly in the direction of the park. Clearly, he was not expecting an answer. Then he lifted his head, and I looked into his large eyes.

"Personally, I don't envy you. May I ask one thing of you? Don't suppose that a little boy is talking to you. If you ever come back here in later years, you'll see for yourself. And even if you don't come back, you'll still have heard—the Jewish world will resound with my fame. My ideas aren't ready yet, or rather, everything is still simmering in a big pot. You can make out the parsley, the vegetables, the beans, the mushrooms—it's all bubbling and seething, but before long it will be ready, a finished dish. I can already taste it. Believe me, I'm not boasting. Jews from every corner of Poland will gather around me, and I shall minister to their spirits with the joy of discovery. Every Jew will become a seer, a thinker, a sage. I won't just carry them on my own shoulders the way my grandfather did. I'll make them stand on their own feet. Nor will they just love one another—everyone will have to earn that love. They will have to rise above themselves, like climbing a ladder. You know how the rabbi of Kozhin interpreted the commandment to love thy neighbor as thyself. 'Is love of oneself such a simple matter?' he used to say. 'You value your eyes more than your legs, and you value your head more than your you-know-what. So if your neighbor is a head, love him as you would your head, and if he is the opposite—well, you get the point. Love him as you love yourself.' That was what the rabbi of Kozhin said."

A man was approaching, very unsteady on his legs. When he got closer, I saw it was my driver. "I'm glad I ran into you," I said. "I want you to take me to the station early in the morning."

"Woe is me," he said. As he opened his mouth the reek of vodka hit me. "And here I am walking around as if the world be damned. You want to make the six o'clock train?" He began to run. "I'm going to get a few hours' sleep," he yelled back. "But don't worry, you can count on me."

I called after him not to forget because I'd be waiting all ready and packed.

"Look not upon me, that I am swarthy,"—he quoted Scripture—"I mean, look not upon me because I've taken a drop or two. After two hours' sleep I'll be a new man. I'm like a horse, I never sleep, I just take naps!"

"Let no one tell you," my companion went on as if he had not been interrupted, "that we Jews need not be better and nobler than our neighbors. Our neighbors do not ask themselves what they are living for, but this is a question we do ask ourselves, and we ask it angrily. Until the great reckoning takes place, we'll be tormenting ourselves with it. We must be in a position to say clearly what is the purpose of our being in this world. In the meantime it is their world, and they let all their Christianity out on us.

"Yes, even my grudging brother," he went on with a happy smile, "even he will have to come and bow to me. Sweet, sweet, is the dream of Joseph—all the others will cross my threshold with their heads held high, but he will have to bow and pay homage before me. No matter how much recognition you get from strangers, it means little until your own come to bow to you. Joseph wanted to break the pride of the envious."

At the entrance to the park, the guard tried to persuade us that it was not worthwhile to go in because he would be closing the park in half an hour anyway, but we assured him that we'd be out before then.

We took a quick walk along the main avenue and sat on a bench near the entrance so as to keep an eye on the guard. He blew his whistle several times and came over to us, obviously pleased at the fact that we had kept our word. "No matter how nice one is to them, it is not enough," he complained, fingering his mustache. "Everyone is out of the park now, except for the young couples. For them the night is always too short."

He blew his whistle again. "My word, I'm going to shut that gate, they can stay on here all night like cats. What can I do?"

Couples began to appear as if crawling out from among the trees around us. It seemed that every tree had sheltered a couple, and every dark and grass-covered path as well. They might all have been playing hide-and-seek. None of them spoke a word. They walked with lowered heads, as though ashamed to have made the guard wait for them till the last minutes.

"Now there's only one couple left. I remember them—I have a good memory. She's a redhead. I'll whistle three times, and if that doesn't fetch them, well, they can have several pairs of twins for all I care."

But before he had whistled the third time, the last couple emerged. Even in the dark I could see the girl's flaming hair and her embarrassment. The tall man who held her arm guided her as though they were passing through a gauntlet of soldiers ready to bring down their whips on sinners who dallied in the park.

When the couple had passed through the gates, the guard looked at us triumphantly. "You see, I did remember them. I keep a mental count of all of them. They can't hide from me."

He gave one last whistle, to be on the safe side. The park now looked the way a synagogue does at night. He wished us a courteous good night, treating us as two decent men whom it had not been necessary to flush out of the bushes to get rid of.

"Don't think that I have nothing to say to you about all those couples, about the evil thoughts they inspire. When I watch them parading out of the park like that, I sometimes have strange dreams afterwards. You must think that I am only half a man. How do I hold my desires in check? How do I tame them? I do just what the Jews did with Solomon's Song of Songs when they transformed it into a song of praise for the community of Israel. So I take my desire to task and transform it into an allegory. It tries to get the upper hand, but I give it an allegorical meaning, to shame it. And what will I do if this fails to work? I'll find myself a wife, and get the better of the temptation that way!"

"Will you be stopping in Paris on your way home?" the rabbi's son asked me when we were close to Buchlerner's hotel. "Tell me, are you taking some important insight back with you, some ideas at least? An ignoramus travels like a horse, but a man, a rational being, must learn something when he makes a long trip. Some people go abroad and then come back home, and in a few weeks it's as though they had never been away. But when travel gives one some new insights, that's different. Then it's profitable."

"If you want to know," I said to myself more than to him, "what I am taking back with me is a riper sadness that comes only after years of looking and listening. There is a sadness that you can hold by the hand like a good companion, not afraid to look it in the face. It is not a terrorizing fear, but a sorrow you can understand. When you look into your eyes in the mirror, you see the talk that has stayed with you, that has left its mark—a groan, a sigh, a smile. You feel that you have finally become your own sorrow that matures, and grows a little wiser from year to year."

"Well, in that case, farewell, and have a good trip." He extended his hand. "Remember me occasionally. Think of your brothers here. Let us look forward to good news from both sides of the ocean."

One window only was still bright among all the dark windows of Buchlerner's hotel. Buchlerner was standing in front of the hotel as if he had been waiting for me all this time.

"Blessed be the true Judge," he said, accenting all the words equally.

"Blessed be the true Judge," the rabbi's son repeated piously and walked away.

"When?" I asked Buchlerner.

"Just now, perhaps a quarter of an hour ago." I walked slowly up the stairs, trying to make as little noise as possible. Finkel came out to meet me. "Have you heard the terrible news? He passed away like a great saint. Blessed be the true Judge."

"So you're really going tomorrow?" Buchlerner asked me the moment I opened the door to my room. I had not even heard him following me. He sat down on the rocking chair and began to rock violently.

"Yes. You may give me my bill."

"Ah, God be with you, who has a head for that? Maybe you'd like a snack? A glass of vodka? I'm starved myself. Let's have a drink—you know it helps the soul of the deceased to ascend to Heaven. And let's eat something too. Believe me, the dead won't have anything against it."

When he saw he couldn't persuade me, he said that he'd be getting up long before me, and that there would be plenty of time for settling my bill.

A tall man with a pointed beard opened the door and stuck in his head. "Is the owner here?" he asked.

"Yes. What can I do for you?"

"Mr. Buchlerner," the other said with piteous expression. "I am here to recite Psalms. I am supposed to stay with the dead the whole night, and I'm simply starved. It will be worse later on. Could I have a piece of herring? And a glass of vodka to pick me up?" He remained standing in the doorway.

"How about a piece of fish, some bread, and a vodka?" Buchlerner asked.

"Ah, ah!" The man smacked his tongue.

"And where shall I serve you?"

"Downstairs, in the dead man's room."

"Downstairs? In his room?" Buchlerner made a face.

"Why not? What is there to fear? The dead man won't take it away from me."

"All right, all right. I'll have it brought to you soon."

The man's head vanished, and Buchlerner got up and left my room. I began slowly to pack my things.

There was a knock at my door, which opened before I had time to say "Come in." It was the driver, his eyes red and sleepy. "I've come to tell you that you need not worry. You can go to bed and sleep at least four hours." He drew an enormous watch from a pocket. "You can sleep for exactly four hours," he said. He opened his worn jacket, unbuttoned his shirt, and began to scratch his hairy chest, like someone who had just gotten up from sleep.

"Ah, Friday I'll go to the bathhouse," he said with anticipated pleasure. "Then I'll go home and during the Sabbath I'll be a man like others. What's the purpose of all the turmoil? Vanity of vanities. You can see now." He pointed with his finger at the door. "The end of all flesh." He scratched himself with greater gusto. "I'll take you to the station, then I'll go to Kazimierz to bring back Neifeld, and I'll go home for the Sabbath with złotys in my pocket and nothing to complain of, thank God."

He sat down on the rocking chair. "You won't mind, will you, if I take a little nap here. Listen to me, take your clothes off and get some sleep."

From below came the sound of quiet sobbing.

"Hear that? Steinman's daughter, poor thing. She's been left all alone, an orphan. No husband, no children, no relatives. Poor, poor thing."

He loosened the rope around his waist and soon began to snore loudly, with hoarse, throaty noises.

It was only half-past two, but a faint blue tinted the skies, the herald of an impatient Polish summer dawn. A bird, as if stirring uneasily from sleep, uttered a few notes and fell silent again. I switched off the lamp: The pale light filtering through the window settled on the half-opened suitcases near my bed, leaving the rest of the room blurred and insubstantial. They were the starkest and most sharply defined objects in the room.

♦♦♦ *Notes*

p. 8   The Sholem Aleichem story in question is "Home for Passover" (Af peysakh aheym, 1903). See Introduction, note 5.

p. 9   The Yiddish term for Lithuanian, *Litvak*, is associated with a number of stereotypical qualities. The reference here is to his reputation for learning and ratiocination rather than physical labor.

p. 9   Steinmetz (1865–1923) was a scientist famous for his research on alternating electric currents. Born in Prussia, he migrated to the United States in 1889 and was employed by General Electric in Schenectady.

p. 11   Barney Ross (1909–1967), born Dov-Ber Rasofsky, world boxing champion in lightweight, junior welterweight, and welterweight divisions.

p. 11   Tsitsit are ritual fringes on the undergarment worn by Jewish men in obedience to the biblical injunctions of Numbers 15:38: "Speak to the children of Israel and you shall say to them that they shall make for themselves fringes on the corners of their garments, throughout their generations, and they shall affix a thread of blue on the fringe of each corner." A similar injunction appears in Deuteronomy 22:12.

p. 14   Richard Dehmel (1863–1920), German poet, whose lyric "Der Arbeitsmann" (The workingman) contains three stanzas, each of which concludes with the words *Nur Zeit*—the workingman has everything but time.

p. 16   The British poet John Masefield (1878–1967) was known for his seafaring poems.

p. 17   Lovestonism was an American offshoot of Communism. Jay Lovestone (b. Jacob Liebstein, 1897–1990), originally a Communist and national secretary of the Workers' Party of America, was expelled from the Communist Party in 1929 and formed his own oppositional branch of the movement.

p. 21   Benjamin Disraeli (1804–1881), British Conservative statesman, author, and twice prime minister of Britain.

p. 22   In Germanic legends, Lohengrin comes to the rescue of Princess Elsa of Brabant.

p. 23   Night of the Long Knives was the term used to describe Hitler's purge of potential Nazi rivals on the night of June 30–July 1, 1934.

p. 24   Haman: villain of the Book of Esther, who urges the killing of the Jews of Persia. Tomas de Torquemada (1420–1498), first grand inquisitor of Spain, notorious for his persecution of Jewish communities. Bogdan Chmielnicki (ca. 1595–1657), Cossack leader who instigated pogroms of Polish Jews as part of his struggle for Ukrainian independence. Pavel Krushevan (1860–1909), anti-Semitic Russian journalist and publisher of the *Protocols of the Elders of Zion*. Jozef Haller (1873–1960), Polish general some of whose units attacked Jewish civilians during World War I.

p. 25   Rabbinic dictum of Rabbi Tarfon from *Ethics of the Fathers*, chapter 2 (trans. Judah Goldin): "The day is short, the work is plentiful, the laborers are sluggish, the reward is abundant, and the master of the house presses."

p. 25   Lao-Tse (b. 604 BCE), Chinese philosopher, author of *Tao Te Ching*—a foundational work of Taoism centered on the principle of "non-action."

p. 26   According to Jewish folk tradition, the unheralded virtue of thirty-six righteous souls in every generation keeps the world in existence. They are referred to as the *lamed-vov* (thirty-six) *tsadikim*.

p. 33   Diapason: in music, an interval of one octave.

p. 34   Jeremiah 31:15.

p. 34   The River Sambatyon, or Sabbath River, in Talmudic literature said to flow with dangerous currents on weekdays and to lie still on Sabbath. The Ten Lost Tribes were believed to have disappeared from history after the destruction of the Kingdom of Israel in the eighth century BCE.

p. 34   Elijah ben Shlomo Zalman (1720–1797), known as the Gaon, or Luminary, of Vilna, was the leading rabbinic scholar and authority of his age. His name is invoked as the epitome of Jewish learnedness.

p. 38   The Kol Nidre prayer opens the service on the eve of Yom Kippur, the holiest day of the Jewish year.

p. 42   The Haggadah (which means "telling") is the story of the exodus from Egypt, read during the Passover seder.

p. 45   The ceremony of Tashlikh, in which sins are symbolically thrown into a body of water, is observed on the first day of the Jewish new year, Rosh Hashanah, or on the second day if the first falls on the Sabbath.

p. 50   Fyodor Ivanovich Chaliapin (1873–1938), famous Russian opera singer.

p. 54   Berek Joselewicz (1764–1809), Jewish merchant who became a colonel in the Polish army during the Kościuszko uprising against Russia, commanded the first Jewish military unit in modern history, and was hailed by the Poles as a hero in their struggle for independence.

p. 57   The Maccabees waged a successful guerrilla war against the Syrian king Antiochus Epiphanes in 168 BCE. The holiday of Hannukah celebrates their victory.

p. 58   There are three traditional calls for the ram's horn: a regular blast, *tekiyah;* a long undulating wail, *truah;* and three staccato blasts, *shvorim.*

p. 62   Deuteronomy 19:19.

p. 64   One of the derogatory terms Jews used for Jesus.

p. 65   Abraham Goldfaden (1840–1908), founder of the first Yiddish language theater, in Romania in 1876, and composer of popular operettas.

p. 66   *Family Tsvi* (1904), by the Yiddish dramatist and novelist David Pinski (1872–1959), written following the pogroms in Kishinev and other Russian cities, sympathetically portrays the younger generation's creation of Jewish self-defense.

p. 66   Dovid Edelstadt (1866–1892), Yiddish poet whose early death from tuberculosis enshrined him as a literary martyr.

p. 70   The Russian journal *Niva* was edited by Vladimir Galaktyonovicz Korolenko (1853–1921), Ukrainian-Russian critic of tsarism, who took a public stand against the 1911 trial of the Jew Mendl Beilis, charged with the ritual murder of a Christian child.

p. 72   *The Swan of Tuonela* is a tone poem by the Finnish composer Jean Sibelius, based on a legend from the Kalevala epic.

p. 78   Shereshevsky, etc., families noted for their wealth.

p. 85   The Hebrew expression the doctor uses is *kema'ayan hamitgaber.*

p. 87   The phrase "and the still, small voice is heard" appears in the High Holidays prayer "Unetaneh Tokef," attributed to Rabbi Amnon of Mainz. The Liebestod, or "love-death," is the final scene of Richard Wagner's opera *Tristan and Isolde.* "Blessed be the true judge," *Borukh dayan emes,* is shorthand for the prayer that is pronounced at the moment of death, or on learning of someone's passing.

p. 90   Here Lawson appears to have erred in his judgment, since Schiff had contributed generously to Jewish causes.

p. 92   Shikse, the Yiddish term for a Gentile woman, may be neutral or derogatory, depending on the context.

p. 93   The International Workers of the World (IWW) was founded in 1905 on the premise that all workers should be united as a class within a single union. Members were called Wobblies.

p. 95   *Red Medicine: Socialized Health in Soviet Russia,* by Sir Arthur Newsholme and John Adams Kingsbury (New York, 1934), presented a glowing account of medical organization and administration in Soviet Russia.

p. 96   Jacob Gordin (1853–1909), pioneering dramatist of the American Yiddish theater, best known for his introduction of social realism in plays like *God, Man, and Devil, Mirele Efros,* and *The Jewish King Lear.*

p. 96   The dentist recalls prominent figures on the Lower East Side in the early decades of the twentieth century. Morris Rosenfeld (1862–1923) was known as a "sweatshop poet" after the theme of some of his best known verses. Abraham Goldfaden (1840–1908) staged the first known Yiddish public entertainment in Galicia in 1876 and was touted as "father of the Yiddish stage." "In the Plow Lies the Blessing," by the popular folk poet and wedding bard Eliakum Zunser (1836–1913), extolled the pioneers who went to till the land of Israel. Goldfaden and Zunser did not fare as well in New York as they had in Europe.

p. 96   Naftali Herz Imber (1856–1909) composed the song *Hatikvah* (The hope), which later became the national anthem of Israel. He, too, died poor and obscure in New York. Louis Miller (1866–1927), American socialist leader and editor of the Yiddish daily *Warheit*, 1905–1916.

p. 96   Abraham Cahan (1860–1951), founder and longtime editor of the Yiddish daily *Forverts* (Forward). The Russian term *molodyets*, "fine fellow," is sometimes used ironically.

p. 96   Dr. Hillel Solotaroff (1865–1921), anarchist theoretician and lecturer.

p. 99   August Ferdinand Bebel (1840–1913), one of the founders of the Social Democratic Party of Germany.

p. 100   *Journey's End,* by R. C. Sheriff, first performed in 1928 and frequently revived, dramatizes the experience of a British Army infantry company in the trenches of France during World War I.

p. 102   Józef Kazimierz Hofmann (1876–1957) was considered one of the finest virtuoso pianists in the world.

p. 110   Levi Yitzhak of Berdichev (d. 1810), was one of the most beloved rabbis of the Hasidic movement. In Hasidic folklore, he is said to have interceded directly with God on behalf of the Jews.

p. 110   Eugeniusz Jagiello, Polish Socialist, was elected to the fourth Russian state parliament in 1912 largely thanks to the Jewish vote.

p. 111   *Growth of the Soil,* by the Norwegian writer Knut Hamsun, was published in 1917. Glatstein left Poland in 1914, so this image must have been imposed retroactively.

p. 111   Hippolyte Taine (1828–1893), Charles Augustin Sainte-Beuve (1804–1869), Vissarion Belinsky (1811–1848), and Georg Morris

Cohen Brandes (1842–1927) were prominent literary critics. "Our" Brandes because he was the Jew among them.

p. 112 Bazarov, hero of Ivan Turgenev's *Fathers and Sons;* Nekhlyudov, of Leo Tolstoy's *Resurrection;* Karamozov of Fyodor Dostoyevsky's *The Brothers Karamazov;* Oblomov and Sanin, eponymous heroes of Ivan Goncharov and Mikhail Artsybashev, respectively.

p. 113 Poem by the Yiddish poet David Einhorn, "Geshtorbn der letster bal-tfile" (The last prayer leader is dead). Glatstein gets the title slightly wrong.

p. 116 The ancient custom of ritual flagellation for one's sins has been observed by some into modern times.

p. 116 Rabbi Israel Meir Kagan (1838–1933) was known as the Chofetz Chaim (Desirer of life), after the title of his best-known work, which instructs in the morality of permissible and impermissible speech. He was a much-beloved rabbi and teacher and ethicist.

p. 124 The man cannot speak because he is still in the midst of his prayers, having not yet removed the phylacteries in which he davens, or prays. From what follows, it seems his piety has its limits.

p. 137 Created by Catherine the Great in 1791, the Pale of Settlement was the Western region of imperial Russia to which Jews were confined. By the end of the nineteenth century, the Pale had a Jewish population of about five million. It was formally abolished by the Russian Revolution in 1917.

p. 138 In 1934 Abraham Faber, a recent graduate of the Massachusetts Institute of Technology, was one of three men accused of shooting two men to death as part of a Boston bank robbery. All three were found guilty and executed by the state of Massachusetts on June 7, 1935.

p. 139 The novels of French writer Joseph Marie Eugène Sue (1804–1857), particularly *Mystères de Paris* (Mysteries of Paris), were hugely popular, including among Jewish readers.

p. 140 Both Guy de Maupassant (1850–1893) and Honoré de Balzac (1799–1850) used Paris as the location for much of their fiction.

p. 140 The Café Dome in Montparnasse was a favored meeting place of American expatriate writers, artists, and intellectuals.

p. 140 The poet Haim Nahman Bialik (1873–1934) was one of the leading figures of the modern Hebrew renaissance. He died on July 4, 1934.

p. 141 Yehuda (Judah) Halevi (c. 1075–c. 1141) was a Spanish Jewish philosopher and poet. He is best known as a poet for his "Songs of Zion," about which one of his translators, T. Carmi, wrote, "No Hebrew poet since the Psalmists had sung the praises of the Holy Land with such passion."

p. 143 There were several conflicts about language in Palestine of the 1920s and 1930s, including over the role of Hebrew as the national language of the Jewish homeland, and the adoption of the Sephardic, or "eastern" pronunciation as opposed to the Ashkenazic or European.

p. 167 This image of emptying the pockets evokes the New Year ritual of *tashlikh*, in which Jews empty their pockets into a naturally flowing body of water, symbolically casting their sins into the sea.

p. 167 Echoes Psalm 137, in which the poet vows never to forget Jerusalem.

p. 167 A makeshift dwelling that Jews build for the harvest festival of Sukkoth, the sukkah is often used as metaphor for material insubstantiality.

BOOK TWO. HOMECOMING AT TWILIGHT

p. 185 Buchlerner in Yiddish means something like "he who studies books."

p. 186 The Biblical Esau, twin brother of Jacob, here represents a generic Gentile alternative to Judaism. The "man in the skullcap" insists that drinking must be sanctified, serve a higher purpose.

p. 187 Havdalah, the ceremony at the end of the Sabbath that marks its separation from the rest of the week, includes a blessing over wine.

p. 192 *L'Arlésienne* is a suite by Georges Bizet to accompany a play of the same name by Alphonse Daudet.

p. 193 Fountain of Love: the Yiddish uses the Polish phrase *źródło miłości*.

p. 194 Israel Ben Eliezer (1698–1760), known as the Ba'al Shem Tov or Master of the Good Name, is the founder of Hasidic Judaism, a movement that changed the primary emphasis from study to direct apprehension of God and joyful celebration of His universe.

p. 196   Observant Jewish women did not show their own hair after marriage.

p. 197   The Cossack tribes of what are now Ukraine and Belarus were famous for their skills as horsemen and soldiers.

p. 197   The Torah is said to contain 613 mitzvot, or commandments, which consist of prescriptions and interdictions.

p. 200   The wife of Lot in Genesis 19 is turned to salt when she looks back at the City of Sodom that they are leaving.

p. 200   Prince Jósef Poniatowski (1763–1813), brother of the last king of Poland, Stanisław. August Poniatowski distinguished himself in one of the battles of the Polish-Russian war of 1792.

p. 202   The patriarch Abraham negotiates with the sons of Heth, or Hittites, to secure a burial place for his wife Sarah in Genesis 23. Ephron is their chief negotiator.

p. 203   After the passage in Genesis 23:1, "These were the years of the life of Sarah."

p. 204   Colloquial for the Russians. Glatstein's father had been called up for temporary service in the tsar's army at a time when Lublin was under Russian rule.

p. 206   Meyer London (1871–1926), Socialist Party representative elected to the United States House of Representatives from his Lower East Side district in 1914.

p. 208   Opening line of famous Yiddish lullaby written by Abraham Goldfaden for his play *Shulamis*.

p. 209   Passover is spring festival, Sukkot, or Tabernacles, is autumn harvest festival.

p. 210   Apparent reference to ladder of Genesis 28:12, where Jacob sees angels ascending and descending.

p. 214   The war between Russia and Japan from February 1904 to September 1905 was fought mostly in Manchuria, and was sometimes called the Manchurian War.

p. 215   Richard Corey, eponymous hero of poem by Edwin Arlington Robinson (1869–1935), is thought to be a successful young man until his suicide forces a reappraisal.

p. 217   Balaam, Numbers 22–24, is sent to curse Israel but after God's repeated intervention ends by pronouncing this blessing, which is traditionally recited by Jews upon entering the synagogue.

p. 218   Menahem David ben Isaac, who bore the honorific title "Maharam" Tiktin, was a Polish rabbi of the sixteenth century. Abraham Abele Gombiner (c. 1633–c. 1683), known by the title of his commentary, Magen Abraham, was a Polish rabbi and Talmudic scholar.

p. 219   Lulav is the palm branch used ceremoniously on Sukkot.

p. 222   The Saxon Garden was a public park founded in Lublin in 1837.

p. 223   Cholent is a stew baked overnight in a slow oven, usually served on the Sabbath when fire cannot be turned either on or off.

p. 224   The feldsher, or barber-surgeon, usually had basic medical knowledge but no formal training.

p. 226   From *treyf,* which means not kosher, comes *trefniak,* one who doesn't keep kosher.

p. 226   A pogrom was perpetrated against the Jews of Kalisz by local residents in 1919.

p. 227   A symbolic representation of a fence to mark out the area within which objects may be carried on a Sabbath without a breach of Jewish law.

p. 227   Baba Bathra is the third tractate of the Talmud, which deals with the laws of damages.

p. 227   The gomel blessing, "Blessed are You, Lord, our God, King of the Universe, who bestows good things on the unworthy, and has bestowed on me every goodness," is recited in recognition of salvation from illness or danger.

p. 227   Bzhezin and Łódź are cities in central Poland.

p. 227   Rabbi Israel Hildesheimer (1820–1899), university-trained scholar and rabbi who became the leader of Orthodox Jewry in Germany.

p. 228   Rabbi Levi Yitzhak of Berdichev (see Book One, note for page 110) addressed God in the familiar second person singular, as *du.*

p. 229   All the cited books are modern historical renditions of ancient biblical and rabbinic texts and legends, some in scholarly and others in fictional form. *The Sages of Israel* (*Toldot gedoley yisroel*), by Solomon Judah Leib Rapoport, applied New Critical methods to the representation of rabbinic figures. *Sins of the Samaritans* (*Ashmot shomron*), *The Hypocrite* (*Ayit tsavua*), and *The Love of Zion* (*Ahavat tsion*) are novels by the Hebrew writer Abraham Mapu (1808–1867) that were very popular in their time.

p. 230   Heinrich Graetz (1817–1891) wrote a comprehensive history of the

Jews and taught history at the Jewish Theological Seminary in Breslau.

p. 230 *Lump* and *Schacherjude*, German derogatory terms for a boor, a person of low status, and a Jewish haggler.

p. 230 *Kiddush* is the blessing recited over wine at the start of the Sabbath meal.

p. 230 Sir Moses Haim Montefiore (1784–1885), renowned Jewish financier and philanthropist.

p. 231 *Nathan the Wise*, by Gotthold Ephraim Lessing (1729–1781), is a drama about an enlightened Jew, apparently based on the figure of the philosopher Moses Mendelssohn, calling for religious tolerance and mutual respect.

p. 231 Steinman is describing the ritual of kapparot, in which the sins of a person are symbolically transferred to a fowl that is swung around the head three times and designated the atonement sacrifice—which is then given to the poor for food.

p. 232 Dating from biblical times, the firstborn son is redeemed from a member of the priesthood. This is now done by symbolic payment. That Steinman performed this ceremony would mean that he was a Kohen or descendant of the priesthood. Hoshana Raba is the seventh day of Sukkot, marked by a special synagogue service.

p. 232 The ram's horn, or shofar, is blown on the Days of Awe, on Rosh Hashanah and Yom Kippur. Steinman is describing a community that has lost the meaning of the ceremonies that it observes.

p. 235 Xanthippe, wife of Socrates, was reputed to be argumentative. Her name is used as a synonym for shrewishness.

p. 236 Sabbatai Zvi (1626–1676), Jewish mystic and rabbi, who proclaimed himself the Messiah and attracted many followers in his native Turkey and across Europe. The movement collapsed after his conversion to Islam in 1666.

p. 236 See Book One, note for page 96. Before immigrating to America where he became a playwright, Gordin founded the Biblical Brotherhood, as described here.

p. 237 Jacob Priluki, Yelisov, Portugalev, and Rabinovich were leaders of several branches of the Brotherhood.

p. 238 The Khazars were a Turkic seminomadic people living in central

Asia. In the seventh century they founded a polity on the Caspian Sea which later adopted Judaism as its religion.

p. 238 Eldad Hadani was a Jewish traveler of the ninth century who professed to have lived among the Lost Tribes of Israel. Hasdai Ibn Shaprut (c. 915–c. 990?), physician and minister at the Spanish Muslim court, exchanged letters with the head of the Khazar kingdom.

p. 239 Theodor Herzl (1860–1904) was the Austro-Hungarian Jewish journalist and political leader who founded the modern Zionist movement in 1897.

p. 239 Leon Pinsker (1821–1891) made out the case for Jewish "auto-emancipation" in an 1882 pamphlet by that name. He founded the Hovevey Zion (Lovers of Zion) movement, which encouraged the building of settlements in the Land of Israel.

p. 241 Swiss city that served as site of the first Zionist Congress, 1897.

p. 250 In Genesis 39 Joseph is rescued from his Ishmaelite captors by Potiphar, who sets him in charge of his household. Joseph resists the advances of Potiphar's wife.

p. 256 *Di Shvue* (The vow, 1900) is a play by Jacob Gordin. Esther Rachel Kaminska (1870–1925) was one of the leading actresses and directors of the Yiddish stage.

p. 257 *Di kishefmakherin* (The witch) is a much-performed operetta by Abraham Goldfaden. *Shulamith,* a play about star-crossed lovers, Shulamith and Absalom, contains what became the best known Yiddish lullaby, "Raisins and Almonds," with the opening line "In a corner room of the Holy Temple . . ."

p. 259 Jews referred to Jesus by other names, Yoshke Pandre or Yosl Panderik, for example.

p. 260 "Woman of Valor," concluding section of Book of Proverbs, traditionally recited on Sabbath eve.

p. 263 Alexander Moissi (1879–1935), famous European actor who championed modern dramas of Strindberg, Chekhov, and others.

p. 263 Babbes—old women, or midwives.

p. 264 The familiar hymn "Ya ribon olam v'olmaya, Ant hu malke melech malchaya . . ." (O God, who created all things, King of Kings, Thy praises shall I recount morning and night).

p. 266　The midnight service, Tikkun chatzot, a Jewish recital of lamentation commemorating the destruction of the Temple in Jerusalem.

p. 271　The etrog, a kind of citrus fruit, was one of the four species that represent the Temple offerings on the holiday of Sukkot, or Tabernacles. It was preserved in a special box to keep it from being damaged.

p. 283　The Polish Socialist Party was a major left-wing party created in 1892 that drew Jews into its platform of workers' rights. The General Jewish Labor Union of Lithuania, Poland, and Russia—known as the Jewish Labor Bund, founded in 1897—maintained that the Jewish working class had to begin by organizing its own ranks.

p. 290　See note for page 236.

p. 290　Jacob Frank (1726–1791), a Polish Jewish merchant who claimed to be the messiah. He preached a form of religion that resembled Christianity and finally urged his followers to convert to Catholicism.

p. 291　See Book One, note for page 9.

p. 292　The mezuzah is a parchment with quotations from the Bible. Enclosed in a box, it is placed on the right doorpost of Jewish homes.

p. 297　Count Leopardi (1798–1837), Italian poet and thinker.

p. 297　Henri Bergson (1859–1941), French philosopher. Paul Verlaine (1844–1896), French symbolist poet. Juliusz Słowacki (1809–1849), Polish romantic poet.

p. 298　A Jewish male would have been expected to keep his head covered at all times. As a courtesy, nontraditional Jews often cover their heads when they are in an observant home.

p. 298　At the Passover seder, the festive meal commemorating the Exodus of the Jews from Egypt, a cup of wine and sometimes a ceremonial chair are set aside for the Prophet Elijah, whom folk belief expects to visit all Jewish homes that night.

p. 302　Nahum Sokolow (1859–1936), Zionist leader and prolific Hebrew writer, editor, journalist, translator.

p. 303　Cheder was the Jewish elementary school, which usually met in the teacher's home.

p. 303　*The Blunderer on the Road of Life* (1868–1870) traces the emergence of a young boy from the traditional Jewish world into enlightenment.

p. 306　The Marranos were Jews of the Iberian Peninsula who converted to Catholicism under duress during the Inquisition but remained secret or crypto-Jews. The term is sometimes used for Jews who conceal their identity.

p. 307　A Russian greeting.

p. 310　Abraham Ibn Ezra (1093–1167) major Spanish-Jewish exegete, philosopher, scientist, and writer.

p. 313　Karet, signifying excision, is the biblical penalty for certain offenses, but the exact nature of the penalty, whether execution or being cut off from the community, remains in dispute.

p. 317　Daniel Khvolson (1819–1911), a Russian Jewish Orientalist who converted to Christianity, but did much to defend Jews from anti-Semitic attacks.

p. 322　Lilith, variously portrayed as Adam's first wife or the consort of Satan, is the chief female demon of Jewish folklore.

p. 323　Phrase signifying ordinary laborer from Joshua 9:21.

p. 325　Communists convicted for crimes against the regime in the 1930s were sent to the Polish concentration camp Kartuz-Bereza, said to be modeled on the German camp at Dachau.

p. 326　Stefan Żeromski (1864–1925) was a noted Polish novelist, whose house at Naleczow has been preserved in his memory.

p. 327　The Mishna, created around 200 CE, is the first codification of Rabbinic Judaism and the first part of the Talmud. The Amoraim were Jewish thinkers of the third to sixth centuries, whose teachings were collected in the Gemara, the later part of the Talmud. The Gaonim were the prominent rabbis of the early Middle Ages who presided over the rabbinical colleges of Sura and Pumbedita in Babylon. Moving through the centuries, the Rambam, acronym for Rabbi Moshe ben Maimon or Maimonides (1135?–1204), is the most influential of all Jewish philosophers, and the Ba'al Shem (see note to page 194) was the founder of Hasidic Judaism. The difference between the rationalist Maimonides and the mystic Ba'al Shem would have sealed the point that every generation developed its own thinkers.

p. 329   The kozatzke, or the Cossack male dance, traditional for Russia and Ukraine, involves a series of jumps and squats.

p. 334   When Poland recovered its independence from Russia in 1918, it changed the official language and language of education from Russian to Polish.

p. 336   Kazimierz Dolny, in Yiddish Kuzmir, is a small town in Lublin province on the Vistula River that attracts tourists for its historical sights and natural beauty.

p. 337   Anatole France (1844–1924) was a French poet and novelist, awarded the Nobel Prize for literature in 1921.

p. 338   Josef Pilsudski (1867–1935), effective head of independent Poland after 1918 and prime minster at the time of his death, was the target of an assassination attempt in 1921 by Stepan Fedak, member of a Ukrainian nationalist group. Poland's National Democratic Party, whose members were called the Endeks, engaged in anti-Semitic politics and agitation.

p. 339   Reference to the burning bush in Exodus 3:4 that burns but is not consumed.

p. 349   The Yiddish folksong "Di goldene pave" (The golden peacock) is said to describe the fate of Esther, the Jewish girl whose legend in one of its variations is recounted here. The legend of Esther, consort of King Casimir, based on the story in the Book of Esther, is a staple of both Polish and Jewish folklore.

p. 351   A shames is the equivalent of a sexton.

p. 354   The first five-year plan was declared by Joseph Stalin in 1928 as a program to build the Soviet economy so as to achieve parity with the advanced Western countries. The tongue-in-cheek addition of "seven-year plan" translates this into an imagined Jewish equivalent, since Jews think in units of seven, including in computing sabbatical cycles.

p. 363   Ramón del Valle-Inclán (1866–1936), Spanish modernist writer, wrote a cycle of *Sonatas*—Spring, Summer, Autumn, Winter—recounting the adventures of the Marquis of Bradomín, who loses one arm in a duel.

p. 364   Probably the Hasidic master Gershon Hanoch Leiner (1839–1891).

p. 365   On the holiday of Simhat Torah, Jews joyfully celebrate the completion of the annual cycle of reading the Pentateuch and starting it afresh.

p. 373   The quotation is from Song of Songs 1:6.

p. 375   See Book One, note to page 87.

♦ ♦ ♦ *Acknowledgments*

When I launched the Library of Yiddish Classics in 1987, I mentioned to Lucy Dawidowicz that I would need to raise independent funds for translation, since Schocken Books required copy-ready manuscripts before it would publish the series. I had spoken to her as a colleague; it never occurred to me that she would try to help, yet shortly after our conversation, Lucy incorporated the Fund for the Translation of Jewish Literature, providing the seed money herself so that we could get the project off and running. The Fund supported five books of the original series, and another seven so far in its expanded sequel, the New Yiddish Library published by Yale University Press under the general editorship of David G. Roskies. Since the present volume will be one of the final books supported by the Fund, this is the moment to salute Lucy's initiative, and to thank my fellow members of the board she assembled—Etta Brandman and Malcolm Thomson—with special gratitude to Neal Kozodoy, who assumed responsibilities for the Fund as Lucy's executor in 1990 and has directed it since. Neal sustained the project and his oversight improved every aspect of every book in both series.

I am very fortunate and thankful to have David Roskies for a brother. I owe him special thanks for including this book in the New Yiddish Library and for his advice and encouragement throughout.

Maier Deshell's translation of the first of these two chronicles was a labor of love and high intelligence. I hope that he will take rightful pride in the part of the book that is wholly his. Norbert Guterman's translation of the second chronicle, *Homecoming at Twilight*, was too good to be superseded, but since he was no longer alive to be consulted, may I be forgiven the few corrections and refinements I made as editor. I am grateful to Yale University Press for publishing this series of modern Yiddish classics, and to Dan Heaton for his editorial help.

This book was so long in the making that I will surely forget to acknowledge all those involved in various stages of conception, translation, editing, and production. Catherine Madsen of the National Yiddish Book Center provided most helpful technical and editorial assistance. Thanks to Kyle Berkman, who helped with research, to Marta Figlerowicz, who helped with footnotes, and to students, past and present, whose appreciation of Glatstein contributed to my own understanding. I doubt that any teacher has ever been more fortunate in her students than I, first at McGill, then at Harvard. This book is for them, and for all readers to come.

OTHER BOOKS IN THE NEW YIDDISH LIBRARY
PUBLISHED BY YALE UNIVERSITY PRESS

Sholem Aleichem, *The Letters of Menakhem-Mendl & Sheyne-Sheyndl and Motl, the Cantor's Son*, translated and with an introduction by Hillel Halkin

S. Ansky, *The Dybbuk and Other Writings*, edited and with an introduction by David G. Roskies

David Bergelson, *The End of Everything*, translated and with an introduction by Joseph Sherman

Itzik Manger, *The World According to Itzik: Selected Poetry and Prose*, translated and edited by Leonard Wolf, with an introduction by David G. Roskies and Leonard Wolf

I. L. Peretz, *The I. L. Peretz Reader*, 2nd revised edition, edited and with an introduction by Ruth Wisse

Yehoshue Perle, *Everyday Jews: Scenes from a Vanished Life*, edited and with an introduction by David G. Roskies

Lamed Shapiro, *The Cross and Other Jewish Stories*, edited and with an introduction by Leah Garrett

Bringing Yiddish works to English readers.

White Goat Press, the Yiddish Book Center's imprint, is committed to bringing newly translated work to the widest readership possible. We publish work in all genres—novels, short stories, drama, poetry, memoirs, essays, reportage, children's literature, plays, and popular fiction, including romance and detective stories.

Editions are published as hardcover, paperback, and ebooks.

To learn more and to see our full list of published and forthcoming titles visit **whitegoatpress.org**